Throwaways

The Claus Chronicles (according to me)

D. R. STRAHAN

authorHOUSE®

AuthorHouse™
1663 Liberty Drive
Bloomington, IN 47403
www.authorhouse.com
Phone: 1-800-839-8640

First published by AuthorHouse   10/26/2010

ISBN: 978-1-4520-8171-7 (hc)
ISBN: 978-1-4520-8172-4 (sc)
ISBN: 978-1-4520-8173-1 (e)

Library of Congress Control Number: 2010914644

Printed in the United States of America

This book is printed on acid-free paper.

In memory of my husband
James R. Strahan
A literary zealot
Influential in my Imaginative Expression

Thank You

This letter is actually an apology, as well as a thank you to my family, friends and acquaintances from Niantic, Connecticut and all along the east coast as well as the west coast on down to San Diego, California and many of the states in between for their encouragement and endurance of my single-mindedness and dedication to the completion of this novel.

As an avid reader from early childhood, I have enjoyed the writing of many authors. The effort put forth or the thrill experienced on their journey in writing had never occurred to me. As the 'Throwaways' fantasy novel developed in my mind then in context, the excitement of creating elevated to a need for sharing some of the moments with others. I thank you all again for continuing as my friends after the two words, 'The End' was written, completing the first novel of the 'Claus Chronicles---'series.

Contents

Chapter One

At il

FOR ONE SPLIT SECOND THE sun faded out the winter darkness and displayed a brilliant sky of blue. Its golden rays of light sifted through soft, white clouds and reflected the brightness on snow covered fields below. Just as quickly as it came the sun flash passed, allowing the darkness to again take over the sky. Daylight season had now begun far north of the Arctic Circle.

Nearing twilight, some weeks later, a thirteen-year-old boy called Fox was frantically pacing back and forth behind a pile of rubble at the city dump. He had been waiting most of the day for his friends. "They should have been here by now," he mumbled under his breath. They were late and he was scared. With anxiety peaking, he glared at the empty path stretching toward the alley below.

Suddenly hearing the distant sound of trampling boots, he cringed, nervously holding his breath. "Oh, no," he whispered, quickly ducking out of sight. "It's the guards---they're already making their rounds." He squeezed between the bundles of garbage and stood perfectly still, trying to control his chattering teeth. With hands pushed against his lips, Fox tried to calm down.

They came closer.

"Ya know tha' boy, Fox," said the first guard.

Hearing his name, an icy shiver slid down Fox's back. "They're looking for me." His body stiffened.

"Yeah, what about him?" said his partner.

"We gotta keep an eye out fer 'im, ya know."

"Why? He seems like an okay kid."

"Wal, that's the word."

"But he's the governor's boy."

"Makes no difrence ef 'e is er not."

Gathering up some nerve, Fox pulled the knit koyt more snuggly over his curly mop of copper red hair and poked his head out. He held his breath, not daring to move, as they came closer.

One of the guards glanced in his direction, then back to his partner. "What did he do?"

"Dunno. Prob'ly stealin'. Ya know how that goes."

"I guess."

They turned at the end of the street.

Fox's knees buckled. "Too close," he shuddered. Sliding to the ground, he pulled his knees tight against his stomach and squeezed them together, heaving a sigh of relief.

An instant later, his thoughts flashed back to his friends. He jumped to his feet, whispering frantically into the dull afternoon. "Wolf! Hawk! Where are you?"

For the thirtieth time it seemed, he had gazed down the empty hill. His friends were not there and he knew it. Dejectedly he turned, forcing his feet back toward the crate where he had spent most of the afternoon, and sat down. Slipping off the koyt, he raked his fingers through the tangled mass of rusty locks beneath, nervously massaging his ears. After turning up the cuff around the edge of it, he pulled it back on.

There was nothing left to do but wait.

Fox had lived most of his life with his parents in At il, an old forgotten city, far north of the Arctic Circle. Although located close to the flat, open tundra, the small community was well protected by a high, thickly-coated barricade of snow and ice. It had a catwalk, leading each direction around the city, with steps to the ground on either side of the wall. Perched on top and to the right of the steps, was a security shack. Directly above the shack hung a roughly-hewn placard of wood, with the engraved letters At il, marking the city entrance. It was better known by residents as the old city.

The city entrance faced south. It overlooked a broad span of spindly, tough growth of vines and small bushes that spiked through the thick layer of ice coating that only melted slightly throughout the year. This wide band of brush, sporadically dotted with low-growing vegetation and occasional small trees, stretched toward the eastern and western horizons. It separated the tree line from the vast northern wilderness of frozen plains, as well as pressing across the valley toward the mountain foothills.

Tempered from view by nearby craggily hills, the city fortress was well camouflaged by broken tree limbs, wood chunks and loose brush which had been driven into the city's outer base by the harsh northern winds.

Early one morning Fox was lying in bed, planning his first day of the three month break from his studies at the university. He would begin his fourth year when classes resumed. Most of his break was already scheduled out and he was anxious to get started.

When he overheard his name mentioned he automatically became more attentive to his parents conversation. His father, the city governor and his mother, the director of city planning, were in the tiny kitchen collecting their lunches and about to leave for work.

"I suppose he's meeting his friends."

"Sandor didn't say---," his mother said.

"They call him Fox, you know," his father pointed out.

"I know. It's a pity," she answered.

"It's safer, though."

"Don't forget your fruit. The market doesn't often stock fresh produce."

"I've got it. Thanks." He reached toward his coat pocket. "Do you have the house key?"

"Um-hum, it's right here."

A few moments later Fox heard the front door close and the click of the lock, as they left. At the window he watched them cross the street, half-noticing the dreary light beaming from the lamp above them as they stepped on the sidewalk and turned, heading toward their offices down town. Turning back toward his room, he thought, "I guess I'd better get ready to go. I have a lot of stops to make this morning. Hawk and Wolf are usually on time---don't want to be late."

He smoothed the down-filled comforter over his half-sized bunk and pushed the worn edge of it between the bed frame and dresser then sat down, still mulling over his plans. Turning slightly, he pulled clean thermal socks and underwear from the upper drawer of his bureau. After a quick glance across the room, he nodded approvingly at the slight morning light. Reaching for his boots from under the window, he sat on the bed to put them on. With a deft twist to straighten the liners, he then buckled them in place.

Once dressed and ready to leave, Fox headed for the pantry to gather food and supplies for the day. He then rifled through the cupboard, in search of a special package from his mother. "I knew she'd leave something," he grinned, pulling it from the back of a drawer. After opening the parcel, he began sorting the contents. "Cheese, dried meat, bread and---let's see what else is in here; oh yeah, some dried fruit. The children will like that." Being careful to re-wrap each item, he packed everything in his knapsack and stashed it with his lantern and other supplies at the front door. He then went to the closet for his coat.

Much to his surprise, his father's old fur coat was hanging there instead of his own. Excitedly, he slipped his arms into the sleeves and tied the belt around his slim waist. Although taller than most of the boys his age, the coat still hung well past his knees. "Wow, my dad kept his promise. This is nice," he said, stroking the fur. "I guess his 'official governor robes' finally arrived. He's been waiting a long time for them."

With a happy grin, Fox scanned the front of the coat then jabbed his hands deep into the pockets, finding them empty. "I'd better get some gloves and stuff," he thought, running back to his room. "It's a good thing I checked before leaving." Sliding to his knees, he dug through the lower drawer of his bureau, pulling out a couple of knit koyts and a pair of gloves. With the spares of each in his pockets, he pushed one of the koyts over his unruly mop of curls and scrunched it down over his ears. Choosing not to be stressed with it falling off, he tied it securely under his chin.

When finished, he tossed the knapsack over his shoulder, locked the front door and crossed the street. Aiming his steps toward the city square, he jogged quickly down the small sidewalk to his first stop.

His plan was to visit a number of targeted grocery stores early that morning, in hopes of salvaging usable produce before it was disposed of. He knew the shop-owners were required, by city law, to burn all excess food and he was in hopes of snatching the good stuff before that happened. If they were caught giving it away, or allowing it to be used illegally, they would be heavily fined or forced to close their shops.

Arriving hours before the stores opened, he immediately ran for the burn containers, behind the stores. The excess or damaged food was usually collected and stacked around the containers then dumped, a little at a time to keep the fire from going out. In each case, the fires had already been set and everything was gone. There were roaring flames boiling out the top of all the large metal drums lined up behind each of the buildings. He ran from store to store, knowing the chances of making a raid were slim to none. Finally giving up, he bagged the meager samples he had salvaged and added them to what he'd gleaned from the family pantry. Quite disappointed, he draped the knapsack across his shoulder and slowly headed across town to meet his friends.

Since his food scavenging took a lot less time than expected, he knew it would be a while before his friends would show up. They were to meet at twilight and it was just past noon. Not to have his spirits dampened, he stayed busy clearing out the mounds of trash from the new meeting place he'd found, making the space inside much more usable.

The security guards had demolished their other hideaway and he had been pressed to find a new one. This location seemed a good choice. With the surrounding trash and debris acting as a barrier, the activities of Fox and his friends would be better hidden from outsiders, especially the guards. They would most likely pass it by without a thought, or so he hoped.

Looking down the hill, with a positive nod, he considered the street lamp at the crossing. The clearing around it was another plus, since it was extremely important that the children have easy accessibility to the gathered food, Fox was well pleased with his choice.

One concern kept popping into his thoughts and he couldn't seem to shake it. His friends, Hawk and Wolf, had never visited this hideaway before and since it was so secluded, they might have a problem finding it. He kept mulling over all the details.

By early afternoon, the sun had slipped toward the western sky. Fox looked about, proud that his cleanup task was finally finished. All the litter had been picked up, bagged and stacked with the rest of the trash. The cleared space was large, but still well hidden. There was nothing more to do but wait.

He stood at the hideaway entrance, pondering the details again. Peering at the street lamp, below, he muttered, "I told Hawk and Wolf how to get here. We went over the instructions a number of times." Squeezing through the small entrance, he headed back toward the crate where he'd been sitting. "I don't know why I'm worried; they've found all the other places we've used." Brushing off the new layer of snow from his seat, he pushed it further into the wall of trash. Thoughtfully, he gazed toward the western horizon. "It's still early, anyway." Giving his koyt a shake, he stretched it back over his head and leaned back. His eyes trailed upward, toward the gray sky, then closed as he waited.

A slow giggle left his throat when spiraling snowflakes drifted into his eyelashes. "Mmm, that tickles." His blue eyes blinked open.

Mesmerized by the scene above, he watched the soft flakes fall lazily down, sprinkling white across his chest. He noticed some had clung to the furry hairs on his sleeve and leaned closer. He began to count. "One second, two seconds, three seconds---gone." After breathing on the flakes, he tilted his head back and waited for the next batch to stick, counting again. Sometime later, the sky had cleared to a golden tan.

Fox gently ran his fingers through the soft layer of fur, draped across his chest. A smile of pride covered his face. He reflected back to the morning. His father's hand-me-down coat was now wrapped around him. Snuggling into the warmth, he looked down and caressed the fur again.

Glancing across the hideaway again, his thoughts slipped back to his friends. "That city lamp is a good landmark," he mused. "Wolf and Hawk just need to turn there and come straight up the hill." He leaned back, comfortably. "I don't know why I keep worrying. As quiet as it is, I should have no trouble hearing them."

The thought had hardly passed his mind when the distant sound of clang, plunk, plunk, clang, clang, clang, reached his ears. An uneven rhythm of wood against metal pealed, like dull bells, through the crisp air. He knew the wooden placard, bearing the city name, was beating against the metal pole again, announcing a change in the wind pattern. He chuckled to himself. "That quiet time didn't last long." He pulled the fur up around his ears, muffling the noise, and leaned back.

A long while later, the incessant racket finally ceased and he sighed. He pulled the collar and hood back off his head and roamed toward the entrance. "Maybe I'd better wait outside. It will be getting dark soon and I don't want to miss them." His eyes rested on the emptiness under the lamp. Dejectedly, he sighed.

Looking up, he watched a shooting star with a long fire-ball tail pass by. Not far to one side was the full moon with a bright ring around it, promising a deep chill before morning light. With a shiver, he sat up, pulling the hood of his coat over the koyt and closer to his chin.

Although the few arctic hours of daylight had brought some warmth, dampness from the slight thaw still hung in the air, causing the near freezing temperature to seem much colder. The biting wind had finally stilled to a slight breeze. He turned slightly, observing the lingering purple-gray haze of twilight that followed the setting sun.

Fox's eyes were drawn again, to the crossing below. Oblivious to the huddles of nondescript dwellings and small, seemingly abandoned igloos sprawled aimlessly across the city grounds, he carefully studied each of the streets and alleys between them. With a slow growl, he muttered, "come on now, it's really getting late. You should have been here by now." He pulled the fur wrap up close, shielding himself from the night chill, as he paced. Near panic had taken over his thoughts.

Although nearly fourteen, he would be the first to admit he was afraid for himself, yes of course, but mainly for his friends, Hawk and Wolf. They would not be out roaming the streets, gathering food for the children, if he had not asked them to do so. Now that the streets were nearly dark, the guards should be doing their rounds. Although they didn't seem to stay on any schedule, Fox knew they were supposed to walk all the streets four times each full day. His father had told him it was to keep the city safe but everyone always hid from them.

With that thought, his fears began to run wild; what if the guards caught his friends toting bags of stolen food. They'd want to know where it came from and what they were planning to do with it.

He knew they couldn't tell the truth; that it was for the children. Of course not! Feeding the children was against the law; everyone knew that. And if they did get caught, what could he do? These thoughts of guilt kept racing through his mind. Added to that, dusk had now set in and the night noises were grating on his nerves. Back and forth, he continued to pace, getting more agitated by the minute.

Before he realized what was happening, he was falling forward; crashing into the snow-coated ground. Without thinking, he yelled. His hands were flailing through the air as he lashed out for something to grab. He dug them into the stacked piles of garbage. One bag began to roll. The rest came tumbling after, knocking him flat against the hard ground.

An eternity later it seemed, they stopped. Gasping and coughing, his head finally broke the surface and he spewed out, "eweu,' holding his nose, "that's some nasty stuff in there." After a lot of squirming and kicking, he pulled himself upright and sat in the midst of it all, laughing. "It's amazing, what I do sometimes, for excitement."

A shuffling sound suddenly cut through the air. "What was that?" He thought. The hair on his neck bristled. Tip-toeing across the hideaway, he peeked down the vacant hill. "I must be hearing things." Then worming his way back through the strewn bundles of refuse, he sat down.

He waited.

He heard the voice again. It ripped through the stillness. "Fox, where are you?"

Startled by the sharpness of the sound, he jerked around. "That's no voice I know," he thought, "but if it isn't Hawk--- or Wolf, who else would it be?"

Feeling his emotions tested, he tried to stay calm. "It can't be security," he thought, "surely not this soon."

Hidden, just outside the hideaway entrance, his eyes traced the hillside, as well as the landing below. His heart raced, wishing he could call back.

The voice rang out again. He stopped.

"Fox are you here? Where are you?"

Recognition finally seeped through his anxiety. "It's Hawk. He's here." Racing outside, he saw the boy standing below and waved excitedly. "Hawk! Hawk, up here," he signaled.

"Hi there, Fox," Hawk yelled, running across the clearing.

Hurrying to meet him, Fox raised his voice. "Am I ever glad to see you? What kept you so long?"

Eight-year-old Hawk was much shorter than Fox, and just as slim. He wore an old wool coat, with a long scarf wrapped three or four times around his neck. The covering on his light brown hair was a stocking koyt, obviously too big by the way it fit. After pushing it away from his eyes, he reached for the two canvas bags, piled at his feet, and began pulling them across the alley. "I didn't think I'd ever get here," he said, excitedly, "Sorry I'm late."

"No worry. You're here and that's the main thing," Fox answered, glancing to either side. After taking one of Hawk's bags, he scrambled across the street, signaling for him to follow.

Hawk tossed the other bag over his shoulder, following closely behind. "What's your hurry?" He panted. "You could slow down a little."

"Sh-h-h," Fox warned. He maneuvered around old crates and snow-covered bunkers, rushing toward the hideaway. Once inside, he stowed Hawk's bag against the wall.

Hawk did the same. "What's going on?" He asked. "Did you run into some kind of trouble?"

"I didn't want you to get caught out there. Security, you know. We never know when they'll show up."

"Say, listen to you. I've been on the lookout for them all afternoon," Hawk giggled, plopping on an old crate. "Don't worry about that."

"I've had a lot of thinking time today," Fox admitted. "The longer I sat here, the more scared I got."

"What about?"

"The situation I put you in, of course. I shouldn't have sent you out scavenging for food---especially by yourself."

"Why not?"

"Because it's too dangerous; you're so young, and you could---."

"I knew what I was getting into," Hawk said, with a sharp nod.

Ignoring the remark, Fox asked. "You're sure you weren't followed?"

"Well, I---," Hawk began.

"You took such a long time."

"Well, you see, I was helping Wolf and---."

"Where is Wolf, anyway?" Fox asked, shoving a tangle of curls from his face. "He should be here. You were both supposed to be here before dusk."

"I'm glad to see you, too," Hawk giggled, breaking the tension. "Wolf was right behind me; I thought he was, anyway." Heading toward the entrance, he added. "He should be here, any time now." He turned, shrugging his shoulders. "He's not out there yet. Don't worry, he'll be here pretty quick, I'll bet."

"Sorry! I didn't mean to snap at you," Fox apologized. "You've just never been this late before."

"No offense taken," Hawk answered. "So, how has the day been for you?"

"Other than anxious, you mean?"

"Yeah, other than that," Hawk laughed.

Well, it's been quiet--- and chilly, of course," Fox answered, shivering slightly.

"That's nothing new," Hawk answered, "it's always gets cooler after dark."

"Yeah, I know. I was mainly worried about you finding this place." Finally sticking his hand out, Fox said, "I'm glad you're safe. There were no patrols, I take it?"

"I haven't seen a thing," Hawk said, accepting the extended handshake. "No people, no police, no anyone. Kind of weird, huh?"

"That kind of news makes me edgy, to tell you the truth." Then putting his arm across Hawk's shoulder, he said, "well come on, we'll wait inside the hideaway for Wolf. It would be a lot warmer out of the wind."

"Great idea," Hawk answered. After dropping down beside the bags, he muffled out an apology. "Sorry, it took so long to get here. Your hiding place was much further out than I thought."

"Forget it. It's all good." Nodding toward the pock-ridden, grimy wall behind him, Fox said, "so what do you think of this place?"

"It's pretty good, I guess," Hawk answered, looking around.

"We shouldn't have surprise visitors here," Fox said, "like those security guards last time."

"It's kind of hard to get to, though."

"Noticing Hawk still leaning into one of his bags, Fox asked, "well, how did you do?"

"Just check it out," he giggled, proudly. "I thought you'd never ask." Immediately opening one of the bags, he stood aside. "Just look at all the good stuff I found. Can you believe it?"

"That's for sure," Fox exclaimed, looking inside. "Felt like it too, coming up the hill."

"Is that your stash?" Hawk asked, pointing toward a knapsack by the wall. "It looks pretty thin to me."

"Yeah, I'm afraid you're right. There wasn't much to choose from," Fox answered, sadly. "I left home really early, too. By the time I got to the markets, they had disposed of everything. Most of what I brought is from our pantry."

"Sometimes it just happens that way," Hawk said, sitting by his bag.

"Did you hear something," Fox asked, looking up? Maybe it's Wolf. You said he was right behind you."

Without thinking, Hawk yelled out, "Are you with us, Wolf?" Not waiting for an answer, he asked. "Where is Storg? I was kind of expecting to see him. You've not seen him?"

"Not yet. I thought he knew the plan; I tried to be detailed. Maybe I wasn't clear enough."

"No problem with that part. I found it, didn't I?" After a hesitation, Hawk added, "he is new around here, though. Maybe he got lost."

"I hope not," Fox answered.

Suddenly, with a sharp twitch, Hawk jerked around, his arms swinging. Aiming at the shadow behind him, he missed by a few inches and, glaring up, found himself staring straight into Wolf's eyes.

Barely ducking the flying fists, Wolf spewed out, "watch it, Hawk, you nearly hit me."

"Oh, my gosh!" Hawk cried, quickly backing away. "Sorry, Wolf. I didn't know you were there."

After collecting his wits, Wolf said, "calm down, little buddy, I wasn't trying to sneak up on you. Why'd you take a swing at me, anyway?"

"You scared me. Why else?"

"Sorry about that."

"It's okay," Hawk said quietly.

Wolf reached back, pulling at his long, auburn ponytail, freeing it from his coat collar. "Wow, what a relief," he laughed. "I didn't want to let go of my knapsack when my koyt fell off." Poking through his pockets, he pulled a blue and green striped one out and stuffed his ponytail inside. After squashing the koyt back on his head, he eyed Hawk, who was standing to one side and said, "Sorry, man, I didn't mean to upset you. I had no idea you'd take offense."

"I should have looked first." Hawk kicked at a dirty clod of snow and watched as it splattered out in front of him. With his big brown eyes glistening, he looked up. "I'm always afraid someone's gonna grab me, again."

"You're safe with us. You should never forget that," Wolf said, gently. Then squeezing Hawk's shoulder, he added, "I know it's hard to get over the fear of being snatched."

Hawk nodded, his eyes lowered. A few minutes later he headed up the path, toward the hideaway.

Feeling the strain between the two, Fox asked, "is there some kind of a problem?"

Wolf looked at him curiously. "You mean between Hawk and me? Oh, we're fine. It's nothing to worry about."

"Is there something I should know?"

"Hawk will tell you when he's ready, I imagine," Wolf said, grabbing at the koyt he had dropped on the ground.

"I'll take your word for it, then," Fox said, decidedly, "as long as the two of you are okay."

Wolf nodded in agreement then pointed at the bag he'd been carrying. "Sorry I'm so late but my knapsack was really heavy. I should have made two bags out of it, I guess." With a grin, he added, "I did get a nice variety of food, though. There was a lot to choose from, today."

"I wasn't so lucky, I'm afraid," Fox said. "Most everything was gone by the time I made my rounds, this morning."

"You gotta get out there early," Wolf grinned, "like I did."

Fox frowned. "I was at the markets, long before they opened."

"Oh!" Wolf said. With a nod, he reached for his bag, and said. "So, what do you want me to do with this?"

"Need some help carrying it?" Fox asked. With a sly grin Fox watched him struggle then asked, "need some help carrying it?"

"I could use some, I think," Wolf whined. "I didn't think I was ever going to get here and that was when I crossed over flat ground."

Fox reached for a corner of the bag then nodded toward Hawk's image moseying up the hill. "That's where the hideaway is. Come on."

"Sure!" Wolf answered, off-handedly. Squatting down, he busily fastened the ropes around his shoulders then stood up.

"I'm surprised you got here without any mishaps," Fox said, getting a better grip on the load. "Say, you're right; this bag is real-ly heavy."

"I know," Wolf answered. "Where did you say we were going?"

"Up there! See where Hawk is standing?" Fox nodded.

"You've got to be kidding!" Wolf howled. "All the way up there?"

Somewhat impatient, Fox said. "Oh, Wolf, come on now, you know I'm going to help you. Hawk and I have already taken the other bags up there."

"Well, I guess," Wolf groaned. Hitching the ropes higher on his shoulders, he directed his feet up the hill. At the entrance, he pulled off the harness and let the load slide to the ground, kneeling beside it. Patting the bulging piece of canvas, he said, "what do you think, Fox? Great, huh?"

"That all depends on what you have inside that duffle." Fox said, pausing for a breather.

Hawk, stepped in closer, interrupting Wolf's moment of glory and said, "I'd say, by the way you two were groaning, it must be full of bricks."

"Of course it's not," Wolf smirked, untying the bag. "I came upon a real find. There was all this nice, fresh food just laid out there for the taking; that's what it looked like, anyway."

"Just teasing," Hawk giggled. "Did you raid a grocery, or what?"

Looking from Hawk to Fox, Wolf laughed, "well, that's a pretty close guess. Then noticing the rest of the bags, he exclaimed excitedly. "By the looks of all those bags, the children will feast tonight."

"Yes, thanks to the two of you," Fox said.

"Just wait 'till Storg gets here, then we'll have lots 'n lots more," Hawk reminded them.

"You didn't ask him to bring anything, did you?" Fox eyed Hawk with a frown.

"Of course not! He just offered and I didn't turn him down," Hawk giggled. "That's okay isn't it?"

"Well, I guess," Fox admitted. "I wouldn't want him to feel obligated, though."

"Now, Fox," Wolf interjected, "we can use all the help we can get, don't you think?"

"That's true," Fox admitted, heading across the hideaway, "as long as Storg doesn't mind."

"Well, I for one, hope he gets here soon. I'm pretty cold, now," Wolf whined. Finding a place to sit, he tucked his knees under his coat-tail and wrapped his arms around them.

"I know. I've been here for most of the day, myself," Fox declared, sitting down next to him. "Scoot over, there's plenty of room for both of us."

After watching the two push into the seat, Hawk ran over and jumped between them, scrunching down as far as he could. "M-m-m, he giggled. Once comfortably settled in, he said, "don't you worry a bit about Storg. He will be here soon. He promised."

"I hope so, Hawk," Fox said, pulling the fur hood over his head. "We can wait a little while longer, I guess."

Wolf leaned back and squiggled down close. "Not much later, Fox. Shouldn't the children be coming soon?"

"Yes, I know," Fox answered, snuggling his coat closer under his chin, "but I think we should give Storg a little extra time." He nodded toward Hawk, lowering his eyes.

"Come on, Storg," Hawk whispered.

There was a little more jostling and squirming then a settling in for the delay.

Quietly, they sat.

Breaking the silence, Fox asked again. "You're sure no one was hanging around?"

Wolf opened his eyes then stretched a bit. "You mean security? No, I don't think so, why?"

"What's the matter Fox? You sound worried about something."

"It's too quiet, Hawk, that's all." Then shifting his thoughts, he asked, "Storg is still coming, isn't he?"

Hawk nodded vigorously. "Yes, he promised."

"Do you know anything about him?"

"Hey! You said no names, remember?" Wolf piped in. "We're not supposed to---."

"I know--- tell each other our real names, or where we live," Fox said. "We did make those rules in the very beginning, and I'm not saying they should change." Rolling his gloved hands together, he continued, "It's just that there's something odd, or different about him, like he's not supposed to be here."

"I'm not sure he is from here," Hawk said cautiously. "Does that make a difference?" He studied their faces then dropped his gaze. Moving to a seat next to the frayed bag of food, he waited for a response.

Quietly, Fox answered, "of course not. It just sounds like you may have information we need to know. We must trust each other."

Hawk studied his expression while listening.

"It's for you to decide." Fox said, finally.

After mulling through his thoughts, Hawk began speaking. "The first time I saw Storg was just a few days ago. Actually, he wasn't alone. There were ten or twelve of them, I guess. I don't know how many, for sure. They just showed up, out of nowhere." Beginning to relax, he continued. "I don't remember ever seeing outsiders come here before."

He waited for a reaction. There was none. He went on.

"I was sitting at my window, watching the mystery lights pass over. It was getting close to daylight by then. When I looked outside, I happened to see this odd looking group of people. Actually, they were hard to miss."

"What do you mean, hard to miss?" Fox asked.

"Well, there was a bunch of sleighs, in the field outside the city, seven or eight maybe. I couldn't count how many because they were parked all scrambled up together, you know. Every one of them was piled high with all kinds of stuff."

"Oh, really," Fox, prodded curiously, "like what?"

"It's hard to describe," Hawk said. "They were all stacked with boxes and crates. I've never seen so much stuff. Oh, and yeah," stretching his arms out, he added, "I saw huge rolls of fur. They were all wrapped up around long poles, and---and---the poles, they were sticking out the ends. That's what it looked like, anyway."

"Watch the arms, Hawk!" Wolf said, ducking his swing.

"Uh, oh yeah. Sorry!"

"We don't have anything like that around here," Fox chuckled. "Are you sure you weren't dreaming?"

"Oh, no, it's true!" Hawk cried out, emphatically.

"That's not even the weird part. Wait till I tell you the rest."
"Where?" Suddenly alert, Wolf demanded. "From what direction did they come?"

"Oh, you know, over where I live; I told you that. I told you I could see them from my window," Hawk answered. "They didn't actually enter town, though. When they got up close to the wall, they stopped. I watched them walk around for a while. Some of them were climbing on top of the sleighs. They were pulling and tugging on long straps and ropes; I guess testing the loads then they just turned all the sleighs around and left. They must have been out there for an hour or more. Strange, huh?"

"That's not possible," Fox cut in. "How could so few people pull such heavy loads? Ten or twelve wouldn't be enough, even if they all did it together. Oh, no! Not enough at all--- and you said you talked them?"

"Sure!" He answered.

"Weren't you afraid of them?" Wolf asked him.

"Nah! They seemed friendly enough," Hawk answered, with a giggle.

"You went outside the wall?" Fox asked, sharply.

"No, of course not," Hawk exclaimed. "I'd never do that. I'd be too scared."

"I just thought I'd ask."

"Oh!" Said Hawk. "Well anyway, what I started to say was that I just waved to them and stuff, when I first saw them. A little later two of them were standing under my window, so I went down and talked to them."

"You said no one came inside the city?"
"I know, but they were just there," he answered.

"Then they must've been inside," Wolf argued. "How did they get there?"

"Dunno. Didn't think to ask."

"Did they say why they had come here? Where they came from?" Fox quizzed.

Hawk shrugged his shoulders. "Didn't ask. Somewhere out there, I guess. They'd been walking in snow up to their knees; I do know that. I could tell by the ridges of ice on their odd-looking leg covers. The weirdest thing I noticed, though, was that they weren't cold. I shook hands with them and their hands were as warm as if they'd been sitting around a fire all day," Hawk tried to explain. "I thought that was pretty strange, too."

"It sounds strange to me," Wolf noted.

"When I first saw them, they were trailing over the hill. You know that long one, just outside the city. It looked like a bunch of animals going along the crest." After rubbing his hands together, Hawk finally tucked them under his arms. Then, noticing Fox and Wolf staring at him, he growled, "can't help it; they're still cold, even with gloves on." For a few moments, he massaged his hands together. "Well, anyway, he continued, "after a while I quit watching them and started hunting for my coat and gloves. Found the ones I have on, under the table." A broad grin covered his face. "My mom, I tell you---she's always hiding my stuff."

"Well, back to your story," Wolf said impatiently, "is there anything else?"

"In the beginning," Hawk said, ignoring Wolf, "I heard all kind of strange noises and looked out the window to see where it was coming from. That was when they first got to town, I guess. You should have seen it. I thought I was dreaming." Hawk search their eyes, then added, "I can't believe I actually met them."

"Go on," Fox invited. "You said there were ten or twelve of them?"

"I'm not sure," Hawk said.

"Did they act mean, you know, like they were going to hurt you?" Wolf questioned, thoughtfully. A moment later, he suddenly blurted out, "you don't think this Storg is a spy, do you? Maybe he's really trying to stop us. Maybe he's with security, or something."

"Nah! Don't worry about that," Hawk quipped. "He said he wanted to help 'n I believe him."

"Ten or twelve people, you said," Fox repeated, frowning at Hawk. "How did they pull the sleighs?"

"With reindeer; would you believe that? They had four, or maybe six of them hitched to each of the sleighs. There was a bunch of reindeer running loose, too. They stayed kind of huddled together, though."

"No kidding?" Wolf spouted. "Like that could happen. Reindeer are wild animals."

"Yeah, true though," Hawk said. Then scooting away from the wall of garbage, he turned. His face squiggled in to wrinkles as he remembered. "There was this old man and an old woman, I'll never forget them. The man was on one side of the reindeer herd--- that's what they called them--- and the woman was on the other side. They were both singing these funny sounding songs, kind of like chants, as they walked along. Most of the time the reindeer didn't pay a bit of attention to them; they just kept digging at the snow, sort of running their noses through it and eating the green moss underneath. It was funny to watch. As long as the singing was going on the reindeer stayed in between the old people. Oh yes, and another thing;

everybody was dressed funny, er different, too. They were covered in fur from head to toe. They wore fur jackets, leg muffs, hoods; all that kind of stuff." He glanced at Fox, with a giggle. "Kind of looked like you."

Wolf looked at Fox, laughing.

Holding his foot up, and pointing, Fox smirked, "I don't have any leg muffs on. I'd never even heard of such a thing until now."

Glaring at the two of them, Hawk whined. "Well, I could go for some of that fur, even if it's not leg muffs. It's getting really cold out here." Scrunching back down between the two, he unwound the shawl from his neck. "Ouch!" He said, rubbing his arm. "Something hit my elbow."

"Yeah, my head," Wolf growled, taking a swat at him.

"Ya missed," Hawk laughed, sliding out of the way.

"All right, you two," Fox warned, pushing his arms between them, "not enough room to be scuffling around."

Hawk ducked, grinning. He flipped the shawl from around his neck and slid it over his head. "Anyway, a couple of them were boys, and one looked like a little girl, I think; couldn't tell by---."

"You're not wearing your mother's shawl, are you?" Wolf sputtered. "Of all the---." Glaring at the floral cloth Hawk was holding, he whipped the wool scarf from his neck and pushed it in Hawk's direction. "Here! Take it. My coat is warmer than yours. Besides, I have two sweaters on."

"I have a spare pair of gloves, too," Fox said with a grin. "You're really having a time of it; keeping up with your clothes."

"Yeah, I know. Thanks, guys," He said, pulling on the gloves. "My mother keeps hiding my stuff. She doesn't want me to hang around with you; says I'm in for trouble, if I do."

"I can tell," Fox answered. "Now, go on with your story."

"Story? Huh! Oh, yeah," he said. "Not much left to tell. Two or three more people, that's all there were. A few of them were taller than me, but not much. It was funny the way the two old folks seemed to waddle when they walked." Quickly jumping up, Hawk began swinging his arms and shuffling his feet back and forth, trying to imitate them.

Moving quickly out of his way, Fox and Wolf both laughed hysterically at his antics.

"Well go on. What else?" Fox urged, still snickering under his breath.

Hawk plopped back down. "I guess they are staying in the mountains, somewhere. That's what Storg told me. He's the one who talked to me. The other guy didn't say a thing."

"You've got to be kidding," Wolf stammered. "They'll freeze to death out there."

"I doubt it. They're probably warmer than we are, especially right now," Hawk answered, with a shiver. "Storg said they had found two caves, pretty close to each other. He said they built special little huts at each of the entrances. He told me all about it. He said the huts were placed in a special way to block off the wind and cold. That was their sleeping rooms, too. He said it was the best living space his family's had in a long time."

"What kind of huts?" Fox asked. "Where did they get them?"

"Made them, I guess," Hawk answered. "Storg said his family carries them everywhere they go."

"I know about the caves," Fox related, thoughtfully. "I've explored some of them."

"What!" Wolf gasped. "That's against the law, Fox. We're not to go outside the city. You know that!"

Ignoring Wolf's criticism, Fox asked, "What do you think of him; Storg, I mean?"

"Oh, he seems like an okay sort." After a thought, Hawk broke his own silence. "There is one more thing."

"Uh, oh, here it comes," Wolf laughed. "I suppose he secretly has pointed ears and a long tail."

"Don't make fun of my ears," Hawk answered, quickly tugging at his koyt. "His ears are kinda tall, but--- but they're rounded on the top." Noticing the look of disbelief in their eyes, he added, "It's true!"

Wolf scoffed, "oh yeah, true, I'm sure." With eyebrows drawn together, he frowned, "and I'm supposed to believe that?"

"You'll see; just wait till he gets here and look for yourself," Hawk said. "They are somewhat pointed, too, I guess." Slipping out of his seat, he turned, "there may have been a few more people than I said. I'm really not sure how many there were."

"Yes," Fox and Wolf said in unison, after sneaking a peek at each other, "go on."

"I'm serious," Hawk stated gruffly. "Well, the sad part is that those few people, according to Storg, are the end of his kind."

"What do you mean," Fox asked, "the end of his kind; the end of what kind?"

"They call themselves Krolls."

"Krolls? Never heard of them," Wolf snickered. He slipped a knowing grin at Fox. "You've got quite a tall tale going there, Hawk."

Fox glanced at Wolf, then back to Hawk, suddenly serious. "It may not be a tall tale, Wolf. I seem to recall reading about a clan of people who lived in the more northern wilderness. It was supposed to be a rather large clan; a few thousand in population, actually. They tamed the reindeer and used them for a good portion of their needs; food, clothing, shelter and many other things." After studying his thoughts, he went on. "If my thinking is correct, the name of the clan did start with a K; Kho, Ktu, Kre or something like that. It could have been Kroll. I wonder if it's the same clan; do you suppose?"

"I wouldn't know," Wolf stated, stiffly rising from his seat, "but I'm tired of waiting for someone who may never show up, and---and now I'm getting v-e-r-y cold!"

Fox unfolded his legs and caught hold of Wolf's hand, pulling himself up as well. Leaning over the pile of crates, he quickly checked out each direction, reporting quietly, "nothing out there." After turning back, he added, "It's just too quiet. There's something going on."

Hawk looked from Fox to Wolf.

"Do you really think he's coming, Hawk?" Wolf asked, with a touch of sarcasm.

"I told you, Storg will be here," Hawk insisted, hotly. "He said he wanted to help."

Slowly dragging his knapsack closer to the wall, Wolf sat down beside it. With a nod to Fox, he said quietly. "Sorry I was late."

"That's okay, you both were," Fox answered. "It gets more difficult all the time; this food gathering, you know---." He sat, looking straight ahead.

Neither, Hawk or Wolf broke the silence.

Fox finally said, "---but it's worth it, I think," he said, looking back at them. "We're all they've got."

"I know," Wolf agreed.

"I wish Storg was here," Hawk said, softly.

After a pause, Wolf said, "I don't think he's coming, Hawk."

"But when I saw him earlier today," Hawk pleaded, "he said he had some errands to do first and then he'd be here. We gotta give him a chance."

"All right, but only a few more minutes," Fox said, nodding to Wolf.

Nervously straightening the gloves on his fingers, Hawk leaned against the wall and pulled his bags up closer. "I wish my mom would quit hiding my clothes."

"Sh-h-h," said the others.

"I thought I heard something," Fox whispered.

"Me too," Wolf agreed.

Sitting perfectly still, their eyes searched the shadows. Finally satisfied with their safety, they all sighed.

"False alarm, I guess," Fox said.

"It's hard to see anything when it gets this dark," Wolf noted quietly.

Fox nodded, "I know, but in another few of weeks we won't have to carry lanterns for a while."

"Yeah, it's about that time of year," Wolf agreed.

"It feels a little warmer, I think," Hawk muttered, straightening the scarf around his neck. "It must be the fog coming in."

"Yeah, that always helps," Fox said.

Wolf pulled his koyt down closer to his ears and leaned against the filth-covered wall. Turning toward Fox, he asked, "what about the other places; have you checked on them, lately?"

"Oh, sure, they are all covered for this week, anyway. Thanks to everyone's help, it's good. As always, I hope it doesn't mess up. I went over to the south location yesterday, and the east one on Monday. It's been a difficult week for both Tim and Matt. Matt had to do all the collecting alone. His two helpers were sick. Tim's always had trouble. Helpers over there never seem to last very long. I usually have to supplement his food supply with some of my own. The other center, the one on the north side, is scheduled for tomorrow. I've never had to worry about Josh, though. He usually has a pretty good spread."

They all sat, quietly waiting.

Fox whispered, "there are a lot of hungry children out there; more and more every day. It does keep us busy, doesn't it?"

"You're spreading yourself kind of thin, partner," Wolf said, tucking his coat closer around him.

"Maybe," Fox smiled, "but it's worth it."

Chapter Two

Children of the Night

WOLF PULLED HIMSELF UP FROM his make-shift chair and stretched out, motioning toward the exit. "I think I'll take a walk and look for myself. Storg may be down there and we just don't know it." He ducked through the opening and ambled down the trail. As he reached the clearing, a sudden gust of wind blasted across his face, causing him to gasp. He shoved his ponytail under the collar of his coat and flipped up the hood. Quick to button his heavy, wool coat up close around his neck, he steadied himself against the lamp post. Hearing them call, he turned, yelling back, "Fox! Hawk! The wind is wicked down here. Whatever you heard; it wasn't Storg. There's no sign of him."

Acknowledging with a wave, Fox said, sadly, "I'm sorry Hawk but it doesn't look like he's going to make it. We've given him plenty of time."

"I know." Hawk's big, brown eyes shifted from Fox's face toward Wolf, who was still waiting at the crossing. "I just knew he'd keep his promise." Digging the toes of his boots through the snow, his head drooped with disappointment. With tears in his eyes, he took off running down the hill, passing Wolf in the clearing. "Storg's got to come," he cried, searching both directions one last time. "He promised."

"Maybe next time, Hawk," Wolf said.

Fox walked on down the hill, pausing beside Wolf. He nodded toward Hawk. "I feel sorry for the little man, you know. He had his heart set."

"I do too," Wolf said. "There's not much to be said, either that would make him feel better." His gaze paused on Hawk then slipped aimlessly down the street. After a long pause, he said, "I have a thought that's been bothering me for some time; I know it's none of my business but I can't seem to get it out of my mind."

"What would that be, Wolf?"

"Oh, I was just wondering whatever got you interested in this food gathering, thing." Reaching up, he pulled off the knit koyt, adjusted his ponytail then slipped it back on. "It's a pretty radical thing to do; your dad being the governor, and all."

"I've been doing it for a long time now, about four years, I guess; almost five. I started when I was eight, nearly nine."

"I'll be nine, my next birthday, see." Hawk quipped, exposing the date on his arm. "You were the same age as me."

Spotting an old ball, Fox reached down and picked it up. He began tossing it in the air and catching it in his lap. "Yeah, I guess I was."

Wolf reached over, intercepting the ball, and tossed it back. After a few rounds, they moved into the alley.

"So-o-o, what happened?"

"What? Oh, you mean the food thing."

"Yeah!" Wolf answered, tossing the ball to Hawk. "What got you started?"

Hawk missed the catch and ran to retrieve it. He passed it back to Wolf then stood in front of Fox, looking up. "I've been curiously about that, too."

Fox looked down, patting him on the shoulder. "Curiously?"

"Yeah," Hawk said, peering into his face.

"I think you mean curious, don't you?"

"Oh!" Hawk said.

"That's alright, Hawk. Curiously is close enough," Fox smiled.

Hawk looked up, his face beaming. "Well!"

"Well, uh---, okay. It all happened a long time ago."

"Before you were eight?"

"Um-hum, Hawk, it was a few months before that."

"When you were little, huh?"

Raising his voice slightly, Wolf said, "So let him talk, alright?"

"When I was little," Fox smiled, "we were walking across town; my mom, my dad and me. We had gone to visit some friends and were on our way home. It was kind of dark; sort of like it is now. We had about three blocks to go before we would get to our house. I was still nibbling on my sandwich when we were suddenly surrounded by all these children. I was scared to death. I didn't know what to think. I had no idea. They just kept circling around us, closer and closer. I felt like I couldn't breathe."

Stunned at what Fox was relating, Wolf asked. "Did they attack you?"

"Oh no, it was nothing like that," Fox answered. "As soon as we got to our house my parents pushed me inside and quickly closed the door. They apologized, explaining to me about these 'children of the night'. That's what they called them."

"Children of the night?" Wolf asked, quite surprised.

"I know, it's what we still call them," Fox answered. "That's how I've always known them.

"So, who are they, these children of the night?" Hawk asked, missing the ball, again. He ran to pick it up then threw it back to Wolf.

"Well as you know, after the age of six, all children must earn their daily food script."

"I guess my parents pay for mine," Wolf said, catching the ball and tossing it to Fox.

"I know my parents do. I've seen the receipt," Fox added, passing it back.

"My mother missed paying for mine, one time. It was awful." A shiver went down Hawk's back. "I now go in to hiding when that happens."

"So, who are they? Who are these children of the night?" Wolf asked. Reaching out, he caught the ball and tossed it toward Hawk.

"Actually, they are the city rejects," Fox answered. "If for any reason, or none at all for that matter, children may be left as charges of the city. After the age of six, though, the city is no longer responsible for them. They must earn script for their food or do without. That law was passed a long, long time ago."

"So then what happens?" Wolf asked. "What if they don't?"

"You know about the perishing pit, right? It's for those who don't make it."

"Of course I---," Wolf began, "a perishing---a what?" His face paled at the thought. "You've got to be kidding."

"It is what you think it is. Need I say more?"

Turning sharply toward Fox, Hawk said quietly, "I know what it is." He tossed the ball to Fox. Fox missed. The ball dropped and rolled across the ground. Wolf rescued it, and tossed it back.

"I had to work at the perishing pit, one time." Speaking in monotone, Hawk's voice was flat and dry.

Fox caught the ball, held it for a few minutes then tossed it again, toward Wolf. Hawk intercepted it with a vengeance. As soon as it touched his hands, he started ripping it to pieces. Finally exhausted, he dropped to the ground, crying, "Storg really needs to get here."

"I know, Hawk. I'm sure he'll come," Fox said, gently. "We'll wait a little longer."

Wolf stared at Fox, without speaking.

Hawk raised his head, blinking his eyes. "Thanks," he said, squirming around to a sitting position. "He's got to come."

Fox then turned toward Wolf and continued with his story. "The children of the night stay in hiding during the day, when all the patrols are out. They come out at night in search of food."

Staring at Fox, Wolf asked. "Do you think that could happen to me? Do you suppose my parents pay for my script? All they ever talk about are the conditions at the university. I've never---."

"I'm sure they must," Fox said.

Pacing around the lamp post, Wolf said. "Then what happened?"

"I was about to tell you," Fox said, quietly. "I couldn't sleep for days, so I started sneaking out at night. I would walk the streets for hours and hours. I wanted to see how the children managed to survive."

"Weren't you terrified? I would have been," Wolf admitted.

"Well, yes at first I was quite afraid," he answered. "What I was more fearful of was the inevitable confrontation with my parents."

Fox turned and headed up the path toward the hideaway. The others followed.

He slid back onto a crate, propped his feet on the edge and draped the tails of his long fur over his knees. Hawk jumped up beside him, tucking his hands under his arms, wriggling up close.

Wolf slid comfortably onto a box across from them and crossed his legs, leaning forward. "Well, go on," he said, "so-o-o, what happened with that?"

"Well, I did work out a plan and tried it for a while," Fox answered. After carefully dusting the layer of snow off the edges around him, he looked up. "I didn't tell them anything about it. They didn't ask, either. They had to know; I was using their food." He pushed himself further back into the bags of garbage. Reaching over, he pulled Hawk a little closer.

Wolf looked at him quite shocked. "You were taking food from your house?"

"Yes! I still do if I'm running short. You know that."

"Yeah, I knew. I wasn't thinking, I guess."

"When I finally got up the courage to tell them, I couldn't get them to listen. They always found a way to change the subject." Fox stared intensely at Wolf.

Hawk squirmed out of his little niche and pushed his legs over the side. "My mom wouldn't have allowed it, even for a minute," he cried, adamantly. Jumping to the ground, with fists flying, he yelled, "I would have been dumped again, I'll bet."

Wolf nodded toward Fox. "Then what happened?" Waiting for an answer, he watched as Hawk stomped his worn boots through the snow, glaring again, toward the alley.

"Well nothing, really. They just said it would be safer for me if they knew nothing about my activities." He looked away, as if visualizing the incident. "As I said before, all the food I gave away was from our pantry. My parents never mentioned the loss. After a while I found ways of collecting from other places."

"You did that all by yourself?" Wolf's eyes glistened in amazement.

"Yes, most of the time. Occasionally, a friend or two would help me out, but not for long. They were always afraid of getting caught." Fox looked at Wolf with a small grin. "It is so much better now that you and Hawk are helping to recruit volunteers."

"Thanks! I just wish we could do more." Wolf said.

"Maybe some of these days, we can, who knows?" Fox said. He slid out of his seat and stood up.

In the stillness, they heard Hawk muttering to himself. "I know he had to chop some wood, and carry it inside. He had other errands to do, as well. Something about breaking up ice for water, too. It's hard to say what else he had to."

Fox looked at Wolf, then back to Hawk. "Hawk," he said, "your friend is much too late. It's well into twilight and the children---."

"The children will be coming soon and we must have everything ready; I know that." Hawk's voice was tight. He stomped toward the bags and dropped to his knees.

"We should start putting out the food, don't you think," Wolf suggested as he headed toward the grimy wall where the bags were stashed. "Whether Storg comes or not, we need to be ready."

"We should do that," Fox agreed, following Wolf. After opening one of the bags, he pulled out a large, thin piece of cloth and placed it on the ground. He then poured the contents onto it. "The children can have everything we brought," touching his pockets, he whispered to himself, "but this. I brought Andrea and Sara Sue a little something extra. Maybe I can visit them tomorrow." Reaching down, he began spreading all of the food very close to the edge of cloth. "It seemed to be a lot of food when I took it from the pantry. It doesn't look like much, now."

Hearing Fox mutter, Hawk said, turning toward him. "I know what you mean. It's always that way." After dragging his bag away from the wall, he sat down and began unpacking it. "I did have a good haul, though." He announced, proudly. "I've been keeping an eye on the grocery, down the street from where I live."

Wolf sidled up next to Fox. He stood, watching him do some of the sorting and placing for a few minutes. Finally, he said. "What do you see in that Sara, anyway? I heard you mention her name. She used to come out here with the rest of the pack. Not your type, I'd say. Agreed?"

"No! I do not agree," Fox spat out, angrily, "and I don't appreciate you saying so. Besides, if it weren't for Sara Sue, the children wouldn't know where to go for the food."

"Well, you know it's true," Wolf admonished. "Her parents didn't want her, it's obvious, and she---."

"---and she was put on the streets to die, like all the other children, I know," Fox cried out. The defensive sting was still in his voice. He took a few moments to cool down then added, "she has a sister. Her name is Andrea. Four years old, and she can't even walk. Pretty little thing, too! Sara goes out--- she's ten, you know. She goes out and earns her script then she goes to their living quarters and takes care of her sister. Her parents have no idea Andrea is still alive. They don't even care, I suppose."

"So, you're taking care of both of them?" Wolf accused. "Don't you think that's going a little far? If you get caught, you could go to jail."

Raising his voice a few octaves, Fox said, defensively, "what do you think we're doing now; it's the same thing, man?"

Overhearing their conversation, Hawk spewed at Wolf, defiantly. "But you've never been tossed out. I have and it's no fun. I know what it's like being so hungry, and-and so cold, you think you're going to die at any moment. I tell you it's scary."

Fox and Wolf turned; their mouths had dropped open, quite in shock at Hawk's outburst.

Wolf, still totally surprised, blurted out. "What do you mean; tossed out?"

"Tossed out; left with no family or home, no anything! That's what I mean," Hawk cried. "These children of the night, they are not out there by choice, you know."

"Sorry, Hawk," Wolf said. "I didn't mean to get you all wound up."

"Well, if you've never been there, you're just lucky, that's all I can say."

"I said I'm sorry."

Hawk's brown eyes glistened. He pressed on. "Well, I'm gonna tell you what happened, anyway."

Wolf reached over, toying with the food he'd been arranging. Then with a nod, he said. "Go on."

"Well, it happened one time when I was really little. I woke up lying on the ground, right out in the middle of a big lot. It was in a place something like this; the trash was all piled up around me." He glared at Wolf, in desperation. "I had no idea where I was; nothing looked familiar at all. All these people were everywhere, just walking around like I wasn't even there." His voice raised in volume as he spoke, nearing hysteria. "It was two or three days before I found my parents. I looked and looked everywhere for them and---and I was so scared." His voice wavered in pain, at the memory.

"It happened a long time ago." He murmured, rubbing his face. "I try to put it out of my mind. That's why I must do this."

Returning to his sorting task, Fox said softly, "we must do this. That's how it's done. We're the older ones; maybe there will be others to continue our quest."

They settled in to finishing their task when Hawk yelled out, holding a tray of muffins over his head and pointing to Wolf's collected. Wolf saw it too. "Fox, come take a look. You're not going to believe what we have."

"What's the matter with the two of you?" Fox asked, quickly turning around. "What is going on with you?"

Hawk crawled over beside Wolf, pointing at his muffins.

"Do you see what Hawk is showing you?" Wolf said, mysteriously. "Now you need to look at mine. We just noticed it. It's really, really weird."

"Okay," Fox said, looking from one to the other, "so, what is this something weird I'm supposed to be noticing?"

"Well, we were over here," Wolf said, "just sorting through the food we brought, you see when, all of a sudden, we noticed that mine was the same as his. It's all too odd. We each have exactly the same things; two dozen cookies, one round cake, one roast chicken--- and-and the rest of the stuff, it all matches, too. It doesn't feel like a coincidence to me."

"It could be a possibility---," Fox noted, seriously.

"---but not a probability," Wolf finished.

"That is true. It's not likely," Fox said, noting and comparing the displays as he spoke.

"All stores, having anything edible, are to dispose of their excess, whether it's fresh, moldy, spoiled, or whatever," Wolf said, reiterating the law, "and it's obvious that was not done, in this case."

"You are correct. By law, no food is to be left available for taking," Fox agreed. A wrinkled frown pressed between his eyes, "and what else did you notice? There's more, I can tell. Just spit it out."

"Well, it's obvious, this food is fresh," Wolf stated. He reached for some samples. "See what I mean; the cookies are not broken and the loaves of bread are soft. That's just two examples. All the food is like that." After examining some bags of dried fruit, he tossed one to Fox. "There's something wrong here. I can sense it."

"I agree. I just can't put my finger on it, yet," Fox said, opening the bag. He dropped a couple of pieces in his hand then tossed it to Hawk. "What do you think?"

"It looks good to me." He answered, taking a sliver of the fruit. As the fruit touched his tongue, Hawk's thoughts went another direction. He spewed it from his mouth and screamed. "I know what it is! I'll bet everything is poisoned. I'll bet that's it."

"Hold it! Hold it there, Hawk! That wouldn't be it," Fox said, quickly. "There is definitely something wrong here; all this duplication cannot be an accident, but whatever the plan, I am certain the food was not poisoned. You see if the grocer, or any other food handler, were to do such a thing they would definitely face a jail sentence, so that's out of the question."

"I didn't know all that stuff," Hawk said, looking up.

"But that was good thinking, Hawk."

Fox then asked, "Have either of you tested the food?" He reached between the two and picked up a sampling from each."

"Oh, I never eat any of it. It's all for the children," Hawk said, fervently. He picked up a hard roll and some meat chips. "Do you think I should?"

"I save everything for them, too," Wolf added, staring dejectedly at the collection. "All this work we did--- and maybe for nothing! What do we do now? We can't give anything to the children until we know for sure it won't hurt them."

"It seems I'll have to test it," Fox said, decidedly. Before anyone realized what he was doing, Fox scooped up a handful of meat chips and tossed them in his mouth.

"NO! No!" Wolf screamed, hysterically. "Fox, no! Don't do it!" Swinging his arm toward Fox's face, Wolf tried to knock the chips out of his hand.

Hawk jammed into Fox, ducking Wolf's swing.

Fox had already bitten into the food. Within seconds he was spewing and coughing, out of control. His throat was burning; it felt like it was set on fire. Tears stung his cheeks. A painful ache in his ribs began to take over, but the coughing wouldn't stop.

Air stopped in his mouth. Wildly, he flailed his arms out, reaching for something--- anything to touch. "I'm going to die. I'm going to die," he choked, clutching his throat. "I can't breathe. No air, uh, no air, o-h, n-o-o-o."

Suddenly something slugged him in the middle of his back, knocking him to his knees. Fragments of food spewed from his mouth, raking his throat like huge, dry rocks. He collapsed on the ground.

From far in the distance he heard a voice cry out, "are you all right?"

Another voice cried out. "There must be something caught in his throat."

"Can you hear me?"

"Answer me!"

"Air," Fox gasped, raking his hands through the air.

After a while, his body began to relax.

"Whew, I can breathe," he croaked. His hand reached up as the air slid past his throat. With a moan, he cried out, again, "oh, oh no! It feels like---hot sand. Burning---burning me---hot."

With the back of his hands, he swiped water from his eyes. "How did my face get so wet?" Rolling to one side, he wiped his face, again.

Cautiously drawing a breath, his mind cried out, "Oh! Oh, that hurts." Teary-eyed, he tried again. With each attempt, the breathing came easier.

After a few attempts, he managed to whisper, "I thought I was going to die." Tears burned his eyes and he wiped them away. "I've never been so scared."

"Here, let me help you up," Wolf said, gently tugging at his arm. "Are you okay, now?"

"What was it; what did you choke on?" Hawk asked, gruffly. He grabbed the other side, trying to steady him. "You were turning blue."

"A definite lack of oxygen," Wolf murmured, with a knowing nod.

Fox stared at the two of them. Tears were still streaming down. Wiping his eyes again, he pointed.

Finally able to speak, Fox cried out, "Vinegar! It was vinegar. It was soaked in vinegar. That's why there was so much of it. That's why it was so available. It was set out, inviting and tantalizing, so we would be sure to take it all. That's what they wanted us to do. The food wasn't poisoned, but it was just as bad. If the children couldn't eat it, they would lose faith in us and stop coming. I guess that's what the city had in mind."

"Why would they want to do that?" Wolf growled. "It doesn't make any sense."

"Children are a waste," Hawk said, stiffly. "That's what I've heard all my life."

Fox slipped between Hawk and Wolf. Grabbing a handful of cookies, he held them up and yelled out, "VINEGAR!!" at the top of his lungs. Tossing them high in the air, he watched each of the cookies fall and bounce on the ground. "Vinegar!" he said again, with a vengeance. "I never did like that stuff."

A sharp, high pitched voice broke through the dull blackness of late evening. Quite shaken at being discovered, the three boys were jarred into motion, searching for the noisy visitor.

"Hi everybody; what's going on?" A fur-clad image had suddenly appeared In front of them. Behind him was a small sled, piled high with leather pouches.

"Storg!" Hawk called out, excitedly running up beside him. "I knew you'd come."

"I said I'd be here," Storg said, patting his shoulder.

"Look who finally made it," he yelled to the others. He turned back to Storg. "Come on over 'n meet Fox 'n Wolf. We've been waitin' 'n waitin' for you."

"Sorry I'm late," Storg said, waving to the others. "I came as fast as I could. Did I miss anything? I hope not." He followed Hawk across the ice-coated ground; the overloaded sled followed smoothly behind him. "I just knew this was the place you were talking about. I'm glad I was right. I didn't have a bit of trouble finding you, either." He parked the sled at the edge of the clearing and quickly began to un-hook the harness from around his waist. "I'm glad you didn't give up on me."

"Storg, we've been worried about you. Did you have trouble with the patrols?" Hawk asked, holding one of the straps.

"Nah! I just had a hard time getting away from our huts. My mom had a huge list of chores for me to do. I told you about that," he said, with a nod. She said I couldn't leave until they were all done. I didn't think I'd ever get finished." He quickly slipped the harness from his shoulders and placed it on the sled. "Actually, I was trying to stay busy until she finished making the meat cakes. It took a lot longer than I thought." He slipped the bags off the sled and passed them along. "They're inside those pouches; the meat cakes. I didn't think you'd mind if I brought some. They're my favorites. Give them a try," he said, proudly. "I brought plenty for everyone. Go ahead. They're really good."

"Well, uh. I don't know," Wolf said, hesitantly. "Didn't you bring them for the children?"

"Oh, sure! But I brought enough for us, too."

"Oh!" He answered. "We-l-l, maybe I might---."

"I'm not shy," Hawk said, plunging his hand into the bag and grabbing one. After biting into it, he exclaimed, "m-m-m, delicious." He stuffed another chunk in his mouth, mumbling, "still warm and crunchy, too." Once his pockets were filled, he turned the bag up and spilled the contents onto the cloth, pushing the tainted food aside.

"What are you doing?" Storg cried out. "Is there something wrong with my meat cakes?"

"Oh no, it's not your food. It's ours," Hawk explained. "Everything we brought was soaked in vinegar. If you had not brought those cakes, the children would have nothing to eat."

"Vinegar? Oh is that all?" Storg laughed. "Why didn't you say so? I have a fix for that little problem." Digging through his pockets, he pulled out a handful of moss-green granules and rubbed them to a powder. He sprinkled the powder over all the discarded food then said, with a quick smile, "There, that should do it."

"Should do what?" Wolf asked. "What was that stuff, anyway?"

"Just some herbs, that's all," Storg answered, rubbing his hands together. Stepping between the blankets of food, he quickly sprinkled more of the herbs on the rest.

Fox stood to one side, watching this strangely clad, unusual looking creature prance around, laughing and talking as if it were an every-day occurrence. When the task was completed, he asked, "Is that all there is to it?"

"That's it! Give it a taste," Storg answered. He emptied his pockets then stuffed the linings back inside. "Tell me what you think."

After testing a sample, Fox looked at Storg. He smiled. "H-m-m," he said, "quite remarkable. How did you know to do that?"

With a shrug, Storg said, "I don't know. My mother has always done it that way. We often use vinegar as a preservative, especially when we're traveling. We just sprinkle the herbs over our food before partaking. The vinegar is diluted, and the flavor is enhanced."

"You're kidding?" Hawk said. "That's an amazing story. Are you for real?"

"No story," Storg laughed. "Go ahead and take a taste. The food is fine."

"O-o-kay? I hope you're right," Hawk said. Cautiously he reached into the center of a biscuit pile and picked one up. After pinching off a tiny piece, he held it to his nose. "H-m-m? There really is no smell of vinegar. That is amazing." Finally conceding to temptation, he bit into the crusty roll. "Wow! I'll have to give you credit, Storg; your herbs worked wonders. The vinegar taste is all gone." Kneeling down, he began to re-arrange the foods he had shoved to one side.

Storg laughed. "I told you no worries, didn't I?"

Fox looked over at Wolf. "Pretty amazing, don't you think?" He then noticed the piece of fruit Wolf was still holding.

Tentatively, Wolf squeezed his eyes shut and plopped the bite into his mouth, chewing into it.

"We-l-l," said Storg, observing the incident, "what do you think?"

"You were watching?" Wolf said, quite embarrassed.

"Sort of," Storg admitted.

"It really does work, though."

"I told you it would," Storg laughed.

Glancing up from his food sorting, Hawk said, "I think this one's about finished." He stood up and stretched.

"That's good," said Storg. "Is your food the last I need to sprinkle?"

"Yeah, I think so. Why?" Hawk answered.

"Well, that was all the herbs I had left in my pocket. I have just enough to finish the job right here," he said with a toss.

While watching the last of the dust fall, Fox asked, "Storg, did you happen to see any patrols as you were coming through town"

"I'm afraid I wasn't looking for any. Should I have been?"

"I guess not," Fox answered. "It's just something we always do. It's been unusually quiet tonight. Kind of worrisome, you know. "

"It does feel strange, doesn't it," Wolf said. "We did have a bit of a scare, a little while ago. "

With a nod, Fox said. "It turned out to be nothing, though."

"I saw no patrols," Storg said, with a wave of his hand. "Actually, the streets were empty. No one seemed to be about."

"That is odd. Security should have been doing their rounds. They are seldom late."

"Oh really, hm-m-m? I guess I'd be a little apprehensive, too," Storg noted. "I see now why you're so concerned."

"By the way Storg, I do have a question," Fox said. "It's been bothering me ever since you arrived."

"Well, maybe I have an answer," he shot back with a grin.

"I'm serious," Fox said, a little too quick.

"Believe me, I'm not taking any of this lightly," Storg answered.

Attentions aroused, Hawk and Wolf looked toward the two.

"You said you saw no guards?" Wolf asked. "That's curious."

"But true," Storg answered.

Hawk then asked, "So, did you come over the wall---like before?"

"I did," Storg said. The corners of his mouth were beginning to curl up. "How else would I get inside?"

"Was it being patrolled?"

"Of course; the guards were doing their job, if that's what you mean."

"And you climbed the steps, over the snow-bank wall?"

"Yes I did; right over the top. Why?"

"Well, what about the guards; what did you do with them?" Cocking his head to one side Hawk waited for the answer.

"I put them to sleep, of course."

"You what?" Wolf shrieked with surprise.

Hawk stared at Storg. Suddenly, things begin to make sense. He cried out. "You know magic!"

Storg grinned, "of course I do."

"You took a big chance, didn't you?" Fox said. A smile of admiration covered his face.

"It was quite an assumption, I know. I figured there was no magic in them, so I gave it a try. As you can see, I was right. How else was I going to get here? I hope you have no problem with it?"

"None at all," Fox answered.

"I wish I had some of that magic," Wolf said, wistfully.

"Don't we all, Fox said, looking at him. "This food gathering would be a lot easier."

"You may have. You never know," Storg quipped.

"I tried one of the tainted biscuits and-and no vinegar taste," Hawk announced. "You did it, Storg."

"Yeah, we saw," Wolf laughed, patting him on the back. "It took a while to get up the nerve, didn't it?"

"And I know what you're thinking," Hawk answered, somewhat embarrassed. "He's my friend 'n I don't trust him."

"Oh, that's not it at all." Turning to Fox, Wolf said, "Hawk finally tried one of the biscuits."

"Oh, that's good," said Fox.

"So," Storg asked, "what do we do, next?"

"Actually, we're pretty well prepared," Fox answered.

"The children should be coming, any time now," Wolf said, quietly.

"Yes, yes! Should we leave now?" Storg asked. "Is that what you're saying?"

"Yes, I think it's time," Fox answered, signaling for them to follow. "We'll take the path behind the crates. Is everyone ready?"

"Sure! I just need to get my knapsack," Wolf said, picking it up.

"Me, too," Hawk answered, reaching for his folded bags.

"I'll just be a minute, okay?" Storg said, zipping the fur collar over his dark, plaited hair. Then kneeling down, he attached the leather bags to the sled and picked up the harness, headed out after them. The glow, from his lantern, made it easy to follow their footprints.

In a rush, he reached Fox's side and frantically whispered in his ear. "You won't believe what just happened to me."

Fox slowed his pace.

Hawk and Wolf came up on the other side.

Storg's eyes seemed as big as his fists. "Just now, while I was following you, I kept feeling these wisps of air---it's hard to explain---they didn't actually touch me but I knew they were there. They were almost like shadows, all around me. It felt like a presence, but not a reality. Did any of you feel it? What was it?"

Fox whispered softly, "We always feel it. It's the children when they come to feed. They don't want anyone to recognize them. We left just in time."

"What do you mean?"

"They won't come out if anyone is around," Hawk answered.

"Why not," Storg asked, "I don't understand."

"Others would recognize them. Others would know they had no script," Wolf added.

"Oh!" Storg said, pausing beneath a city lamp. "Fox," he said, cautiously, "there's something else that's bothering me." He watched the flicker of dull yellow glow on the snow and kicked into it. Unconsciously, he listened to the crunch.

"What's that?" Fox asked, watching the slush fall from his boot.

Studying his words carefully, Storg said, "These uh, children of the night, as you call them---it seems they have no home. Why is that?"

"Yes, that's true. Most of them are throwaways. They have no place to go," Fox said, meeting his gaze. "We have a facility that takes care of them until the age of six then they must leave; they must care for themselves after that. It's the law. I'm sure Hawk told you about it."

"He did, but I don't understand how a city could turn on small children like that."

"When they don't earn their script," Wolf said, "they come to us."

"Oh! But there's so many."

"I know," Fox nodded. "It really keeps us busy." After a quick glance at the crossing, he made a signal. "Security is not far away. We should get out of sight."

"Are we going back to the hideaway?" Hawk asked, running between Storg and Fox.

"I think it would be better if we found a place to hide; somewhere close by until we head home," Fox answered, with a slight grin. "After security does their rounds, we could walk Storg to the steps, if he'd like."

Hawk's nose crinkled into a grin. "Is that okay?"

"Sounds fine to me," Storg answered, smiling down. "I can make my way back to our camp from there."

Chapter Three

The Tunnel

Fox ROLLED OVER AND REACHED for his blanket, tucking it under his chin. With a start, his eyes flew open and he sat straight up in bed. "Oh, my gosh, what did I get myself into?" He growled, massaging his face. "I must have been out of my mind. I told Storg we would come visit his family. What a stupid thing to even consider." He plopped back across the bed. "How am I ever going to get out this fix?"

He rolled to his side, lifting his head on his hand. "If we visit the Kroll campsite, that means we would have to leave the old city. We could get caught; probably would and I'd be the one to blame. Sometimes I wonder where my smarts are. Hawk and Wolf---why they've never been outside the city before! If I hadn't told them about my leaving, they would never have considered it; I know they wouldn't." Dropping to his back again, he glared at the ceiling. "Oh man, what if we get caught? It would be all three of us in trouble, not just me."

Sliding his hand across the table by the bed, he searched for his timepiece. Once located, he picked it up. "Not that I wouldn't like to. If it were only me, I'd go in a second." He reached for the lamp and lit it. "I knew from the start it was a bad idea but I let Storg talk me into it, anyway. What a mess!" Glancing at the time, he groaned and rolled over. "Two hours," he stammered, "I was asleep for only two hours?" After scrunching the pillow, he pushed his head into it, whining. "That is not enough sleeping time for anyone."

After giving his pillow a hefty toss, it landed on the end of the bed.

He flopped across it, staring at the ceiling, again. "There's no way to leave the old city, anyway; security is always there. H-m-m-m, that's a thought. Every time I've left before, there was an opening of some kind to go through." He grinned slightly. "That must be the answer. We cannot leave if there is no way to get out."

While mulling through these thoughts, he heard the front door squeak, then click. That meant his parents had left for the day. He dozed off. Once again, he awoke and checked the time. It was only twenty minutes later. "I'd just as well get up," he growled, dropping his feet to the floor. Grabbing a robe off the end of the bed, he slouched out of the room.

In the pantry, he found some bread and cheese to munch on then went back to his room and sat on the edge of the bed. "I don't know what's gotten into me," he muttered, putting the snack on the table beside him.

With a slight groan, he reached under the bed and pulled out a lantern. After cleaning the suet from the mirror inside, he polished the outer windows and slipped them back inside the slots and tapped them in place. "It's too late now," he thought. We've already made plans; Hawk and Wolf will be waiting for me to show up." He trimmed the wick and turned it low, not wanting the flame to smoke when the lantern was lit. Once that was done, he filled the reservoir with oil and wiped down the outside casing then set it aside.

Going back to the pantry, he scrounged around until he found a couple of spare pouches and filled them with extra oil. After attaching them to the rope around his waist, he took a length of wick and a handful of matches, stuffing them in his pocket. "Well, I guess I've got about everything I need." Picking up the gathered supplies, his snack and the lantern, he headed for the front door.

It was late morning and the visible horizon was nothing more than a slight haze separating the sky from the gray-white ground. Fox locked the door and went down the steps, heading toward the sidewalk that led down town. The illuminated street lamps had been dulled with suet and wear, allowed only a meager beam to touch the ground. He glanced up, automatically counting them as he walked. After passing the city square, he reached the snowy ridge and turned, following it to the next crossing. Without realizing it, his attitude had begun to change.

He crossed two more streets then aimed for the red brick office building where his parents worked. "Mom and Dad should be having first meal about now," he thought. Making another turn at the end of the street, he passed a large, yellow building with a cupola on top. Security Quarters was written in large, block lettering above the double doors. "I'd better hurry before they see me," he thought. "Probably shouldn't have come this way." Standing up straight and walking with a purpose, he passed the building without mishap.

He reached the next intersection and turned toward the tall barricade of snow that wrapped around the city. The crossover bridge was now in sight and he quickened his steps. "I wonder if Wolf and Hawk have gotten there yet?" He breathed. "I hope so."

After rounding the last corner, he saw Hawk racing toward the steps. Then he shot a quick glance to the top of the barricade, finding no guards outside the shack. "That's good, now to find Wolf." Before the thought had passed his mind, Wolf stepped forward.

"Come on, you two," he laughed, motioning from beneath the steps. "You're both late."

"Yeah, but not by much, I'll bet," Hawk giggled.

"We're not late," Fox smiled, greeting the two. "You're just early."

"Yeah, but not by much," Hawk repeated.

"I know! I know! I just got here, too," Wolf snickered. He then turned toward Fox. "I saw the guards out, a few minutes ago. So-o-o, how do we get over the bridge?"

"We don't. We'll have to find another way. I was thinking about a tunnel. I only know of one that goes all the way through the wall. It's not far from here. Nodding toward the snow-covered barricade, he said. "That bridge is always too dangerous to cross over. We'd have a hard time passing those guards without getting caught. They're always there."

Startled at his remark, Wolf turned, staring at Fox. "It sounds like you've tried it before. Is that true?"

"I'm afraid so," he answered. "I wouldn't try it again, though."

"Say! I know where there's a tunnel," Hawk piped up. "I used to hide my clothes in it. You want to see?"

"You should hide them there all the time," Fox laughed. "Sure, where is it?"

"The same way we're going, only further down the street," Hawk said excitedly. "It's behind where I live. I can't use it anymore, though. Everything gets stolen."

"Oh really?" Wolf said, casually slipping his koyt more snugly on his head. "You don't still use it for storage, do you?"

"Of course not," Hawk answered, "It's bad." Then pointing toward the second street corner, he said. "Do you see those buildings? We just go a few blocks further on down the street. See---over there."

"On second thought, maybe we should come back that way," Fox said, noting the location. "Storg should be directly on the other side of the bridge steps. We wouldn't want to miss him by going too far out."

"Yeah," Hawk said, slightly disappointed, "that's good." He then looked up. "So what's next? Guards are on the---."

Wolf nipped back, "we can't use the bridge; there are guards everywhere. Didn't you hear Fox say he knew about a tunnel?"

"Yeah, but---" Said Hawk.

"He's been outside the barricade, you know."

Whipping around, Hawk's face paled. "Oh---you have?"

"I mentioned it when you were telling about Storg's caves, remember?"

"Well... I guess," Hawk stuttered, with eyes glued to his face.

Noticing the fear in his eyes, Fox said, quietly. "Listen, Hawk, it may seem scary but people do leave the city occasionally. My parents took me to the outside when I was very small. For some reason, they had to leave for a while and took me with them. I don't remember much about it, though."

"So you went out of the city---and you didn't become a monster?" Hawk shuddered.

"That's what I'm trying to tell you," Fox answered.

"But--- but, what about getting caught on the bridge," Wolf reminded him.

"Oh, that happened the last time I left. But every time before that," he said, turning back to Hawk, "I would stay close to where I went out then come straight back in." He smiled. "I was afraid I'd change into a monster, too."

"Did you?"

"Did I what?"

"Turn into a monster?"

"No, but it was a real fear I had." Fox said, gently.

"Well-l-l, I've been really worried about that," Hawk said, seriously, "still am."

"I know. It's hard not to be."

"What about the bridge?" Wolf interrupted, kicking at a clump of snow. "How do we get past the guards?"

Fox looked back at him. "It's not easy. I got caught when I tried it."

"Wolf's voice fell. "Is that all there was to it?"

"Of course not; I wish it were, though." Back to studying the ice-coated barricade, Fox pointed, slightly raising his voice. "There they are; some of my markers. I keep them pretty well hidden. Come on!"

"You really got caught?" Hawk quizzed, running along beside him.

"Yeah, but it wasn't when I left the city; that was pretty easy. When I got caught was when I tried to sneak by the guards, to get back in."

"I don't get it? This is not the easiest place to leave or we'd probably have gone out before now." Wolf stated. "What did you do?"

"I didn't do anything. I just happened to be in the right place at the right time, I guess. Anyway, there was this crew of men; they were standing right over there---," he said, pointing toward the steps leading to the guard shack, "---and I got to watching them. I was curious to see what they were up to. They had all these strange looking tools, like I'd never seen before, and began digging into the side of the wall. After a while I heard them talking about some wire fencing inside that needed to be repaired. That was a real surprise; I had no idea about any fencing, you know," Fox related, "so I kept watching. It took some time but they finally drilled through all the ice and snow, making a big hole in the wall. When they stopped and walked off---maybe for lunch, I don't know---I couldn't stand it any longer; I had to see what they were doing, so when they weren't looking, I just walked inside. That's when I found the opening all the way through."

"Really?" Hawk exclaimed. "Weren't you scared to go in there?"

"I guess, a little. I didn't think much about it, though," Fox answered. "I was too excited."

"What did you see out there?" Hawk asked, with a shiver.

Fox's mouth curled up into a huge smile. "There was snow...lots and lots of snow. You've never seen anything like it in here though. It was clean, white and pretty and sparkly, just like a million lights had been sprinkled all over everything."

"You could see all that in the dark?" Wolf asked, noting the afternoon's dull light.

"Of course not, it was summer time; no sunset, you know. If you could have seen the way it reflected off those wide, white fields." He looked toward each of them, his eyes glowing. "It was a beautiful sight, for as far out into the openness as I could see." Slowly he breathed in---then out. A smile covered his face.

"Oh," Said Hawk. "Wish I'd been there."

"I can't even imagine anything like that," Wolf admitted, looking away. His field of vision registered on some randomly placed igloos, as they walked by. "Then what did you do...you know, when you were on the outside?"

With a silly grin, Fox admitted, "well, I have always wanted to see trees; to touch them and to smell them. All my books have pictures of these... these big and beautiful trees, with green leaves all over them. I have always dreamed of sitting under one of them and looking up through the branches, you know. I was so disappointed the first time I stepped outside the barricade and found no trees; not even little ones. There is that ridge of hills on the south side of town and---."

Suddenly noticing where they were, Fox signaled for them to stop. "We nearly passed it," he said. "Come on, hurry! We don't want to be seen leaving town."

"Do trees smell?" Hawk asked, peering up at Wolf.

Wolf shrugged. "I have no idea."

"Me either." Hawk pushed his koyt further off his forehead. "I hope Storg isn't late."

"Not like the last time, I hope," Wolf agreed. Suddenly, as if in slow motion, he found his feet spiraling over his head as he tumbled to the ground.

"A-o-ouch," Hawk screeched, sliding into Fox. "Your boot...it hit me!!"

"Watch it," Fox cried out. "Umf!" He crashed into the ground.

Hawk fell over him.

Pulling out from beneath the others, Wolf rolled to his knees and climbed to the top. He sat up, laughing. "I can't believe it," he said, leaning over to rub his knees. "All of a sudden I saw my feet where my head should have been," he giggled again. "It's funny now, but it sure wasn't when I landed."

"I felt myself slip," Hawk said, sitting up and shaking his koyt, "but didn't have time to say anything." Tucking his ears inside, he pulled it back over his head. "I thought we were goners that time."

"Anyone hurt?" Fox asked, shaking the snow off his coat.

"Nah! Not me," Hawk said, dusting his jacket with his hand. "It takes more than a little spill to put me down."

"What about you, Wolf? "I saw you land pretty hard."

"I'm good," Wolf said. "I'll be alright."

"That's good. We need to get out of sight," Fox said. "You know how the security is."

"Yeah, I know! They might have heard us…all the noise we made," Wolf agreed.

"They'd get mad at us, too, I'll bet," Hawk said.

"I'm sure they would," Fox agreed. He caught Wolf's eyes and glared.

Wolf looked back with a smirk, but only said, "I wouldn't doubt it a bit…probably get really mad, especially if they knew what we were doing."

"Yeah," Hawk said.

Fox nodded. "That's right."

Hawk looked toward the entrance. "Is that the hole they drilled?"

Not to be outdone, Wolf stepped forward.

They both stopped when Fox held up a cautioning hand.

"Don't go inside yet," Fox said, digging through his pockets. "Give me a minute and I'll light the lantern." Once lit, he held the light slightly ahead, walking slowly. "Follow close behind me; it's hard to tell what we might find."

"Okay," Hawk said, snuggling up close.

Gently swinging the lantern back and forth, Fox guided them inside. They had just passed the entrance when his hands shot out. Quickly turning, he snapped. "Stop, we can't go in there. Go! Get out of here, right now!"

"Why?" Wolf blurted, before thinking. "What's in there?"

"It's full of sleepers," Fox whispered. "Go! Hurry!"

"What are sleepers?" Hawk panted; his face white with fear.

"Just go," Fox urged. "I'll tell you later."

"Uh, where to?" Hawk asked, backing away.

"The tunnel; where you hide your clothes," Fox said, decidedly. "Where is it? Not far, I hope." He extinguished the flame and hurried toward the walkway.

"It's only a few blocks from here," Hawk said, running ahead. "Come on, I'll show you."

"Okay then, we'll follow," Fox said, quickly. "I hope security didn't see us coming out. They'd make those children leave."

Hawk pointed toward a dilapidated housing project, some blocks ahead. "I live on down from those buildings," he pointed, "and the tunnel is behind it; just down from my house."

"You don't have to whisper, Hawk," Wolf smirked, sarcastically. "They can't hear us anymore."

"Oh, okay," Hawk said, somewhat self-conscious. "My mom and I; we live up on the third floor." After making a signal, he ran ahead. "Come on. I'll show you."

"Is your tunnel big or small?" Wolf asked, looking beyond the first housing project.

"It's a pretty good size, I think," Hawk answered. "Why?"

"We're a lot bigger than you are. Do you think we can fit inside of it?"

"I hope so! I used to think it was huge---when I was a little kid." After thinking for a bit, he said. "It may not be all that big, anymore. We'll probably have to crawl through it." He stopped, turning again, "I've hidden my stuff in there a bunch of times, though."

"Does it go all the way to the outside?" Fox asked.

"I dunno! It used to, I guess," Hawk said, "but I've never done it."

"I hope so," Fox said, somewhat uneasy. "Someone told me about another one, but I never could find it."

"Sorry I'm no help. I didn't know about any of them," Wolf said, walking along beside them.

"Well, trying to find it now would be a nightmare," Fox murmured, "and besides, the day patrol would see us."

"You're probably right," Wolf said. "Hawk's tunnel sounds like our only option."

"Yeah, I know. We'll have to make it work."

Following Hawks lead, they slipped quietly behind the apartment complex, heading toward his cache.

Breaking the tense silence, Wolf whispered to himself. "Hang on a minute." Lagging a few steps behind, he reached down, pulling a length of rope from the snow. After coiling it into loops, he tossed it over his shoulder. "It could be useful."

Catching up, he overheard Hawk say, "Fox, you nearly scared me to death when you've found those sleepers." After walking for a while, he looked up. "What are sleepers, anyway?"

"Some of them are children of the night," Fox said, with a nod, "and others are the children who have done something wrong."

"What do you mean?" Hawk asked. "Is that why they are out for food, instead of in the bedding hall? I don't understand."

"You remember the bedding hall? I'm surprised about that." Fox said, shaking his head. "You were just a little kid."

"When I was dumped? Yeah, I know," Hawk said, sharply. "That was the only good thing that happened to me. It was when I followed a bunch of people into a big building. I had such a hard time climbing those steps; they were really tall. I had to put my foot up then push," his leg lifted, slightly, "to get onto each step. When I got inside, I saw rows and rows of mats on the floor. Each of them had a blanket on top. I was so-o-o sleepy, so when I saw an empty one, I crawled right into it. The next thing I knew, I was waking up. Oh yes, now I remember why. I saw somebody standing on a box. They were blowing a whistle and everybody was running for the door. I was so scared. Mostly, I was afraid all those people were going to step on me, so I got up and ran, too." Hawk looked up at Fox. "Was that where I was? Was that the bedding hall?"

"It sounds like it might be." Looking back at him, Fox answered, "but I've never been there. When the guards caught me going over the steps, I wasn't allowed to use the bedding hall. That was part of my punishment, you see. I had to earn my script for the day, of course, but I had to hunt for a place to sleep. I wasn't allowed to go home, or to even see my parents or anything, for two whole weeks."

Wolf finally interrupted their conversation. "I had never heard of sleepers either, until just now. Fox, you said you've been one. Why were you a sleeper?"

"I was just telling Hawk about that," Fox laughed, glancing toward him.

"Oh, I guess I missed it."

"Not really," Fox said, with a nod. He hesitated then took a deep breath and began, again. "As I was saying before, I slipped through the barricade wall. There was an opening and I couldn't resist going out." Looking at the two, he grinned. "But who would have thought how hard it would be to find the same place again when I got ready to come back in. I sure didn't."

"Why was that?" Hawk asked.

"From the outside of this town, everything looks different."

"Well, what about landmarks?" Wolf suggested, somewhat sarcastically. "We had a class about that, one time."

"I thought of that, of course. But that's the other thing. Landmarks are so huge, and look so much alike, that the only thing I knew for sure was which side of the city I was on. It's really not that easy."

"What about hills, fence posts, lanterns or something like that?"

"That's what I mean. It seemed like everything had moved---except the steps." Fox said, kicking at a clump of old snow. It rolled in front of Wolf.

"Curious." Wolf said, thoughtfully. When he kicked it back, the clump of dirty ice broke into pieces.

"I know, but true. Anyway, I used the steps where the guard shack is, you know, and counted my paces to where the repair was supposed to be. It was a lot of walking, and I had to repeat it a number of times, before I found the right spot. When I finally did and tried to slip back through, the damaged fence had been mended, even though the opening was still there. So the only way out of my situation was to take the steps."

"But Fox, you can't get around the guards," Hawk said, quite distraught. "You know they're always on the wall."

"Yes, I knew that, but I had to get back inside. You see, I'd been away for almost a week and my supplies were nearly gone. I didn't have a choice."

"So what did you do?" Wolf asked. With a quick swing of his foot, he knocked another chunk of ice out of the way.

"The only thing I could do," Fox answered, shrugging his shoulders. "I was hoping to sneak by the security shack."

"Did you get caught?" Hawk asked, staring into Fox's eyes.

"Of course he got caught," Wolf sneered, "you silly ninny."

"Wolf!" Fox eyed him cautiously.

"Well!"

"He's eight."

"Sorry, Hawk," Wolf said, looking down. "I wasn't thinking."

"That's okay."

"Funny thing, though, I nearly made it." Fox smiled, smugly. "I got all the way up to the crossover before they saw me. It was when I was coming back down the steps; that was when the guards caught me."

"What did they do?" Wolf asked, quickly. "Did they kick you around or something? They're mean enough."

"Nah," Fox answered. "They put me in a holding room until the next day. That's when I went before the board."

"What's a board?" Hawk asked, curiously staring at Fox's face, Fox raised his voice, saying. "I had to go before the board," he paused, adding with emphasis, "the governor---my father!"

"Oh-h!"

"He's the one who made the final decision on my punishment," Fox said. "He gave me the two weeks as a sleeper." Lowering his voice, he added, "It could've been worse, you know."

"That's for sure," Wolf said.

A shudder went down Hawk's back. He dropped his eyes to the ground, watching his feet move in front of him. Finally looking up, he said quietly, "Being a sleeper would be scary."

Studying their faces, Fox continued, "I was just glad he knew I was okay. That was a good thing. It was hard for me to wait that whole two weeks, though. I was so anxious to tell my parents about what all I'd seen."

"Weren't you afraid---being a sleeper, I mean?"

"I guess---a little, but I deserved it."

"Quickly changing the subject, Hawk asked, "Did you find any trees?"

"No, I'm afraid not," Fox grinned. "That's the sad part. There were some scrubby bushes and stuff, but nothing like the pictures in my books."

"Where did you go?" Wolf asked.

"When I got to the other side, you mean?"

"Yeah."

"Oh, I headed toward our mountain, of course; you know the one," he nodded slightly. "That was my plan, once I got to the outside. All we can see from here is the very top of it. I could never visualize what the rest might be like. I wanted to see as much of it as possible since I finally had the chance." He snickered to himself. "I had this big plan, you see. I was going to run right over to it and go all the way around. I was so surprised at how far away it was."

Listening attentively to Fox's description, Hawk finally interrupted him by saying, "I can hardly see even the top of it, unless I stretch high on my tip-toes."

"I never gave it much thought, myself," Wolf said, casually.

Fox continued, paying no attention to Wolf's remark. "The very top of the mountain was quite flat, you know. That was pretty disappointing to find out."

"Why?" Hawk asked, curiously.

"I just imagined it being so different. I expected it to be tall and grand looking, you know, like the pictures in my books, but it wasn't like that at all," Fox said. "When I saw the whole mountain, from top to bottom, it didn't seem very tall. I guess, because it's so wide at the bottom. It's odd looking, really."

"Odd! How so?" Wolf asked, showing a bit more interest.

Fox laughed, slightly. "Well, the one side was scooped out, kind of like a big spoon had sliced into it."

"Did you go all around the bottom of it? I would have," Hawk said, excitedly.

"I couldn't. I told you, it's huge," Fox exclaimed, spreading his arms out. "You have no idea how big that mountain is. The bottom of it spreads way out, nearly reaching this big, icy pond I walked across. It's all squiggly and stuff, too."

"Were there any trees on the mountain?" Hawk asked.

Wolf swatted at him. "He said he didn't see any trees, right, Fox?"

"No, Hawk, there weren't any trees, just scrubby bushes and stuff. But wait till I tell you the best part," Fox insisted, excitedly. "When I got closer to the scooped out part, I saw how slick and shiny it was, all the way from the bottom to the top; covered with ice, I guess. Then when the sun reflected off that slope, I saw this beautiful rainbow. It was hanging right above my head. No kidding!"

"Was it raining?" Wolf asked.

"No, I don't think so. Why?" Fox asked.

"Just wondering; something must have put moisture in the air," Wolf said, logically. Picking up the pace, he stepped into the lead. An all-knowing frown crossed his forehead. "It takes the sun and moisture to make rainbows, you know."

"To be sure," Fox answered. "It was a real moment, though."

"Was it where sleepers were?" Hawk asked. "Was that where you went out?"

"No, huh-uh. I'll show you some time, though," Fox answered. "That's a hard thing to forget."

"Sleepers are just children, aren't they?" Wolf asked, flanking Fox on the other side.

"Sure, what else would they be?"

"I don't know," he grinned slightly, turning toward Hawk, "thought they might be monsters."

"They are not…," Hawk yelped, staring at Fox, "…are they?"

"Oh, come on," Fox said, "I told you I was a sleeper, once. I am no monster."

"So, what made you a sleeper?"

"I broke the rules."

"Going out of the city without permission; that rule makes sense," Wolf said. "You could have been killed."

"I know, but there are a lot of other rules, too."

"Like what?" Hawk quizzed.

"Being late to the bedding hall, not having your script, trying to use someone else's script, possessing food your script didn't list. There are a lot of things...." His voice trailed off.

"Nobody's supposed to leave the city, anyway," Wolf said, sharply. "That's the law."

"One time when my parents had to leave...," Fox began, "...and took me with them...."

"No kidding," Hawk said, looking up at Fox.

"I think you told me about it," Wolf said.

"This was a different time, Wolf."

"Oh."

"For some reason, we had to leave the old city in a hurry. My mother had our belongings all packed up when my father came home. They bundled me up and strapped me to a seat. I remember that because something kept pinching my leg. It hurt so bad, I couldn't stop crying. My mother held her hand over my mouth. I could hardly breathe. They were acting really scared."

"What else do you remember, Fox?" Wolf asked. "Where were you?"

"I don't know. I don't remember very much about it. I was two or three years old, maybe four, I guess." He stared at his feet, shuffling them through the snow. "We stayed in a room, a really dark room, my mother and me. Once in a while my father would come and visit us for a few days."

"I don't know how I got back here. My mother and I had been playing some kind of game one night, just before bedtime. I remember her picking me up that evening and holding me in her lap. When I stretched really hard, I could touch the floor on both sides of her knees. We had so much fun. A little while later my father came in, unexpectedly. Right at first, she seemed so happy to see him. A little later, she was crying."

"I don't remember going to sleep, either but when I woke up she was putting food in our pantry where we live now." Fox glanced toward each of them then stared down the street. "I've never been told why they were so afraid.

"Did you ever ask them?" Hawk asked, curiously.

"No, I never felt like I should," Fox answered.

Wolf glanced over at the two then scraped up a handful of snow. He squeezed it into a ball and tossed it at an old discarded sign. He then asked, thoughtfully. "Were you born here, Fox?"

"I'm not sure. I've never thought about it. Why?"

"Oh I was just wondering," he answered. "My parents said I was born somewhere else."

"Oh really?" Fox said, turning toward him. "What brought that up, anyway?"

"Oh, I was just thinking about what you said."

"You mean my not knowing how I got here?"

"Yeah, I guess," Wolf said.

"Do you remember the name of your home town, Wolf?" He asked, curiously.

With a small laugh, Wolf answered, "well I don't know how to pronounce it, but I can find it on a map. I've looked it up before."

Skipping along, just in front of the two, Hawk suddenly pointed ahead, saying, "we're almost there." Excitedly, he started running toward the corner. About half way there, he slowed down, pausing in front of the last two windows. They were both facing the street and boarded up. He turned, waving in anticipation and called back, "come on! I'll show you where I hide my stuff."

"It's about time," Wolf growled, scraping up another handful of new snow. Giving it a toss, the slush splattered right behind Hawk's heels.

Fox shot him a fiery glare.

Wolf shuffled on past Fox, slowly closing the space between himself and Hawk.

Oblivious to the event, Hawk yelled back. "All we have to do is turn at the next corner. We'll be going right in front of my apartment. It's not very far away, now."

Hanging a few steps behind, Fox watched Hawk bound excitedly down the street. There seemed to be something brewing between Wolf and Hawk, but he couldn't put his finger on it. He saw Wolf getting closer. He then saw Hawk turn and point at the apartment above them. He couldn't hear the conversation but it seemed friendly enough. "Maybe it's just the age difference," he pondered. "Wolf should be a bit more accommodating, though. He's quite a bit older and needs to keep that in mind."

The apartment complex stretched along three full city blocks; all in need of repair. Most of the paint had worn away, leaving any color that might have been there to the imagination. Most of the windows had been boarded up. A few transparent panes still had frames around them, but were dulled to an opaque gray. Most were covered with wide strips of tape covering the cracks and breaks, precariously holding them in place.

Still following at a distance, Fox's attention was diverted by rippling waves of pale green light dancing above him. He could feel the energy as the mystery lights passed by. A steady, magnetic force pressed through him, sending with it, a surge of well being. He watched the lights slip over the city and fade away. "Wow! I've not had that happen in a while," he said, reveling in the moment.

Released from the pressure, he looked ahead, noticing Wolf and Hawk deep in conversation. They were passing the last apartment on the street. "Maybe it's my imagination," he thought. "Everything seems fine, now."

He saw Hawk pointing directions to Wolf. They both turned at the end of the street, cutting across a narrow field. By the time he arrived, they were already clearing debris away from the tunnel entrance.

Wolf looked up and grinned. "Got caught in the mystery waves, didn't you?"

"Yeah, it's been a while," Fox admitted. "My legs felt heavy as I crossed under them."

"This is it! This is the place," Hawk giggled, excitedly. "It's pretty small, like I was telling you, but I'll bet we can get through. Come on!"

"Need any help?" Fox asked. He picked up an armload of trash and dumped it out of the way.

"Nah! We're good," Hawk said, dropping to his knees. He pushed away the last of the garbage and quickly slithered into the opening. "I've never been through the fence part, though. It's in the center of the wall, you know."

Crawling on his stomach, Wolf wriggled through the entrance. "Umf! Ouch!" he squawked, forcing himself inside. "I'm right behind you. Keep going. You're doing fine." Squirming around to look back, his head connected with something hard. "O-o-che," he cried out.

"Sor-r-y!" Hawk called back. "I'm going as fast as I can, but there's a bunch of wire wound up in here. It has all kind of poky things sticking out everywhere. I don't know if I can push it out of the way."

"Just get hold of it and---" Wolf called out.

"Ou-e-e, they jabbed me in the arm--- them poky things! Now they're in front of my face!" Hawk yelled back. "Just a minute---I'll try to go under them."

"Yikes, Hawk, watch it! Your boots are wicked on my nose!" Wolf bellowed. "Did you get through the wire?"

"I'm past all that. I'm in this slick part now. Move back. I'm going to try something." Turning around, he began stomping his boots over and over into the ice-coated tunnel walls, forming ridges deep enough to push against. With a sharp kick, he boosted himself part way around the last of the wire mesh. Finally, he yelled out triumphantly, "I got it, I got it. I got my legs through!"

"Go ahead. Don't stop now. You're going make it," Wolf urged. "Watch that other piece of wire, swinging over there beside you. Don't let it hit you in the face." Sliding a little further back, he gave Hawk space to move around.

R-I-P! "Did you hear that?" Hawk groaned, pulling at the fabric stretched against his legs. "I think I tore my pants." There was a short silence then he said. "Where's Fox? Is he still behind you?"

"M-m hum, still back here." Fox grunted. "Do you have much farther to go?"

"Can you see the outside, yet?" Wolf asked.

"Not really. I hear the wind blowing, though."

"You must be getting close."

"I know!"

"These walls are as slick as glass," Wolf groaned. "I can't get hold of a thing. My boot keeps slipping around."

"I know. It's all smooth there, but when you get a little farther, you can use those ridges I made," Hawk grunted. "The other side of that poky wire was a lot easier to get through."

"What do you mean?"

"Now I've gotta use my elbows to stay straight," Hawk groaned. "It's slick in here. I keep sliding in all directions."

"Well, keep on moving, anyway." With a little more patience, Wolf then asked, "Do you need a boost?"

"It might help."

Wolf jammed his feet into the ridges, pushing Hawk a few inches ahead. After a slight twist and a shove, he finally cleared the rest of the mesh divider. "Did that help?"

"A little bit! Don't push so hard, though. These walls are really slippery, and I nearly spun around, that time," Hawk whined. "Now, try it again, but a little softer."

"Okay, grumpy," Wolf teased. "Any better?"

"Oh yeah, a lot. I can reach the sides with my feet, now."

"Well, it must be getting narrower if you can do that. I sure hope we don't get stuck in here," Wolf said. Kicking off against the wall, he slid up behind Hawk.

Fox suddenly cried out in pain, "Hey there, Wolf, watch where you're kicking. I'm still back here."

"Oops! Sorry! Are you still having a problem with that ball of wire?"

"I would say so! I'm really in a tight squeeze back here."

"Oh, but we're fine!" Wolf snickered, looking back at him. "We've got plenty of space up here."

"Yeah, so you say," Fox groaned. "You're both a lot smaller than me."

"How far back are you?" Wolf called, twisting around to look.

"Right behind you---this wire is awful to get through."

"Just be careful, Fox. Go slow and easy. There are a lot of sharp, pokey pieces sticking up." Wolf turned a little to one side and reached back. "Let me see if I can twist them around you."

"Uh, that's a little better," Fox grunted. "I think I've got one arm loose."

"Hang on! Let me hold the whole thing up. Maybe you can get through it that way. Okay?"

"Got it," Fox muffled an answer.

"Give me a minute," Wolf cautioned. "Don't move for a minute. Let me get a better hold on it."

"Okay, go ahead. I'm just about through it, I think."

"Here! Grab hold of this mesh and push it out of the way."

"I've got it," Fox said, reaching out.

"Good," Wolf said. After turning back he shoved against the wall, slipping forward.

"Is Hawk out, yet?" Fox called out.

"No!" Hawk shouted back. "I'm stuck."

"How far are you from the exit?"

"I'm at the exit. It's right in front of me."

"What's the problem?" Fox grunted, giving himself another boost. "Is something blocking it?"

"Oh---. Uh---no, not really," Hawk answered, looking out. "I can see the snow."

"Then what's going on? Why can't you get out?"

"I'm---uh--- I'm afraid."

"You are---what?" Wolf yelped. With his face right next to Hawk's boots, Wolf slid to one side, trying to see past him. "Afraid of what?"

"I'm afraid I'll---uh, turn into a monster," Hawk's voice trembled.

Listening from behind, Fox thought for a second then he called out, "You know, Hawk, the first time I went out, I was afraid, too. It's not an easy thing to do."

"I've always been afraid I'd turn into a monster, even when I was little."

"That's okay, Hawk," Fox said. "You don't have to go. We'll just back up so you can get out. Don't worry about it.

"Just give me a minute, okay?"

"Sure. Take your time," Fox said, wriggling slightly to give Wolf more room for his feet. "If you close your eyes and---."

"Hello in there. Fox! Wolf!" Hawk yelled, excitedly, "Come on out, the snow really is sparkly out here."

"He's out," Wolf cried. "Hawk's made it out."

"You okay, Hawk?" Fox yelled. Pushing on the tunnel walls with both hands, he slid right up behind Wolf's boots.

"Yeah, I'm good," Hawk answered.

Wolf scrambled out, jumping to his feet. Leaning down, he yelled into the tunnel," Come on out of there, Fox. We made it."

"I'm right here," Fox laughed, looking up from the opening. "It would be nice if you gave me a boost."

Wolf reached down and tugged, pulling first one hand then the other. "I'd say it's a good thing you're not any bigger."

"Thanks for dragging me out. That was a pretty tight fit." Fox said, getting to his feet. After shaking the snow and grit off his coat, he stared in wonder at all the sights. His vision slowly traced the furthest distance of the space in front of him. Finally releasing a heavy sigh, he said. "It must have taken a lot longer than I thought to get through. I was hoping it would still be daylight."

"It probably took a couple of hours or more," Wolf said, anxiously.

Noticing an odd grind in Wolf's voice, Fox turned, and at the sight, cried out. "What's wrong? You look like you've seen a ghost."

"I don't feel so good either." Then glaring at Fox, he blurted out, "This is nothing like I expected. After all you've been telling us, I had all these visions and expectations---and this isn't it." He hesitated, weaving back and forth, while staring out across the dimly lit fields. "I feel really strange, too."

"Does your stomach feel fluttery and unsettled?"

"Yeah, I guess," Wolf tucked his arms across his midriff. "My head feels kind of woozy, too."

"I'm not surprised. It hit me about the same way; my first time." Taking hold of Wolf's arm, he guided him to a large boulder. "Why don't you sit down for a few minutes?"

"Oh," Wolf said, rubbing his temples, "maybe I should."

"It still makes me feel strange, but not as much." He then noticed the blank stare in Wolf's eyes, and the unsteady way he was acting. "Do you feel any better, sitting down?"

"Yeah, I think so."

"Give yourself some time."

"I think it's beautiful out here," Hawk giggled excitedly. He slid between the two of them then took off running across the open field.

Fox watched Hawk's antics, with a grin. "My, my, my, it didn't take long for him to adjust."

Fox sat down beside Wolf. "It was during the summer months when I was here before. It was daylight the whole time. That may have been what you were expecting. I'm sorry if you're disappointed."

"I'm not sure I'm so disappointed. It's my stomach. Feels like I'm going to get sick," Wolf answered. "It's just so different; seeing so much open space. It's almost---scary. You know, a feeling---of the never-ending, I guess."

Looking away for a moment, Fox searched around until he spotted Hawk, far off in the distance, gliding across the field. He smiled.

Back to Wolf, he said, hesitantly, "I know. It's like another world, isn't it?"

"M-m-m-hm," Wolf murmured, tightening his arms across his stomach.

"Look, Wolf, look just above your head," Fox said. "It's a beautiful experience out here."

Shades of purple had transformed the broad space above into brilliant color. The aurora borealis mystery lights had suddenly appeared. They were skipping and dancing across the wide spacious fields of white, from one horizon to the other. Alive with shades of green and gold, the coursing lights energetically spun and pulsed back and forth. Continuously, the colorful display swayed, filling the massive tundra with a musical rhythm from within. In perfect rotation, they spiraled and stretched, upward through the atmosphere, to finally meld into the star-filled blackness of arctic night.

Then far to the east, and high above, a giant spill of violet and purple brightness began to flow downward. With a rush, it tumbled into the waiting river of cranberry and variegated pinks, seeming to crash like a waterfall over a rocky precipice. The energy of light then pushed into a waiting lake of red, as it pooled and spread across the lower sky.

Blending into the musical tempo of green and gold energy passing below, the dancing light phenomenon gracefully slipped over the western horizon and out of sight.

Tearing his eyes from the scene above, Fox asked with concern, "Where did Hawk go?"

"I'm here," Hawk giggled, "right behind you. I was trying to catch up with the mystery lights. They were too far away, though."

"Careful in doing that Hawk, you might get lost," Fox cautioned.

"I went way out there, but I could still see you and Wolf. I didn't want any monsters coming after me."

"Where's your lantern?"

"It's right here. Do I need to light it?"

"Not if you can see without it," Fox answered, swinging his lantern around as he turned. "One may be enough."

"Not much to see, anyway," Wolf growled.

"I guess you're feeling better," Hawk giggled.

"I suppose," Wolf answered, "still not much to see."

"Grumpy," Hawk said, looking up.

"Good!" Fox said, ignoring Wolf's whining. "If we can get by with one lantern, it will conserve our fuel."

"Fine with me," Hawk giggled, sliding back and forth between them. "This is fun."

"Sorry about the view, Wolf," Fox said. "Daylight makes a difference, I promise."

"You didn't like the mystery lights?"

"Didn't see them; I was kinda busy," Wolf whimpered, folding his arms across his stomach, again.

With Fox in the lead, the three continued along the city's outer edge, hoping to soon rendezvous with Storg. The sky was now a clear, crisp, cloudless blue-black. It reached far out across the broad fields with nothing but a few spiny bushes to hinder the view. The distant ridge of rolling hills wrapped the tundra's edge, giving a stopping point to the eyes. With the stars and moon reflecting off the fields of new snow, the night still held the glow of twilight. They followed along the southern perimeter of the compound wall, toward the steps. Last year's ice and snow were beginning to thin slightly. Much of the new snow had already blown away. Having no idea what lay in their path, they proceeded cautiously.

"I've never been here, before," Fox muttered, holding the lamp in front of him.

"You said you'd been out here," Wolf muttered. "You should know---."

"Not on this side of the steps, Wolf. I went west, toward the mountain."

"Oh!"

"Where's Storg?" Hawk grunted. "I thought he was supposed to be waiting."

"He shouldn't be too far away,"

"I haven't seen any steps yet." Wolf reminded him.

"Hey, this is fun," Hawk giggled, running to the front. He slid a short distance on the ice then stopped and waited.

"How are you feeling, now?" Fox asked.

"Okay, I guess. Being on the outside sure is more different than I thought. I had no idea it would be so dark." Wolf grumbled.

"Once your eyes get fully adjusted, you should be more able to see. It may take a little while, though."

"I hope so. Following behind you is pretty boring," Wolf groaned. "I can hardly see my feet."

"Just watch my lantern," Fox said, lightly. "Hawk's not complaining."

"The moon's out 'n everything's glowing," Hawk said, happily.

Wolf suddenly cried out, "What is that shadowy thing up ahead?"

"I saw it, Wolf. You don't have to watch your feet all the time," Fox said, with a snicker. "It's some kind of a big boulder; a huge rock." He broke a trail through the snow then walked up close to the edge and around it. "Like I said before, this is all new to me, too. Just stay close and we'll be fine."

"Uh, okay," Wolf said, stepping up close to it.

Hawk took off, sliding around the two of them. "Oh my gosh!" He shrieked. "The wind---the wind is lifting me. I'm all the way off the ground. I can't get down."

"Hawk," Fox yelled, jumping up, he grabbed at Hawk's flailing arms and pulled him to the ground. "It kinda gave you a big toss, didn't it? You'd better hold on to me, okay?"

Seconds later, they were all jolted by an unusual scraping noise that cut through the wind. Fox quickly jerked Hawk in behind him. Looking up, he saw a row of lamps, hanging at intervals, along the top of the compound wall. When a gust of wind struck the lamps, they began swinging back and forth on the hook. With the metal rubbing against metal, it caused a hollow, scraping sound that cut through the crisp air. They were there to light the catwalk for the guards walking their rounds. A hint of the brightness filtered down the edge of the outside wall.

"What was that?" Wolf and Hawk yelped in unison. Holding a finger to his lips, Fox pointed above his head.

"Oh!" Hawk said, his teeth chattering uncontrollably, "I thought it was a monster."

"It was a creepy sound, all right," Wolf admitted, patting Hawk on the shoulder.

Looking up again, Fox saw a guard passing by. His heart skipped a beat. Automatically, as if it made a difference, he tucked his unruly locks of red under his koyt and slipped closer to the wall, motioning for the others to do the same.

Catching an image below, the guard yelled, "Yoh, who goes there?" Flashing his beam over the side, he searched for the movement that had attracted him.

"Hurry, get out of sight," Fox commanded, edging up closer to the wall.

Hawk and Wolf quickly jumped behind the massive boulder and slipped beneath the edge of it. Nervously shoving his ponytail tightly under his koyt, Wolf settled into a stiff crouch, just out of the beam as it swung by. Hawk tucked his feet further under the edge of the rocky ledge and snuggled up close to Wolf.

For the next few seconds they held their breath. Finally realizing Fox was not with them, Hawk and Wolf peeked out of hiding. Then they heard his voice.

Fox was standing in the guard's light beam, yelling back at him."Yoh, yourself! This is Brog. I am assigned to the outer perimeter, tonight. I've gotta walk the whole miffin thing."

"When'd they start that? Never done it before, Rob," the guard yelled back, swinging the beam toward Fox's shadow.

"Yeah, tonight, I guess," Fox answered, swinging his lantern. "I got the draw, though. Miffin cold out here, too. Wanna swap?"

"Nah! Don' think so," the guard laughed. "Som'thin' wrong with your lamp?"

"It just blew out," Fox lifted his lantern, swinging it in front of him. "Gotta find a place to light it. The wind's fierce down here."

"Good luck, 'ole buddy."

"Thanks for nothing," Fox called back. "Better get goin' or I won't get the round done in time. See ya!" He swaggered out of the guard's light and ducked behind the boulder with the others. "We'd better get a move on."

"I can't believe what you did," Wolf said, staring at him in awe.

"Go on! Hurry! Both of you, run for the steps while I light this lantern. He's going to be checking on me. I've got to try and trick him." Fox crawled under the ledge, after digging through his pockets for some matches.

"What are you doing?" Wolf whispered, loudly.

"I'm going the other way. Just go!"

Hawk crawled out of hiding and follow Wolf without saying a word. After going a short distance they both looked back. They saw Fox strutting arrogantly along, in the opposite direction, swinging his lighted lantern as he went. He raised it high above his head and waved at the guard. "Got it lit," he yelled, "See ya."

The guard waved back and headed toward the steps.

When Fox reached the border path, he retraced his steps, running back toward the others. Out of breath, he whispered to Hawk and Wolf, "he's not going to believe that line I gave him for long. He'll be asking about me, you know. We'd better get to Storg before he reaches the shack. Come on!"

Chapter Four
The Elf

"MY EARS! MY EARS!" HAWK screamed, frantically holding the sides of his face. His normally small, ordinary ears had suddenly become unusually long and slender. Extending off the sides of his head, they were pointing straight up. "What's happening to my ears?" he wailed, attempting to push them back inside his koyt. It flew off again, landing in a pile of snow. After bending and twisting the odd growths, Hawk found they were securely connected to the sides of his head. That didn't help at all. He tried over and over again to pull them off; they were quite attached. Feeling totally helpless and alone, tears started rolling from his eyes.

Noticing that Fox and Wolf were watching from a distance, he tried to hide them under his koyt, but it flew off. "What am I going to do? I can't let them see these things," he thought. "I don't even know what they are." He glared at his friends, standing in the distance. They were still waiting. "I've got to do something." With an angry twist, he reached down and raked at the koyt, crammed the unwanted extensions inside then stretched it as far over his face as he could. When he let go, the koyt flew off, again. He looked down, glaring.

"They're going to laugh when they see I've been crying. They'll think I'm a baby." Mad at the thought, he said defiantly. "They don't have these things hanging off of them. Just let them laugh and see if I care."

"So, self," he scolded, "what are you going to do?"

Wiping his eyes on his sleeves, Hawk said, decisively, "I must have gotten into something. I guess I'd better see what it is before I really panic." Pulling one of the protrusions across his cheek, he tried to inspect it. "O-ou-ch!" he cried out, immediately letting go, "that hurt!" After a quick release, the ear regained its stature.

Hawk thought again about the situation. "Well, if something is on me and I can't get it off, I guess I'll have to hide it. I'll just have to try a little harder to keep my koyt on, that's all." Searching the grounds around him, he growled. "So now, where did I lose that koyt? I know it's here, somewhere." Spying it on top of a snow bank, he growled. "There you are," and snatched it up. After squishing both ears inside, he stretched the koyt all the way under his chin, trying to tie it together. As soon as he let go, the koyt immediately bounced off his head again. Picking it up, he tried again and again.

Fox looked back, watching Hawk bend down then raise back up, over and over again. "What is he doing?" He thought. Determined to get Hawk's attention, Fox waved his koyt over his head, yelling at the top of his voice. "Come on, Hawk! You'd better hurry or were never going to connect with Storg."

Noticing Fox, Wolf turned as well. "What's up with Hawk?"

"I don't know. We should probably wait for him, though," Fox decided. "He's a lot smaller than we are. Maybe he's having a hard time getting through the snow."

"Oh, I'm in no hurry. I was just wondering," Wolf said. "I was in needing a breather, anyway. It's hard work trying to navigate through all this snow. I hate to admit it but I'm exhausted and we've not even reached Storg, yet. Pretty sad, huh?"

"Yeah, I know. I'd forgotten about that part." Taking note of their location, Fox pointed toward the steps. "Traveling in snow is always difficult. I wouldn't like to make a long trip through it."

"The guard shack…just ahead; yeah, I see it," Wolf said. "I thought we'd have seen Storg by now."

"He's probably hiding near the old tunnel entrance," Fox answered. "It shouldn't be much further, now?"

"That's what I was thinking, too. I've been kind of watching for him."

"Well, it is a logical place to wait, I'd think."

Looking back, Wolf said, sounding relieved. "Here comes Hawk. It's about time, too."

"I wonder what his problem was?"

"Whatever it was, he seems okay, now." Wolf said.

"He kept yelling and yelling, but I couldn't make out what he was saying."

"Me either," Wolf said. "It sounded like he said deer. I've not seen any, though."

"I've never seen any reindeer this close to the city, but I guess it could happen," Fox said. "They are around, though. I saw some when I tried to reach the mountain. They were skittish and ran away from me." Looking back, he saw Hawk running toward them. "What is he doing with that koyt? He's got it pulled over his eyes. Oops, it fell off---and now he's stomping it into the ground. Good grief, what's the matter with that boy?"

While they were watching, Hawk pulled another one from his pocket. It bounced off his head as soon as he let go. He then held it in place with both hands. Seconds later, he was standing beside Fox

"What were you doing back there?" Fox asked, surprised at his appearance. "I was afraid you might get lost."

Trying to be casual, he murmured, "oh, nothing! I was just trying to keep this thing on."

"I saw you running this way," Wolf said, curiously. "How did you get here so fast?"

"Oh, I dunno; I just did. Why?" Hawk pulled a scarf from his pocket and began tying it under his chin

Fox, noticing Hawk's struggle, began digging through his pockets. "That koyt must be too small; try this one," tossing it to him. He snickered, "some of these days I'm going to run out of spares then what are you going to do?"

"This one doesn't fit, either," Hawk pouted. "I keep putting them on and they just bounce off. This is the fifth time I've tried."

"Say, isn't that the one I loaned you the other day? What's the matter with it? Are you getting picky, or something?" Fox teased.

"No, I'm telling you," Hawk argued, nervously pushing at his hair, "I was just trying to keep my ears warm but it won't stay on."

"Hey there, everyone," a merry voice greeted, "it's good to see all of you." Climbing out of the old tunnel entrance, Storg quickly beat his gloved hands together then stuck one out toward Hawk. "I've been waiting out here for a couple of hours. I was afraid you had changed your mind."

Startled at Storg's arrival, Hawk let go of his koyt. It fell to the ground. Ducking quickly, he scraped it off the ground and stretched it over his head. It flew off again.

"Oh no, we wouldn't do that," Fox replied, extending his hand. "It took a lot longer than expected. We had to find a different exit since sleepers were on the other side of this one."

"I thought that might have been the problem," Storg said, "so I went looking for another exit. Did you know there are only two? You must have come through the one close to Hawk's apartment, right?"

"Uh, yes. How did you know?"

"Well, Fox, it's just logical. The north side of town is too far away, and the icy drifts are enormous. You'd have never gotten through."

"I've never been there," Fox admitted.

"I have! Take my word for it," Storg laughed. "Did you like the improvements I made on Hawk's tunnel?"

"What kind of improvements?" Wolf asked, his eyes glaring with suspicion. "How did you find the tunnel, anyway?"

With a mischievous glint in his eye, Storg turned toward Wolf. "I just went looking around. The tunnel was too small anyway, so I just stretched it a bit."

"You what?" Wolf cried out.

"How did you do that?" Fox asked.

Without answering, Storg reached down and scooped up the knit koyt off the ground. He turned to Hawk. "Is this yours?" he asked.

"I can't get it to stay on," Hawk said, slowly reaching toward Storg. His ears immediately sprung back up.

"My, oh my," Storg grinned, "look what we have here." While scrutinizing Hawk from every direction, he pulled off his fur hood and koyt then smoothed his brown plaited hair. In admiration, he let out a low whistle. "Pretty good ones, I'd say."

"Pretty good 'what'?" Hawk cried out, desperately trying to cover his anomaly. "Don't stare at me. My koyt, give it back."

Storg turned and said. "Fox, would you bring the lantern over here?" When he turned back to Hawk, he was still grinning.

"What are you doing?" Hawk quizzed. His body ached with humiliation. "Where's my koyt, Storg? Give it back."

"It's right here," Storg teased. "I'll give it to you in a minute." Then noticing the agony in Hawk's face, he said, "Oh, well, here. You can have it; just don't put it on, yet."

"Why not?"

"It won't stay."

"I know. That's what I've been telling you. So?"

Fox held up the light. Then seeing what Storg was so adamant about, his mouth gaped open. He sputtered. "You really are an elf."

"I am a 'WHAT'?" screeched Hawk. He lashed out at Fox, in a fury, "I am no such thing---there is no such thing as elves!"

Fox reached out, trying to calm him. "You shouldn't get so upset, Hawk---", he began.

Swinging around, Hawk glared into his face, saying with a vengeance, "I am NOT an elf!!! I just got into something. Do you understand?"

Not knowing what else to do, Fox and the others backed off, escaping his tantrum.

Suddenly, Hawk's body began to shake uncontrollably. Fox grabbed him on one side and Storg caught him on the other. They guided him toward a place to sit. "Okay now, Hawk, you've got to take it easy," Fox said, gently. "You're going to be all right. Just sit here for a few minutes."

"How can I take it easy? Just tell me that," Hawk cried out, wrestling to get loose. "You just told me I've turned into a monster."

"Hey there," Wolf said, rescuing the koyt from the ground. He shook it a few times then held it out to Hawk. "You're acting like a four year old."

"I am not," he cried. His face was wet with tears. "I'm nine---well, almost nine. So there!"

"There's nothing wrong with elves, Hawk. I wouldn't mind being one, myself," Fox said, placing a soothing hand on his shoulder. His eyes were drawn to the ears, again. "They're just different. Elves are magical, too, or so I've been told."

"Yep! That's for sure," Storg stated with pride. "Only people with ears, such as yours, are elves. Why did you hide it? I don't have a problem with elves. Some of my best friends are elves."

"What made me an elf?" Hawk snubbed, wiping his cheeks. Automatically his hands reached for the unwanted extensions then dropped to his sides. With pleading eyes, he looked at Storg, searching his face. "I don't wanna be an elf! I wanna be like you. I just wanna be me."

"Luck of the draw, I guess," Storg said, with a grin. He reached up, casually straightening the deer hide koyt between his tall, rounded ears.

With fists squeezed tight at his sides, Hawk's body shook with anger.

"You didn't know you were an elf, I presume?" Storg's expression changed to surprise.

"Of course not; how would I?" Hawk growled softly. Still glaring at him, he jammed the knit covering back on his head.

It bounced to the ground. Looking down, his eyes brimmed with tears again, as he scooped it up.

"I don't know. Just thought I'd ask," Storg answered gently.

"My koyts have fit just fine, all my life," he sobbed, "an' I just knew I'd be a monster if I ever came to the outside. I was right!" He wrestled with the koyt again, trying to make it fit.

"Being an elf is not uncommon to me. The Kroll species have similar attributes, you know."

Paying no attention to Storg's explanation, Hawk grabbed the useless headgear off the ground and shoved it in his pocket. Glowering at the others, he raised his voice, snubbing as he spoke. "But what's my mother gonna to say? She'll ditch me like everyone else does their children."

"Nonsense," Fox said, trying to console him. "Your mother had you rescued, the time she left you behind. Remember?"

"No," Hawk cried, throwing his hands up in desperation, "I don't know that at all. I was left behind when I was really small." With tear filled eyes he looked toward Fox. "I thought I was going to die."

"She had to do that to spare you," Fox said, gently reaching toward him. "My father told her how to go about it so you wouldn't get hurt. There were people watching you all the time."

Defiantly, Hawk pushed the hand away. "You don't know," his voice shot out. "You weren't even there."

"Of course I was. I found food for you…on two different occasions, remember? I also made sure you were picked up and taken home, safely."

"No-o-o, that can't be," Hawk gasped. After wiping his face on his koyt, he stared at Fox. "All I remember was this tall guy with red, curly hair. He picked me up and put me on a sled." A shiver went down his back at the memory. "I was so scared."

"Scared? Why?" Fox asked, somewhat surprised. "It was the quickest way to get you home."

"I had never been on a sled before." With an unconscious twist of his wrists, Hawk pulled his locked hands apart. "That tall guy put me on that big sled and tied me down. You would have been scared, too."

Fox pulled off his koyt, shaking it at his side. "Sorry about that. I didn't want to take any chances of you falling off."

Hawk raised his eyes. "What do you mean?"

With a grin, Fox said. "That was me." The curly mass of red sprang around the edges of his koyt.

Hawk's eyes lit up with recognition. All he could sputter out was, "Oh!"

Fox smiled. "I was told to keep you safe. You had to be left for three days, with all the other throwaways and fend for yourself, so your mother would be allowed to keep you. It has been very hard for her to live in At il."

As if in slow motion, the city steps slipped on by as they walked. Looking past Hawk, Fox's eyes traveled upward, tracing each snow-covered plank of the steps and resting in front of the guard shack. Slightly curious, he noticed the absence of any guards. "Kind of odd," he thought, extinguishing the lantern's flame. While swinging it between them, he studied the sparse layer of brambles across the fields.

"You know, Hawk," he said, thoughtfully, "now that you have been transformed into your real self, your elf self, you're free---and so is your mother."

"What do you mean, 'free'?" Hawk asked, curiously. He reached up to his face, and slowly brought his hands back down to his sides.

"Your dad was not an elf. He was banned from his tribe when he went against their rules."

"I don't understand," Hawk said. His voice was just above a whisper.

"I know this is a lot of information, but I'm trying to explain it to you, okay?"

Hawk plodded along beside Fox, saying nothing as they continued down the small path along the compound wall. Deep in thought, Fox gazed across the snow-covered field of spindly bushes and broken twigs.

"When your father and mother married they came to At il because his tribe would not sanction their union. They were to be left behind or to be exterminated, that was the tribe's unbroken rule. This was a place where they could hide and still be together."

"So, you're saying my mom's an elf?" Hawk blurted out in shock. Fear and disbelief jumbled through his mind. "This has to be just a fantasy; it's not me he's talking about."

"Yes," Fox said, interrupting his thoughts, "that's exactly what I'm saying. She used to be, anyway. When your parents came to the old city, your mother had to have her ears clipped to hide her elf identity. According to my dad when they first arrived she was a real beauty; had the finest set of ears he'd ever seen, he said. He called them 'knock-out gorgeous'." A silly smirk crossed Fox's face while remembering. Taking a breath, he continued. "I guess she had a really rough time getting past the surgery and everything. It caused her to lose her magic, you know. When she began to age, like common humans, your father lost interest. She was devastated. According to my parents, had you not been born, she would have surely died."

Unaware he had touched his ears, Hawk looked toward Fox, saying, "I don't remember ever seeing my father. My mom has some old pictures. She said they were of her and my father. She doesn't look anything like the pictures, though, so I don't know for sure if it is. She's smiling up at him and he's got his arm around her. They both have really fancy koyts on; they seem to be all dressed up for some special occasion." He stared into nothingness for a moment. Finally focusing on Fox, he said, "there's something odd about it, though; something about the picture. Every time she picks it up, she begins to cry. Do you suppose it was taken the day he died?"

"I don't know that he died," Fox answered.

Hawk's vision disappeared. Quickly pulling his hand back down, he said, raising his voice slightly. "What do you mean? Of course he died. It was a long time ago when I was just a baby. My mother told me all about it."

Fox's eyes swept downward, resting momentarily on Hawk's ears. He then said, "I have an old memory about your father." After a slight hesitation he went on, "I must have been about five."

Hawk's head jerked upward, staring at Fox. "You knew my father?"

"Yes," Fox answered.

"How--- how did you know him?" Hawk stuttered.

"Your parents and mine knew each other."

"Why didn't you tell me before now?"

"I didn't know who you were," Fox answered. "It was a long time ago---when they were friends."

"Oh!" Hawk answered.

"One time, my parents allowed me to go to your house, alone," Fox began. Looking down, he watched Hawk walking beside him. They continued along the city boundary; the path Wolf and Storg had followed ahead of them. "We usually went together, you see. It was when you were just a baby; probably no more than a year old. You were crawling around on the floor; I guess I was fascinated by it."

"I can't imagine being a baby." Hawk giggled, sneaking a peek at Fox's face.

Fox nodded, lost in thought. He was visualizing Hawk's parents, sitting on the living room floor. Pillows had been scattered all around and Hawk was sitting in the middle of them. With an outstretched hand, a beautiful woman with slightly tall, iridescent ears, reached out, shaking a blue, fluffy rabbit in front of the baby's face. She was laughing and patting the floor between the pillows, tempting him to crawl toward her. She then looked toward a young, dark-haired man as he took the rabbit from her hand and rolled it across the floor. He seemed to be talking and laughing at the same time. Smiling at the vision, Fox watched them crawl, snuggling the rabbit under the baby's chin. He grabbed at the man's nose and they all laughed, mocking the baby's gurgling sounds.

A long moment later, Fox looked down at Hawk and continued, "After that, I often went to see you by myself. We'd always played this one game you liked so much. Your dad and I would chase around behind you…for hours, it seemed; it was kind of like hide and seek. Oh, we played other games, you know; all kinds of stuff." Snickering to himself, he went on, "There were times you'd crawl as fast as you could, chasing after us. We'd crawl in front of you then stop, really quick so you could catch us. You would lose your balance and roll over. It was so funny. You would try and try to get up…then when you did all of a sudden you'd fall over again." He nodded, with a quick grin. "You would get so-o mad. I'd tickle you and get you to giggling, and then you wouldn't be mad anymore. After that, your mom and dad would race across the floor, trying to see who could reach you first. We always laughed so hard at you. It was so much fun when I visited your family." His eyes crinkled at the thought. "You were my only friend, back then."

"Then what happened?" Hawk asked, grasping for details.

"Oh, nothing much," Fox answered, looking down at him. "After a while, I'd finally go home."

"I meant---uh, that was it?"

"Uh---well, sort of. Later on, I went to your house a few times, but your dad was never around. After a while I just stopped going.

"Oh, what happened to him?" Hawk asked, anxiously. "Is that when he died?"

"I don't know, really. I don't remember ever seeing him again."

"But you knew him. You should know if he died or not." The pitch of Hawk's voice got louder. "What about your dad--- he's the governor, he should know."

"He lost track of your dad, too, as far as I know." Fox looked toward

Hawk. With a sharp sound of authority, he said, "Okay, Hawk, what is this really all about?"

Looking up toward Fox, Hawk's eyes were blazing behind the tears. "You knew I was an elf, all along and didn't tell me?" Hawk barked out his anger with contempt. "You're the one who has all the answers; the one who's been everywhere and done everything, why am I not surprised?"

"No, that's not true!" Fox reached out, trying to console him.

Hawk pushed his hand away.

Drawing it back, Fox placed one hand in the other. "Only since we came out of the tunnel, had I wondered about it. I've only known for sure these last few minutes."

"That's a lie! Of course you knew. You were right there. You saw everything," Hawk cried out, fiercely. Tears welled up in his eyes, again. He scoured Fox's face for the truth. "You saw my mom and dad. What about my mother's ears? She was right there in front of you. You had to know."

"Hawk, I was only five years old! How was I supposed to know?" Fox reminded him.

"Oh, well---I guess," Hawk snubbed, wiping his face with his sleeve. Glaring at the ground, he stomped away. Moments later, he turned back toward Fox.

Just above a whisper, Fox began to speak, again. His eyes followed all the movements of the small, dark-haired boy who was now beside him. "What I'll never forget about your mother was those beautiful scarves she always wore. I remember this one time though, when we were playing, I accidentally bumped into her and her scarf fell off. She jumped right up and ran out of the room, crying. I never did that again."

"Like the ones she wears now?"

"I don't know, maybe."

"I have never seen her without one wrapped around her head."

"Did you ever ask her about them?"

"Why would I do that, Fox? She always wears them. "

"Just thought I'd ask."

Gazing up the path, marking At il's perimeter, Fox said, "I've not seen Wolf and Storg in a while. I wonder where they took off to?"

"They've been ahead of us all the time," Hawk answered.

Then Fox pointed. "Oh, there they are…over by the wall. Do you see them?"

"Not yet. It's kinda dark out there."

"Do you want me to light the lantern so you can see?" Fox teased, swinging it forward.

"Nah! I see them," Hawk pointed, "right up there."

"They found something to sit on; it looks like a big rock."

"I know. Hawk looked up. "They must be waitin' on us."

"That's alright," Fox smiled, "we have quite a walk ahead of us."

Hawk then said. "Didn't mean to get mad."

"That's okay," Fox answered.

Hawk reached up and rested a hand on Fox's shoulder. An instant later, they appeared next to a rather large tree trunk pressed into the compound wall. Wolf and Storg were sitting on the edge of it, deep in conversation. Distracted by the sound of ice crunching next to them, they turned.

"Hi, fellas," Hawk giggled. "Waiting on us?"

Before they could answer, Fox cried out, "How did you do that?" A look of shock covered his face. "How---how did we get here so fast?"

"I dunno." Hawk said, just as stunned.. "It's happened a few times before."

"But--- but how did you make us move like that? We just seemed to glide on top of snow," Fox stammered.

"I know," Hawk answered, shyly shrugging his shoulders. "It just happens."

Noticing the huge stump beside them, Fox blurted out. "Where did that come from?"

"I have no idea; it was just here." Wolf laughed, sliding off the edge.

For only a second, his thoughts had detached from the conversation and Fox envisioned himself reclining under a tree from his book. He saw branches, gorged with shiny green leaves, gently swaying in the warm, sunny breeze all around him. Just as quickly, his eyes flashed across the valley. Where could that stump have come from? For as far away as he could see, there was no timber of such large growth, not even from the big mountain; he'd already been there. Of course, there was the long mountain range ahead, but the surface looked too smooth. Glancing forward, he noted a few small saplings still hanging on, with wind-whipped stubs of green, he thought, "with the warmer temperature, they might make it."

His eyes wandered back to the stump. Most of the bark had fallen away, making an uneven ridge around the base. He then noticed a few chunks had been imbedded in the city wall, with the fall-off from it buried under heavy layers of ice and snow. "I guess that stump has been here for a while."

Jolted back to the present, Fox heard Storg say, "Skimming, huh?" He was nodding toward Hawk. "I see you've been trying out your magic. What do you think? Works pretty good, doesn't it?"

Momentarily confused, he heard Hawk stammer a reply. "But I don't know how it happened; I didn't do anything."

"Of course you did," Storg said.

"So, what did I do?"

"Can't say; I don't know your magic. I'd have to watch you in action," Storg decided. "Don't worry, though, you'll get the hang of it."

"So it's called skimming, huh?" Wolf said, staring toward Hawk. "You were doing it before we met up with Storg, remember---when you're koyt kept flying off?"

"Yeah! I don't know how I did it then, either. It just happened."

"Catch me up, here," Fox interrupted. "It seems I missed out; I was daydreaming, I'm afraid."

"We were talking about this skimming thing," Wolf answered. "That's how you got here so fast; Storg calls it skimming; some kind of magic Hawk has been using."

"We could use it to go to my camp. It will be a long walk, otherwise." Storg said.

"Where is your camp?" Fox asked.

"Over toward those mountains," Storg said, pointing to the right of them.

"Did you use skimming when you came here?" Hawk asked.

"Oh no; it takes too long," Storg answered, quickly. "I usually transport when I go a long distance."

"Transport," Hawk asked, "what's that?"

Storg looked from Hawk to the others. "I'll tell you how, if you want to give it a try."

"I don't know---," Hawk began.

"It really isn't very hard," Storg said, "and we could be at my home in no time."

"Sure! I guess, but---."

"It's easy. I'll tell you exactly what you need to do. Don't worry about it, okay?" He then placed a hand on Hawk's shoulder, motioning for Fox and Wolf to do the same. "It's your turn, okay? Just put your hand on his shoulder. Yes, that's good. Now, everyone close their eyes."

Hawk stared at Storg, "I---I don't---."

"Eyes closed? Now just think where were going." He saw the fear in Hawk's face. "You'll be fine; you can do it."

"O-o-ka-ay," Hawk murmured, squeezing his eyes closed. He stood there. He waited. Nothing happened; no movement, no noise, no anything. "It didn't work," he thought. Finally blinking his eyes open he saw a cloud of blue light swirling around him. Straining to see what was pulling on his shoulder, he saw Fox's clinging hand. Wolf and Storg then slipped by his vision, swirling in the same cloud of blue. "Where are we? How did we get here?" He thought, frantically forcing his eyes closed. He cried out. There was no sound. He cried, again. There was nothing. Nothing! Everything went black---quiet---nothing. Then he heard his name being called from a distance.

"He'll be all right," Storg said, looking down at Hawk's still body. "Give him a minute. I don't think he's ever transported before."

"Don't be stupid! Of course he hasn't. He's never been outside the old city before," Wolf croaked, angrily. "You may have killed him."

"How was I to know?" Storg answered, fiercely. "I just met him the other day."

"No excuse, you duff; get out of my way," Wolf spat. Pushing by Storg, he dropped to his knees and reached toward Hawk's face. Holding a hand close to his nose, he test his breathing.

Pushed out of the way, Storg said, tried to reassure them. "He'll come around. He's going to be fine, I tell you."

"He doesn't look fine," Fox answered, sharply. He attentively watched as Wolf completed the examination. "It looks like he might be hurt pretty badly. He's not responding to anything Wolf is doing."

Wolf lifted then released each of his arms, testing for a response. They dropped to the ground. Then using the tips of his fingers, he examined Hawk for other possible injuries.

"Is there anything I can do to help?" Storg asked, feeling the strain.

"Wh-where am I?" Hawk whimpered, lifting his head from the ground.

Storg dropped down to Hawk's side and grabbed his hand. "Hey man, I'm sorry. I didn't mean to set you up like that. How are you doing?"

"I've been better. What happened?" Hawk asked, still somewhat dazed.

"I didn't realize you had never transported, before," Storg began, visibly shaken. "I would have never---."

"Save it!" Hawk said, quite embarrassed. "I'm fine! Help me up. Okay?" With a small grin he lifted up a hand for Storg to pull him to his feet. "That was quite a trip you took me on."

Chapter Five

The Camp

STORG LOOKED DOWN AT HIS small friend. Halfheartedly, he stuck his hand out to pull Hawk up from the ground, but shaking his head, dropped it back to his side. "Actually, Hawk, you look a little disoriented. Why don't you just sit for a few minutes and pull yourself together?"

"Maybe you're right," Hawk winced, pressing each side of his face. "I think I bumped my head on something." Palming the ground, he touched something hard. It tilted slightly, rolling into his hand. "This must be it," he said, glaring at a rock about the size of his hand. "No wonder it knocked it me silly."

"That's enough to give anyone a headache," Storg said.

Giving the small boulder a hefty toss down the hill, Hawk reached up, accepting Storg's help. "I've got a pretty good lump---and a headache to match," he said, but I don't plan on sitting here all day."

"Are you sure you're okay?" Fox asked, reaching out.

Ignoring the offer, Hawk pushed himself up from the ground, looking about. "Where are we, anyway?"

"We're at the caves, where I live" Storg said, full of excitement. "You did a good job transporting, for your first time."

"What are you all looking at?" Hawk said to Fox and Wolf. He then noticed the trail where they were standing. It led down the long slope, intersecting a narrow crevice stretched out between two hills.

"Did you notice how the holding pens are mirrored on either side with barricades crossing the crevice?" He heard Storg describing to Wolf and Fox. "Well, in that narrow passage the moss grows thicker, so the reindeer are always coming through there to graze. We just detain them for a while."

"How unique," Wolf said, studying the layout. He noticed that the pens had been constructed of long, wooden poles tied closely together. One end of it was buried in the snow and the other was used to brace the strips of hide at intervals along the full length of the barricade. "So the animals run down the ravine and straight into your trap."

"Yeah, I guess," Storg answered. "We've done it that way for years."

Noticing movement inside the barricade, Fox was caught up watching the animals. Intently, he followed their steady shuffling, as they moseyed from one side of the pen to the other. "So those are reindeer?" He asked. With eyes still glued to the scene, he noticed them nudging, nose first, through the layers of snow.

"They must be, Fox," Hawk said, giggling, they're acting just like you said." His eyes shifted to the other side of the pen. "What are they doing now, Storg?" He asked, watching some of them circle around one particularly large male specimen, who was standing up close to the barricade. He kept swaying his head, racked with antlers, from side to side.

Before Storg could answer, everyone looked up, distracted by a strange, switching sound overhead. They saw three pair of eagles in flight. They were flying in full circle, seeming to have an unusual interest in them. Then gliding low, with tail feathers rippling and broad wings flattened by the wind, they slipped across the valley then over the mountain, out of sight.

"Say, Hawk? It's getting late and everyone has already left. We'd better get going." Storg interrupted. "Come on."

The noise shattered Hawk's thoughts. He jerked around. "Sorry, I was watching the birds." Unconsciously reaching up, he touched his suddenly warm ears, and headed out to join them.

"This is our new home." Storg said, proudly walking toward a small round hut.

"Is this where you live?" Hawk said, admiringly. "I've never seen anything like it." Sliding between the others, he scrutinized the small building from all angles.

"Yeah! Great, huh?" Storg answered, with a grin. "Just like I described, isn't it?"

"I'd say---only better." Then speeding to the other side, he strained to get another peek toward the holding pens---well, actually what was in them. On the way, his sight glided across the open fields, he caught glimpses of small bushes and brambles, all crunched to the ground and small, broken limbs all loaded with new-fallen snow. Looking closer, he noticed an occasional scrawny hand-full of sticks, overlooking the brambles, not much taller than his head.

Rounding the hut again, he slid up beside Storg, while rubbing his stomach. "Wow! I just got a whiff of something that smells so good."

"Oh, that's my mom's cooking," Storg laughed. "She's the best."

"The aroma is outstanding," Fox admitted. "I didn't realize I was hungry until just now."

"Well, come on then," Storg urged, excitedly. "Come and meet my family. They are so anxious to meet you."

"Oh-h-h! Is this where you live?" Wolf asked, staring at the hut in amazement. "It's so small. How did you make it so round?"

Fox glared at him, in shock.

"Well!" Wolf answered, staring back at him.

"Oh, oh! This is just the entry room; not the whole house," Storg said excitedly. "Wait till you see the rest of the place." He nodded, extending a hand toward it. "The first thing we do is to make the shape by placing long poles in a circle and pulling them together at the top. After tying them all together, we stretch reindeer hides over the outside. Sometimes we have other kinds of animal hides but we use those for special wraps or clothing; seldom for such things as roof covering, you know." As an afterthought, he grinned at Wolf, "but it's not an orb; it's flat on the bottom."

"My mistake," muttered Wolf, examining the exterior. "How do you get inside? Where is the---?"

"---the door? Oh, it's over here! I'll show you. We put it on the south side, of course, to keep the wind and cold out," Storg announced, stepping aside for Fox and Hawk to enter.

"Wolf, are you coming with us?" Fox asked, looking over his shoulder. "I thought you wanted to---."

"Sure! I just---ao-e-ch," Wolf cried, clutching his forehead. Stretching his hand out, for support, he began to reel.

"Watch out!" Storg shouted. Quickly jumping to one side, he grabbed for Wolf's arm.

"Oh, what was that?" Wolf barked. His eyes were watering with pain, stinging his face. "What hit me?"

"Oh, I'm sorry, Wolf. I didn't think to warn you," Storg said, quickly. "You jammed into the door heading. We make them low to conserve the heat."

"I should have been paying more attention," he said, rubbing his forehead.

"The room was about to collapse," Storg said, slipping in the last pin on the door frame. "It really is stable, but as you see, it's made to come apart easily." He waited for Wolf to go through then stepped beside him. "If you push the door handle down and pull it toward you, the latch will hold. Okay?"

"Got it." Wolf said, letting out a breath of relief when he heard the click.

"Good! Now everyone, please come in and meet my parents," Storg said, excitedly.

Following closely behind Storg, Wolf stepped onto the soft layer of fur, covering the floor.

"Be careful and lower your head; the entry is not very high I'm afraid. You'll have to stoop all the way through the passage as well, until we reach the cave interior."

"Are we still in the hut?" Wolf asked.

"Of course not, Wolf. The hut doubles as my parents bedroom and it's entirely too small for family gatherings. If you'll follow me, the main entry is just ahead."

Dutifully, Wolf followed Storg, with Fox and Hawk coming up from behind.

Once there, Storg flourished his hand, saying, "this is the grand room of the cave. Isn't it wonderful?"

"It's huge in here," Wolf said, looking quite astonished.

"It's one of the nicest caves we've ever found," Storg said. "It's the one our hut is attached to."

"Uh, oh! Fox did say something about caves up in these mountains."

"I told you about Storg's hut," Hawk smirked. "Remember?"

"Uh, yeah!" Wolf admitted. "I guess I wasn't listening."

"Oh, sure!" Hawk criticized. "You just didn't believe me, that's all!"

"I know! Sorry about that!"

"Hang it up, boys! We're guests in Storg's home. It's time to mind your manners." Fox hissed, quite embarrassed.

The young visitors followed Storg into the grand room. Having no idea what to expect, they were surprised at what they saw. The large, circular, ice-coated floor had been covered with layers of fur, from one wall to the other. Numerous small lamps had been placed on ledges around the cave walls. The soft glow gave it a look and feel of warmth throughout. Colorful, sheer fabric had been draped from the cave ceiling, attached in place by beaded hangers. Along the wall were two large, elaborately carved trunks. One had the lid ajar, showing linens and pillows stacked inside. A long, rock table lay in the middle of the room, with a bench on either side. A man with long, dark plaited hair was sitting at the far end of it. He wore a light colored robe that draped to the floor. A beautiful, stone encrusted medallion lay just above the neckline of his robe. Not far from him, a woman was kneeling beside a large, flat stone with small flames flickering around it. She wore a matching medallion in her meticulously groomed, plaited hair. She was also attired in a light colored robe.

Storg walked toward them, conversing in a language unknown to the visitors. He then turned toward his friends and said, quite embarrassed, "when Wolf stumbled, I forgot my manners. We're to leave our coats and boots in the hut. So, if you please?"

"It's done!" Fox said, in agreement. When he turned and looked down, he gasped. He was clothed in similar robes as the hosts. "What! How did that happen?"

"We look like triplets," Wolf snickered.

"I just needed your permission," Storg smiled, "then I could make the correction."

"Oh, I see!" Fox answered, not knowing what else to say.

Turning back toward the couple in the grand room, Storg walked to the head of the table. The man and woman stood as he approached. He went first to the woman and touched each of her cheeks with his nose. She reciprocated. He and the man did the same. Turning toward his friends and pointing to each of them, he said, in a language they did not understand, "Mayita! Dinato! I'd like for you to meet the friends I've been telling you about. This is Fox, Wolf and Hawk. At your request, I've talked them into visiting us for a while. Although their habits are quite different than ours, I think you'll find my friends to your liking."

Standing to greet the guests, his parents nodded with a smile toward each of the boys.

Storg turned to his friends and said, proudly, "I'd like for you to meet my parents. They are happy you decided to visit." Looking from his mother, then back to them, he said. "This is my mayita. She made those wonderful meat cakes you liked so much."

They looked toward Storg, then back toward his parents with a smile.

Storg then said with a slight bow, "Mayita means mother." He walked toward them and stepped behind the tall chair, "and this is my dinato; my father. They have both given permission for you to call them mayita and dinato. Their names are very hard to pronounce. I hope you don't mind?"

"Of course not," Fox answered for the three of them.

"Well then, please come and sit. They want you to be happy while you visit." Stepping toward the benches, on either side of the table, Storg motioned toward them with a smile. "Mayita has prepared a meal for us."

With a nod, Fox led the others toward the table. When Hawk leaned forward, nudging his arm, Fox turned toward him.

Hawk looked up then toward Storg's parents

"What?" Fox whispered.

"No shoes!"

"I noticed!" Fox said with a grin. "We don't have any on either."

"Oh!" Hawk said, pulling up the long gown. That's strange. I didn't even notice they were gone."

They both stopped and looked toward Wolf, when they heard the distress in his voice. "Why are your parents staring at me?" He asked. "They have been ever since we got here."

"Oh, it's nothing really," Storg answered, shifting his feet slightly. He glanced quickly toward his parents.

"It is to me," Wolf said, sharply. "What am I doing wrong?"

"They were wondering what was wrong with your ears. Fox's too, for that matter!"

"What!!!" Wolf yelped, in surprise. Suddenly realizing what had been said, he grabbed each side of his face. "What's wrong with my ears?"

Fox automatically reached for his ears, as well. He traced them with his fingers and shrugged his shoulders. After dropping his arms to his sides, he looked at Storg. "What are you talking about? They feel just like they did when I woke up."

"Not a thing! They've just never seen anyone without a set of ears, before."

"We do have ears! I don't get it!" Fox stated, raising his voice slightly.

"I hope you can forgive them for such a rude remark," Storg said, quite embarrassed. "As with the elves, the Kroll ears show the family heritage of magical powers and status. They are quite revered."

"We are not of the same species," Fox said in a soft, tightly strung voice. "Our differences should be taken into consideration and appreciated; not ridiculed."

"Thank you! That's good! You're right!" Storg said, stumbling over his words. He searched for understanding in Fox's eyes. "They didn't mean to hurt your feelings."

A few tense moments passed. No one moved. Hawk and Wolf looked from Fox to Storg, then back to Fox.

When Storg took a step back, Fox stepped forward with his hand extended. "Storg, it seems I am at fault here, as well. I should practice the words I speak. Please accept my apology."

Storg nodded, accepting the handshake. They both turned to Storg's parents and bowed, slightly.

"Wh-a, what happened here?" Hawk stuttered. His eyes flashed from Fox and Storg, then back to Wolf. "I don't understand! Everybody was mad---then---then! Now it's all over? What did I miss?"

"Why nothing, I guess," Wolf answered, quietly. "I guess the issue has been put to rest." He turned toward Fox and Storg with a nod.

Fox joined the others, sitting down to a fine assortment of food in front of them. After a moment of wonder, he looked toward Storg. "Your mother sets quite the inviting table." He touched his ear again, sliding his hand down the side of his face and rested it by his bowl, waiting.

"She does enjoy having company." Storg smiled toward his mother.

Fox then asked, "are your parents not dining with us, Storg?"

"Oh, no. This is soup was left from the noon meal. I hope you don't mind. Everyone will come for the evening's dining when the day's work is finished."

"Of course!" Fox then took a sampling the hot liquid. After tasting, he said, "m-m-m, this is delicious! Quite an extraordinary flavor, I must say."

"It's yummy!" Hawk said, slurping a mouthful of the broth.

"Hawk, mind your manners," Fox reminded him.

"M-m, sorry," Hawk said, glancing toward Storg's mother.

She nodded, with a smile.

A few days later, Storg's eyes were sparkling with excitement. "When we're finished with our meal, we are going to tour another part of our campsite. It was my father's idea. He thought you might be interested in watching us cull the herds."

Turning to Fox, Hawk asked, "cull the herds; what's that?"

"I don't know, but I'm sure we'll find out."

Storg placed a warming pot of fragrant herbs on the cleared table and led his visitors from the grand room, toward the door. "Don't forget to duck as you leave."

"Thanks," Wolf said, rubbing his head again.

"Where are we going?" Hawk asked, crowding in between the others.

"Come on and I'll show you," Storg grinned.

"Uh, okay."

Once outside the hut, they followed Storg to the back side of it. He stopped and pointed to a flat knoll, on a hill past the valley. Turning to Hawk then the others, he said, "we're going to the top of that hill."

"That's a long way," Hawk whined, looking across the valley.

Wolf growled, as he passed.

After crossing a large open field, Storg pointed down the slope toward a small herd of reindeer. "If you'll notice, we've got---."

"Hey! Give me a break!" Hawk panted, rushing from behind. "You all have longer legs than I do. That's not fair!"

"You didn't miss anything. Quit your whining," Wolf scowled.

Fox sent a harsh stare toward Wolf then said, "what were you saying, Storg?"

"Oh, just that we have divided the reindeer into small groups, with the main herd set a distance from here. This is our sorting and training ground."

"That's not your grandparents down there, is it?" Fox asked, studying the people at the bottom of the hill. From what I can see, they're not much older than you."

"Oh, no! My Grands took the main herd to the other side of the hill."

"Why is that?" Wolf asked, slightly interested.

"We didn't want them exposed to these animals. It's easy for them to pick up on the wildness, again."

Excitedly, Hawk asked, "can I pet one?"

"They're wild animals, Hawk," Fox said.

"After they're not wild, could I pet one?"

"I'm not sure my Grands would let you."

"Oh!" Said Hawk.

"Would you like to watch the others?" Storg suggested.

"The others? You mean those people down there?" Fox asked. "Sure!"

"Yes! Two of the men are my uncles. The other three are neighbors, from where we used to live. They are training some of the reindeer we plan on adding to the herd. It's really very interesting."

"That sounds like a great idea," Fox answered, turning to Hawk and Wolf. "What do you think?"

"Everything is really different out here," Wolf said, "nothing like the old city."

After a few moments of thought, Fox asked, "Are these people all that's left of your clan?"

"Yes, all but those who are helping with the evening meal."

"Oh, I see," Fox said, "and who are they?"

"Well, there's my Aunt Maribell and my cousin Jen. Beth Ann is around here somewhere, too. She lost both her parents so we all take care of her."

"What's wrong with her?" Fox asked.

"Not a thing. She's five years old and hard to keep up with, that's all."

"Oh! I've not seen her, I guess."

"She's probably with my Grands. She likes the animals." Looking toward Hawk, Storg's face wrinkled into a grin.

"Hey! Does she get to pet them?" Hawk yelled. "That would be fun! Do you think I could pet them, too? Huh? Do you? I've never petted an animal before."

With a frown, Wolf shrugged, "well, I wouldn't plan on it this time either. It probably won't happen."

"You're mean!" Hawk frowned back.

"Am not! I'm just telling the truth. You can't just walk up to an animal and pet it. It'll bite you, or something."

"I'm afraid Wolf is right, Hawk. My Grands may allow you to pet one of the tamed reindeer, but they're not here, right now. The ones you see below were just rounded up. They're wild. That's why we have them in a holding pen," Storg explained. "You can't get too close to them, either. They might spook and start running. They can get crazy, you know."

"What do you mean 'spook'? How would I do that?"

"Scare them! Don't you know anything?" Wolf sneered.

Stepping up beside him, Fox whispered savagely, "what's going on with you?"

"Nothing!" Wolf said, angrily.

"Whatever the 'nothing' is, fix it!" Fox said, sharply.

Having overheard Wolf's remark, and noticing that Fox was confronting him, Storg went over to Hawk and led him aside, saying quietly, "the reindeer are wild animals, as I told you before, and if you run toward them, or talk loud, or sneeze, or something unexpected such as that, they'll spook. It's kind of like being scared, but not really. They could hurt us---or my uncles, down there. We wouldn't want that to happen. Just be careful."

"I will! I promise," Hawk whispered.

Storg nodded, with a grin. "If we're quiet, maybe we can get a little closer."

"Really?"

Hawk dropped down, waiting on Storg to do the same. They began creeping toward the animals.

Storg grinned and motioned to the others.

Fox nodded to Storg, but declined the invitation. He and Wolf stayed some distance behind. "Are you going to tell me what your problem is or do I have to guess? I don't think you'd like what my guess would be," Fox said, somewhat short-tempered.

Wolf's face turned red. His voice was strung tight, when he spoke. "The runt's taking over, that's what! Since he got those---those odd-looking growths---well---uh, on the sides of his head, he talks like he can do anything." Scowling at his feet, he muttered, "probably can, too---since he's got magic---since he's not like us anymore."

"He didn't ask for it; he didn't want it---it just happened. It's who he is," Fox said, quietly.

"Well, what are we going to do?" Wolf said, still tense but slightly more rational. "You and me---we're outcasts. Storg---the rest of the Krolls; they all have magic. That's what Storg said, anyway. They're all looking down on us, like we're nothing. Don't you get it?"

"Sure, I get it. Until I thought about it, I kind of had the same opinion. But you see, I like being who I am. Be it Kroll, human or elf---or whatever; I'm me. In whatever suit I'm wrapped up in, I'll be the best me I can. That's what I think is important, you know."

"So, you're not jealous?"

"I don't think so," Fox answered, softly.

"I don't want to be; I just am." Wolf admitted.

"Well, you're in charge of that, you know."

"I keep trying but it just won't go away."

"Well, you'll have to try harder," Fox warned.

"I'm working on it."

Fox looked across the meadow. Nudging Wolf, he pointed at Hawk, who was slithering toward the holding pen.

"I know," Wolf said, "he's been out with those reindeer for days."

"I've noticed that, too," Fox said. "He can't seem to get enough of them."

"Each day, he edges up closer."

Fox's thoughts were interrupted by a flock of noisy birds as they flew over. Looking up, he said, "Daylight is getting brighter; had you noticed?"

"Yeah, and longer. Are you thinking about school?"

"Um-hum. We can't get out of it. The university has a numbered attendance count and we'd be missed," Fox reminded him.

"Yeah, that's true," Wolf agreed. "How long?"

"Two or three weeks, I'm guessing. School starts the first week of September."

"Would you look at that Hawk, now?" Wolf said, pointing. "He's jumping up and down, all over the place."

"I see that," Fox said, with a nod. "Now what about Hawk---or runt, as you seem to favor---you still have a problem, correct? I know you're jealous but there seems to be more."

"He's such a show-off. With all that magic, you know."

"Wolf, I can't believe you're saying that. He's just had a whole new world open up to him. If you were him, would you hide all that newness in a basket? I don't think so! Get real! You'd try it out---maybe cautiously at first, but you know you'd explore! Am I right?"

"I know, but he's too young to know how to handle it."

"Maybe so, but I think Storg is a good teacher. He has magical experience, and they trust each other. They're friends."

"You're right, as always," Wolf conceded.

After a few moments, Fox said, "shall we join the others?" Without hesitation, he headed toward the top of the hill and stopped beside Storg.

Wolf watched Fox walk away. "I don't know how he does it. He always knows exactly what to say."

"Is there anything we can do to help?" Fox asked.

Storg grinned at him. "No, I don't think so. They won't even let me help. They have already started training our new stock. It is tedious work and I'm not very good at it, yet."

"New stock?" Fox asked, curiously.

"Yes, when you first came, remember? We had the holding pens, separating the---."

"Yes, yes of course, but where did you get them?"

"Oh, I guess I didn't tell you about that," Storg admitted. "You see, most reindeer are born in the wild. They don't belong to anyone. When they infest our herd, and they do it all the time, we must train them, or weed them out. We do the same with our new calves, too. When they're flighty and uncooperative, the rest of the herd is difficult to manage. It doesn't take much for wild traits in the animals to reappear."

Fox stood, half listening to Storg. His mind wandered. "This world is free, and clear, and calm. It belongs to those animals out there---and us. It's as if there was no old city, at all."

"We depend on the reindeer for most of our life necessities. We use their meat for food, and their fur for shelter and clothing. As you've already noticed, we even fashion utensils out of their antlers and bones. Nothing goes to waste." While walking down the hill, Storg pointed toward a young buck and a couple of does, "just like that fine animal there, the choice ones are used to improve the quality of our herd."

"They are beautiful," Fox whispered. Nearing the fence, he watched them prance across the field. "I've never seen such a beautiful sight in my life."

"The reindeer are very high-spirited animals, and if not trained to follow the theme of the herd, can tear it apart with one battle of wills. Have you spent much time with wild animals?"

"No! Never! I've had no experience with animals; just what you've taught me. I had only seen a few of them, in my whole life."

"Me either," Wolf said, finally joining them. "I had never actually seen a live animal before. I had seen pictures of wolves and rabbits, though,"

"Where from? What kind of pictures?" Hawk asked, overhearing the conversation.

"From my mother's science book, silly; she leaves it on the shelf," Wolf said, still a bit edgy. "I can look at it any time I want to."

"Oh!" said Hawk. His eyes trailed back to the reindeer, again. "I'd really like to touch one. They look so soft and smooth." He scrunched back down on the ground.

"After they lose their winter coat," Storg laughed. "When it's long and shaggy it looks pretty ugly to me."

Thinking about what he'd just said, Wolf crept over beside Hawk. "Would you mind having company?"

"Sh-h-h!" Hawk said. "We don't want to scare them. Reindeer spook, you know!"

"Yeah, sorry." Wolf whispered.

"Do you see that one---the one with the huge set of antlers?"

"What about him?" Wolf said.

"Well, I've been talking to him. He said his name was Dalt, and he's the boss, or king or something." Suddenly, Hawk turned to Wolf and laughed. "Did you see that? I told him you were looking for him and to shake his head. Did you see him?"

"No! Tell him again."

"He said he'd shake his butt," Hawk giggled. "See there---he did, too."

"You've got to be kidding. That is the weirdest thing I have ever seen," Wolf gasped. "What else will he do?"

"I asked if I could pet him," Hawk said, turning serious. "He told me his girls needed to get to know me first."

"His girls???"

"Yeah! He said he had the prettiest 'crop' of girls ever, and if they liked me they'd let me pet any of them I wanted to. Of course it would take some time, he said."

"Why is that?" Wolf asked. All the while he was thinking, "I must be going out of my mind, listening to all this---and believing it!"

"You're not crazy! That is what Dalt told me---for sure!" Hawk said, with a grin. "Dalt has a lot of girls for me to meet. Some of them are a bit aloof, he said, but when I get to know them, I'll like them. His girls are the prime choice of the does, from everywhere here in the north. He said that any of the young, he sires with his girls, will be the elite offspring."

Stepping behind Wolf and Hawk, Storg looked toward the herd. "Take a look over to the right," he said to Fox, pointing at a well-racked reindeer. "Do you see that buck? He's switching his tail, right now. See him? He's right there."

"Yes, I think so," Fox answered, not sure of what he was looking for.

"He's the one with the huge rack---on top of his head, you see—the horns. He has all those does hanging around him," Storg said, pointing again.

"Sure! I see him. What about him?"

"We call him Dalt and---."

Wolf spun up from the ground and shook in amazement at Storg. "What did you say?"

"Well, I started to say that Dalt, that reindeer---," he pointed again, "---down there, seems to have a hold on all those does. We have tried to breed them with other bucks, but nothing works. They just prance and dance around old Dalt. I don't know what's going to happen. He's getting pretty old and---."

"Dalt said his girls would foal elite offspring, whatever that means," Hawk related, casually.

Wolf nodded to Fox, then turned to Storg with a knowing shrug, and said, "he talks to Dalt. Weird, huh!"

"I kind of suspected Hawk might be a whisperer," Storg said. "He has an unusual determination to touch the animals; an almost fearless need."

"Don't you think it's kind of odd---having no fear? He knows nothing about them," Fox said, quite surprised at Storg's complacency."

"Of course not," Storg said, briskly walking back up the hill, "because they can communicate; Hawk and Dalt can understand each other. There's no need for fear."

Hawk jumped up, racing after them, and yelled, "what happened with the sorting and training your uncles were supposed to do? I wanted to see that, too!"

Storg called back to him. "The sorting was finished yesterday. Come on! Hurry! We don't want to be late for dining."

"What is wrong with you, Hawk?" Fox asked, totally surprised at his outburst. "Storg's uncles finished feeding and watering all the animals a little while ago. After that, they had to bed them down for the night. It took a long time to get them settled. We were all trying to help out! Don't you remember?"

"No! I don't guess I do," Hawk answered, somewhat dazed.

"Storg's uncles worked really hard, today. I can't believe you missed it."

"Wow! Maybe that's why I'm so hungry," Hawk giggled. "I didn't even realize how hungry I was, until just this minute."

"Right on time, too!" Fox laughed. "I think everyone is in the grand room but us. We shouldn't keep them waiting."

Chapter Six

The Return

"Now, HAWK," STORG INSTRUCTED, "IF you're going to transport Wolf and Fox back into the old city with you, don't forget to put your hand on each of their shoulders---use a good strong grip, you know. You don't want to lose them on the way. Oh, yes, and when you take them over that tall city wall---. Oh, my! Oh, my, that could be a problem. I didn't think about that. You didn't have it to cross over when you came out."

"We came out through a tunnel," Hawk reminded him. "Why couldn't---?"

Ignoring Hawk's interruption, Storg continued with his description. "Of course, you left the old city through a tunnel, but it could be very dangerous for you to go back the same way. If any of you were missed, during your visit with us, the guards would surely be on the lookout for your return and---."

About that time Fox and Wolf came out of the small, round hut, all prepared to leave. They overheard the last part of Storg's discussion with Hawk. Fox interrupted him by saying, "you know we've been gone for nearly three months and---and we're probably considered---."

"I know, Fox," Storg said, "but when Hawk tries to get the three of you over that awful wall---well, he may not make it since he's never done it before---I don't know what he---."

Fox heard Storg's mother call his name and turned, meeting her at the bottom of the hill. In her native language, "sa mayita toh," he said, in greeting. She pressed a small bundle into his hands. After another moment or two of conversation, Fox touched his nose to each of her cheeks. She returned the familiarity then they parted. When he rejoined the others, he said to Storg, "your mother is quite a character." His eyes sparkled.

"What do you mean? Is that good---or bad?" Storg asked. A grin flickered across his lips.

"It was definitely good." Wanting to savor the moment, he hesitated a few seconds before continuing. "Did you hear what she told me?" A grin spread over all his face.

"Of course not! I don't eavesdrop." He teased.

"She told me to be patient. She said that someday I would have a pair of ears; beautiful, strong, magical ears! What do you think of that?"

"I wouldn't doubt she's right; not at all. That's what I think." Storg laughed. "Did she give you meat cakes in that package?"

"She sure did."

"I knew she would. She knows how much you like them."

With a heavy sigh, Fox finally said, "we really must be going." He turned toward the small hut, where the rest of Storg's family was standing, and waved goodbye, calling out, "aloike av tu marsku, (Until we meet again.)" After hugs were exchanged, he said to Storg, "it has been an honor to visit with you, your family and friends. I wish we could extend such an invitation to you."

"What about your return entrance to the old city?" Storg began. "Hawk has never---."

"I have confidence in Hawk's abilities. The magical capabilities, you have taught him already, are quite admirable."

"But---but!"

"We can never thank you enough for these fine fur coats we're wearing," Fox said, changing the subject. Patting his knapsack, he added, "I'm taking my father's coat back home, at your mother suggestion."

"Aunt Maribel made the coats, you know," Storg said, with a smile, "after we finished tanning all the hides."

"That was only one of our many challenges," Wolf chimed in. He raked his fingers through the fur across his chest then patted it gently.

"They're the best I've ever seen!" Fox said, smiling toward Hawk and Wolf, who were nodding in agreement. "Should we meet up with those guards, they will probably think we're visiting diplomats, as distinguished as we look."

"Yeah!" Hawk grinned, straightening the fur cap between his ears.

Shaking Storg's hand, Fox said, "aloike av tu marsku," then he turned to the others. "Are you ready boys? We've got a trip to make!"

Hawk reached up and placed a hand on Fox and Wolf's shoulder then closed his eyes. A bold, sharp blackness immediately surrounded them as they felt the pressure of standing leave their feet. Slowly, they began to spin. As moments passed, the speed increased, with a smooth, rolling spin that seemed quite comfortable. The air slipped by them as if it were made of silk.

Suddenly bouncing into something hard, Wolf cried out in pain.

Fox forced his eyes to stay shut. He heard Hawk scream. "Up! Up!"

The spinning had stopped.

Cautiously, Fox opened his eyes to total darkness. "I can't be blind," his mind cried out. Slowly his vision adjusted to the darkness. Dim images began to appear. Willing himself to focus, his eyes traced the edges of long, narrow forms above him. "I must be under some kind of roof," he thought, "but where, I don't know."

Closing his eyes again, he visualized his presence. "I'm lying in a prone position---on what? It feels like something really narrow. I sure don't want to fall off." Cautiously dropping his legs to either side, he pulled himself to a sitting position. "M-m-m, that's better. I must be on some kind of bench or table, I guess."

He tried to gather his thoughts. "Everything is all scrambled; I don't recognize a thing. I wonder why it feels so familiar? Now Fox," he scolded, "you're making no sense!"

Looking down, he saw the planked flooring just below his swinging feet. While stretching his legs to step down, he thought, "I hope this is no mistake. One squeaky board could cause big trouble." After taking a couple of steps and making no noise, he let out a deep breath and sat back down.

"I can't imagine what happened to Wolf and Hawk," he thought, staring into the darkness. "I wish I knew where they were. I can't see anything, though. They could be right under my nose and I wouldn't be able to find them. Not to worry," he said, nervously, "they'd let me know. Hawk would probably be yelling or something, by now, I'm sure."

"Come to think of it, I've not heard any noise at all. I wonder if I'm alone? Couldn't hear anything over my heartbeat, anyway---guess that means I'm scared! Um-hum, that's a huge understatement!!"

Trying to think what to do, he leaned over and cradled his head in his hands. He heard a noise. "Hey! What was that?" His mind whispered. "It sounded like someone talking. It might be Hawk and Wolf; I hope."

Excited at the thought, he got to his feet and slipped across the walkway.

He heard the voices again. He began to panic. "It's not them!! What am I going to do? I've got to find a place to hide." Spinning around, he ran blindly across the walkway, jammed into the safety-fence, losing his balance.

He slipped. His feet were over the side. Then reaching for the cat-walk safety-bar, he toppled over the edge. Seconds later, he hung suspended with only air around him. Squeezing his hands around the bar, he looked down. "Uh-ho! That's way too far down to drop! I'd better find a place to put my feet."

Finding some courage, he let go with one hand, grabbing for the top rung. His other hand began to slip. Clamping both hands together, he tightened his grip and tried again. Over and over, his attempts were not successful.

Sweat filled his eyes. His arms ached. "Too tired. Blisters!" The metal rung had ripped through the skin on his hands; he could feel it. "I've got to do it!" He grabbed again and caught hold.

"I have no pain, no pain," his mind cried. "I feel no pain."

He climbed the railing, rolled over the top and dropped to the walkway.

"Hmuf!!!" He winced, as his body smashed into the wooden planks.

"Ouch," he thought, "that hurt!"

Sitting up, he inspected his aching hands. "It could be worse," he thought. "That was a long way to the ground. I can't imagine what was below; too busy to look, before."

With a bit of mental prodding and a lot of curiosity, he pulled himself off the wooden planks and leaned over the railing. Looking down, he gasped. "Oh my gosh," he cried, "I'm on the old city wall!" He stared in disbelief at the city of At il stretched out below. "It is no wonder everything felt so familiar," he murmured.

The not-so-distant sound of creaking boards and trampling feet, immediately pushed all else from his mind. The danger was real and he knew of no way to escape---yet.

"Oh, oh! Those voices are getting closer," he whispered, "and I've got to hide, right now. Quickly looking about, he spied a walk-through in the wall across the catwalk. He ran for it.

Quickly swinging inside, he found himself in a very long room. There was a row of toilet stalls, with a shallow trench beneath, along the length of the room.

"Yech!" He coughed, holding his hand over his mouth while side-stepping puddles of muck on the floor. "This place is beyond awful. I don't know how anyone could stand to use it."

Far above his head were two soot-filled lamps hanging on the wall. They cast a dull yellow glow across the drab greenish-gray walls and on to the floor. Covering his nose with the other hand, he backed toward the entrance.

Before he could turn around, he heard the voices again---right behind him. They had turned into the walk-through right behind him.

Without another thought, Fox ran back inside, frantically searching for a place to hide.

"Gotta stop in here, Mog!" A gruff voice said.

"Toilets!" Fox whispered, standing in one of the stalls. "Yuck! Slippery!"

"Well go!" Said Mog. "No funny stuff, this time."

"Just watch!" Ro laughed, stomping his feet and pointing toward one of the open stalls. "To that last crapper. Bet?"

"What'cha got?" Mog asked.

Going through his pockets, Ro held out his find. "Two buttons!"

"Hands on yer head?"

"Guess so."

"Yer on!" Mog agreed.

Stomping again, Ro's voice roared with excitement. Placing one foot in front of the other, he crouched down and leaned forward. "I'm waitin'," he laughed. "Ya gotta say 'go'!"

Looking back at Mog, Ro noticed the occupied stall. "Yoh, Bud," he growled, heading toward Fox. "What yer doin' in here? Yer lost, er sumthin'?"

"Oh, I don't think so. I just needed some relief," Fox said, politely. "The office is the next floor down, isn't it?"

"Thas a fine coat, yer got there," Ro said, stepping next to him. Immediately wrapping his fingers around Fox's neck, he pressed down between the muscles. "I like fine coats."

"Don't do that Ro," Mog said, softly. "He's not one of us."

Loosening his grip, Ro said, "awe, Mog, ye take the fun outta everthin'. Wasn' gonna hurt him much. Jis scare 'im a little."

"Get your own," Fox said, calmly moving Ro's hands away. "There's plenty more."

"Getting' pushy there, Bud. Think I'll be takin' that one," Ro demanded, stepping toward him, again.

"It's too small for you," Fox said, mildly tugging the sleeve out of his grasp. "Get one that fits, why don't you?"

"I'll bet he's an inspector, Ro. Look at him," Mog argued, "he's not from here."

"Nah! He's no inspector," glaring at Fox, he said, "are ye?"

"A new coat issue just came in," Fox stated, crisply. "Better get yours before shift change."

Ro looked at Fox, then at Mog. "What's he talkin 'bout?"

"Do what ye gotta do, Ro," said Mog, "but I'm goin' for a new issue coat, meself." He turned and left the room.

Ro glared at his captive, then at the entrance.

"Ya think he's an inspector?" Ro yelled, running up beside Mog.

"Dunno. Maybe."

"Never seen an inspector before."

"Me neither," Mog admitted. "Didn't wanna chance it."

"Think there's any coat issue?" Ro asked.

"Mine's comfortable."

"Oh!" Ro thought for a second then said. "Yer goin back to the galley?"

"Yeah."

"Not me. Got me heart set on that soft, new coat."

"Too small," Mog said.

"Don't care; never seen a new one before."

"Ef yer determined, guess I'll go back wit ya," Mog said.

Fox watched them walk away. "That was too easy. I'd better get out of here. This is no place to be cornered, twice."

Before the thought had settled, he heard their voices again.

"I knew it! I knew they'd be back." he whispered, looking about for an escape.

In desperation, he cried out, "Up! Up!" As soon as the words came out of his mouth, his body slammed into the rafters.

"What---what happened?"

When the spinning in his head started to ease, he opened his eyes, forcing them to focus on something. The planked floor was now directly in front of him. "What's going on?" He gasped, raking his hands across his face. "How did I get up here? Oh, oh, my head---my head. It's so scrambled."

Fox heard Ro's deep raspy laugh again. It was exploding down the walkway. He watched the two guards come back in view.

"Can'wait ta get ma hands on that fine fur. That little twirp has'ta be close by."

"Whut ya plannin' ta do wit 'em?" Mog asked.

"Awe! Toss'em 'round a little. Not gonna hurt 'em---much."

"He didn' do anythin' to you, Ro. He was just---."

"Thas right! He stopped me game." Ro growled.

"He didn' stop yer game, Ro."

"Ho! Ho! Got me an idea, Mog. A good one, too!" Ro rolled his eyes toward Mog then stomped his foot, with gusto. "Know whut I'm gonna do, huh? Listen ta this! Think I'll send'em 'cross the room---jest fur fun. See ef he'll slide 'n hit that last stall. What'cha think 'bout that one?"

Watching from above, Fox shuddered.

"I wouldn' do that. He might be an inspector."

"He not an inspector. Betcha!"

"Could be."

Stomping out of the walk-through, Ro looked at Mog and growled. "He not here. He got me coat."

Fox squeezed himself closer into the rafters, hoping they wouldn't hear him breathe.

"Ye check the stall?" Mog said, mildly. "Maybe he's there."

"Ef ya say so." Ro ran toward the wall and disappeared from sight. "One o' these lights er out, in here. Hard ta see anythin'." He bellowed. "Gonna take a minute ta see in ever one 'o them, ya know."

"We got time." Mog called.

"Ya see 'em out there?" Ro yelled back.

"Not a sign."

Ro ran back out. "Did'ja see'em anywhere?"

"Not anywhere. I told you, already."

"Whut 'er we gonna do now?"

"Go back to the galley, I guess. There's nothing else to do," Mog answered, heading away.

"Sure wanted tha' soft, fur coat," Ro whined, catching up with him. "I know. There may be some of them left," Mog answered.

Fox watched them shuffle down the hall.

"They're gone," he thought, "now how to get down from here---I have no idea."

He turned to face the beam, pushing against it with both hands. As soon as he let go, his face smashed up against it. "Obviously, this is not working," he thought. "Just as well stop!"

Twisting around, he looked down. "If I knew what I did to get up here, it might help me get down. I don't know that either."

Rolling from side to side, he caught hold of a rafter. "Maybe I didn't push hard enough." Loosening his grip, his body slammed into the beam, again. "I had to try." he said, gingerly touching the scrape on his cheek.

"Okay! It's time to get serious," he said, closing his eyes. "Let me think what happened before. Those two guys were coming this way. I was afraid they'd catch me. M-m-m, what else? Oh, yes! I heard myself say Up! Up! I---."

"Ouch! Owech," he cried, squeezing his eyes closed and massaged the back of his head. "That hurt. I wish I knew how to get down from here."

His eyes flew open when he felt a sudden drop. Looking up, he found himself hanging in mid-air.

"That's it, that's it! I just need to say down," he cried, excitedly. "Here goes." With his eyes glued to the walkway below, he said firmly. "Down! Down!"

Nothing happened.

"So! What now? That didn't work."

Fox leaned his head back, studying the structure under the roof. "I'm not up there, anymore. That's an improvement---I guess." Leaning forward, he pulled his feet apart for a better view below. "Nothing's helping. I'm still stuck up here."

Peering over the old city from his airy perch, he noticed a gray-blue haze in the midnight black sky. "Oh my gosh!" He exclaimed, "I had no idea I'd been here so long. We left Storg's camp, this time yesterday?"

"Brilliant rays of light suddenly spilled through the haze, just as he looked up.

With a crash, he landed on the plank, below.

He sat up, totally surprised. "Wow! What a drop. I guess I did something right," he muttered, rubbing the back of his head. "That's pretty obvious."

"Oh! Yes, of course! Now I know what to do," he said, suddenly remembering. "Hawk did it, yesterday! He told us to close our eyes. The next thing I knew, he was yelling, 'Up! Up!' When I opened my eyes, I was scared. I thought I was blind. Pretty soon though, I saw waves of green and blue coming up from below. "

"That's it! That's it! I'll bet anything," he said, excitedly. Running over to the railing, he quickly closed his eyes.

His eyes sprung back open, and he gasped, "I'm no elf. What am I thinking?"

Anxiously he paced back and forth, trying to sort everything out. Finally, going back to the railing, he gazed into the dull street lighting of the old city. "What do I have to lose?" He said. "It can't hurt to try."

Squeezing his eyes closed, he commanded. "Up! Up!"

A split second later, a surge of energy passed through his body. A wash of silky smoothness slid across his face and pleasant memories began to drift through his mind.

"Where are you going?" Asked a deep, mellow voice.

Jarred to reality, Fox shouted, "what? What? Who are you?" His eyes flashed open.

"Where are you going, Fox?"

"I can't find you," Fox managed to say. "How did you get up here?"

"I belong up here. Where are you going?" The voice asked, again.

"Who's talking to me?"

"I'm right behind you," the voice answered. "You must tell your mind where you're going."

Fox turned toward the voice.

Two eyes appeared directly in front of him, with the body of a fowl materializing behind it.

"Are you---are you the voice I heard?"

"Of course I am. When I noticed you were in trouble, I sent my mate and my flock on ahead. I thought you may need some assistance."

"What? Who?" Fox stammered, "but---but you're an eagle---and I'm talking to you?"

"Yes to all. My name is Ari. You are Fox, I believe. My family and I are migrating south for the winter. We had to leave a little later than usual this year. That happens sometimes, you know. A bit of different scenery may be nice, though. I'm kind of looking forward to it."

"You know my name? How do you---? Only my friends know me as Fox."

"You have many beings watching over you," Ari answered. Looking forward, his attention followed his eyesight. "I must be going now. The flock has made good speed."

"Will I see you again?"

"For certain," he answered. "Remember, your mind is your guide."

"Thanks, Ari."

"Oh yes, there is one other thing. For landing, it is down, down, gently." After flying a circle around Fox, Ari tilted a wing and left.

Watching the huge bird fly out of sight, Fox whispered to the wind, "I can't wait to tell Wolf and Hawk about Ari."

Looking down, he saw the old city below and began his descent.

"Nah! They'd never believe it."

Chapter Seven

The Meeting Place

AT THE SIGHT OF A small boy, with slightly tall ears, standing in the alley just ahead, Fox shouted out, excitedly, "H-e-ll-o-o, Hawk!" He raced toward him, yelling and laughing at the same time. "How did you get here?" He cried, throwing his arms out to give him a spin. "I had no idea where you were." Then, from the top of the hill, he heard a voice call his name. He turned, yelling and waving at the silhouette. "Hey there, Wolf, it sure is a sight to see you."

"You, too," Wolf shouted back. "We just got here. Come on up."

"What is all that noise behind you, Wolf? It sounds like you're having a party."

"We sure are. Everybody's here." Wolf yelled back. "We're making toys. You've got to come and see"

"I'll be right there." Fox answered. Nearly exploding with excitement, he ran toward the hill, yelling for Hawk to come along.

"Well, hurry," Wolf yelled urgently. "I don't want you to miss anything."

As soon as they reached the summit, Fox laid a hand on Hawk's shoulder, saying earnestly, "I'm glad you and Wolf are alright. Yesterday, when the two of you disappeared, I nearly---,"

Hawk wriggled out of Fox's grasp and backed away. "That wasn't yesterday. What are you talking about? It was just a few minutes ago."

"Uh, what?" Fox stammered. "But---but the light. I saw a---,"

"---a big fireball, yeah, I know. It happened just a few minutes ago. We saw it, too." Hawk said. "It might have been a shooting star."

"Whatever it was nearly blinded me. It wasn't the sun, either," Fox reasoned. "You know how it flashes sometimes, before we go into the dark season."

"Uh-huh, I guess." Hawk motioned for Fox to follow. "I'll bet it was a shooting star."

"I don't know. It seemed really close to the ground, though." Fox mused. "Whatever it was, just flashed and was gone."

"I know! That's what we saw, too," Hawk said.

"You mean Wolf saw it, too?"

"Yeah! We hadn't even gotten inside."

"Who's up there with him?"

"Dunno; hadn't got there yet. I saw you in the alley and thought I'd wait."

"Oh, thanks," Fox said, "I appreciate that."

"No problem. Thought you'd want to know we were here."

"Say! How did your mom like your ears? Was she impressed?"

"She's not seen them, yet," Hawk said. "We came straight over here."

"How did you know to come here? Just a guess?"

"Nuh-uh. When we were landing, we saw all the lights and decided to come and check."

"Oh!" Fox answered.

"You know, hearing all the noise and laughing made us curious."

"Where is all the light coming from: it wasn't like that before." Fox noted, peering about.

"Hey there, Wolf!" Hawk shouted, running through the hideaway door. "We made it! I told you Fox was down there."

"Yeah! I saw you racing up the hill---both of you," Wolf cried. While holding one hand over his shoulder, he glanced toward it then gently curled his fingers into his jacket.

"I'm glad we're all here and intact," Fox grinned, reaching a hand out to Wolf. Then noticing his strange behavior, he asked. "Is there something wrong with your arm?"

"Oh no, Fox, I'm fine," Wolf said. Mysteriously, a smile curved his lips. "I want to show you something, though. You won't believe what I've got."

"Sure! What is it?" Fox said, watching his hand slide down.

"It's not an 'It', it's a 'He'!"

"Wolf, you're not making a bit of sense."

"Just take a peek. You'll see what I mean."

"Sure!" Fox said, going toward him. "You'll have to move your hand, though. Is it going to jump out at me?"

"Be careful," Wolf said, sharply. "Oh, oh there he is." Lifting each finger up, slightly, he stretched both hands toward Fox, one cupped over the other. "He's fragile."

"I may be small but I'm not fragile!" A squeaky voice growled.

"Ouch! He bit me." Wolf cried out; his hands slipping apart. The prize fell loose. "Oh,oh, you've gotta catch---."

"I've got him!" Fox said, scooping both hands into the fall.

"Thanks!" The voice said, shakily.

Quite speechless, Fox marveled at the small being, standing in the palm of his hand. Finding his voice, he said, curiously. "Who---what are you? Do you have a name?"

After gaining composure, the voice answered defiantly. "It's obvious, I'm an elf! My name, if you must know, is Mr. Twiddler---and---and they ruined my home. I had everything just like I wanted. It took years of hard work, too. They came right in and ripped it all apart."

"Who would do such a thing?" Fox asked, sympathetically.

"Why, those boys in there," he squeaked, angrily shaking his fist toward the hideaway.

"We'll see about this." Fox said, quite distraught, "I can't imagine."

"I'm afraid we did," a young man said, coming toward them.

"Josh! What are you doing here? How is the north side doing?"

"It's all good. Everything's ready for tomorrow, including the children's gifts. Come see what we've done. Mr. Twiddler has been showing us how to make dolls, birds, animals; all kinds of nice toys."

"What about his home?" Fox asked. Standing in awe, he watched a crowd of boys shuffle stacks of wrapped gifts and unwrapped toys from place to place.

"It was an accident," two other boys said, simultaneously, "but he has a new home now. Do you want to see?" They pointed at a completely furnished two-story house, sitting on a bench behind them. "It has lighting, heat and everything. It's all furnished, too."

"Matt! Tim! It's beautiful," Fox exclaimed. "Your helpers; how are they?"

"We're over here, Fox," they chorused. "We're making toys!"

"Oh, my goodness," Fox shouted, ecstatically. "This is unbelievable."

Mr. Twiddler squirmed in Fox's hand. "Hey there," he said, holding a piece of purple string, "watch the squeezing."

"Sorry about that," Fox said, quickly loosening his grip.

"We found him," Josh began, "up in the street lamp yesterday when Matt and Andy decided to clean the flu. Soot and bugs, you know. They dumped all that stuff out---and he fell out, as well."

"Yeah," Andy confirmed, "and he was really mad; I didn't blame him either. The light made him a perfect home, since he's only four and one half inches tall."

"It WAS perfect," Mr. Twiddler pouted, "I've been living there for years."

"You do have a nice, new home now," Fox said, gently. "Don't you like it?"

"I'll get used to it, I suppose," Mr. Twiddler conceded, folding his arms across his chest.

"Would you like to ride in my pocket?" Fox asked, gently. "It should be nice and warm in there."

"Well, I guess so," Mr. Twiddler squeaked. To everyone's surprise, he quickly jumped through the furry pocket opening and slid to the bottom. After stretching out comfortably, he yawned, "he, he, he, this is too good."

Climbing to the top, a few moments later, he whined, pathetically. "Could I have my pillow, please? It's the only personal item I have left."

"Of course," Fox answered, reaching into the small house.

Grabbing the pillow from Fox's fingers, Mr. Twiddler dropped back inside, stuffed it in the pocket corner and stretched out, again. "M-m-m, this is the life," he twittered.

"Fox," Wolf called out, trying to get his attention. With arms loaded down with packages, he shuffled through the noisy crowd, "from what everyone is telling me, tomorrow has been set aside for the children. Is that right?"

"They've never had a special day, so tomorrow it is," Fox answered, quite elated. "We have plenty of food---,"

"---and toys, Hawk reminded him.

"Oh yes, and toys for all the children. Because of everyone's help, we will give them a little happiness." Fox said, softly. "Quite remarkable, isn't it." Peering across the smiling faces, he nodded. "You are the best; thanks to all of you."

Wolf leaned toward Fox and whispered in his ear.

"Oh, yes. Thanks Wolf."

Turning back, Fox called out. "Wolf just reminded me of something you don't want to forget! Tell no one of your secret hiding places for the food and gifts. Since everything seems to be pretty well completed, we should close down our festivities and meet here tomorrow at the same time. Everyone, please be safe."

They soon began to leave, in twos and threes, slipping quietly through the dark arctic back streets, toward their homes.

Fox looked back toward the hideout, as they left. "That street lamp kind of focuses on our hideaway, doesn't it?"

"Our stuff has never been bothered here, before," Hawk mentioned. "Do you think we should be worried?"

"A little, I suppose. How much is there; the toys and food, I mean?" Fox asked.

"Everything for our place is well hidden on site. We didn't put it all in the same spot, though," Wolf said. "All the other locations take care of their own stuff."

"I see you've got it covered. Thanks!" Fox said.

The three walked toward the second street corner, noticing every shadow along the way. "You know, Wolf, we have quite a dilemma here," Fox said, just above a whisper.

"You mean, about the university?" Wolf mentioned, quietly. "Yeah, I know. The session has already begun, according to Josh and the others."

"I don't go to school, yet," Hawk said, listening in.

"I didn't think so," Fox said, patting the top of his head. "You may not have been missed. That would be a good thing."

"Any ideas?" Wolf asked.

"Not yet," Fox admitted. "While visiting Storg's family, there were so many new things to do and see, I lost track of the time; that was early on---and then I didn't try to catch up." Huddled together, the three of them quietly walked toward the next street lamp, watching the yellowed light make flickering shapes on the snow. "If we had counted our sleep cycles, like I do at home---,"

"How long do you think it's been," Wolf asked, "a couple of months, maybe?"

"It must have been longer than that," said Fox, trying to make an educated guess. "We left a few weeks after the sun flash. The day we left, it had been light for some time: long before we even started for Hawk's tunnel."

"It's a good thing no sleepers were in it," Hawk snickered, or we'd have never met Storg."

"Because of sleepers in the other one, yeah I know," Wolf said, "It was dark when we came out, though."

"It took a long time to go through," Fox reminded him, "then you were sick."

"Yech, don't remind me," Wolf grimaced.

"Speaking of sleepers, what do you think about the 'Gift Day' we're to celebrate tomorrow?

Wolf and Hawks spun toward him. "'Gift Day'," Wolf spouted, "where did that come from?"

"Are those toys just for the sleepers?" Hawk asked, curiously.

"Of course not, they're for all the children."

"You've already named it?" Wolf stammered. "It sounds like you've got something spinning in that head of yours. "Yeah, kinda. It's been there for a while, though."

"Well keep it there, we've got to figure out this school thing for now," Wolf said, decidedly.

"Yeah, I know." Fox grinned.

"So, what is the plan?"

"Maybe we should just go to our classes and act like we've always been there."

"It sounds pretty radical to me," Wolf said, solemnly.

"I can't think of anything better," Fox said.

Who knows," Wolf grinned, "it might just work." Dragging his feet through the new layer of snow, he looked down. "It always takes a long time to get home, doesn't it?"

"When we split up, it does," Fox agreed, "I don't mind it so much until then."

"I know," said Wolf. "There has been times I've ran the rest of the way home."

Hawk turned to Fox then to Wolf. "I run home every time. Does that mean I'm a scaredy?"

Peering down, Fox patted Hawk on the shoulder. "I don't think so, little man."

"I miss Storg," Hawk whispered, wistfully.

"I think I do too," Wolf said, with a chuckle. "I can't believe I'm saying that."

"It seems like we've been gone forever," Fox muttered, softly.

"Three or four months is a long time," said Wolf.

"How long is that?" Hawk asked.

"Since we left," Fox smiled.

"Do you think I'm nine, yet?" Hawk asked, thoughtfully.

"I don't know. What does say on your wrist?"

"I don't know how to read," Hawk said.

"Someday you will."

"I wonder if we've all missed our birthdays," Wolf said.

"Mine is in the winter," Fox said.

Slowly scuffing their boots through the snow, they walked down the dimly lit street.

"I hope my mom's not asleep," Hawk whispered, touching his ears.

"Sh-h-h," Fox warned.

"Oops!" Hawk whispered.

"How's the koyt mayita made for you?" Fox asked.

"You mean with the ear holes? It works great! You want to see?" Hawk asked, pulling at the knot under his chin. "I put this old scarf on top."

"I know. You don't need to take it off. I was just asking," Fox said, quickly.

"Oh, okay." Hawk said, retying the knot.

When they reached the intersection, Fox turned to Hawk and Wolf. "Tomorrow should be pretty exciting. I'll see you then."

"I gotta go." Hawk said, glancing up at Fox then into the darkness. A few seconds later he was running across the field.

Watching him leave, Wolf said. "He really is scared."

"He's not the only one," Fox answered, watching his own shadow slide under the street lamp.

Without turning around, Wolf said, "I'll see you tomorrow." Picking up speed, he left Fox standing alone at the corner.

"See you," Fox answered, watching the image of his friends grow smaller and smaller. A few minutes later, he headed toward home.

Chapter Eight

Home at Last

Fox left the street and crossed through the back lot, as always. When he reached the foot-path, where his swing used to be, he headed toward the porch and ran up the steps. Glancing toward the window, he thought, "hm-m, I wonder why there's no light inside?" While standing on the top step, he reached toward the window sill for the door key. "Mom and dad must be visiting. Maybe she left me a note. She always does." He traced his fingers along the sill, again. "Where is that key?" He growled. "It should be right here…," The edge of the window's ledge slid beneath his fingertips. "…and it's not." Looking about, he snapped out irritably. "It is too dark out here. I can't see a thing."

Noticing the cause, he ranted, under his breath, "no wonder; the street lamp is out again. Dad will be furious when I tell him about it."

"Oh, well, first things first; I can't get in without a key. It must be here, somewhere," he thought. Then leaning again toward the sill, he fell against the door. It sprang open and as it did, something attached to the door swung hard against him. He cried out, rubbing the side of his face. Not able to identify the object, he finally said, "Mom must have been doing a little decorating."

After ducking around the open door, he went inside. "I hope I can find a candle or lamp somewhere; I can't see a thing out here." Hands outstretched, he headed across the room. "Mom keeps all that stuff in the pantry. It would be nice if the lamp has oil in it. It would be hard to fill in the dark. I may have to hunt for a candle if---."

"Hmuf!" He groaned, falling to the floor. "What did I step into? That's not right?" Twisting and turning, he finally pulled his foot loose and stood up.

Cautiously, he took another step and stumbled, raking his knee. "Ouch," he muttered, reaching down.

"There should be matches in the cupboard, if I can find it. It's closer than the pantry. I'll try to get there first." Feeling his way across the room he stumbled again, raking his knee. "Ouch," he muttered, reaching down. Intent on going on, he managed to find a wall and followed the smooth surface with his hands. After passing his parents' bedroom, he reached for the kitchen doorway and went inside. "I found a drawer...," he muttered, rummaging through the contents. Finding a small container, he gently shook it, "---and matches, I hope. Good!" After opening the lid, he felt inside. "There's only three," he thought, "but it's good to leave one behind."

With matches in hand, he reached for a lamp and removed the glass covering. When he lit the first match, it flamed up and went out. After adjusting the wick, he held his breath, striking the match.

"Success is good," he said, lifting up the lamp. It filled the room with light.

At first sight, Fox gasped in horror at the destruction. He tried to scream but the skin had tightened around his throat then groveling sounds began to spew from his mouth. "Vandalized; my parents' home---destroyed." Fury coursed through his body as his eyes darted about, searching for some kind of comfort. None was there.

"What---what happened? Who would do a thing like this?" Suddenly realizing his fingers were aching, he loosened his grip on the lamp and raised it up.

Escaping reality for a moment, he forced the image of his mother's tidy kitchen to his mind. When he blinked, the vision disappeared. The dishes now lay broken on the floor with the cupboard smashed to pieces across the contents. Table linens, towels and window coverings were flung all about and stomped into the floor. A single cooking pot was still hanging in place. "Mom's going to have a fit when she sees this mess."

Slowly, his mobility returned and he guided the lamp light across the room. Looking down, he discovered what had caused him to stumble. A huge hole was in the middle of the floor. The family food supply was now an assemblage of smoke-coated bulging cans, broken jars and singed boxes, surrounded by charred pieces of wood. The floor had been burned through to the ground. "Why?" He whispered. "None of this makes any sense. I don't understand."

Tearing his eyes from the sight, he scoured the rest of the house, checking out each room. He found the devastation similar throughout. Slowly heading toward the front door, he paused at his parents' bedroom then entered. Lying beneath the dresser, he saw a small figurine and dropped it in his pocket. With one last glance, he quietly left, closing the door behind him.

Mr. Twiddler peeked out of Fox's pocket. "What was that?"

"It's a gift that belonged to my mother. Sh-h-h."

Mr. Twiddler stared up at him. "What did you say?" Busily tying the purple string around his long ears, he asked. "Where are we?"

"We're at my house."

"Oh!" Mr. Twiddler said, squirming around until his elbows dangled out of the pocket opening.

"Don't come out, Mr. Twiddler. It's too dangerous! My parents' house has been ransacked and demolished. The whole place is trashed; the furniture, the dishes, everything, even the floor is gone."

"I can see that," Mr. Twiddler answered. "What do we do now?"

At the front door, Fox noticed his parents reading lamp, lying on the floor, between the two chairs. He picked it up and placed it back on the small table, carefully straightening the shade. "Huh, what did you say?"

"I said what do we do now?"

Heading back toward the kitchen, he said stiffly, "we get out of here."

"You're going the wrong way. The front door is behind you."

"I know," Fox answered. "I need to get a couple of things, first." He reached inside the pantry door and took the oil bags off the pegs, and threw them over his shoulder, muttering to himself. "They're nearly empty. Oh well, I'm taking them anyway." Looking up, he took a book from the top shelf and hid it inside his shirt. "I'd have thought there would be a note somewhere. Mom has always left a note for me." Reaching down, he picked up a yellow rag and stuffed it in with the figurine. "That's it, there's nothing left."

When he got to the front door, it wouldn't open. He tugged again and again. Resisting his efforts, it scraped slightly; budging no more than an inch. As soon as he lifted the door's edge, it released and slammed open, knocking him off-balance. Thrown to the step landing, he barely managed to get to his feet when something slammed into his head. He cried out, "o-u-ch, it hit me again." Sliding to his knees, he hit the wooden planks of the landing with a crunch. Looking up, his eyes focused on the object suspended from the door.

"Get that light back on, you idiots!" A loud voice shrieked.

Fox pressed a hand over his mouth to muffle the scream he felt rising up. "It's the guards---the guards from the wall. What are they doing here?" Breathing hard, he crawled back inside and slipped behind the door.

Looking down, his eyes traced the flickers of light streaking across the floor. "Oh my gosh, the window," he croaked, "it's been boarded up."

"We gotta git them boys. Fire up that lamp," the voice yelled, "can't do anythin' in the dark. Come on, time's a-wastin'," the voice said again.

"I need some oil up here," another voice yelled. "I ran out."

"It'll have to do then. Come on down."

"No oil anywhere? Check again; gotta have some for this one," a third voice said. "It's the governor's house. His kid, the one called Fox, lives here."

"He'll be back---if he's not already here," another voice shouted.

"Get in there, then. Go on, check out the house," squawked the first voice. "While you're at it, see if you can find the oil stash."

"Boots er' still on the door. Not been here yet, I'll bet."

"Boots," Fox mouthed. "It was boots that hit me on the head?" Sudden understanding churned through his stomach and into his throat. Nearly choking, a gurgling sound came from his mouth. "Oh, no," he moaned, "that can't be. Not my father." Hot tears sprung from his eyes and flooded his face. "That can't be."

"Fox? Quiet," Mr. Twiddler warned, pushing his head through the pocket opening. "They'll hear you."

Working to control his voice, Fox answered, "You're right. Just give me a minute."

"You've got to pull yourself together," Mr. Twiddler said, sharply.

"I know, I know," Fox answered, shakily. "We've got to get out of here."

"Yeah, I figured you'd say that," Mr. Twiddler quipped, "and right now sounds like a very good time to do that."

"Ye still want me to go inside?" A voice cried out.

"Sh-h-h," Fox warned. "They're right outside the door."

"I hear them," said Mr. Twiddler said, dropping back in the pocket.

"Nah, just go over and look around. We had plenty o' oil in this other bag."

"I need some oil up here. What's the hold up, anyway?"

"We gotta keep th' gov'ners street lamp burnin', ya know."

"Yeah, I know, I know. Just get it lit and come on down. Mog n' Ro 'er gonna keep an eye on this place after we leave."

"Good plan!"

"I need to warn the others," Fox said, gruffly. Getting to his knees, he pulled the rag out of his pocket and wiped his face. "I've got to find a way out of here, first." Pushing it back in his pocket, he touched the figurine. A surge of anger went through him. "That belonged to my mother," he hissed, defiantly. "Whoever did this is going to pay."

"Get mad later," Mr. Twiddler said, peeking out. "Not good timing. This is not a good place to be, either."

"Don't you think I know that," Fox barked, "but we're kind of trapped?"

Calmly, Mr. Twiddler answered, "go out the door and leave, right now before the street lamp is lit."

"Out the front door," Fox cried in horror. "You must be out of your mind."

"Right. Well maybe so. Do it anyway." Mr. Twiddler urged.

"That's better than any idea I've come up with," Fox said, jumping to his feet. "Before I lose my courage, here we go."

"Don't fall in that hole again," Mr. Twiddler squawked, anxiously. "You nearly broke my nose the last time."

"Well, hang on then," Fox said, taking a leap toward the door, "this will likely be a rough ride." Seconds later he was jumping down the front steps. Without slowing down, he raced around the side of the house and across the back lot.

"Don't get in the light," Mr. Twiddler warned, "they'll be looking for you everywhere."

"They already are, from what I'm hearing," Fox said. Aiming for the dark alleys, he slowed to a walk.

"Wow! I'm glad you're here." a voice shouted.

"Uh, who?" Fox cried out, quite surprised.

"It's me! It's me, Hawk. I'm down here."

Fox followed the sound of the voice, looking in several of the boxes, pushed against the building. "Why are you hiding out here, Hawk? I thought you'd be home by now."

"I tried! I got close but couldn't get in. I even went through the back way, like you showed me. Remember?" He said, crawling from beneath a crate.

"Sure, I remember. What happened?" Fox asked, trying to keep his voice steady.

"When I got there, it looked like daylight. All the street lamps had been cleaned I guess. I saw guards everywhere. They were holding these big bright lights and shining them all over the place. They were coming out of every one of the apartments, two and three at a time. It was really scary."

"Where were you?" Fox asked, kneeling down in front of him.

"I was up close to the wall, across from my apartment," Hawk said, bouncing from one foot to the other. "There was this big sign on our door. I couldn't read it so I drew the letters down." Slowing down, for a moment, he pulled a scrap of paper from his coat and handed it to Fox. "What does it say?"

"I don't know yet." He stood up, reaching in his pocket. "Give me a minute; I may still have a match."

"You need a light?" Someone said, coming up from behind.

"Josh, what are you doing here?" Fox cried, pushing the note in his pocket.

"The guards are out hunting for you. I just wanted to warn you," Josh said, accepting the handshake. "I wanted to tell you earlier but didn't get the chance."

"What is happening around here? My dad---?"

"There was an overthrow of power and your father was arrested. He's no longer the governor. I don't know where he's being held."

"His boots were nailed to our front door," Fox said quietly. "Does it mean what I think?"

"Oh, that's awful," Josh gasped. "It means he's up for execution. I'm so sorry, Fox."

"When I overheard the guards, in front of my house, I thought that's what it meant," Fox moaned. His body shuddered, uncontrollably, and tears began to flow down his cheeks. "My father---gone? It can't be. Not my dad."

"We don't know that, for sure." Josh grabbed for him.

"My mother," Fox sobbed, pushing away from him. "Where is she?"

"I don't know," Josh answered, gently touching him on the back. "I've heard nothing about her."

"I've got to go find her," Fox cried, writhing hysterically.

"No, you can't. You're our only hope. Fox, listen to me, please," Josh begged. "You've got to leave before they arrest you, too."

"I can't, I can't. I've got to find my family," Fox moaned. "My family; my mom and dad, I did this to them. It's all my fault."

"You must leave now," Josh insisted, firmly.

"But I can't leave without Wolf; what about him?" Fox cried. "I won't---!"

Coming into view, Wolf said, "I'm right here, Fox. What do you need?"

"Josh said the guards are looking for us. He said we need to leave… immediately."

"That is true. That's why I'm here," Wolf answered. "Josh and I; we've already talked. I'll catch you up on everything when we're in a safer place."

"Fox, I'm so sorry," Josh said, softly.

"But my mom," he sobbed.

"We'll do what we can. We must hurry."

"I'm ready, then. Let's go." Fox said, drying his eyes.

"Follow me," Josh said, quickly. "I'll show you another way to get past the barricade. You can't use magic in here. It doesn't work."

Quite surprised, Hawk said, pushing up beside him. "How do you know that?"

"You're not the only elves around here," Josh nodded. Turning to the others, he said. "We don't have much time. I've got to be back before the guards miss me."

"What about the children; the food, the toys?" Fox asked. "If you get in trouble because of that, I'd never forgive myself."

"Oh, that," Josh said, "with all the violence that's going on; your dad being ousted, and all the rest. Believe me, our toy and food program won't even be noticed."

"Then why was my father punished, maybe even killed?"

"Think about it, Fox," Josh said, "he was the governor; the one in charge and in this case, the fall guy. He could be easily blamed for everything."

"So, then when we left---."

"When the three of you left the grounds, and were gone more than a month---,"

"More than three months," Fox corrected.

"---and then came back of your own accord, with no one being the wiser."

"We didn't hurt anyone, and-and we did come back. So?" Said Hawk.

"You outsmarted the guards," Josh pointed out. "Don't you see what that means?"

"Well, I---," Fox began.

"And on top of that, management's census count system failed," Wolf added, "incompetence all around."

"That's it," Josh agreed, "and they're all furious."

"Where are you taking us?" Fox asked, looking about uneasily.

"It's not much further," Josh urged. "Come on."

"But I see a lot of guards and most of them are coming this way," Fox argued, getting quite concerned. "Being here is not a good idea."

"I'd planned on you escaping before they caught sight of you," Josh said, running ahead.

"They haven't yet," Fox said, anxiously looking behind. "We're too close to the wall and about to be boxed in if we don't do something quick."

"I have an idea," Wolf said, quickly. "Come on!"

"Whatever it is, hurry!" Fox said.

"Right up there," Wolf pointed to the guard shack, "we take the steps," he grinned. "Are you coming with us, Josh?"

"I can't leave, yet. If all goes well, I'll be with you some day. Be safe." He waved goodbye and turned back toward the city.

"What did he mean by that?" Hawk asked.

"I'm not sure," Fox answered. "Get over those steps and don't slow down until you're on the other side."

"I'm outta here." Tying the scarf under his chin, Hawk took off running.

Wolf was right behind him.

Fox was just a few paces behind them when familiar voices reached his ears. "Oh my gosh," he thought, "the one thing I don't need." Beyond the top step, he saw Mog and Ro cleaning lanterns in the walkway.

"Jus' like I always say, Mog, them there uppity's over in them offices don' appreciate nothin' we do. Ef they did, we'd have one o' them issue coats, ye know."

"I know, Ro," Mog answered, handing the lantern up to him. "Are you ready for this?"

"Guess so," he said, looking down.

"Some of the soot's out," Mog began.

"Yoh!" Ro cried, jumping off the ladder.

"What?" Mog yelled, backing away.

Ro hit the walkway with a crash. "Me coat! There goes me coat!" Seeing Fox, he took off after him.

Fox jumped to the middle of the catwalk, squeezed his eyes closed, screaming, "up, up!"

Nothing happened.

"It worked before," he thought, frantically.

Trying again, he cried out, "up, up."

The catwalk was still there.

"Me coat. Ye got me coat," Ro screamed, reaching toward him.

Ducking his flailing arms, Fox raced back toward the steps.

Quite unconcerned, Mr. Twiddler poked his nose out of the pocket and let off a long, high pitched, screeching howl then dropped back inside.

"What---what was that?" Ro stammered. Stopping as if he'd run into a wall, he pointed at Fox.

"What are you so all-fired about?" Mog said, walking up behind him.

"He-he got spirits. You shoulda heard it!" Ro's mouth was still quivering from fear. "Never heard anythin' to beat it."

"Is that why you ran off?"

"No! Course not! It's me coat." Pointing down the stairs, Ro yelled in agitation. "See, down there. They all got issue coats."

Mog stared at the boys, then at Ro. "Too small," he said, walking away.

"Look where they're standin'," Ro yelled, again.

"And so?" Mog said mildly, "out of my jurisdiction."

"What'cha meanin'?"

"Outside the wall; not my job," Mog stated.

"Whut 'bout me coat?"

"Too small," Mog said. "Hope you didn't break the ladder."

Opening his pocket, Fox looked in and grinned. "Some voice you got there."

"When it's needed," Mr. Twiddler answered, with a chuckle.

Fox turned to the others. "I thought I was going to get caught that time. Did you see what happened?"

"I know I heard an awful screeching sound coming over the steps. I thought my eardrums were going to fly out of my head," Hawk said.

"That was Mr. Twiddler," Fox laughed. "Quite a set of lungs, he's got."

"Yeah, I'd say," Hawk answered.

"He can sure make a lot of noise, for his size." Fox laughed.

"You've got Mr. Twiddler with you?" Hawk asked, quite surprised.

"Sure! Where else would he be?"

"Where is he?"

"In my pocket."

"Oh!" Hawk stammered.

"He's been riding in my pocket ever since Wolf gave him to me."

"Who are you talking about, Mr. Twiddler?" Wolf asked.. "Is he with you?"

"Yes! I was just telling Hawk."

"That guard nearly caught you up there, didn't he?" Wolf said. "Was it Mr. Twiddler that scared him off?"

Fox nodded.

"You shouldn't have gotten so far behind us?" Wolf pointed out.

"I thought I'd fly across the steps but it didn't work," Fox answered, somewhat embarrassed.

"What do you mean," Wolf asked, "what didn't work?"

"You know, when Hawk transported us here from Storg's campsite."

"Yeah?"

"You know magic doesn't work inside the city." Hawk reminded him.

"Of course I do, but when you dropped me and I was stuck on top of the wall; it worked then!" Fox argued.

"That wasn't your magic!"

"What do you mean?" Fox said.

"That was Ari's magic. You saw Ari, didn't you?" Hawk said.

"Yes, but how do you know him?" Fox asked, quite stunned.

"We landed on top of the roof and he came to our rescue. That's how we got down." Hawk explained, "I guess we'd still be up there."

"I know that feeling," Fox said. "It was a long way down from that railing."

"Is Mr. Twiddler going with us?" Hawk asked.

"If he wants to. Why?"

"He's so little. He could get hurt!"

"He's an elf,"said Mr. Twiddler, sarcastically. "There are a lot of us elves around, Hawk. You'd better get used to it."

"He's new at the game," Fox said, with a brash edge to his voice. "Don't be so hard on him."

"Oh, by the way," said Mr. Twiddler, "I would be interested in knowing where we are going?"

"To Storg's campsite," Fox responded, without thinking.

"Well, get on with it," Mr. Twiddler said, decidedly. He dropped back into the pocket.

Fox turned to Hawk and said. "Do you think you can get us there?"

"I'll try not to drop you this time." Hawk said, nervously.

"I'm sure you'll do fine," Fox said, with a grin.

Chapter Nine

The Raid

"WHAT DID THAT NOTE SAY that I gave you?" Hawk asked. "I'm just curious."

"I've not read it yet." Fox said, pulling it from his pocket. "Where did you land us, anyway? I don't recognize this place at all."

"I don't either." Hawk answered, looking for a landmark. "We're supposed to be on Storg's hill."

Spreading the crumbled paper on a flat rock, Fox moved his lantern next to it. "All you wrote was your name, Hawk."

"My name's not like that. I've seen it before; it looks different than that," Hawk answered, sharply.

"Sorry Hawk, that's what I'm reading. That's all you have on here."

"A sign was stuck on my front door, too---just like the one you have, there." Wolf said, looking over Fox's shoulder. "It was in big, block printing just like Hawk's drawing." He nodded toward Fox, adding. "I'll bet you had one, too."

"Maybe," he whispered. "The boots were all I noticed."

"I'm sure," Wolf said, reverently. He stood silent.

Raising his voice, Fox said. "So, I think they were markers." Gingerly pacing, his voice bounced along with it.

With a breath of relief, Wolf answered, "for the guards, I suppose. That would make it a lot easier for them to find us."

"Probably so." After forcing the loosened curls back under his koyt, he tugged on the sides, covering his ears. "So, where are we, Hawk?" He asked.

"On the hill in front of Storg's hut, I hope," Hawk answered, looking to either side. His voice turned heavy with disappointment. "I must have done something wrong. I don't see it anywhere."

"Hold on; wait a minute," Fox cried out, pointing stubbornly. "Turn around, Hawk; see up there---the two caves, hidden right behind those bushes. See?"

"Oh! I was looking for the hut."

"I know, but it isn't here anymore."

"---but that was our landmark."

"They must have moved---I wonder why?" Wolf looked from Fox to Hawk. "They really liked this place."

"I know," Fox said, pacing the perimeter of the hut's foundation. "They didn't have to leave in a hurry. That's a good sign."

"How can you tell?" Hawk asked. "I don't see anything."

"That's just it, there's nothing left behind. The reindeer pens are gone and so is the hut and everything else. There's no trace of where it was, either. It's as if they were never here."

"Oh, I'm not surprised at that," Hawk snickered. "Storg told me they could trip a camp, that's what he called it, in a matter of minutes. They've had a lot of practice, you know."

"Maybe so but I still don't see how they can do it."

"There were fourteen of them, don't forget," Hawk said, "and they all knew exactly what to do. I watched them, some of the time."

"Well, I guess!" Fox said, apprehensively. Finally he said. "There's something about all this---that just doesn't feel right."

"Probably a reaction to what we left behind." Wolf suggested.

"I guess." Fox said. A shiver went down his spine.

Suddenly Wolf's attention shifted. "Where is Hawk?"

Realizing where Wolf's thoughts were, he looked toward the caves. Hawk was racing up the hill. "Hawk, stop," he screamed, "don't go in there."

"I'm going inside," Hawk yelled out, pausing for a moment. "I have to see if Storg's in there."

"Not so fast, Hawk. What if there's an animal in there?"

"Oh, I guess," Hawk answered, slowing down with a shudder. "I didn't think about that."

"Storg doesn't live here anymore."

"I know, but what if he's in there?" Hawk said. "I've got to see."

"All right," Fox conceded, "but we're coming with you. Just be careful."

"I will," Hawk answered, running ahead.

Wolf and Fox held their lanterns high, following Hawk into the grand hall. At the entrance they stopped, blinking and covering their eyes; a golden aura permeated the cavern.

Once his vision cleared, Hawk ran toward the back. "I need to see if Storg's here."

"Watch your step," Fox called back. In amazement, he gazed at the empty room. " I could never even dream of anything like this."

The dull light of the lantern radiated a pale glow across the room, softly illuminating the grand hall interior.

"Where do you suppose it's coming from?" Fox said, turning toward Wolf. "These lanterns don't have enough brightness."

"That question nudged the back of my mind when we were visiting, but I never put any real thought to it." Wolf said, rubbing his ears. While investigating the illuminated surfaces, he stumbled over an object in the shadows. "You remember how mayita only had that small fire where she prepared meals? That seemed curious to me, too."

"I know! I wondered about that---oh, and how it was always so warm and comfortable; those fine-spun robes we wore--- were almost weightless, you know." Fox commented. "They weren't made for warmth."

"Yeah---and the whole place was always so well lit." Wolf reminded him.

"There were lanterns setting about."

"I know, but that wasn't all she had; come look."

"Um, sorry," Fox said, stumbling toward Wolf.

"See what I mean---those little flecks all over the wall," Wolf said, excitedly. He held the lantern up.

Taking a closer look, Fox cried out excitedly. "Oh my gosh, this whole cave is covered with fragments of gold. So, what we have is reflected light; quite amazing." Stepping back, he stumbled again.

"That's not all, Fox. Why do you think it's so warm in here?"

"We were already commenting on that, but caves are always warm, he answered.

"Not like this."

"Well---that is true."

"I don't know for sure, but my guess is that the flecks are gold---and gold is a metal---,"

"We already said that," Fox said.

I know, but maybe it generates heat from the lanterns." Wolf reached up, massaging his ears, again. "What do you think?" Stepping back, he tripped, again. "What keeps getting in my way?"

"You know more about that than I do," Fox answered, lifting up the lantern.

"What am I tripping on?" Wolf complained, swinging his lantern into the shadows. "Well, would you look at that," he cried. "Fox, you'll never believe what I just found."

Swinging around, Fox looked toward Wolf's discovery. The light flashed up. "Wolf," he said, excitedly. "Wolf, you've got ears. When did you notice them?"

"Ears; what are you talking about?" Wolf said, reaching up. "Oh," he shrieked. "I didn't know---until just now."

"You're kidding---really?" Fox cried, ecstatically. "They're beautiful."

"Are they really?" Wolf touched his hands to them, not knowing what else to do. "I wish I could see them."

"Do they feel funny---or, or anything?"

"No. Not that I can tell."

Just then Hawk came racing into the grand room, yelling. "You've got to see, you've got to see! I didn't find Storg, but you'll never guess what's here."

"Hawk, look at Wolf---he's got ears." Fox said, staring in awe. "Can you believe it?"

Just then Dalt came prancing through the grand room. "I see you've met my girls," he bowed, tilting his antlers.

"Hawk," Fox cried," did you hear that?" With a nudge from the reindeer, Fox turned. "Dalt, it's so good to see you."

Dalt bowed to Fox. "Welcome to our home."

"They're back here," Hawk shouted, pacing impatiently. "The momma deer have babies. Just wait 'till you see them."

"Hold on, Hawk," Fox reminded him, "Dalt said you're going to scare them if you don't speak softly."

Hawk stopped. He then said, "Oh, I forgot. Sorry Dalt."

Dalt bowed his antlers to Hawk then turned back to Fox.

"Staring curiously at Dalt, Fox said, "this is strange, why can I hear you speak now when I couldn't before? I don't understand."

"Your power to know languages was just beginning," Dalt bowed. "I am not at all surprised."

Nodding toward Wolf, he said. "Three of my girls are now ladies. The two of you may visit my children, if you wish. They're just inside."

"Your---your children?" Fox stammered.

Dalt nodded proudly.

"Come on, Wolf! Dalt invited us to visit his families."Fox said with a grin.

"You mean there are more in the back?" Wolf stammered. "There are four here in the grand room"

Dalt tilted his antlers toward Fox. "Those girls are too young. They may be ladies next season. Time will tell."

"Isn't it a little early for your season." Fox asked.

"Perhaps! We had to prepare a bit early this year. It happens sometime." Dalt answered. He shook his antlers and the four girls stood then walked toward him. They bowed as they left for the room behind him. "My girls are quite spirited. They are taking the children out to play. This will give my ladies a chance to rest."

Bowing toward Fox, Dalt said. "You're looking for Storg and his family?"

Fox nodded. "Yes! Do you know where they are?"

Dalt shook his antlers and pawed at the ground. "They had to leave, just minutes after your departure."

"Ask him where Storg is?" Wolf requested.

"I just did." Fox answered."

"The deer could be hiding from his family."

"Wolf, he's trying to tell me."

"Oh," Wolf said.

"It was suggested we come here," Dalt answered. He turned to Fox. "Your mother was with them."

"My mother's alive?" His voice broke with relief.

"Yes, but she was badly injured."

"Could you take me to her," Fox pleaded. His eyes filled with tears.

"We're not to go, yet," Dalt stated.

"Why?" He snubbed. "Why? She needs me."

"Storg's family took her to a hiding place. They are trying to save her life." Shaking his antlers at Fox, he said, sharply. "Fox, you must listen to me. She was very weak when she got here."

"She came here? Why?" Fox stared at him in disbelief. "She knew about Storg's campsite?"

"Yes! She knew all about it. As soon as your father was apprehended, she escaped the compound and came straight over here. She wanted to warn you not to come home. One of the guards shot her when he saw her leaving."

"How did she know where we were?" Fox asked.

"I guess you didn't know she was an elf. She was gifted in languages, like you."

"No, I didn't," he murmured. "Were her ears clipped like Hawk's mom, to destroy her magical powers? I never noticed, I guess."

"No, she had all the powers without the ears."

Fox automatically reached up.

Dalt shook his antlers and smiled. He then said. "If the report is good, when my girls and the children return, we should leave. I sent them out to see if anyone may have followed you."

"Well, uh, okay." Still trying to digest Dalts information, Fox shook his head. "My dad, he was human, then?"

"That's right. He was a good man." Shaking his antlers again, Dalt said, "I see the girls returning; all is well. Oh, one more thing; you need to fasten your pocket or Mr. Twiddler may fall out when you transport."

"You're right," he said, quickly making it secure, "thanks. Come on, Wolf, it's time to go. Where is Hawk?"

"I'm right here." Hawk's face was covered with smiles. He skipped across the room, stopping beside Wolf. "You know what I was doing? I was in the back room with all the mommas' and they let me pet their babies."

Fox's eyes wrinkled with a smile. "So, you finally got to pet them, huh? That's great." Then nodding to Wolf, he said. "We really do need to leave. Are you both ready?"

"Uh-huh," Hawk said, bounding through the door.

"Uh, sure I guess." Wolf growled, following Fox outside. "I wish I knew what everyone was talking about. I felt like a lump."

"Sorry about that," Fox said "I was surprised I understood."

"Hawk didn't even notice my ears."

"He will."

"How do we know where we're going?" Hawk asked. "I don't know what to say."

"Elf magic is out of my realm of understanding. I'm afraid you're on your own." Dalt said, following his family back into the cave.

"Hey," a squeaky voice cried out, "I can't get out."

"This is not a good time, Mr. Twiddler," Fox warned, "we are going to find Storg. You'll have to stay in my pocket for a little while longer."

"Okay, fine," he growled, dropping to the bottom of the pocket. "This is boring. You could give me a light or something."

"You have lights in your house. Just settle in there for now."

"Oh, that must be it," Hawk yelled, quite relieved, "I thought of a way to get us there. Hang on."

"We are already," Wolf said. "I hope you've got this transporting a bit more perfected."

"I'm working on it," Hawk said, placing a hand on Fox and Wolf's shoulders. He yelled out, quite distinctly, "find Storg." The familiar dark cloud consumed the three as they began to move. Streaks of red and yellow pushed up from below. Seconds later, they crashed to the ground.

"Ouch! Oh!" Fox cried out, gingerly picking himself up.

"What are you trying to do, kill me?" The voice from his pocket yelled.

"Mr. Twiddler, are you all right?" Fox called out, frantically. He pulled at the pocket opening.

"I could be better," he growled, poking his head out. "Where are we anyway?"

"I don't know, yet," Fox answered. "Sorry about the bumpy landing. Do you want to come out?"

"Nah!" He said, slipping back inside the pocket. "Just watch those sudden stops, will you?"

"I'll try."

"What happened?" Hawk yelled, jumping up from the fall.

"You're on a hill behind our camp," a voice answered, dryly. "What are you doing here?"

"Storg, it's you. I've been so worried. Are you okay?" Hawk cried, excitedly. "I'm so happy we found you."

"How did you find this place?" He asked, without emotion.

"We transported, of course," Hawk answered.

"You shouldn't have come."

"Oh, but we had to," Hawk argued. "We were worried about you---and your family---when you were gone from the caves. We didn't know what to think when we found Dalt and his ladies in your home."

"I didn't think anyone could find us. How did you do it?"

"I just said 'find Storg' that's all."

He looked back at the group and muttered. "Well, since you're here, you'd better follow me back to camp."

Hawk stared up into his friend's face. "What's going on?"

"Oh, I didn't think about using a name," Storg said to himself. His shoulders began to droop as he mellowed.

"Why did you have to move?" Wolf asked. "I thought you liked the caves."

"I did. We all did. A lot of things have happened since you left."

"What kind of things?" Fox asked. "We heard you'd had some trouble."

"Our camp was raided right after your mother came. We nearly got caught. We were attacked on the way here. My mayita and dacco and my grandfather were all killed. Two cousins and an uncle were injured. It's been bad."

"Oh my gosh," Hawk blurted out, "we didn't know."

"Was it my mother? Did she lead the guards to your camp?" Fox questioned sharply. "She only came to warn me."

"Fox!" Storg interrupted. "If your mother hadn't come, we would probably all be dead." Tears sparkled under his eyelids as they fell.

Oblivious to Storg's voice, Fox continued, defensively. "She came to warn me about the uprising in the old city. She wouldn't have---."

Storg raised his voice slightly, getting Fox's attention. "It wasn't your guards who attacked us."

"It wasn't?" Fox answered. "Oh, then who was it? I thought---. I was afraid---."

"Who would be after you?" Hawk asked.

Joining the others, Wolf asked. "How far is it back to your camp? I took a walk, quite a distance out and didn't see anyone."

"We're almost there. We've been walking the perimeter," Storg answered. "As you have surely noticed, we are well hidden."

"Isn't it dangerous to be so far out?" Wolf cautioned.

"Actually, it's pretty safe," Storg said. "No one knows our location. I just need to leave once in a while, to clear my head."

"We found you." Wolf reminded him.

"I know, but you transported. Our enemies don't have powers like that."

"Your enemies can't transport?" Hawk said, quite amazed.

"No! They don't know magic," Storg answered, "just like your guards."

"Oh, I see," Hawk answered.

"But this place is still dangerous for you. Your guards don't care about us," Storg explained. "They only raided our camp while hunting for all of you. Now that they've left, I'm not expecting them back." As an afterthought, Storg added, "we're planning to move back to the other camp in a few days."

"It has reindeer living in it," Wolf mentioned. "Did you know that?"

"Of course. We asked them to."

"I'm confused, Storg," Fox said. "Tell me again, what happened."

"As soon as your mother arrived at our camp, my mayita took her inside and dressed her in the magical Kroll robe and jewels for curing wounds. Almost immediately, your guards from the old city came into the hut. When one of them, I think he was called Ro, saw a fur coat hanging on the wall, he started jumping and dancing and yelling. "Me coat! Me coat!" I thought he had lost his mind. After that, he and his partner ransacked the camp and left."

"So, how did they know about your camp?" Wolf asked.

"Oh, it was no secret. Your city officials knew where we were located," Storg answered, quickly. "We visited the governor about living in your city."

"Really, you came to see my dad?" Fox blurted out. "Why?"

"For safety, of course," Storg answered. "We had traveled many days; remember the first time I saw you, Hawk?"

"Yes, of course I do," Hawk answered.

"We had been told about your city and how secure it was. We thought it might be a way to escape our enemies."

"You didn't tell me that," Hawk said.

"After seeing the living conditions, we thought it wiser to just camp a distance away."

"What about these enemies of yours?" Fox asked. "You never said anything about them. Were we in danger at your camp?"

"I don't know. I didn't think you were." Storg answered

"Who are they---," Wolf asked, "these enemies?"

"They're the remains of a band of humans; two or three, maybe. They turned outlaw after our clan was disbanded, a long time ago. They don't usually attack unless they're hungry or in need of something. This time they turned vicious."

"What about my mother, Storg?" Fox asked, finally getting his courage up.

"I'm not sure. When my mayita was killed, her magic stopped working. She was having a problem with it anyway, since your mother was an elf. I just don't know." Storg answered. "Turn here. The camp is below."

Quietly walking single file, Storg led the others toward his family campsite. Apprehensively, they were all lost in thought.

As they arrived, Storg finally broke the silence with a noted sigh of relief. "I see no red flag at your mother's tent; that is a good sign." He looked about. "Everything seems to be as I left it." He then motioned to Fox. "Come, I'll take you to your mother."

Wolf immediately said. "Hawk and I will stay out here."

"It would please my mother if you came in to meet her," Fox invited. "I've told her many things about you both."

Following Fox inside, they found her robed in a gown and reclining on ornate pillows. Two Kroll women were attending her. Her pale face lit up at the sight of her son.

Pulling his cap off, Fox ran to her side and gently kissed her forehead. "Momma, I am so sorry."

"You are free my son, you are free." She whispered, caressing his matted spires of red with her fingers. "My beautiful son, let me take a look at you."

He touched her hand then held it gently. "I'd like for you to meet my friends." Pointing to each of them, he said. "This is Hawk, Wolf and Storg. Of course you've met Storg. We were visiting his camp."

"I am very happy to meet your friends." Turning to the attending ladies, she requested they leave.

"Momma?"

"They know my needs," she replied, quietly.

"But---?"

She looked at him with pleading eyes. "What I have to say is important. You must carry it with you, always. I have little time."

"You mean?" Fox moaned, softly.

"Yes," she whispered. "You are my son; my only child." Holding her hand up, she stroked his face. "You will no longer be a number in the old city books. I took care of that."

"But Momma---?"

"Just listen, I have much to say." Nodding toward the other three, she said. "Please stay."

"We thought you might want to be alone," Hawk said, lowering his head.

Looking back to her son, she stroked his hand. "I understand your friends' call you Fox."

"Yes, It's just a code name."

"Your true name is Sandor. Sandor is from your father. My name is Sadria."

"I didn't know."

"We were never allowed to use true names," she said. Our sir name is Claus. You will be known by that name from now on."

"It sounds like I'm going somewhere."

"You are. You cannot stay here, or anywhere close by. When you escaped and returned undetected, it made the security here a laughingstock. You will always be in danger."

Looking across the bed she addressed Hawk. "Your mother is no longer at the old city. She is now in hiding and doing well. I see by the stature of your ears, you are one of thought and reflective reasoning. Your true name is Hermes Potts."

With the hand of Fox between hers, she squeezed it gently. Turning her eyes toward the other side, she continued. "I believe you've been going by the name of Wolf," she said. "Was there a reason for that?"

Somewhat embarrassed, he answered. "My mother used to say I howled like one, when I was a baby. It seemed to be a good choice."

She smiled at him. "That's a pretty good reason. I remember those days."

"Your true name is Robert David Jax. I see your ears are developing nicely. It's taking a while, isn't it? I find it no surprise, since you'll be following in your parents footsteps."

"What do you mean?" Wolf asked. "I've hardly ever seen them."

"I'm sure that's true. They are held in high esteem for their scientific contributions, at the university and in the science world."

"Do you know where they are? Are they all right?"

"As far as I know, they are well," Sadria told him. "At the present time they are in a lockdown at the university."

"Did they do something wrong?" Wolf asked.

"Oh no, it's for their safety," she answered. "The guards are still hunting for the three of you."

"Are they going to be all right?" He asked,.

"I believe they will." Turning again, Sadria said. "Storg, it looks like you and your family got caught up in our difficulty."

"You didn't cause anything. It would have been worse if you had not warned us. His voice trailed off. "We've been running for a long while. We're pretty good at it most of the time."

"If you should choose to go with my son and his friends, changing your name might be advisable since Storg is known by association."

"Storg is a made-up name. Fox---u-m-m, your son, Sandor had all of us use fictitious names. He didn't want anyone to know where we lived, either. It was my idea for them to come visit me."

"Do you have a true name?" She asked.

"Oh, yes! It's an old family name, from my great-great grandfather. My name is Claudius. It's Claudius Cee."

"Claudius, it is an honor to meet you."

Sadria turned again toward her son, holding out her hand. "Do not tarry long, my Sandor. I fear for your life."

He looked long into her eyes then kissed her hands and left. The others followed.

"Please have the ladies return. I am so very tired," Sadria requested. While watching them leave, tears covered her cheeks.

Once the boys reached the top of the hill, they looked back at the camp. Wolf said, quietly. "The red flag is out. I'm so sorry, Sandor. Your mother was a beautiful lady."

Chapter Ten

What's in a Name

"WHAT DO YOU THINK ABOUT our names?" Wolf said. "My mother called me Robye once in a while but I didn't know it was my name." He smoothed the knapsack out on the ground and began packing supplies in it.

"Robye seems like an alright name. I wouldn't mind calling you that" Hawk said, dropping another stack of provisions beside him. "Here are some more blankets. Will they go in your bag?"

"I think there's enough room," Wolf answered, picking one up and tucking it on top of the others. "Actually, I like Robye. So Claudius, what do you think?" He said, nodding toward Storg.

"I think it fits you pretty well, if that's what you're asking."

"Yeah, I guess. I never thought about that part."

"Sure you did," Hawk laughed. Dropping to his knees, he held the knapsack open. "That's why you called yourself Wolf."

"Did you really howl like a wolf when you were small, Robye?" Claudius snickered. After tying up the bag, he stacked it with the others.

"That was what my mother said. How would I remember? I was just a baby."

"Can you still do it?" Asked Hawk. He scrunched his nose and cocked his head to one side, waiting for an answer.

"Do what?" Robye questioned, looking up."

"Howl like a wolf?" Hawk laughed, stroking his right ear. "I want to hear you."

"Yeah, me too," Claudius urged. "Come on with it."

"Oh, well, I'll give it a try." Robye cupped both hands on the sides of his mouth and let out a mournful cry. "A-a-o-o-o!"

"From across the campsite, Fox ran toward them. "What was that horrible noise?" He cried.

"Sorry, I didn't mean to scare you, Fox---er, Sandor," Robye laughed. "We were talking about our names and they wanted to hear me howl."

"That was enough to make my hair curl," Fox scolded, peering over the load of supplies he was carrying. Slightly hesitating, he then dropped everything to the ground, saying, "well?"

"Well, what?" Robye asked. His eyes followed the drop then slipped back to Fox's face.

"Your names; do you have a problem with them?"

"Not with mine, I don't. Actually, I'm getting used to Robye already," he laughed, observing his friends reactions. "Robye Jax, that's me; it fits don't you think?" Standing up, he took a deep bow. "Without the howl, of course," he laughed.

"Well, that's good to know. When I knew you before, I was too young to care, I guess," Fox quipped. "That howl would have scared me half to death."

"Well I'm glad to know my true name," Hermes chimed in. "It was fun being called Hawk, though. That used to be my imaginary friend when I was really little. We would do everything together." A trace of sadness crept across his face. "I didn't even know I had a true name. All I ever knew was my number---3779." He looked up. "My mother told me a story one time, about a hawk who rescued a little boy from a monster dragon. I could always see myself fighting that dragon and taking the little boy to safety. Later, when I was six years old and could choose a name, Hawk was the one I decided on."

"It's too dangerous to call you Hawk," Fox said, quietly.

"Oh, that's alright. Hawk will always be my friend. I still talk to him when I'm afraid of monsters, or something." With a quick grin, he added, "my parents chose Hermes Potts as my true name and that means I'm real; I'm not just a number anymore."

"It's funny how names affect us. Take mine, for example." Fox began.

"Yeah, take yours," Robye snickered. "Sandor sounds like a wicked bird."

Surprised at his candor, Fox said. "You're talking about my family name. My father's true name was Sandor."

"I know, but don't you agree?" Robye argued.

"Well, I guess," Fox admitted. "It's not my favorite---but it was his name---and-and I inherited it."

"I know but---." Robye stammered.

"---and I don't have a middle one to fall back on, like you do; Robert Da-vi-d Jax."

"So-r-r-y!! Couldn't we just nick it a little, though?" Robye pleaded.

A grin crept to the corners of Fox's mouth. "It's a good thing you're an old friend. That's all I have to say."

"Oh, okay Foxie. I didn't mean to stir you up," Robye teased, backing off. "Well, what do you think?"

"I must admit, the thought had crossed my mind," Fox snickered.

Claudius turned toward the two and said in a matter-of-fact voice. "If anyone is interested in my opinion, I think Sandy would be more suitable, considering the hank of red that keeps springing from under your koyt all the time. It seems fitting to me, somehow."

"H-m-m, Sandy---Sandy Claus. I think my mother would approve. I've heard her call my father Sandy, before. He seemed to like it." With a grin, Fox said. "Claudius, sometimes you just seem to know the right thing to say."

"Hmf! Just leave me out of the big decisions, would you?" Mr. Twiddler snipped, climbing out of Fox's pocket. He leaned against the furry edge of the sleeve and frowned up at the foursome.

"Mr. Twiddler? I haven't seen you all day. Where have you been hiding?" Hermes cried. He dropped another load of supplies beside Robye and dusted the fur on his coat front. "What is it you do in that pocket, besides sleep?"

"What do you mean, Hermes?" Fox responded in surprise. "He lives in there of course!"

"He what?"

"He lives there. His house is in my pocket, of course; the one our friends built for him at the hideout, remember?" Fox opened the pocket with his fingers. "See, it fits perfectly. He's been in there ever since we left."

"That's impossible," Hermes sputtered. "How did you do that?"

"How did I do what, the interior lighting? Oh that was a bit tricky but we finally got it to work. For a while I thought there was a flaw in the system but Mr. Twiddler found the problem; we hadn't activated it. He lived in the dark for a couple of days before we found the solution, I'm afraid."

"I'm not talking about the lighting; what about the whole house, how did you do it? How did you get it to fit in your pocket?"

"Oh, "said Fox, "I just picked it up and slipped it inside."

"The whole house?" He cried, grabbing at the furry opening and staring inside.

"Let me see, too," Robye said, wedging up beside Hermes. "Well, I'll be; you sure did. That's the most amazing thing I think I've ever seen."

"Of course and everything works quite nicely, according to Mr. Twiddler," Fox answered with a smile.

"Unbelievable!" Claudius said, peeking around the others.

"I know! After some prodding, he even admitted that it was more comfortable than his old place. My pocket insulates it from the wind and the cold so he hardly ever needs to light the fireplace."

"That too?"

"Sure!" Fox answered. His eyes twinkled.

Mr. Twiddler popped through the pocket opening, just as the fur began to slide together. Busily tying the purple string around his ears, he said, "ahem," clearing his throat. "If you don't mind, I am a private elf. I do have a front door and you could knock. It's rude to peek in on someone."

"Sorry, Mr. Twiddler, I didn't mean to pry." Hermes apologized, stepping back.

"Me too," Claudius and Robye chimed in, holding their hands up in defense.

"Well, enough of that; just so you know," Mr. Twiddler scolded. "Now back to Fox, um-m-m Sandor, and this nick you're all trying to put on his name. Sandy is not a name I'll be riding with. Nothing against your father," he glanced up at Fox, somewhat apologetically, "but I'm not the Sandy type."

"I'm guessing you have a suggestion," Sandor grinned."

"Of course I do or I wouldn't be out here in the cold. B-r-r-r," Mr. Twiddler quivered. "I may have to light that fireplace after all."

"It's getting close to spring. It's been pretty warm today, Mr. Twiddler, can't you tell? The mystery lights have not been as bright as usual."

"Well, whatever," Mr. Twiddler snipped. "As I was about to say, before the weather report," he glared at Sandor then went on, "Santa, which means saint, would be of some renown."

"Special, you mean?" Robye interrupted.

"Of course, Mr. Twiddler raked, sarcastically. "Not that he'll ever be one, but it sounds good. I don't travel second class, you know."

"Oh, ho," Robye said, quickly, "just listen to the little guy!"

"Ahem," Mr. Twiddler said, loudly, "may I go on?"

"Sorry!" Robye quipped, apologetically.

Clearing his throat again, Mr. Twiddler continued. "Santa is different enough from Sandor that those lazy lugs who seem to be chasing you, would probably never get the connection to your father---and it is certainly nothing like Fox."

"I see---I think?" Hermes said, looking a bit lost to the explanation.

Mr. Twiddler glared at Hermes, then at the others. He then said, quite annoyed, "Governor Sandor Claus known as Governor by most! You got it, now?"

"Yes," Hermes said, meekly.

"Sandor Claus Jr. known as Fox---?" Said Mr. Twiddler, with a nod.

"I get it."

"The authorities searching for Fox would have a hard time connecting the name Santa Claus to it. Besides I happen to like the name," Mr. Twiddler stated, in a matter-of fact tone. He nodded his head again and dropped back into the pocket.

"Well, he does have an attitude," Robye giggled.

"I kind of like his suggestion," Hermes said, kneeling beside Robye's bag. He began packing supplies into it.

"Hey! What are you doing there? I can do that," Robye scolded.

"I know, but I've run out of space in this other bag," Hermes frowned. "I didn't think you'd mind."

"I think I could get used to Santa Claus, I really do," Fox laughed. He grabbed Hermes bag and tossed it over his shoulder.

"Thanks, Santa," Hermes said with a crooked grin.

"Welcome," Santa answered, heading toward the sleigh. "I guess I can drop the 'Fox' name then."

"Good idea," Claudius agreed. "I'm glad to have my real name back, too."

"I'm sure you are," Santa commented. "Storg wasn't too bad though, was it?"

"M-m-m, no, I guess," he answered, "but I felt like I was losing my identity."

"I understand that feeling," Santa answered. "We all do. We're just finding ours."

"It's a good feeling, isn't it," Claudius said quietly, "to know who you are."

"It sure is!" Santa replied.

"This bag's finished," Robye said, tying it closed.

"I'll take it for you," Hermes offered, reaching to pick it up.

"It's going to take both of us to carry this one, Hermes. You added all that extra stuff---and now it's really heavy." Robye whined. He stood up and grabbed the knot. "Grab that end. I've got this one."

"Sure!" Hermes said, grabbing one of the corners. "Hmf," he groaned. "I've got it! I've got it!" Trying to lift it up, he pulled his end of the load toward the sled.

"We've got just enough room for three more bags," Claudius yelled, standing on the end of the sled. "Robye! You and Hermes bring that one over here and we'll try to hoist it up together. Okay?"

"We're trying! We're trying," Robye yelled back.

"So, Claudius, do you think changing Sandor to Santa is a fitting thing to do, for my family heritage, that is?" Santa asked. "I respect your opinion."

Claudius caught Santa's eye, in passing and said. "If Santa Claus feels comfortable, and you like it, I think it's a very good choice."

"It feels like I was born to it, if that's what you mean."

"Exactly!" Claudius answered with a smile.

"Claudius said we have room for two more bags," Santa announced, returning from the sleigh.

"That's a good thing, Santa! That's all the room we have," Robye called back, swinging a small one over his shoulder.

"This is the last one, Santa," Hermes said, struggling with his load.

"Here! Let me help," Santa said, with a grin. "It's almost as big as you are."

"This is everything for Claudius's family, isn't it?" Hermes said.

"Sure is!" Santa answered. "After we deliver it, we only need to pick up our knapsacks and be on our way."

"Do you think we could visit Dalt and his ladies before we leave the caves?" Hermes queried. "I'd like to say goodbye to them."

"We need to do that," Santa answered. "This time of season they are probably out with the rest of the herd. We're getting five to six hours of daylight, now."

"So, we'll be leaving tomorrow?" Robye asked, turning toward the two.

"Probably," Santa said, "If everything goes well."

"So, where are we going?" Asked Hermes.

"To tell you the truth, I don't know," Santa answered. "With longer days coming on, each day we spend here makes our escape more dangerous. The guards will soon be roaming further and further out from the old city, if they've not started already."

"What about Claudius? Is he coming with us?" Asked Robye, curiously.

"It's up to him. He may want to stay and protect his family," Santa said, thoughtfully.

"Everything is ready to go," Claudius announced, coming up behind the three. "All the supplies are secured and the reindeer are hitched to the sleigh. We should probably get to the caves and have all this stuff unloaded before it gets dark; that is if we don't dally." Looking at Santa, he added. "We're leaving in the morning; is that the plan?"

"We were just discussing that. Are you sure you're not needed here?" Santa asked. "You may be leaving your family behind, forever."

"Now, if you don't want me to go with you just say the word," Claudius stated. "I've already talked it over with my family. They have decided I should travel with you."

"Then you are and happy we are to have you." Santa said, pushing a hand out in welcome.

"That's better!" Claudius said, accepting the handshake. "I wouldn't miss this adventure for anything. Where are we going?"

"I thought we'd head northeast," Santa answered, "but I'm open for suggestions."

"I've been out that way. Once you get past the scrubs, it's flatter than a stonecake." Claudius said, climbing on the sleigh and picking up the reins. "Come on! The seat's big enough for all of us."

"What are stonecakes?" Hermes asked, struggling to reach the seat. Robye gave him a boost.

"Oh!" Claudius laughed, reaching out to help. "They're kind of like my meat cakes only made of dough. It's an old saying that means there's nothing out there."

"Oh!" Hermes said quietly. Sliding toward Claudius, he asked. "Are they good?"

"What? Oh, the stonecakes; they sure are," Claudius said, quickly. Suddenly his voice tightened. "My mayita always made them in the summer when the berries were ripe. She'd take roots and berries and make a sweet sauce to pour over them."

"Sorry about your mayita," Hermes said. Tears welled up in his eyes. "I miss my mother, too."

"We'll find her! I promise," Claudius said gently.

"Hey! Squeeze on over," Robye said, dropping onto the small plank seat. "We need room for one more."

"Okay! Okay! Give me a minute," Hermes said, sliding closer to Claudius.

"Come on, Santa," Claudius called. "Let's get going."

Robye extended a hand toward Santa and tugged him toward the top of the sleigh. Landing on the edge of the seat, Santa nearly lost his balance, just as Claudius signaled for the reindeer to take off. Robye pulled him back on.

"Wh-e-e-e! I've never ridden in a sleigh before," Hermes yelled excitedly. "This is fun! Are we going to our new home by sleigh? Will we get there tomorrow?"

"I'm sure we will be traveling for more than one day, Hermes," Santa answered. "We need more distance from At il than that, to be safe."

"At il?" Hermes questioned. "Where is that?"

"That's the real name of the old city," Robye cut in.

"Oh! I don't guess I ever knew that," Hermes answered. "I just thought it was the old city, you know."

"Hermes did bring up a good question, Claudius," Robye said.

"What's that?"

"My question, as well," Santa added, "the sleigh for our travels?"

"I wish we could but this is the only one my family has left," Claudius said, "and we have no reindeer to pull it."

"What about Dalt and his ladies," Hermes asked.

"They don't belong to me," Claudius answered. "They would have to choose to go with us, with my family's approval. Besides all that, their young would have to ride in the sleigh. By the time they are old enough to travel on their own, we should be far, far away."

"You're kidding! Right?" Hermes said, staring up at Claudius. Robye and Santa glanced at Claudius as well.

"Not kidding," Claudius said. "We protect our stock."

"What about a sleigh?" Robye asked.

"When we round up reindeer of our own and tame them, we may have need of a sleigh, so we'll build one, of course."

"So, that means we're walking?" Asked Robye.

"That means we're walking," Santa confirmed.

"What about transporting? We could do that," Hermes suggested. "I'm pretty good at it, you know."

"We have to know where we're going and right now I have no idea where that might be." Santa explained, patiently.

"Right ahead is our caves," Claudius said, waving excitedly to his family. A signal with the reins had the reindeer heading toward them. "It looks like they've got the hut and everything all set up."

Santa waved to the family, calling out a greeting in the Kroll language.

"Where are Dalt and his ladies? I don't see them," Hermes cried out. Suddenly standing, he tried to get a better view of the reindeer herd.

"Sit down, Hermes; you're going to fall," Robye warned, quickly grabbing at his coat. "They're here somewhere. We'll see them before we leave, I'm sure."

"O-kay," Hermes whined. Resigning himself to patience, he dropped back into the seat. As soon as Claudius parked the sleigh he jumped out, yelling. "Grandmother will know where they are, I bet." He took off running toward the holding pen at the bottom of the hill.

Chapter Eleven

The Long Walk

DAWN HAD COME EARLY, PROMISING a clear and sunny day. Across the fields of melting snow, spindly fragments of vegetation had taken on shades of green with the budding of new growth. A show of animal and bird tracks had appeared overnight and seemed to be randomly scattered throughout the valley, tracing around the edge of every small bush and sprout that had the slightest hint of new growth with the warmer season's arrival. As the morning sun broke across the horizon, chirping birds welcomed the light.

It had now been days since Fox and his friends had left the Cee family campsite at the twin caves. Only the mountain tops could now be seen. Beyond it was the old city, At il, and although they had traveled some distance, they still had the fear of being caught.

"Last night, Claudius, at the campsite," said Santa, "you were talking again about the northeast tundra."

"Yes, I mentioned it."

"From your description, the flatness of it is far-reaching and covered with ice."

"That's true. It goes right over the cap of the North Pole."

"You said you had traveled it; what is it like?" Santa asked, pulling at the straps to his knapsack.

"Like I said before, there's a tree line that melds into a brushy band, which we're actually in right now. Much north of this would be mainly flatland with no place to hide. It's covered with ice that never melts, why?" Claudius answered.

"I'm not fond of the idea but we need to go where we're least likely to be followed. It's the best season for us to be traveling but it's also a good time for the guards to be out hunting for us. They won't give up easily, you know." He pulled at the straps again.

"What's wrong with your knapsack? Can't you get it to settle onto your shoulders?" Claudius asked, reaching toward Santa's back. He ran his fingers down the length of the straps. "Is that better?"

"Not really. I must have packed it wrong," Santa said. "When we find a place to stop, I'll check it out."

"How far do you think we've gone?" Hermes whined, plodding along beside Robye. He looked up, scrunching his face into a frown. "I'm tired---and-and hungry." Shifting his eyes toward Santa, he added. "Can we stop now?"

"Maybe, if we find a good place to set up camp," Santa answered, looking toward Claudius for confirmation.

"Good," Hermes said, jumping into a narrow bank of snow.

"I think we are all a little weary," Robye said, glancing toward Santa and Claudius.

"It is a little early, but I know of a place not far from here," Claudius offered. "It's not a cave but we'd be out of the weather."

"Did I hear someone suggest we stop?" Mr. Twiddler quipped, poking his head out of Santa's pocket. "It's about time. Every time I lean back for a nap, I get dumped out of my chair."

"I'm sorry, Mr. Twiddler," Santa apologized, looking down at him.

"You should be!" Mr. Twiddler growled, dropping back into the pocket.

"Is he all right?" Robye asked, staring at the pocket opening.

"I think so. Traveling like this will take some getting used to for all of us," Santa said. "Is Hermes still pouting?"

"I'm afraid so. He was really looking forward to visiting with Dalt, you know."

"I was, too," Santa admitted. "I was glad to see Claudius's family doing as well as they were."

"Me too," Hermes interrupted, catching up with them. His arms were loaded with snow balls.

"Where did you find enough snow?" Santa laughed.

Hermes pointed toward some rocky mounds. "I got most of it over there," he said, giggling. "There's still plenty of snow, between the rock crevices and stuff."

"What are you going to do with them?" Robye asked, with a grin. "Are you planning to beat off monsters or something?"

"Nah! I got bored, just walking behind you all day and thought I'd work on my pitching arm." He threw one of the snowballs at a nearby bush. "See! I'm getting better. I hit that dried up old twig with three out of five. Not bad, huh?"

"Not too bad. How did you do before?"

"I only got two out of five."

"An improvement, already."

Hermes leaned down and scooped up two of the balls he had dropped, yelling at Claudius. "Here it comes."

Claudius turned just in time to get smacked right in the face. "Hey, why did you do that?" Squeezing some snow into a ball, he whipped it back at Hermes.

Hermes turned to run but got caught in the backside. "I said 'catch'. Didn't you hear me?" He laughed, aiming one at Robye. Santa stepped in and caught it, whizzing it back at Hermes. Soon snowballs were flying in everywhere.

"Wow, I've not had that much fun in a while," Robye exclaimed, when they finally called a truce.

"I know," Hermes said, with a giggle. "Walking and walking and walking gets boring."

"We all needed the break," Santa agreed.

"What's Claudius doing?" Hermes yelled, pointing at a ledge a few yards away.

"I didn't know he left," Robye cried out. "He sure is excited about something; just look at him. He's going to lose his arm if he doesn't watch out."

"What are you doing over there?" Santa called, waving back at him.

"Hey everybody, this is it---the place I was telling you about." He was standing in front of a tall bank of craggily rocks

"Hey, Claudius," Robye yelled back, "I can see you. Did you find us a good camping spot?" After jumping over a pile of rocks and splashing through a big puddle of slushy snow, he reached the base of the ledge where Claudius was standing. His eyes immediately shot up the rocky wall behind him then registered on Claudius's face, full of disappointment. "I don't see anything. Where is it?"

"Right behind me," Claudius laughed. "I nearly missed it, too. It's a good thing I had memorized the location or I'd have never found it again. Come check it out!"

Behind him was an indention in the rock formation that took on the shape of a shadow and not easy to identify. He stepped aside and pointed at it. "See what I mean? It's really hidden from everything!"

Santa ducked his head inside the shaded overhang. What he saw was a large orb with smooth and rounded walls covered by a heavy coating of ice. "Do you think we can all fit in here?" His voice echoed. "It's awfully small." He withdrew his head and turned around. "I don't know if it's big enough, Claudius."

"Of course it is," Claudius answered, quickly. "There were nine of us, the last time I was here. It's bigger than it looks." Noticing what Santa was staring at, he quickly added. "We only need to pack the opening with snow. We'll stay warm as toast. Don't worry about keeping the cold from seeping in."

"The getting inside doesn't seem to be too much of a problem," Santa said, crawling inside, "but who may have occupied this place before us, does bother me a bit."

"Are you thinking the same thing I am?" Robye said, crawling in behind him.

"Probably."

"Bear cave?"

"I'm pretty sure of it," Santa answered. "Where is Hermes?"

"He's right behind me," Claudius answered. "This is an old hibernating cave for bears. I'm sure they won't be coming back for a while but I put out a barrier, anyway."

"I've got a candle," Hermes offered, crawling into the space.

"We may not need it," Claudius answered, "with all our body heat."

"I mean, so we can see," Hermes said.

"Oh! Yeah," Claudius grinned. "There won't be any room for monsters."

"What's toast?" Hermes asked, changing the subject.

"Toast? Oh, its dough that's cooked on a hot, flat rock," Claudius answered. "It's pretty tasty."

"Oh," Hermes answered, "I think I'm still hungry."

"I think we all are," Santa said, climbing through the opening. "We'll eat from our supplies tonight."

"I think I'll make a skid while we're here. That way we can pull our supplies, rather than carry them. They were pretty heavy today. What do you think?" Claudius asked, following Santa across the opening.

"It's worth a try," Santa agreed.

"Do you want to help me, Hermes?" Claudius called.

"Sure, what do I have to do?" Hermes answered, as they left.

"Well Santa, it seems we're stuck with cooking, huh?" Robye said, with a crooked grin.

"That's all right. You know how Mr. Twiddler likes to help with that," Santa laughed.

"Did I hear my name in vain?" Mr. Twiddler piped up. "What was that I heard about a bear cave?"

"Don't worry your little head about that," Santa laughed, patting his pocket, "you're not big enough for a good bite."

Walking away from the others, Claudius turned toward Hermes. "First, we've got to find some flat sticks---about that long," he said, measuring with stretched-out arms, "and hopefully they'll be pretty straight." Heading toward some bushes, he reached down and picked up a long flat strip of wood. "Something like this might work"

"What else do we need?" Hermes asked, trying to keep up with Claudius's long stride.

Robye watched as the two left. He turned to Santa with a smile. "Hermes is a piece of work. He's not said a word about Dalt."

"I smell food out there," Mr. Twiddler said, scrambling from the coat pocket.

Santa reached down and picked up the small elf, placing him on his shoulder. "It seems that your nose is still working. We're putting some of my famous soup together. Would you like to join us?"

"I thought you'd never ask," Mr. Twiddler said, casually tying the purple string around his ears.

"Glad to have some help," Santa remarked.

Observing Santa's work, as he added herbs, Mr. Twiddler asked. "What do you have in that pot, anyway?"

"Oh, I have some meat and vegetables, so far. I'm working on a stew. Why?"

Mr. Twiddler immediately began to stress. Finally, he could control himself no longer and cried out,"you're going to ruin it!"

"What do you mean?" Santa said, mildly. "It needs the herbs to bring out the flavor."

"I know," Mr. Twiddler squeaked, "but you don't want to destroy it in the process."

"Of course not," Santa said, "So, how should it be done?"

"Gently press those herbs between your palms then sprinkle evenly across the soup."

"Why is that?" Santa asked.

"To tantalize the taste-buds with the aroma, of course."

"So, you're a gourmet cook."

"I do enjoy the challenge," Said Mr. Twiddler. "You know what you see and smell is a large portion of the eating pleasure." He casually leaned against Santa's bushy locks and adjusted the purple string around his ears, then said. "One time, when I was in Paris, I observed a chef preparing a soup similar to yours. He had a special ingredient that enhanced the---."

"Look! Look at the skid we made," Hermes yelled, running toward the campfire. A long, flat bundle of sticks bounced along behind him. "Claudius showed me how to tie everything together with a special knot. All you have to do is---." He came to a sudden stop and pointed his, now slightly long, nose up in the air. "M-m-m, something smells good! Is it time to eat? I am rea-l-ly hungry."

"Slow down, slow down, Hermes," Santa laughed. "Our dinner will be ready soon."

"Where is that boy's manners?" Mr. Twiddler said, dryly. "I was in the middle of a great remembrance."

"Well, go on with it, Mr. Twiddler," Santa invited.

"I'm likely not to recall the incident, after such an interruption."

"You said something about a chef in Paris," Santa reminded him. Dipping a ladle into the soup, he began to briskly stir.

"Gently, gently, Santa; you'll damage the aroma."

"Oh! Yeah," Santa said, slowing his movement. "The story, Mr. Twiddler, the story; you were in Paris."

"Paris? What's a Paris?" Hermes quizzed, eyeing the small elf sitting on Santa's shoulder.

"Paris is not a what, it's a where," Mr. Twiddler corrected. "Paris is a city where chefs are taught the fine art of food preparation and presentation for royalty; earls and kings and queens and such. They must go to the university---." Looking down, he noticed his audience walking away. "Hey there Hermes, where are you going?"

"Claudius needs me to help him carry in some firewood." Kicking a clump of snow in front of him, Hermes muttered, drooping along. "I only asked a question."

With kind of a shock, Mr. Twiddler turned toward Santa. "What happened? Was it something I said?"

"I would say so," Santa said, sharply. "Hermes didn't understand a thing you were talking about. He's not even ten years old, you know."

"I wasn't thinking," Mr. Twiddler said, slightly embarrassed. "He wanted to know what a Paris was and I thought the question quite foolish, but if---."

Suddenly Mr. Twiddler's voice was interrupted by a raspy growl directly behind them.

"G-r-r-r."

"What was that?" He squeaked, pushing Santa's fur collar around him.

"I don't know," Santa whispered. "Some kind of animal, I think." Reaching up, he opened his hand and Mr. Twiddler climbed into it. "It didn't sound very friendly, either."

Suddenly, growling and scraping was heard from the opposite direction.

"There's more than one something out there," Mr. Twiddler tweaked, shaking violently.

Santa placed his hand over the pocket opening and Mr. Twiddler climbed inside. "I'm afraid you're right," he said under his breath. Nervously rubbing his arms, he glanced about.

"G-r-r-r." He heard again.

"From behind our camp, I think. We're surrounded," Santa muttered.

"Did you say something?" Mr. Twiddler squeaked, sticking his head through the fur.

"Get back in there!"

"Oh," Mr. Twiddler whispered, "you don't have to tell me twice."

He dropped back into the pocket.

With Mr. Twiddler safe, Santa's thoughts raced to the others. "Where is Robye?---Claudius?" His eyes darted frantically about. "I don't see them anywhere. Where are they?" He whispered, feverishly. "Hermes is with Claudius, ---I hope?" Every twig and leaf seemed to move. Every noise was like an explosion. "They've got to be all right."

Finally he spotted Claudius and Hermes, ambling quite unconcerned toward the camp, deep in a conversation. As usual, Hermes hands were flailing all about.

When his eyes swept forward, an icy shiver went down his spine. Two huge, shaggy wolves were hidden, just ahead of them. They separated and went to either side. The boys were being stalked. He opened his mouth and tried to scream but no noise came out. Standing rigid, he watched the beasts slip through the brush.

Claudius heard a twig snap. Casually, he glanced ahead but saw nothing.

Suddenly, a long, throaty howl broke the silence. Santa jerked as he turned. Directly behind him, perched on a small knoll, was a pair of eyes staring down at him. "We're completely surrounded." A shudder went down his back, again. "We've got to find a way out of here---and fast."

Hearing the spine-chilling howl, Claudius leaped to one side, pulling Hermes along with him. Shoving him to the ground, Claudius dropped on top of him. "Wolves," he hissed, raising his head. "Where are they?"

Hermes cried out in surprise.

"Quiet!" Claudius warned.

"Awg," gurgled Hermes, behind Claudius's hand.

"Sh-h-h!" Claudius whispered, holding him down. "Don't move!"

"M-m-muf," Hermes groaned, trying to pull loose, "you're squashing me."

"Sh-h-h!"

Hermes pushed his head from under Claudius. "What is it?"

"Wolves."

"Yeah, I see them," Hermes whispered. "We've gotta get out of here."

"That's obvious," Claudius snapped. "Any ideas?"

"Sure!" Hermes answered. "Transporting."

"That's not a choice. We must all leave together," Claudius said, sharply.

"I know---we will!"

"Where will we go?"

"Dunno! Up is out---that beats here!"

"It's all of us, or none," Claudius answered. "Stay down!"

"I am," Hermes whimpered, dropping his head to the ground.

Claudius raised his head and peeked up. Santa's signal caught his eye and he rolled off Hermes, muttering gruffly, "Santa's not far from here. Come on! Stay down and close---and don't make a sound."

"Oh! Okay," Hermes said, between chattering teeth. "I'm scared."

"Me too," Claudius said, firmly holding Hermes arm. "We've got to hang in there."

"I know," Hermes said, shaking uncontrollably.

Claudius patted him gently then rolled to his stomach. "Just do what I do, okay?"

"I will." Hermes reached for his sleeve, sliding up beside him.

Pressing flat to the ground, they cautiously slithered across the open ground toward the bush where Santa was hiding. Maneuvering around old brush and sparse new growth of spindly bushes, they crawled cautiously toward Santa's location.

Resisting the urge to wipe cold sweat from his burning eyes, Claudius leaned down to swipe his face on one of his coat sleeves. Continuing across the damp ground he felt, more than knew, that Hermes was trailing close behind.

Periodically glancing up, Claudius watched for Santa's discrete gestures that kept him aware of the wolves locations. As soon as they arrived, a fountain of words tumbled from Santa's mouth. "I'm glad you made it. I was watching---! I can't find Robye? I've not seen him--- anywhere."

"Looking for me?" Robye whispered, coming up from behind.

Startled at his voice, Santa's body jerked, slightly. "Oh, yes! I've been looking everywhere for you. What happened to you? Where have you been?"

"I got caught on the other side and had to circle around, behind all those wolves, to get here. It wasn't easy but I don't think they even noticed me."

"Oh, I'm sure they saw every move you made," Santa told him. "They've been watching us too, I'm afraid. We really need to stick together. We've got to find a way out of here."

"Do you hear that scraping sound? What is it?" Hermes whispered, squeezing up beside Santa. "It sounds scary."

"Sh-h-h!" Santa warned.

"Oh! Oh! There's one of them! See him? See that wolf? He's right behind us." Hermes squeaked, between chattering teeth.

Cautiously turning, and motioning for the others to do the same, Santa saw the wolf Hermes had spotted. Flanking it on either side were two more.

"Down," Santa whispered, forcefully.

They all dropped to the ground, wrapping their arms around their heads. Side by side, moment by moment, they lay there, waiting.

"What do we do now?" Robye whispered, under his arm.

"We stay quiet," Santa answered, softly.

"Hopefully we can sneak out of here," Claudius said, looking toward them.

Finally, Hermes looked up. "They're gone! Where did they go?"

"Sh-h-h, Hermes, I don't know," Santa said, looking at him, "but we'd better get out of here before they change their minds. I do know that. Come on! Let's go."

"What about transporting?" Hermes suggested, again. "We could get out quick."

"Not unless we have to. We don't have a place to go" Santa reminded him. "If we should get separated, we'd never find each other."

"And all our supplies are back there," Robye added.

"No, they're not. I slipped through the campsite and grabbed the skid," Said Claudius, with a stiff grin.

"What about the soup? I'm hungry," Hermes whined, rubbing his stomach, as he got to his feet.

"Soup's right here. Those wolves weren't interested in it at all. They just stood out there, staring at each other, growling."

"Kind of dangerous, what you did, Claudius," Santa said, with a frown.

"Not really," He answered. "They're working up to a fight. I wasn't a threat to them so it was pretty safe."

"How do you know that?" Hermes asked. He watched Claudius dig through one of the supply bags. "Whatcha lookin' for, Claudius?"

"Our soup bowls, silly. You said you were hungry. You change your mind?"

"No! I'm still hungry," He answered, grabbing the bowl. "You still didn't answer my question, Claudius."

"Oh! I guess I missed it."

"About the wolves---fighting, you know."

Santa and Robye turned. "Yeah, how did you know?" Robye asked.

"Was it a territorial thing?" Santa questioned. "I was so busy, I didn't think about why."

"Well, yes---sorta," he answered. "It had nothing to do with us---unless we got in their way, that is."

"So, we weren't in any danger?"

"Oh, I didn't mean that at all. We could have been torn apart."

"Then why did you think it was safe for you to get the skid?" Santa asked.

"They're not hungry," he said. "Did you not notice that some of the wolves were quite shaggy and others had a smooth shiny coat of fur?"

"Yes," said Santa. "Some had not lost their winter coat---like some of your reindeer. That's what you said."

"We're in mid-summer; twenty-four hours of sun, remember?"

"Well---?" Santa said. "Do the animals all lose their winter coat? How do they stay warm?"

"It doesn't take long for a new one to grow," Claudius answered. "Besides, animals don't get cold like we do."

"I guess you can tell that I'm rather inexperienced."

"You did tell me, I just forgot. Sorry!" Claudius apologized. Taking a deep breath, he continued. "Well, in this case it's the old wolves, the ones with the ugly looking fur, that are trying to hang onto their territory---,"

"---while the young ones are trying to take over," Robye finished.

"That's right," Claudius agreed.

"So, this isn't over?"

"Oh, no," Claudius answered, "there will be a battle."

"You have quite an understanding of wild animals."

"Just things I've observed from my family," Claudius said. "We should probably have our meal. I don't think we'll be leaving here for a while."

"Oh, good," Hermes said, quickly dipping soup into a bowl.

"You're always hungry," Robye teased, tipping the bowl of soup to his lips.

"I know! I can't help it. I just am," Hermes said, taking another swallow of the liquid then popped the last chunk of stone cake in his mouth. "Pretty good soup even if it was cold."

"You're finished already?" Robye laughed.

"M-m-huh."

"Sh-h-h! Stop it, you two," Santa warned. "Listen for a minute. It sounds like the fight has already started."

"What? Oh, no! They're really crying. They can't do that," Hermes screamed, pressing his hands over his ears. "I think they're killing each other."

"I know. That's what we've been waiting on," Robye yelled back. "Right, Claudius?"

"Yes! It's time to leave---right now!" Claudius said, sharply.

"We've got to go help them," Hermes cried, turning to run toward the animals.

"Right now, go!" Claudius commanded.

"No!" Hermes cried out, as Robye caught him around the waist and pushed him through the brush.

"Follow Santa, Hermes. Go! Those wolves are wicked, mad. You'd be dead in two seconds. Go!" Robye pushed Hermes through the brushy growth, trailing him close behind Santa.

Claudius yelled, grabbing the supply skid and racing after them. "We've got to get out of here. Go!"

Howls of pain were still ringing in the air as they scrambled out of the heavy thickets and dried brush, into a field of prickly thistles and vine-covered weeds.

"Oh, oh, we're in a mess, now!" Robye howled, stomping at the vines around his legs.

"Yeah! They keep tying my feet up," Hermes squealed. He fell to the ground, pulling at the vines that had twisted around him.

"Hey somebody, I need help back here," Claudius cried out. "I can't get the skid loose; we're all wound up."

Looking back, Santa saw the dilemma Claudius was in and yelled, "Keep moving straight ahead, everybody. I've got to help Claudius."

"Thanks, Santa," Claudius panted, "it's all bogged down; I can't move it because of the weeds; they're all twisted up in it."

"Grab hold; I'll get one end and you get the other, okay?" He said, reaching out.

"It looks like Robye and Hermes are loose," Claudius said. He turned and waited while Santa got the skid loose from another patch of vines then they started weaving through the vines again. "This could take us a while to get through all this mess."

"We've just got to be persistent, you know," Santa said, puffing along behind Claudius.

"I know," Claudius said, ripping away at the vines, still tangled between his feet. "We'll get there."

Tenaciously, they followed the others across the field.

Once they reached the clearing, Santa looked ahead and pointed. "Keep going toward that boulder but don't get too close to the edge. It seems we're on a plateau and that valley is much further down than it looks. There's also something around the base at this level, so be careful."

After some observation, they stopped a distance from the boulder. There was a thick layer of green slime that had mixed in the slushy ice puddles, and spread out around the base. Toward the top of the rock monolith, all the edges and ridges were covered with mossy green vegetation that hung, dripping down the sides. Walking closer to the ledge, they noticed the rock formation was nearly straight down into the valley.

Claudius pulled the skid into the edge of the shadow and untied the small bush. He busily dragged it up the trail and back. After re-tying it, he looked at Santa. "I don't know if it helps, but it makes me think so."

"It can't hurt," Santa answered.

"I was wondering why you always do that," Hermes asked. "Is it to keep the monsters away?"

"Well, sorta," Claudius grinned. "Monsters like those wolves, I hope."

"Oh," Hermes answered, softly. "I thought it was to keep real monsters away."

"It does that too, I guess," Claudius said.

Looking toward Santa, Hermes said, "what are we going to do now? We lost our bear hole."

Santa stared at Hermes. "You knew all the time?"

"That it was a place for bears to hibernate? Not all the time," Hermes answered. I guess I just knew."

"Oh," said Santa.

"You were all so worried about staying there---," Hermes said.

"---and you weren't?" Santa asked.

"Well, somebody had to keep the monsters away---and-and they don't like candles."

"That's a good thing to know," Santa said.

"So, where are we going to stay?" Hermes asked.

"The sun will be shining for a few more weeks," Santa answered. I'm sure we'll find a place, soon. Don't worry."

Turning at a noise behind him, Santa cried out excitedly, "Dalt! Oh, my goodness, it's good to see you!." He ran and threw his arms around the reindeer's neck. "How have you been?"

Dalt nuzzled the back of Santa's neck then shook his antlers, "I am doing well.

"And your girls?"

"All but two are ladies now." he nodded, excitedly "the two from last season, if you remember?"

"Of course I do. Their fawns were born in the back cave, just before we left."

"Yes! They're already getting their spots. They'll be yearlings, soon. It doesn't seem possible, does it?"

"It certainly doesn't," Santa laughed, "until I get to thinking about some of the experiences we've traveled through."

Dalt cocked his head to one side. "You are doing well, I see." He then continued. "Two of my ladies have fawned this season, already. Fasha and her Malo. Oh, my goodness, he is so smart, --- and handsome like me." Dalt shook his antlers, strutting around Santa with pride. "Then there is Kada. She is having a time with the twins. She's a very good mother, though; patient but strict. Those girls are quite special. You know how first-borns are."

"I guess," Santa answered, hesitantly.

Dalt cocked his head to one side, observing Santa's expression. "You miss your parents. I'm sorry I brought it up."

"I think about them often," he admitted. After a few moments he asked, "what about the other girls---there were seven, right?"

"Yes! Seven! They are all doing very well." He paced around Santa, again then stopped in front of him. "Mika should be delivering soon. Sweet Emm and Yalla are yet too young to be in season. None of my family came with me, of course."

Hearing a noise behind them, they turned in time to see Hermes and Claudius return to camp.

"Dalt! Dalt! Oh, how I've missed you," Hermes squealed, excitedly running past Santa and the rest. He threw his arms around Dalt's neck and stroked his shoulders. "I really wanted to say goodbye before we left. I didn't think I'd ever see you again. How did you find us all the way out here, anyway?"

Dalt gently shook his antlers and stepped back. "Ari and his flock have been keeping track of you, of course," he gazed at Santa, shaking his antlers again. "You are going too far north. You must aim your travels toward the shadows below the rising sun. Daylight is nearly continuous so set your sights carefully."

"Do you know where we're to go?" Santa asked, anxiously.

"I know only what I know." He paused then bowed slightly. "I must return to my family now. Take heed of my directions." Shaking his antlers, he turned and galloped away.

After watching Dalt leave, Robye approached the others, still holding the wooden bowls he had unpacked. "It was the weirdest thing. I was standing down there," he pointed at a small crest in the snow bank, "and all of a sudden I felt a nudge in the middle of my back. "I nearly jumped out of my skin, I tell you. When I turned around, why, there was Dalt standing right behind me. I hadn't heard a sound."

"I wish he could have stayed longer," Hermes whined. "I've missed him so much."

"He had to get back to his family," Santa reminded him.

"Oh, did he tell you that?" Hermes asked.

"Why, yes. Didn't you hear him?"

"No! I didn't hear him say a thing."

"Maybe it was before you got here," Santa said.

"I guess," Hermes drew his brows together. "How did he know where to find us?"

"He said Ari had been following us."

"Oh," Hermes said, slowly.

Looking toward the others, Santa said, "the days are long, I know and we need to get some rest, but with the sun is rising and setting so quickly right now, it may take all of us to find the shadows. We must continue in that direction. Dalt said we were traveling too far north."

"That's fine with me," Robye said with a grin. "It would be a nice change from all this brush and flatland we've been crossing---m-m-m, not counting this ridge we're camping on."

"It won't be as easy to spot followers, though." Claudius remarked, handing the stack of bowls to Robye.

"Where are we going?" Hermes asked, throwing snowballs into the campfire.

"You ask that question every time we make camp," Robye laughed.

"I never get an answer, though," Hermes grunted.

"We'll know---," Santa began.

"---when we know," Hermes finished. He threw another snow ball at the dark circle. "The fire's out."

"How many times did you hit it?" Robye asked, pulling out his bedding.

"Every one of them," Hermes said, proudly, "from all the way out here."

"You're getting better. That's a long way."

"I know," Hermes grinned. "It only took eleven snowballs this time."

After pulling his bedding from a knapsack, he ran over and plopped himself down beside Robye. "I miss my mother," he said, climbing inside.

"I know you do," Robye wriggled down into his nest of coverings, trying to get comfortable. Pillowing his head on his hands, he stretched out. Finally he said, "I miss mine, too."

"Stars are coming out," Hermes said.

"Not for long. Go to sleep. Tomorrow will be another long day."

"I know. Wish I was like Mr. Twiddler," Hermes said.

"Why's that?" Robye asked.

"I wouldn't have to walk so much. I could just ride around in Santa's pocket all day," Hermes snickered, "in my own house."

"It wouldn't be too bad, I guess," Robye answered. "I don't think I'd like to be four and one-half inches tall, though."

"I guess so," Hermes answered, staring at the darkening sky. "Did you see that?" He said, quickly pointing up. "I just saw a shooting star. It had a fiery tail, too."

"You're lucky to see it. We don't often see them this time of year," Robye answered, lazily stretching his arms over his head.

"Why's that?"

"There's such a short night time, right now."

"Do they go away?" Hermes asked, turning to his side.

"The stars? Of course not! The sun is too bright for you to see them."

"I know, I was just kidding," Hermes giggled.

"Go to sleep."

"Why didn't I hear Dalt talking?"

"I don't know. I've never heard him talk."

"He didn't even nuzzle my neck."

"To sleep."

"Okay," Hermes said quietly. He turned over and stared at the small hill where Dalt had stood. "Wish he didn't have to leave.

Chapter Twelve

The Shadows

"Santa, you're up awfully early. What's going on?" Robye asked, rubbing his eyes.

"I couldn't go to sleep. I'm to find the shadows under the sun," Santa answered. "I was afraid I'd miss them. I was told to look for them at sunrise."

"Dalt told you that?" Hermes looked up, questioningly. "He doesn't talk to me, anymore."

"You can't receive. He told me that." Looking around, Santa added. "Where is Claudius?"

"He's making our meal," Robye answered, "stone-cakes, I think."

"I'll go help," Hermes yelled, running toward the campfire. "I like the way he makes them brown around the edges. Sometimes he puts surprises in them too."

"Hermes! Not so loud." Santa groaned. "It's much too early."

"Oh! Uh, okay." Walking off, he giggled to himself. "Sometimes he's an old grouch when he wakes up."

"I heard that call for food," Mr. Twiddler said, sticking his head out of Santa's pocket. "I'll get my plate."

"It sounds like you're hungry, Mr. Twiddler," Santa grunted. "I hope I didn't wake you." Quite distracted by the rising sun, he carefully scanned the mountain ranges to the east. "Wish I knew what I was looking for--- not just shadows."

"Yeah, I went to sleep in my chair and just woke up." With plate in hand, Mr. Twiddler climbed aboard Santa's open hand. "I found that Claudius makes a pretty fair stone-cake. I can hardly wait."

"That's quite a compliment, coming from you." Robye laughed, passing the plates around.

"Is this sauce ready?" Hermes asked, peering into the kettle. "It has bubbles on top."

"It should be." Claudius called back. "Go ahead and pour it into the pitcher, Hermes."

"It sure smells good, Claudius. What do you have in it this time?" Robye asked.

Oh, a few berries I found along the way," Claudius grinned, "and a little of the honey we found in that old hollow tree."

"You still had some of that honey? That is amazing." Santa said, somewhat more mellow.

"Now Santa, you should know me by now." Claudius laughed. "Good things are much better, or tastier in this case, if they are in small amounts. The raspberries and blackberries---,"

"plus my special herbs." Mr. Twiddler reminded him.

"Yes, Mr. Twiddler, plus your special herbs gave the sauce---,"

"---the gourmet touch," Hermes giggled.

"You're right, Mr. Potts." Mr. Twiddler said with a smile.

Claudius placed the platter of food on the table then said, reaching over Santa's shoulder, "these are for Mr. Twiddler."

"Just my size," Mr. Twiddler smiled. Then holding a tiny pitcher, he said to Santa. "Some sauce if you please."

"Of course, Mr. Twiddler," Santa said, filling it to the brim.

After cutting into the stack of tiny cakes and taking a bite, Mr. Twiddler said with a sigh, "m-m-m, delightfully tasty. Your sauce is the perfect touch."

"Sure is," they all said between bites.

After helping himself to another stack of cakes, Robye asked. "What else did Dalt have to say?"

"He's quite the father," Santa said, passing him the sauce. "One buck and two does. Kada had twins, you know. There's one more doe to birth very soon. That's why he had to go back so quickly." Looking toward Claudius, he added. "M-m-m, these are quite delicious."

"I'm glad you are enjoying the meal," Claudius grinned.

"Really delicious, thanks Claudius," Robye said, taking another bite. "It's my turn to do the clean up."

"There were two does that birthed before we left," Hermes reminded Santa.

"I know, Hermes. They are all doing fine. Dalt talked like his whole family is going to follow us as soon as the fawns were mature enough to travel."

As soon as everyone was finished with the meal, Robye began cleaning the tableware and packing it in the knapsack. "I wonder why?" He said, stacking it with the other equipment.

"I don't know, Robye. I didn't ask," Santa answered. "He said Ari, and some of his flock had been following us. That's how he knew where we were."

"What are you looking for, Santa?" Claudius asked. He finished wiping down the cooking stone then stood up. "You keep staring at those mountains."

"I know." Santa answered. "Dalt told me we were going too far north. He said we should change our course and head toward the shadows under the sun.

"On the mountains?"

"I guess. He didn't say anything else.

We're making the correction today, that is, if I can find any shadows. When the sun crests the mountains is what he said. I don't understand how we can see shadows with the rising sun, though. If we can, it should be any moment now, so help me watch."

"We're going back into the brush?" Robye questioned. He stood, with both hands shielding his eyes, gazing toward the mountains.

"Probably," Santa said. "We'll soon see."

"That's where the wolves were," Robye said, shivering.

"and there's the shadows---can you believe it?" Santa cried out, excitedly.

"I think I see the place you're talking about," Claudius said, holding his hands above his eyes. "Are you talking about those dark spots almost to the peak---you think that's the place?"

"Yes, I'm pretty sure of it," Santa said.

"That's a long way up," Claudius exclaimed. "Are you sure it's the right shadows?"

"I didn't see any others, did you?"

"I'm afraid not," Claudius admitted. "That's going to be some kind of trip, though."

Santa glanced at Robye for confirmation. "What do you think about our chances?"

Robye looked back, saying thoughtfully. "That mountain is almost straight up and, any way you look at it, we're going to have a tough time getting that close to the peak---if we can do it at all." After tossing his backpack to one side, he began brushing the campsite with a hand full of twigs. "There will probably be more challenges with wild animals, too."

"Maybe not, Robye. This is the warmer part of the season and most animals have gotten kind of lazy," Claudius stated. "We might see some rabbits, though. They hunt and store food. They dig a new hole or repair the old one, you know. That's just what they do this time of year."

"It wasn't rabbits I was thinking about, Claudius," Robye pointed out. "It was more like moose and sheep and stuff---and maybe even wolves." He shuddered at the old memories.

"I'm not promising anything but the chances of us meeting up with those kind of animals are less likely, other than mountain sheep and goats, than it has been for most of this trip."

"You think?"

"Just a minute, Claudius," Santa said, turning toward Robye with a frown. "Are you backing out on us? You don't want to go up the mountain?"

"Of course not, Santa, I'm with you all the way." Putting his backpack on, Robye said, somewhat surprised. "I was just making a comment."

"You had me worried for a moment," Santa said, quite relieved. "Is everyone ready?"

"I still have to tie everything down then I'll be ready to go," Claudius answered, kneeling beside the skid.

Spotting Hermes sitting on the ground, Santa went over and sat down beside him. "What are you doing, old buddy? You look kind of down."

"I was just sitting here, waiting on the rest of you," Hermes said dolefully. "I was thinking about my mom; wondering if I'd ever see her again."

"I wish I could answer that."

"I wish Dalt would talk to me."

"I'm sure he misses it, too." Santa said, giving him a hug. "He let you pet his babies, though. He wouldn't have done that if you weren't special."

"I guess."

"Are you about ready to leave?"

"I've been ready. You were all talking and I got bored."

Santa laughed. "Well, come on then. Robye and Claudius are getting pretty far ahead of us."

"Is this a rabbit hole?" Hermes questioned, kneeling down by a mound of leaves and twigs. He began poking at it with a stick; knocking the damp soil from around the hole.

"I'm not sure," Santa said, "but you shouldn't disturb it."

"Oh, okay. Will it hurt the rabbit?"

"Maybe so; it could be the animal's home."

"When are we going to find our new home?"

"It may be on top of the mountain; I don't know, Hermes."

"That's a long way from here."

"But we're getting closer."

"I know," Hermes said, jumping over a small pile of damp brush.

Walking up on Robye and Claudius, Santa and Hermes overheard them still discussing the trip up the mountain.

"One good thing about it though, there's been bushes and undergrowth most of the way today. We're not in to the rocky cliffs yet," Claudius pointed out. "Maybe it won't be all that bad."

"All I was saying was that from here, it looks like a steep climb. I didn't mean we couldn't do it," Robye stated.

"You know how it is. We'll be following trails along the way, just like we've been doing on this whole trip. There won't be much of a difference, really."

"Boys, boys, you've been into this discussion most of the day. Hermes and I would like a change of topic, if you don't mind," Santa suggested.

"Yeah, I'm hungry! Can we eat?" Hermes asked, wistfully staring at Santa's face.

"I'm sure we can," Santa grinned, glancing up at Claudius and Robye. "Have either of you seen a place to stop? We've gone a long distance today."

"We haven't seen anything yet," Claudius said, turning to Robye. "Do you want to help me find something?"

"Sure! I hope we don't have to hunt for long," Robye answered, sauntering over to Claudius, "I'm ready for a break."

"Me too," Claudius agreed. He straightened the straps on his backpack as they walked off.

Hermes watched the two of them leave then looked up at Santa." My feet are really tired." Matching Santa's stride, he stretched his pace as they walked along side by side.

"I know, mine are too," Santa smiled, stroking his chin. "That's how I know we've traveled further than usual."

"Why did we have to go so far?" Hermes asked. "We've been walking forever and---."

"When Dalt had us change directions, we had to calculate when the snows should begin. We need to prepare with food and shelter for the long winter."

"But the sun's still out most of the time."

"I know, but it won't last much longer," Santa reminded him.

"You keep doing that," Hermes said, watching him curiously.

"Doing what?"

"Oh, rubbing your chin. You do it all the time," Hermes answered. "Did you hurt yourself?"

"Of course not, why?" Santa asked.

"I was just wondering. That's all." Before Santa knew what was going on, Hermes had stepped in front of him. With his head cocked to one side, and looking into Santa's eyes, he said. "Well?"

"Uh?" Santa grunted, starting to go around him. He then stopped and stared back. "What? Oh, the chin," he said, rubbing it again. "I decided to stop pulling out all those chin hairs. They kept popping out, anyway. They're quite irritating either way."

"How do you get chin hairs?" Hermes asked, stepping aside.

"I don't know," Santa laughed, massaging his chin again. "They just started appearing."

"I hope I get red ones just like yours."

"You won't like them," Santa nodded decisively. "For a while I pulled them all out but before I knew it, they were right back."

"Why don't you just let them grow?" Hermes said. With his head turned to one side, he scrutinized Santa's face. "They make you look extinguished."

Santa looked down; his eyes twinkled. "I think you meant distinguished, didn't you?"

"Well, yeah, distinguished," Hermes' voice dropped slightly. "Anyway, that red on your chin looks okay."

"Thanks! Guess I'll leave it alone since you approve," Santa grinned, slightly embarrassed.

Hearing the rustle of broken twigs, Santa hesitated slightly and looked up. He saw Robye crashing through the bushes, toward him. "Uh, oh, something is going on," he thought. "he's sure in a big hurry."

"Maybe he found us a place to camp," Hermes said hopefully. "I sure am hungry."

"I found it; I really did! I found our new home," Robye yelled out, racing wildly toward them. "It's just what we've been looking for---all this time. It's got everything---wait till you see." Flinging his arms out with excitement, he motioned toward the opening. "Hidden behind---see that pile of dead brush---," he gasped, "there's a place back there---I found a place---it's phenomenal!" Nearly running into the others, he danced around on one foot, then on the other. "You'll never believe what I found until you see it. It's sunny, and it's green, and it's warm. It's loaded with all kinds of bushes and flowers and---," aiming his vision toward Santa, "---and huge trees, like the pictures in your book. There's all kind of stuff---even a small pond. There may be some fish in it---I didn't take time to look. Animal tracks everywhere." He caught his breath, again. "All kinds of stuff---it's amazing." Laughing and talking at the same time, with hands flailing through the air, he cried out, urgently. "Come on, come on! You've got to see this place."

"That's a good sign," Santa said, following him at a distance. "No big animal tracks, I hope?"

"All I saw were small ones," Robye answered, impatiently. Turning, he started back down the trail then looked back. "Come on! I'm not kidding. It's like another world."

After a slight hesitation Santa called out, motioning for the others to follow, "Robye may have found us a new campsite. Let's see what he's so excited about."

Hermes paced around Claudius; looking up with a huge grin. "That means we're finally stopping---an-and food! My stomach says I'm ready."

"Got your second wind, I see," Claudius said, following Hermes's antics with his eyes. With a smirk, he added. "So, are you going to dance around here all day or do you want to see what all the excitement's about?"

"Huh," Hermes answered, "I was waiting on you."

"Come on, then!"

"Wait up, wait up! We're right behind you," Hermes yelled, hanging on to Claudius's hand. Chasing after each other they nearly ran into Santa and Robye, who were pulling a pile of dried brush out of the way. With the growth of vines and weeds tangled through it, they were making very little progress.

"Robye, how did you get in there, anyway?" Santa asked. He groaned and he tugged, pushing the nettles and weeds into a pile behind him while Robye dragged it further away from the thicket of bushes they had to pass through.

"Actually, I didn't," he answered. "I just parted some of those limbs on the top of the bushes and looked inside. That was when I saw the huge green valley on the other side. Wait 'till you see. You won't believe it either."

"Let us help," Claudius and Hermes said in unison, picking up armloads of damp brush and prickly vines.

"Ouch," Hermes cried out. Dropping his load, he began pulling at the vines twining around his face, "that big old ropey thing's got stickers all over it. Get it off of me; it's all stuck in my hair. Claudius help me, I can't---get out."

"Just a minute little guy, you've got to hold still so I can unwind it," cautioned Claudius, busily . "It's going to scratch all over you if you keep wriggling all over the place."

"I'm trying---but it's itching my ears," Hermes whined, "and it's stuck on my koyt. I can't get my hands loose."

"Here, let me help," Santa said, turning toward the two. He began tugging at the weather-worn tangle of briars, securing some of them beneath his feet while twisting others off Hermes arms with either hand and holding them back. Robye got on the other side and began doing the same.

After some time and a lot of whining from Hermes, he was freed of the thorn covered vines that had wrapped and twined all over him. Following Robye, they all set out again, toward the thicket of bushes just ahead. One by one, twisting through the limbs, they stepped inside. What they saw was a world they had no knowledge of existing. In awe they gazed, spellbound at the sight.

Stretching as far as their eyes could see were lush, green meadows bathed in a golden hue of warm sunlight, reflecting off the surrounding mountain range. Standing tall in the grass was a generous sprinkling of colorful wildflowers, swaying gently in the breeze while butterflies and hummingbirds bounced from blossom to blossom seemingly unaware of any human presence. Dropping their eyes further down, they watched rabbits and other small animals tunnel and skip through the damp grass in a meandering fashion, leaving a narrow shadow of bent greenery behind.

Further out, they saw deer and elk, and other herbivores, sedately grazing side by side.

"Oh, my goodness," Santa exclaimed, pulling his eyes away from the view. "I had no idea."

"I know," Claudius murmured, standing quietly beside him.

Without warning a soft mist began to fall, filling the sweet smelling air with a rainbow of color. Santa leaned back, feeling each drop of dampness spread over his face. "This is better than any dream I could ever imagine."

"I'm surprised Mr. Twiddler's not out here," Hermes said. "He's probably busy, reading or something."

"Maybe so, but I'll see if I can get his attention." Gently shaking his pocket, Santa said. "What are you doing in there, Mr. Twiddler? You must come see this place."

"You bounced me out of my bath," Mr. Twiddler retorted, pushing his head through the furry exit. The purple string was missing and his ears flopped on either side of his head. "What's going on? Can't you see I'm quite unavailable?" After pulling at a purple towel and tucking it tightly under his chin, he dropped back into the pocket.

"I wasn't trying to disturb him. I thought he'd enjoy the sights," Santa said, noting frowns from the others. "Maybe he's getting dressed."

"Well, uh---," Robye began.

"I'm right here," Mr. Twiddler announced, sharply interrupting Robye's response. Realizing that everyone was staring at him, his mood began to change. "What?" He said, reaching for Santa's outstretched finger. After jumping into his hand, Mr. Twiddler's eyes followed the direction everyone was pointing. Within moments, he was standing quite still, gazing across the grassy meadow. "My, my---oh my goodness," he exclaimed.

"I told you," Santa said, placing the fully clothed Mr. Twiddler on his shoulder.

"I know! I'm still stunned," Robye said. A little later, he caught Santa's eye and pointed to the left of where they were standing. "Did you see your tree?"

"My tree?" A damp breeze rifled through Santa's sparsely covered chin as he turned his head. "Oh, my gosh," he stammered, "I had no idea trees grew to such an enormous size. None of the pictures in my book did them justice."

Startled by a small flock of birds, flying into the tree and disappearing through the leaves, his eyes immediately flitted up. "What was that?"

"Oh, no," yelped Mr. Twiddler, glaring at Santa's nose, "birds!"

"Birds? I know! I saw them. Aren't they beautiful?"

Shaking Santa's ear, he squawked into it. "They could eat me, you know?"

Santa reached up. "It's not food they want."

"Oh, you think?" Mr. Twiddler said, his voice quivering.

"Of course not, they want your purple string," Santa laughed.

Covering his ears, Mr. Twiddler screeched, "my what?"

"The string around your ears, of course; they're nesting."

"It's almost fall; not the right season," Mr. Twiddler barked.

"It is here."

Ducking under Santa's collar, he peeked around the edge. "How do you know?"

"They told me, of course."

"Oh!"

"Come on, Mr. Twiddler," Santa urged. "The birds are gone now. They flew behind all those branches and leaves."

Cautiously looking about, Mr. Twiddler came out and plopped on Santa's shoulder.

Without warning the birds began to sing, almost like a signal to the rest of the creatures. Santa reached an open hand to Mr. Twiddler. The singing continued and he again looked up, listening. The musical chirping fostered an array of sounds throughout the valley. Crickets and frogs, as well as other small beings, joined the serenade. His eyes wandered as a peaceful serenity surrounded him. With a smile, he nodded. "H-m-m-m--my tree, finally," quite contented, Santa said. "Yes, this is where we're to stop for a while."

Like a gentle breeze, the summer warmth washed over him. The others stared at him, as if he'd gone mad, when he began removing layers of clothing and stacking everything on the small skid. "What?" He said, noticing the surprised look on their faces.

"What are you doing?" Hermes cried out.

"Mr. Twiddler and I are going for a walk," Santa answered mildly, and it's far too warm for all this." Turning to each of them, he added. "You can join us if you like."

"We can't go in there! It's dangerous! It may have monsters! It---it could swallow us up! We can't---!" Hermes staunchly pressed his feet to the ground and pulled his fur coat tight against him.

Understanding his fear, Santa said quietly. "Hermes, you don't have to enter if you choose not to."

"I choose not to," he barked.

Both Robye and Claudius stood aside for a moment. Finally Robye broke the silence. "Hermes, I've read about places like this. It's called an oasis."

"You're making that up," he yelped. Tears were flowing down his face.

Robye reached for him. "I wouldn't do that."

"Don't touch me!" Hermes cried, tightening his arms around his coat.

"All right," Robye said, gently pulling his hands back. "I wouldn't make up something like that."

After a few moments of consideration, Hermes answered, "I know you wouldn't." His voice snubbed and he cleared his throat.

"Better?"

"Yeah," Hermes said, quietly, "but I'm still not going in there."

"That's okay."

"So, tell me about o-a-sis."

"Well, yeah," Robye began, "an oasis is a place that is sometime found, but not always, when all the elements for survival are correct. They are usually in very unique locations, such as the one we have here."

"What do you mean, elements?" Hermes asked, still somewhat distraught.

"Heat, water, light, ---things that sustain life," Robye answered. "The elements have to be in the proper proportion for an oasis to occur."

"I've only seen one before and it was much smaller than this one," Claudius added. "This place is safe, Hermes. You shouldn't worry about that."

"How do you know?" Hermes asked, looking up at his friend.

"Because of the plants and animals, and the fact that they are here," Claudius answered, nodding toward Robye. "Don't you agree?"

"That's true. The presence of wildlife is the best way to know if a place is habitable."

"Well---, I don't know," Hermes said, shifting from one leg to another. "What about monsters, and---?"

"I think I have an idea that could solve your problem about that, too," Santa said. His eyes twinkled at the thought. "Think back, Hermes. When we were at the old city we could use no magic."

"No! It didn't work," Hermes said, quickly. "Actually I didn't even know I had magic."

"You didn't have any magic within the walls of the old city---none of us did," Santa confirmed. "Being inside stripped the older people of their powers and it also stunted or stopped the youth from developing theirs."

Everyone nodded in affirmation.

"So, where are you going with this?" Hermes blurted out.

"Well---I was just thinking---you might like to try your ears out," Santa smiled. "Maybe you could do a bit of transporting."

Hermes's stalwart disposition changed to one of excitement. "How can I do that?"

"I'm sure there must be a few caves in this valley. It would be nice to have one to live in for a while, don't you think?"

Hermes slipped his hand along the length of his left ear then, with an anxious giggle, said. "Oh! Yeah! I can do that." He looked at the others then giggled. "I'm out of here!" Glancing across the valley, he yelled, "Up, up," and disappeared from sight.

Claudius and Robye glared anxiously at Santa.

"He'll be fine." Claudius said fiercely.

"Of course he will," Santa agreed, mildly. "Young men need to have challenges. It's what gives them tenacity."

Robye nodded, unfastening his jacket. "We've had a bit of that lately." Placing his bundle of clothing on the skid, he said, "should we wait here for Hermes?"

Santa thought for a moment then answered. "We shouldn't need to. What do you think, Claudius?"

"He'll be able to find us, I'm sure."

"Well, now that our accommodations are being taken care of, I'd like to check out that pond," Santa twittered, heading toward it. "I don't think it's as mellow as it looks."

"You've noticed that too, huh?" Robye said, quickly catching up. "The spout of water, I mean."

"I've not seen any water spouts. I was talking about a mist that seems to appear out of nowhere. I've seen it twice, now," Santa said.

"Hey, you two, hold up," Claudius cried out, unexpectedly. "I need some help back here."

Quickly turning, Robye and Santa saw two eyes peeking out from under a jumble of fur. Neither of them could stop laughing.

"Why do you have all those coats on?" Santa quipped, reaching toward him. "Did you get a little chill?"

"No, it's not funny," Claudius grumbled, climbing to his feet. "The skid fell over. It started to roll---," mimicking his actions, his arms flailed out, "and I tried to stop it." Finally, somewhat mellowed, he growled. "You try pulling that thing for a while."

"I guess we were taking you for granted," Santa apologized, picking up one of the coats. "You seemed to have chosen the task." He placed it on the small carrier.

They picked up all the coats and piling them back on the skid. When finished, Robye wrapped himself in the harness. "I'll take it on for a while, Claudius."

"I don't think you---," Claudius began.

"Hmuf!" Robye groaned, bouncing against the straps. "It won't budge!"

"Why didn't you say something?" Santa asked, earnestly.

"It wasn't that heavy before all those coats were piled on top," Claudius answered.

"Then I suggest we take them back off. We'll have to carry the coats separately," Santa said, decidedly.

Following Santa's lead, Claudius tucked a few of the garments under his arms.

"Oh yes! It's not so heavy, now," Robye said, pulling against the harness. After a couple of tugs, the skid began to move smoothly behind him.

Toting all the winter discards, Claudius and Santa lagged behind Robye and the skid. Mr. Twiddler rode in the cuff of Santa's cap, quite content with it all.

"I think we got the worst of this deal," Claudius said, blinking sweat from his eyes.

"You're right," Santa answered, wiping his brow. "I'm glad Hermes is still wearing his stuff."

"I know," Claudius said. After a few steps, he muttered. "Are we there yet?"

Chapter Thirteen
The Pond

Every step Santa took brought on another layer of sweat until it was trickling down his back and dripping off each of his elbows. He swiped the beads of water off his face then began adjusting the coats to a little more comfortable position. After raking his hands under the prickly, wet fur, he tightened his hold and continued on his way. He glanced at the clear, blue sky then back at his destination beyond the meadow with a sigh. "Still have quite a long walk ahead of me, it seems." When he reached the sandy beach, Santa dumped the jackets on top of the ones Claudius had brought. "Surprising how heavy they are in warm weather," he chuckled.

"I didn't think we'd ever get here," Claudius moaned, wiping the sweat from his face. Plopping down, he reached for the laces that held his leg covers in place and let them drop loose, tossing them behind him. The boots and stockings were next. Once the bare toes were exposed, he let out a sigh of relief and leaned back. "Oh, this is the life. I didn't realize how heavy those boots were until I took them off.

"I didn't either," Santa declared, heading toward the pond's rocky ledge. He sat down and pulled the fur covers off his legs. "It was a lot further than I thought." Leaning over, he picked up a small stick.

"What are you doing---got a problem?" Claudius asked, curiously. Slowly he rolled off the pile of fur and watched Santa poke at the end of his boot.

"No! No problem. Why?"

"You've been doubled over like that for a while. I thought you might be having a twinge, or something."

"Oh, no," Santa laughed, straightening back up. "It's nothing like that. I can't seem to loosen the knot in my shoestring."

"Oh, I see," Claudius said, still watching. "Did you know Mr. Twiddler was caught up in your koyt?"

"He's been there for a while," Santa answered. "Why? What's he doing?"

"Oh nothing, it looks like he's asleep."

"I'm not asleep. I'm just resting," Mr. Twiddler answered, lazily.

After pulling the boot off, Santa raised up, saying, "oh, finally! I didn't think I'd ever get that string untied." He dropped the stockings on the top of his boots and stood up. Looking down, he watched his toes wriggling through the warm, white sand and said, with a grin, "do you know what I'm about to do?"

"Couldn't guess," Claudius said, opening his eyes to answer. Rolling to his back, he noticed a flock of birds circling over a tree top.

"I'm taking Mr. Twiddler for a walk." Santa started dragging his feet through the warm sand, smiling as the grains trickled between his toes. Whistling softly, he thought. "Wow, this is nice."

After landing on the hidden limbs, they disappeared into the foliage soon to return and fly off again. "Be careful of the birds," Claudius reminded him. "Mr. Twiddler, you know."

"Yeah, I know."

Looking over the cuff of Santa's koyt, Mr. Twiddler asked. "Where are we going?"

"I thought we'd see if there were any fish in the pond."

"Oh," said Mr. Twiddler, closing his eyes again. "Fish, hmf, I doubt it."

Santa circled the beach then slipped his feet across the rocky ledge, dangling them in the water. "They're probably hiding beneath those rocks," he thought, watching quietly. Within moments schools of fish began slithering out of hiding, slipping through the rippling waves around the water's edge. "I knew it," he whispered excitedly. "Did you see that, Mr. Twiddler? This place is loaded with fish."

"Careful! Care-full," Mr. Twiddler yelped, rocking precariously forward. "Watch what you're doing, will you? Don't be poking your nose over that water hole. I'm not dressed for a swim."

"Uh, yeah, sorry," Santa grunted, reaching up toward the koyt. "Would you rather sit on my shoulder?"

"I'm fine, right where I am," Mr. Twiddler quipped. "Just mind what you're doing. Bathing is as much water as I need in a day."

It took Robye some time to get out of the harnass. He then placed it on top of the skid and went over toward Santa. "Did you see any fish in there?" He asked, looking into the water.

"Yes, of course," Santa grinned, pointing toward the ripples around the edge. "Just look at them."

Robye looked up. He screamed. Mr. Twiddler was dangling on the edge of Santa's koyt---his fingers twisted into the knit cuff. "Santa, move back, hurry! Mr. Twiddler is about to fall."

Santa automatically raised his hands to the koyt.

"Yes! It's Mr. Twiddler! He's losing his grip." Pointing and shaking his finger, Robye yelled. "Catch him! Catch him. Hurry! He's dangling off your koyt"

"I checked him just a few seconds ago. He said he was fine." Carefully leaning away from the water, Santa reached up and allowed Mr. Twiddler drop into his hand. "Thanks."

"It's a good thing I saw him," Robye said, quit distraught. He sat down and pulled his knees up. "That was a scary moment."

"For me, too," said Mr. Twiddler. "Those fish might consider me bate, if I had fallen in."

"What happened, Mr. Twiddler, you said you were fine? You about scared us to death."

"I was fine then the koyt slipped over to the side of your head---it happened so fast I couldn't even yell." Mr. Twiddler's hands shook so bad he could hardly tie the purple string around his ears.

"We must be more careful about you riding in that cuff."

The near accident went undetected by Claudius, who had been napping. Waking up, when Santa pulled the coat from under him, he cried out. "What?"

"Mr. Twiddler's house is in my pocket."

Groggily, Claudius stared up at Santa. "Oh, sorry," he croaked. "Did I miss anything?"

"Oh, not much," Santa answered. "Mr. Twiddler's had enough excitement, though."

"I see," he answered, rubbing his eyes. "Has Hermes come back, yet?"

"No, not yet," Santa answered, opening his pocket. Mr. Twiddler jumped inside. After hanging the coat on a nearby bush, he caught sight of Claudius standing by the pond.

"You're right! There are a lot of fish in there," he said, standing a distance from the water's edge. "It looks kind of deep, though."

"It's hard to know without going in," Santa said, noting the hesitation in Claudius's voice. "Are you afraid of the water?"

"A bit, why?" Claudius answered, staring into the pool. "It looks really different without ice on top."

"Swimming was one of my classes at the university." Santa answered. "I could teach you, if you like."

Claudius sat on the edge of the pool, dipping his hand into the water. Sliding his hand along the shelf of rock, he said. "These stones are slick and really cold, too." He looked up. "I don't know. I'll have to think about it."

Leaning over the rock ledge, Robye looked underneath it while dangling his arms deep into the water. "This pond must be fed by an underground river," he said, following the ripples along the edge with his eyes.

Claudius dropped his hand over the side of the pond and watched the tiny waves roll smoothly across his fingers. "You think these little waves may be caused by a river beneath us?" Looking up, he said, "I don't understand how that's possible."

"We already know there is a lot of water flowing underground, right? There are tunnels all over the place."

"Well, uh! I never thought about it, I guess," Claudius answered, slipping off the stone edge and into the sand.

"Well there are, believe me, and they can cause a lot of things to happen on the surface, such as whirlpools and waterspouts." With Claudius still showing interest, Robye continued. "Whirlpools suck the water in and waterspouts push it out," he nodded. "Now flowing water, such as this pond, has little growth of moss or algae on or around it. I noticed that first off. That's why I suggested the underground river theory."

"Did you go to the university, too?"

"Um, hum," Robye answered. "Why?"

"I was just wondering if you could swim."

"Well, yeah, but not very good. I was only in my second year."

"I went to classes, before my clan was attacked," Claudius said, quietly. "We didn't learn to swim, though."

Hearing the pain in his voice, Robye said. "We can't give up, Claudius. We will all find our families, some day."

"I didn't know you had one; a family, that is."

"Oh sure, I have my parents. They were two of the professors stuck in a lockdown at the university. Don't you remember?"

"I don't guess I knew. Sorry."

"That's all right. Just know we're going to get back together."

Stretching out his legs, Santa said to Robye, "Claudius wasn't with us at the time. He wouldn't have known about your parents."

"Oh, that's right. We met him some time later. I wasn't thinking."

"I was listening in on your conversation. I hope you don't mind." Santa said. I've been considering your underground river theory and it seems pretty sound. Do you think that same theory might be applied to the pond's circular shape? For some reason, that seems odd to me."

"Actually, I hadn't thought about it." Robye admitted. "I suppose it could cause the water to swirl but I don't think so." After rolling over to his knees, he stood up. "Do you need a hand, Santa?"

Just as Santa reached up, his eyes flicked toward a distant movement. "I thought I heard something."

"I know," Mr. Twiddler called out from the bush. "It was Hermes. He's on his way back." He climbed to the edge of Santa's pocket then dangled over the furry edge. "You could come and get me any time, now."

"Sorry, Mr. Twiddler," Santa said, reaching for his coat.

"The cuff on your koyt would be nice, if you don't mind," Mr. Twiddler said, jumping into Santa's hand.

"Are you sure you want to ride up there?"

"Of course," Mr. Twiddler snapped, "just be more careful."

"Hey there, Santa," a voice yelled. "Hel-l-o out there, I'm over here! I found a cave."

Santa lifted Mr. Twiddler up to his koyt and tucked him behind the cuff. Then turning toward Hermes voice, he searched the rocks until he found where Hermes was standing. Behind him were boulders of all sizes, piled high like a mountain. Beneath him was a dome shaped hill that seemed to be attached. On either side of the cave opening were vines covered in flowers.

"I think Hermes found us a place," Claudius said, excitedly, "but his voice is echoing so much I can't seem to find him."

"He's right over there---see that little hill?" Robye yelled, pointing across the meadow. "It must be good news by all that waving that's going on."

"Oh, I see him now," Claudius said, turning to Santa. "You know I was getting a bit worried."

"He was on a mission," Santa reminded him.

With relief, Claudius sighed, "Yeah, I know. I couldn't help it though." He then turned and yelled back excitedly. "Sa-y-y, Hermes, we'll be right there." He turned to Santa. "I'm going to see what he's found."

"I'm right behind you."

After passing through the field of tall grass, Claudius aimed for a narrow path that led up the side of the hill. "Santa and Robye are on their way," he panted.

"Why didn't you use your magic?" Hermes giggled. "It's too hot to be running."

"Didn't think about it, I guess. You find something good?"

"It looks like Mr. Twiddler is having a problem."

"Again? He's been having trouble nearly from the time we got here."

"Like what?" Hermes asked.

"Like nearly falling in the pond---that was the last thing." Claudius growled. "Shouldn't be riding on that koyt. Too dangerous, you know."

Claudius turned to hear Mr. Twiddler still squawking at Santa. "I think you completely forgot I was up here. You nearly jiggled me to death. It was so bad I had to count all my fingers and toes, to make sure I was still together. Why, I---!"

"Oh, I'm so sorry, Mr. Twiddler. I didn't mean to shake your innards loose," Santa said, slowing his pace. "Is this better?"

"Well, I guess," Mr. Twiddler answered, settling himself behind the cuff. With a soft giggle, he added. "Not moving at all would be better."

By the time Santa and Mr. Twiddler arrived, everyone was standing in a row, patting their feet impatiently. "Well," he said, looking back at them, "I was kind of held up."

"Come on, everybody," Hermes cried, excitedly prancing around in front of them. "This place is really spectacular."

"Has anyone had a chance to look inside, yet?" Santa asked, heading toward the entrance.

"Just Hermes," Claudius said. "We've been waiting for you to get here."

"Well then, Hermes," Santa said, clearing his throat, "I guess you'd better lead the way."

Hermes grinned. Automatically, his shoulders straightened as he went toward the cave entrance. He paused at the opening with his hands on his hips. "Come on in and I'll show you around," he said, with eyes sparkling. "This place is great. It reminds me of Claudius's old home."

"Really?" Robye said sarcasticlly. "It would take a lot to do that." Pushing by the others he stepped inside. After a moment of silence, he stammered, breathlessly. "Wow, you're right Hermes, this is unbelievable. How did you find it?"

In unison, Claudius and Robye said. "Well!"

"Oh, there is a bunch of caves around here. I liked this one the best, though. Did I do good?"

"You did great, Hermes," Santa said, noticing all the details as he entered. "Nice sized opening, large grand room, wide smooth floors, high ceilings---does it have connecting rooms?"

"There are two that I know of; maybe more. I didn't explore that far back."

"Monsters?" Robye quipped.

"Well, there could be," Hermes answered. His voice quivered slightly.

"Could be," Claudius agreed. "We should be with a partner when exploring new territory. It's safer that way."

"That's true," Santa said. "There are all kinds of monsters."

His eyes were drawn upward. "Hmmm, filtered light is coming through the ceiling, for some reason. That's quite unusual." Getting Robye's attention, he pointed at his discovery. "What do you think?"

"This cave must be under a mound of crystal rock," Robye nodded thoughtfully. "The soil, covering the outer surface, must have eroded which allowed light to come through. I think I'll go out and take a look."

"That's a good idea," Santa agreed. "Let me know what you find."

"Sure," Robye said, heading out. With a small leap upward, he tapped the entrance rim and laughed. "I don't have to worry about hitting my head, do I?"

Claudius growled back at him. "But I kept warning you about the low entrances, didn't I?"

"I know, I know," Robye laughed. "I just had to say that."

Santa watched the two of them, with a slight grin. He then turned to Hermes, saying. "Are you ready to go exploring?"

"I sure am, Santa," he answered, with a quick smile. "This cave has everything, doesn't it? It's the greatest place I've ever seen."

Robye stopped Santa as he passed by and said softly. "Do you think we could make this our new home? It would be perfect for all of us."

Santa looked into Robye's pleading eyes, answering quietly. "It seems to be so."

"We've been searching for such a long time---and-and I really like it here."

"Me, too," Claudius said, overhearing the request.

"I don't know," Santa answered, slowing his pace further.

"This is our new home? Is it really?" Hermes squealed, running between the others and clapping his hands. "I can't believe it! We're finally here."

Santa hesitated, letting Hermes run ahead. "I wish," he whispered under his breath.

"But probably not," Mr. Twiddler finished the thought.

"It's the children, Mr. Twiddler. We can't leave them behind."

"I knew you'd think that way."

"I-er-we made a promise."

"I remember," said Mr. Twiddler.

Chapter Fourteen

Gone Fishing

"SAY THERE, ALL YOU SLEEPYHEADS," Santa sang out, happily. With a spring in his step, he strolled across the castle room of the new cave, heading toward one of the sleeping rooms in the back. "It's time to get up and enjoy the beautiful day."

"What do we have to do, now?" Hermes whined, blearing up at him through layers of eyelashes. Finally forcing his eyes open, he saw Santa towering over his mat and looking down. "I don't wanna get up," he muttered, turning his face to the wall. "All we do is work."

"Hermes, what do you mean? We do things that are fun all the time," Santa declared, his spirits slightly wilted.

"Well, yeah, cutting those apples up for pie was kinda fun, I guess," he answered, rolling to his back, "but it gave me a stomach ache."

"Four pieces, though. I warned you, Hermes."

"But I wanted it," he growled.

"I know," Santa said, gently. "How are you feeling now?"

"Okay, I guess," Hermes answered, closing his eyes. "I'm going back to sleep. There's nothing to do around here."

With a slight grin, Santa said brightly, "Our meal is ready. I thought you might be hungry."

After a moment of consideration, Hermes tossed his blanket on the floor and sat up. "I guess I am," he answered. "So what are we having, this time; the same old stuff? Not pie, I hope." With heels perched on the edge of his sleeping mat, he waited for an answer.

179

"Well, grumpy, I've just had a fantastic idea," Santa laughed, shaking the mat with his foot.

"What's that?" Robye asked, staggering in from his sleeping room. After raking through his matted, auburn locks, he shoved it all behind his ears and sat down. Glowering up at Santa, through half-opened eyes, he muttered. "Yeah, what did you dream up this time?"

"I thought we might go fishing. Wouldn't that be fun?"

"Why? There's no fish down there," Claudius said, leaning against the wall. "You said we scared them away when we were learning to swim. Remember?"

"I thought so, too," Santa answered, "but they're all back. I went down to the pond a little while ago. I saw probably a hundred or more in it. I guess they stopped hiding since you've not been stirring up the water."

"Oh really," said Claudius. He poked at Hermes to move over and plopped on the other end of his mat. Looking up, he asked. "What was it like? Sometimes it's really humid down there."

"I never thought about it," Santa said.

"It was the other day, didn't you think?" He said, nudging Hermes."

"I don't know; I guess," Hermes answered, stretching his legs.

Looking toward Santa, Robye asked. "What did you have in mind for us to eat? I'm getting a little hungry."

"So am I. Eating is a much better idea than fishing," Hermes said, sitting forward. "I'm real-ly hungry."

"You always are," Claudius smirked, looking sideways at him.

"Well, that's the other fun part," Santa said, with a grin. "We're going to eat fish---after we catch them."

"There's no way we can have fish," Hermes whined.

"Of course we can," Santa said, patiently. "We can go to the pond and catch them for our meal."

"But there isn't any, remember?" Claudius said.

"Yes there is," Santa argued. "We've all seen them."

"But they disappeared."

"I just told you, they're back," Santa countered. "The pond is loaded with fish."

"I knew there was a trick to all this," Hermes squealed, angrily. "There you go with that work stuff, again."

"Hermes, you wanted something to do," Santa said mildly, "and fishing isn't work. You'll have a great time, trust me."

Claudius and Robye glanced at each other then at Santa.

"I doubt it," Hermes said, with a frown.

"You don't have to fish if you don't want to," Santa said.

"I don't want to," Hermes answered, pouncing back into the middle of the cot.

"Oh, that's fine," Santa said, watching him squirm under the blanket and close his eyes. "We're going to leave now."

Hermes turned over and forced his eyes toward Santa. "What's the catch?"

"Oh, there's no catch."

"Really?"

"Of course not. We'll be glad to let you watch while were eating a fine meal."

"What about me?"

"Well, Hermes---," Santa said, thoughtfully, "we wouldn't be needing the heads or entrails. I guess the wild animals wouldn't mind sharing."

"But I'm hungry!" He cried.

"There is some leftover pie, I think," Santa offered.

"Yech! I don't think so," Hermes yelled.

"That's a good thing," Robye and Claudius said, quickly. "We ate it for a snack."

"Then it's up to you," Santa said. He waited for a response.

"Oh, I guess you're right," Hermes whimpered. "It won't be any fun but I'll help you catch the fish."

Looking at Hermes, he said, "that's the right answer," and walked away.

"What do you suppose he meant by that?" Robye asked, looking from Hermes to Claudius. "He brought us here and now we're supposed to do everything? That's not right."

"I hadn't even thought about it," Claudius said, "but you've got a point."

"Where do you suppose he went?" Hermes asked, looking at the two.

"To the pond, I suppose." Heading for the door, Robye said. "Come on! We'd better go see what he's got on his mind."

"There's probably no fish in there. He just wanted us to get up, you know the way he is." Claudius said, raising his eyebrows at Robye. It wouldn't surprise me."

"Then we all may go hungry," Hermes squealed, angrily. After giving his blanket a pitch toward the mat, he ran after them.

"Are you over that stomach ache, little buddy?" Claudius asked, slowing his pace as they went down the hill toward the pond.

"Yeah, I guess. I'm still hungry, though," he growled, stretching tall beside Claudius. "I'm nearly as big as you are. That little buddy stuff's got to go."

"Hey, it took me thirteen years to get this tall. Don't rush it, my friend. What's your hurry?"

"Uh, well, everybody's bigger n' taller than me," Hermes whined. "All you do is tell me what to do."

Overhearing Hermes complaint, Robye turned sharply. "We do not! It's you that's been acting like a whining butt lately. When we left At il, we treated you as an equal because, uh, because you were one then," he stammered, angrily. "It has nothing to do with size, or, or anything else--- and you know it." Glaring at Claudius, then at Hermes, he added, more in control of his voice. "I must admit we've gotten pretty sloppy, and useless, lately---." With a sheepish look toward the two, he added," maybe that's why I got so mad."

Jarring himself from the mood, Claudius spoke up. "I'll bet Santa's wondering where we are. Come on!"

First to reach the edge of the pond, Hermes stood and watched as Santa tossed a fish to the shore. He yelled. "Hey, Santa, how did you catch it?"

"Hi there Hermes, take off your shirt and bring it with you. I'll show you how to catch them." Santa called back. "Careful! It's slippery on those rocks."

Not listening to the warning, Hermes ran across the sandy beach and onto the slick bank of rock. As his feet touched the damp boundary, they were suddenly out from under him and he was sliding feet first over the rim. Clutching for the shirt as it disappeared, he was pulled under water. A few moments later, sputtering and flailing his arms, his head finally bobbed to the surface. He yelled out, "wow, that was fun."

Pulling his legs against the weight of the water, he managed to half-walk, half-swim toward the center of the pond, where Santa was standing. Once there, he used the shirt to wipe his face off, then he asked. "Now what do I do?"

"Oh, it's easy. Just use your shirt like a net and throw it over the fish as it swims by."

"You're kidding?"

"Nope, I'm not kidding at all." After pushing his wet hair behind his ears, Santa pointed past the water barrier. "See up there on the beach? I've got three nice big fish already, just waiting to be eaten."

Holding his shirt by each of the sleeves, Hermes looked toward the water. "Okay, we'll see about this." Turning back to Santa, he said, "I don't see any fish. I told you there wasn't any fish in here."

"Give them a minute," he answered, "The fish will come." After a few minutes, he pointed to Hermes left. "I see one, it's right over there. Do you see it?"

"Oh, oh, I sure do. What do I do now?"

"Hold your shirt up."

"Like this?" Hermes pulled the dripping shirt out of the water and held it under his chin.

"M-m hum. Sh-h-h, be quiet," he whispered.

"Okay, now what?" Hermes said, gently turning toward Santa.

"Now keep your eye on the fish; don't lose sight of it."

"I am! I am. I see it right there," he yelled back, excitedly.

"Sh-h-h! Wait until it gets closer, Hermes. Don't rush it!"

"I'm trying," Hermes whined, wagging the shirt closer to the water.

"Don't do that," Santa warned, glancing up. "You'll scare it away."

"I was just getting it to move."

"That's okay." He looked down again, saying softly. "Not yet. Not yet. It's almost there."

Hermes stared into the water. The shirt moved slightly, in the breeze.

"Now," Santa cried, "toss that shirt right over top. Quick! Catch it! Now! Get hold of your shirt. Don't let go. Don't---."

"It got away," Hermes whined.

"I know. I'm sorry. You'll see another one in a min---. There you go, Hermes. He's just waiting to be caught."

Hermes threw the shirt, flat against the surface of the water and wrapped his fingers under the catch. "I've got'em! I've got'em," he yelled excitedly.

"Hang on! Grab it from underneath."

"Grab what?" Hermes screamed.

"The shirt Hermes; the fish in the shirt, hang on to it; hold it tight. Hermes! You're going to lose your fish. Don't drop the shirt!"

"I know," Hermes yelled back, "I've got hold of 'em. Now what do I do? He's in my shirt."

"I know. Hang on to him," Santa laughed, motioning toward the shore. "Just run it up to the bank and let it loose."

Hermes jumped over the rocks and across the sand. "Claudius, look what I caught," he cried. "It's the biggest fish I ever caught."

"It's the only one you ever caught, silly." Claudius laughed, carrying a bucket of water to the bench.

With eyes dancing, Hermes said, excitedly. "Um---give my shirt back. I've got to go n' catch another one. This is fun!" Jumping back over the rocks, he splashed through the water with the shirt dangling in front of him.

Nodding toward Claudius, Robye snickered, "well, what do you know." They stood on the edge of the sandy beach watching as Hermes took aim for another catch. Reaching inside the bucket, Robye pulled out another fish and dropped it on the cutting board.

"Hey there, Santa," Claudius called out, "we have plenty of fish for our meal. You can stop any time."

"I kind of figured we did."

"There are two for each of us and a couple of spares."

"Hermes," they laughed.

"What?" Hermes smirked. "Can't help if I'm always hungry."

"A growing spurt," Santa smiled, patting him on the shoulder. After climbing out of the pond, they followed Claudius and Robye toward the cave.

A few days later, Santa caught up with Hermes, saying. "You're getting to be quite the fisherman, Hermes. How many did you catch, today?"

"I dunno, more than ten, I'll bet," he giggled, flaring out his fingers.

"Are you going to eat that many?"

"Probably, why?"

Claudius and Robye mentioned that you're spending a lot of time at the pond and they're a bit concerned."

"Why? It's a lot of fun to catch fish."

"I know it is, but we have a good supply of them already. We'll be leaving soon and there are other things to do."

Hermes stopped in the middle of the path, allowing Santa to go a few steps ahead. "I didn't know we'd be going anywhere. I thought you said this was our new home. You promised!"

Santa turned around, speaking softly. "I did not promise such a thing. What about the children?"

"Children, that's all I hear from you." Full of anger and disappointment, he cut across the field and up the hill, screaming impatiently. "Robye! Claudius! Did Santa tell you he wants to leave?" Short of breath, he ran through the cave entrance. "Not here," he screeched at Santa. "Where are they?" With a quick turn, he chased out the door again and around to the back. Racing over a small rise, he nearly collided with them. "I've been looking everywhere for you!" He yelled, skidding to a halt. "Didn't you hear me?"

"Yeah, but you didn't sound hurt, though." Robye looked up as he spoke. "What's got you all tied up in knots?"

"Santa wants to leave. Did he tell you?" Hermes yelled angrily. "He said we could stay; he promised. I don't want to go." Stomping through the grass, he kicked at a piece of wood. "Ouch!" He cried, kicking at it again.

"Sit down, Hermes, before you break your leg on something," Claudius suggested. Holding up a tall limb, he pulled the top toward him and began trimming it with his knife.

"How many does that make?" Robye asked, casually. Without turning, he continued to work on another one.

"So, what's your problem?" Claudius asked.

"I don't wanna leave."

"I don't suppose you'd have to," Claudius said, continuing to trim, "but you'll get a bit lonely, I suppose."

"You might get a little hungry, and a little cold too, with no one around," Robye added.

"There's not any winter here," Hermes barked.

"We don't know that." Reaching the pole toward Robye, Claudius said. "Are you ready for this one?"

"Almost. Put it back there with the rest of them, okay?"

"Sure." Claudius gave it a slight toss in the air, catching the lower half. He ambled around Robye and leaned the pole against the wall. "You've only got two more over here."

"What'er you makin'?" Hermes asked, curiously.

"Do you think it's enough?" Ignoring Hermes, Robye glanced toward Claudius. "I hope so," he added, holding his hand up for inspection. "I'm getting blisters on my thumb. See!"

"I showed you how to do it! You're supposed to scrape with---."

"Hey," Hermes yelled, "I told you Santa wants to leave. Did you know that?"

"He hadn't mentioned it. No," Claudius said. "I'm not surprised, though."

"You're not!" Hermes stared at him in disbelief. "He said we were going to stay here."

"For a little while and rest up. We've been here for a good part of the summer---a lot longer than I thought, actually," Robye said. He turned toward Claudius. "I'm finished. What's next?"

"Wrap and tie, wrap and tie," Claudius laughed, picking up two of the poles. "It takes a long while to do but it isn't hard, it's just bor-ing."

"So, are you going to tell me what you're making?" Hermes demanded. His eyes followed the strips as Claudius formed a knot around the pole. He said, somewhat excited. "Oh, that's the knot you showed me how to make. Remember, Claudius, when we built the skid? I still know how to do it."

"Would you like to help?" Claudius asked. Nodding to Robye, he grinned.

"Sure! What 'cha building, anyway?"

"A surprise for Santa," Claudius answered.

"Oh, really, what is it?"

"Can you keep a secret?"

"Try me," Hermes giggled. "I'm good at secrets."

"I'll bet you are," Robye said, smiling back at Claudius.

"We're building Santa a sleigh."

"What for?" Hermes said, quite disappointed. "We don't have any reindeer. Claudius, you said we needed reindeer to pull a sleigh. Where are we going to get some?"

"Hold it, hold it. Slow down a minute."

"Well, do we?" Hermes said, staring Claudius straight in the eye. "Well?" He glared from Claudius to Robye. "They don't just fall out of the sky, you know."

"Well, maybe not out of the sky. You're right, but---," Claudius grinned at Robye, then back to Hermes, "---but we do have some reindeer right here."

"Claudius has been teaching me how to tame them," Robye said.

Hermes eyes popped wide open, staring at the two. "You-you have?"

"Sure! You've been so busy, catching all those fish, you didn't even miss us."

"Oh, oh! The fish," Hermes fidgeted.

"Don't worry about that," Claudius said. "They're all cleaned, and dried, and packed ready to eat."

"I forgot." He stared at his feet. "I didn't mean to."

"We know," Robye said, picking up some of the poles and laying them side by side. "Are you going to help us out---or just stand there?"

"Oh, I'm helping," Hermes said decidedly. Dropping down between the two of them, he looked toward Robye. "Where did you hide the reindeer?"

"We didn't hide them. Claudius and I made a holding pen on the other side of the hill, just like his family used to do," Robye said, twisting a strip of hide around two poles. "I'm surprised you didn't miss them in the pasture. I thought you had given them names."

"I did. I've not been out there for a while."

"I noticed. A couple of them have babies. If you had been to visit, you'd have known."

Hermes finished tying his knot and watched Robye work on his.

"Are the reindeer in the pen?"

"Yeah, that's what I said. It's kind of like the one his uncles made. That's where we've been training---Uh---!" Pulling the strip of hide loose, Robye began again. "I can't get the knot to set. I keep doing something wrong."

"You want me to show you?" Hermes asked, picking up the pieces. "It's really easy."

"I don't know if I'm trainable," Robye sighed, watching Hermes make the perfect knot.

"A little practice makes perfect," Hermes grinned. "That's what you tell me all the time."

"I know, I know. I think I need to listen to my own advice, sometimes," He laughed.

"It wouldn't hurt," Claudius said, with a grin.

Chapter Fifteen

The Sleigh

"M-m-m, this roast is quite delicious," Claudius said, taking another slice of the venison. "Nearly as good as my mayita's."

"Why, thank you Claudius," Santa smiled. "I take that as a compliment. Your mother was quite an excellent cook."

"As it should be," he said with a nod. "What kind of treatment did you use? It's too tasty for the fare we're accustomed to around here."

"Oh, just a little fine tuning. Mr. Twiddler has been teaching me the fine art of gourmet cooking, using fresh herbs from his garden."

"How soon will we be leaving the valley?" Robye asked between bites. "Hermes mentioned something about it."

"In a few days, I'm sure," Santa answered. He bit into an ear of corn then placed it on his tray. "We'll have to gather and pack the food we've prepared for the trip."

"My fish---," Hermes began, "was that why we dried so much of it?"

"Yes, of course---and the other meat, as well," Santa smiled. "We also have the fruits and vegetables drying on the roof, and the bags of nuts and roots we gathered."

"Don't forget the bag of grain---,"

"---and my herbs," Mr. Twiddler squeaked.

"And your herbs, of course," Claudius laughed.

"We've had enough time for the gathering, but the carrying will be a challenge," Santa reminded them. "The trip up that mountain will be long and hard. I really have no suggestions about that."

"We were wondering if the mountain was still a part of your plan," Claudius said.

"It is," Santa nodded. "Dalt has been a faithful friend. It was his request that we go to the shadows on the mountain."

"Then we have something to show you," Claudius said. "Robye! Hermes! Are you ready to do the unveiling?"

"We sure are," they chorused.

"Me too," Mr. Twiddler shrieked, stomping his foot. "I supervised, you know!"

"Of course, Mr. Twiddler," Claudius said, guiding Santa toward the made-to-scale house. Mr. Twiddler jumped from the steps of it onto Santa's hand.

"If you're ready, Santa," Robye said, with a formal bow.

"You four are leading the parade. I'm just the spectator," Santa laughed, holding his arm up for Mr. Twiddler.

After jumping aboard, Mr. Twiddler plopped down on Santa's shoulder.

Claudius led them out of the cave and behind the hill where the completed sleigh had been hidden.

Santa stood spellbound, staring in awe at the sight. The base of the sleigh had been layered with polished limbs, thatched together with strips of deer hide, and covered with a moss and root paste to make it strong. It had then been soaked in oil, for maneuverability and speed. The ends of the limbs had been rolled upward across the front and thatched in place, then trimmed and polished to protect the passengers as they rode. Finally finding his voice, Santa cried, throwing his hands to his cheeks, "my goodness, where did you find such a fine sleigh?"

"We made it!" The four yelled out in unison.

"We've been working on it for weeks," Robye laughed. "That's why we've had a hard time waking up for first meal."

"How do you like the way we designed the seats?" Claudius pointed out.

"I was getting to that," Santa laughed. "I would have never thought to make the backs so high but I'm sure it would make a safer and more comfortable ride."

"Uh, yeah, they are more comfortable that way." Looking up, he went on. "I meant the other seats; the ones facing the back."

"Say, you're right. Quite clever, I think," Santa grinned. "The passengers can watch what is going on behind while someone else is doing the driving."

"Not only that, Santa, don't you see how Claudius designed them?" Robye sputtered.

"I've never had a sleigh," Santa said. Looking at them curiously, he added, "I wouldn't know how to judge a good sleigh from a bad one, I'm afraid."

"I wasn't thinking," Claudius apologized. Reaching out, he caressed the bent poles across the seat back. "Normally, if there is a seat, it's flat with no back and you hope you can hold on, even if you're the driver."

"I see," said Santa. "I want to appreciate this work of art and all the labors put into it. Go on with your description."

"Good! It was work but we've had the greatest time building it."

"Speak for yourself." Robye and Hermes interrupted, holding up their blistered hands."

"I showed you both how to tie those knots," Claudius growled. "Hermes seemed to manage but you, Robye, just couldn't get the hang of it."

"I know Claudius," Robye answered, still glaring at his hands. He dropped them to his sides.

"Yeah, there were so many knots to do," Hermes added, rubbing his calloused hands together, and then I had to help fix the others when they didn't know how to do it; they're tricky to make."

"But we didn't want it to fall apart," Claudius said, defending himself.

"Hey, Claudius," Hermes said, impatiently, "you didn't tell him how we made the poles bend, did you, huh?" He traced his fingers along the inside of the front poles and let them slide across the surface. "They feel so-o smooth, too."

"That's from all the scraping and sanding we had to do," Claudius said. "I'm sure he knows about soaking them in the water, though."

"Do you?" Hermes asked, nodding toward Santa. "That makes them pli-a-ble. Right, Claudius!"

"Pliable is correct, Hermes."

"The wood doesn't split out that way," Hermes said, excitedly.

"I would have never thought there was so much to do---and so many steps," Santa said, testing the smoothness across the seat back. "So you sanded these poles first?"

"Yeah! Then we soaked them in the pond overnight and by the next day we could bend them in those curves, and after that---after they dry, of course, we had to sand them all over again."

"It's a beautiful piece of work," Santa said, walking slowly around the sleigh. "I do have one question, though."

"What's that?" Hermes asked, turning his head to one side.

"I was just wondering how we were going to pull it?"

"With reindeer, of course," Robye piped in. "We thought of that, too. We have them all trained, and everything. Do you want to see them?"

Santa looked from one to the other, questioningly," you say they're already trained to pull the sleigh?"

"I didn't know we'd have to do that!" Searching for a sign from Claudius, Hermes questioned. "Is that right? Do we still have to train them to pull the sleigh?"

"That is mainly what we've been doing, Hermes. They were pretty tame already." Claudius answered.

"But we just finished the sleigh."

"While you were fishing, Hermes, Robye and I had them pulling those big rocks and the loads of wood---,"

"---in place of the sleigh, don't you get it!" Robye laughed. Looking to Santa, he said. "Claudius said yes, this was how they often tamed the animals."

"I heard," Santa said, quickly looking around, "so, where are they?"

"They're not here. We have them in a holding pen," Robye answered, beckoning excitedly. "Come on and I'll show you."

Tucking Mr. Twiddler in his hat band, Santa said, "let's go then. I'm anxious to see them."

Running ahead of the others, Robye led the way toward a small valley behind the cave.

"Hey Robye?" Hermes cried, "can we go to the pond, too?"

"What for," Robye said, quickly, "I thought we were going to see the reindeer?"

"I know, but---," Hermes began.

"I'm not going to that pond," Mr. Twiddler squeaked, shaking Santa's ear.

"Why?" Santa asked, reaching toward him. "You're safe in the band of my koyt."

"I don't think so," he answered, "I nearly fell out of your cuff the last time we were close to the water."

"Why do you need to go to the pond?" Claudius asked.

"He doesn't know how to bend those poles; I wanted to show him," Hermes squealed, dancing excitedly in front of him. There are still some soaking in the bottom of the water. It wouldn't take long---and it would be fun. Come on, please."

"Oh, Hermes, come on now. He wants to try out the sleigh," Said Robye.

Walking between the them, Santa finally said, "there is a solution, you know."

They all looked at Santa.

He smiled as he said, "what if we drove the sleigh to the pond. We need to try it with the team, anyway."

"A very good idea," they agreed.

After the reindeer were hitched to the sleigh, everyone climbed aboard. With Claudius instructing him, Santa picked up the reins and shook them gently. "Ho," he cried, and the sleigh began to move. With a deft hand he guided the team across the fields and valleys, the hills and the paths, and then along the trees far away from their home. At the journey's end, he aimed the reindeer toward the small pond, and drew the sleigh to a stop.

"A fine sleigh, it is," he said, happily clapping his hands, as soon as his feet touched the ground. "I'll have to say that's the most fun I've had in a long time."

"It sure was, Santa," Robye cried, jumping to the ground. "That is the first time we've seen this whole place, since we've been here, too."

Claudius looked Santa over, from head to toe, then exclaimed with a grin," I'll have to say, you handled that team like a professional."

Santa laughed, "I had a good teacher."

"Well, I guess," Claudius laughed

"Where is Hermes?" Robye said, anxiously searching the grounds.

"He jumped out of the sleigh as soon as it stopped," Mr. Twiddler squeaked, "and ran toward the pond like a flash. I tell you, I don't know about that boy."

Robye and Claudius glanced at each other then headed toward the rock ledge, yelling for Hermes to wait up.

Mr. Twiddler was wriggling further under the cuff as Santa followed the others toward the pond. "What is the hurry, anyway?" He growled.

"Oh you know, Mr. Twiddler," Santa laughed, "how impatient we can get." Having reached the pond, he glanced over the edge. Hermes was busily digging through the silt covered bottom of the pond when everyone arrived.

"That's no pole, Hermes," Claudius yelled, watching him crawl through the shallow water. "What did you find?"

Looking up, Hermes yelled back. "I found it! My mother's brooch! She always pinned her scarf on with it. I lost it when I was fishing." Bending over he kept on digging and tossing muddy sediment in all directions. Furiously, he cried out again. "It's stuck in all this slimy yuck. I can't get it loose!"

"Twist your fingers around it," Claudius yelled back, cautiously kneeling on the narrow ledge of rocks. He reached toward Hermes. "Don't let go of the brooch; you'll get it." He urged.

"I'm trying," squealed Hermes.

Tearing his eyes away from Hermes for a moment, Santa glanced at the dried vegetation on the inner bank. He looked up at Robye. "Had you noticed that wide layer of moss and algae growth around the rim of the pond? I wonder how long the water level has been low, like this?"

"Oh, for a while, I guess. Not quite this low, though," Robye answered, his eyes still peeled on Hermes and his battle with the soggy weeds piled all around him. "We were here a few days ago and the water was almost waist high." He looked up, with a grin. "That's how Hermes was catching so many fish. Didn't he tell you?"

"No, I didn't know," Santa said, looking back at Hermes. "When I taught him how to fish was my last time down here."

"I think he's getting it untangled!" Robye nudged Santa and pointed. "Hey, it looks like he finally got that big pin loose. Good for him."

Without notice, the pond was again filling with water, Hermes stood with his hands extended over his head and squealing with delight. "I got it! I got it! See, here is my mother's brooch," he cried, swinging it over his head.

The water had now begun to swirl higher against the pond's edge.

With his face beaming, Hermes held the brooch high then stuffed it in his pocket and headed toward the long poles, laying a few feet away.

The roar of the water's rotation caught Santa's attention.

"Hermes!" He screamed in terror. "Get out of there! Quick!"

Hermes heard Santa's urgent cry.

He looked up.

He saw Claudius reaching toward him.

The waves rolled over Claudius, knocking him off the wall.

Robye was holding on to Santa, pulling him back from the wall.

Santa's hands were wrapped over Mr. Twiddler.

In slow motion, Hermes saw everything. Then a sudden sensation of weight pulling at his feet, forced him to look down. Slick, muddy clay, sliding between his toes, began to drop into a void of darkness below.

A wave of fear enveloped him.

He screamed.

He disappeared.

In a daze, his friends stared at the hole where Hermes no longer stood. They did not dare to look away; or believe what their eyes had photographed, or their minds had committed to memory.

Interrupting the trance, Santa let out a blood-curdling scream that echoed, over and over again, across the valley. Robye and Claudius ran to his side. Wracking and screaming they cried, clinging to each other.

The air suddenly became heavy with the smell of acrid, boiling water, making it difficult for them to breathe. It forced them to break away from each other, coughing and crying. They looked toward the pond. An enormous cloud of gray-white steam was building; layer by layer it towered so high the blueness of the sky had blended into it.

"To the sleigh---now," Santa screamed, grabbing the reins as he jumped to the seat. "We've got to get out of here!"

Falling into the back seat as the sleigh began to move, Robye cried out, "what about Hermes? We can't leave him behind."

"I don't know! We can't stay here," Santa yelled back. We're no good for him dead!"

"He's gone," Claudius moaned into his hands. "He didn't have a chance."

"Get it together!" Santa screamed, racing the sleigh toward the cave. "We can't help Hermes. This place is not safe; we could all die."

Claudius looked up. "Santa we can't---."

"When I stop this sleigh, we will take what we must and we will leave. I don't know what to expect from that pond, or the cloud hanging over it, but we're taking no chances." Santa's voice was tight with emotion. "If you intend to be leaving with me, you'll be ready when I am." As soon as they reached the cave entrance, he stopped the reindeer team and jumped to the ground.

A few minutes later, they were piling the last of their supplies in the back of the sleigh and climbing inside. Robye gently placed Hermes coat beside him. Santa opened his coat pocket for Mr. Twiddler to get settled inside his house. When his fingers touched the small figurine, tears fell down his cheeks.

Claudius slipped into the seat beside Santa, saying, "I think we have everything we need; food, herbs and the flat stone for cooking."

"That's good."

"It seems very quiet," Robye whispered.

Santa drew in a heavy breath then picked up the reins. With shoulders drooping, he looked first to Robye then to Claudius, and said softly, "we'd better go." With a slight shake of his hand the reindeer began to draw the sleigh down the familiar path, away from the cave.

Everyone was silent as they traveled across the fields, passing the ominous cloud of steam over the pond and on toward the entry point of the valley. When they arrived he pulled in the reins and peered across the valley. Above his head the leaves had turned brown and the chirping of the birds was no longer. "My tree," he murmured. "It doesn't seem so friendly anymore."

"What did you say?" Mr. Twiddler said, poking his head out. "Oh, the birds are gone. Hmf!" He snorted, dropping back inside.

Reaching for the reins again, Santa guided the sleigh toward the valley's point of entry.

The reindeer came to a halt.

After many attempts to get them to move again, Santa threw down the reins in frustration. "I don't understand," he cried, hopping from the sleigh. "We've gone everywhere in this valley with no trouble at all, now nothing seems to persuade them.

Watching Santa pace in front of the team, Claudius said, "maybe there's something wrong with the harness straps." Climbing out of his seat, he walked toward the team while checking the leathers along the way. "I don't find any twisting, and there's nothing binding them, either." He walked to the front, stroking the reindeer as he passed. "I don't know, Santa. It's a mystery to me."

From his seat on the sleigh, Robye watched Santa and Claudius circle the team. All of a sudden he yelled out, excitedly, "I know what the problem is. I'll bet they're hungry." Quickly pulling the bag of fruit from a box, he dug out a handful of the tidbits and jumped down, running toward them.

"We didn't even think of that, Robye," Santa laughed, taking the bag and reaching inside. "You're probably right."

When the fruit fell at Santa's feet and the bag disappeared, a look of surprise and shock spread over their faces.

"What?" Robye cried out, in disbelief.

Beyond the two, Claudius glanced toward the valley. When a scream of panic spewed from his mouth, both Santa and Claudius flashed their attention toward him.

"The valley," he cried. "Look behind you! It's fading away. The pond and everything has disappeared."

"The valley," Santa questioned, quickly turning to see. "Oh no," he screamed, "we must have entered a porthole. We've got to get out of here. Run!"

Chapter Sixteen

The Storm

"The mountain seems a lot closer, doesn't it?" Santa remarked, adjusting the straps to his backpack. "It shouldn't take but a few more days to get there."

Claudius laughed, "Santa, that's what you said yesterday."

"I know," he said, gazing down the brush-covered path they were following.

"I've got some of the meat strips left. You want some?" Robye asked, holding out the opened bag. "Help yourselves. I've been nibbling on it all day."

"I have some in my pocket," Santa said, gazing back at the mountain.

"Some of that fish would be tasty about now," Mr. Twiddler said, peeking out of Santa's pocket.

"Yeah, I do too but his tastes better," Claudius muttered, reaching into the bag. "It was strange to find all our belongings stacked outside that porthole, though; then all those empty bags and stuff."

"It's a shame we had to leave the sleigh behind," Robye added. "We could have been up that mountain, already." He looked down, watching his feet drag through the late-season slush, and said, quietly. "I feel as if it were all a dream."

"It does to me, too," Claudius said, shifting the bag on his back.

"It could seem so if Hermes were still with us," Santa said. He pushed a scrubby bush aside and stepped around it, looking up. "We are in the foothills. It will be harder to travel but more interesting, I think."

"It's colder too, and there's a lot more slushy snow everywhere," Robye muttered.

"Robye, look at the positive," Santa laughed, "it could be snowing."

"I know," he answered, peering up the mountain side. "Maybe this will be our new home, do you think?"

"I have no idea. Dalt said we should go."

"It seems weird, having a reindeer as a guide," Robye stated.

"I know," Santa said, "but it was more weird the first time I talked to him."

"That makes it real?" Claudius said, gruffly. "Hermes is not with us makes it real."

"Yes Claudius, it does," Santa said.

"I have Hermes coat. It's in my bag," Robye said. "I don't know why. I just couldn't leave it behind."

"I know," Santa said quietly.

Mr. Twiddler stuck his head out, again. "Don't you think it's about time for a break? I'd like to sit in my chair and rock it by myself." Looking past Santa's elbow, he said. "Besides that, I can smell a storm brewing."

Automatically, Santa's eyes flicked up. "What are you talking about, Mr. Twiddler? The sky is as clear as it can be. Actually, this has been a pretty nice day."

"Well, if you'll take notice, the weather is changing already," Mr. Twiddler growled, jumping into Santa's hand.

"You're right, Mr. Twiddler," Santa agreed, placing the small elf on his shoulder. Glancing up, he watched as a blanket of blackness began to slip across the sky. "How odd," he whispered. "Every ray of sunlight is being blocked out as that black cloud slides by." He looked again. "But that is not clouds. It's like midnight with no stars, suddenly moving in. It has nothing to do with weather, Mr. Twiddler."

"I'm seldom wrong about the weather," Mr. Twiddler squeaked, frantically pacing on Santa's palm. "This one is going to be fierce."

"I'll take your word for it but it doesn't look like weather to me," he said, slipping Mr. Twiddler back in his pocket.

"Hey Santa, have you been watching that cloud?" Robye yelled, running up beside him. "Claudius and I were out hunting around for a place to camp. Claudius said he was getting hungry. Me too, kinda," Robye laughed. "We happened to duck under this rocky ledge that didn't seem to be occupied, you know, with bears and stuff so we thought maybe it would be a place to---,"

"So where is Claudius?" Santa interrupted.

"Oh, he's still up there."

"Where is this place?" Santa asked, trying to be calm.

"Come on! I'll show you," he said, turning back the direction he had come, waving for him to follow. "When we came out, it was already dark; you know strange dark. It's not the right season for that, is it?"

"No, it's not. Robye, where is this place?" Santa cried out. "We've got to hurry, right now! We're about to get hit."

"Oh, why didn't you say so?" He said, anxiously. "Are you talking about a storm, storm or a what?"

"Yes, it's a storm, but I don't know what kind. The foothills are known for spawning ferocious ones and this one looks bad. Run!"

"It's right up here. Follow me! It's kind of steep. The footing is not too bad, though, just a little slick."

"Just go and I'll follow. I've never seen one move in so fast or look so ugly." Santa's foot slid out from under him. Skipping it up until he regained his balance, he kept from falling." "Now you tell me!" He yelled. "Don't slow down, Robye, I'm fine, we're right behind you. Hurry!"

Claudius saw them coming and cried out. "That cloud has nearly covered the sun. Robye, get in here before you get lost."

"I'm in! I'm in, already! Move over for Santa. He's right behind me.

Mr. Twiddler peeked out and squeaked, frantically waving his arms. "The storm is already on top of us." He dropped out of sight.

"Where is Claudius?" Santa yelled at Robye. "I don't see him. Where---?"

"I'm inside!" Claudius cried, holding out his hand. "Grab hold! I'll pull you in! We're being attacked by long blades of ice."

"Ice blades? I've been hit. O-o-o, one got my leg," Santa screamed. "Get me out of here. They're---everywhere. I---can't reach you. I'm hit!"

"Claudius," Robye cried out, "his arm---grab his arm. Pull! You've got-to get-him in here. Those blades are coming down fast, hurry!"

Claudius grabbed Santa's arm. Robye reached out, dodging the blades as they fell straight down on either side and grabbed his hand. Within minutes, they had him pulled inside.

As if in slow motion, Claudius leaned over him and wailed. "Oh Santa, you could have frozen out there!" Gently picking up his limp head, he tucked it against him and began rocking back and forth.

"Claudius, get a grip!" Robye snapped, "don't you dare panic on me." His eyes immediately darted across the room. "I need Hermes coat---it's in my backpack. Bring it here." Quickly, he added. "I need the lantern, too. Hurry up with that."

With persistence, Claudius slowly crawled toward the backpack. He watched his hands move forward, finally touching the bag and pulling the coat out. After pushing it toward Robye, he found a place close by and sat down.

Without thinking, Robye pulled off his own coat and tucked it under Santa's head. He quickly moved the lantern closer to check Santa's eyes for a response then looked up, saying, "I saw him blink, Claudius. I think he's coming around." Reaching down, he began to untie the fur covering from Santa's leg and pulled it away. "I guess he took a hit on the head, too. He was out for a minute."

Without warning, Claudius let out a low moan, causing Robye to turn.

"Oh no," Robye cried, watching Claudius fall to his side. "I didn't think about you getting hurt."

"Oh, my head," Santa moaned, trying to get up. "What happened?"

"Don't move, Santa. Your leg; it could be broken." Robye warned.

"What happened to Claudius? Why is he on the floor?"

"There's blood seeping through his coat," Robye said, glancing up. "Stay still, Santa. I'll take care of it." Looking back toward Claudius, he began peeling the coat sleeve off his arm.

"How is he?" Santa groaned, rolling his head to one side.

"Not a puncture; just a graze. That's good," Robye answered. "I'll pack it with ice to stop the bleeding."

"Ouch! Careful," Claudius growled, glaring up at Robye. "What do you think you're doing?"

"I'm just trying to wake you up," Robye said sharply. He picked up more ice and packed it around Claudius's arm. "I'm glad you're back."

Turning toward Santa, he said. "You have a huge bruise on the upper part of your leg. I'm not sure if it's broken but you shouldn't take any chances."

"What do you mean?" Santa cried, watching Robye come toward him, holding more ice in his hands.

"You're not moving from that spot for a while," Robye grinned. "Ice is good treatment for bruises too, so the two of you are out of commission for a while."

"You're loving this, aren't you?" Claudius growled.

"Oh, yeah!" Robye grinned. "You know how payback is." He slipped over beside Claudius and sat down.

"What now?" Claudius asked, looking up.

"I need to see if the bleeding has stopped."

"Oh!" Claudius said, looking away. "I didn't know bleeding was so painful."

"What do you mean?" Robye asked, removing the ice pack. "I think you're going to make it. The bleeding has already stopped."

As Robye exposed the wound, Claudius quickly turned away again, with a groan. "When I saw the blood on my coat, my head started spinning."

"I thought I heard you say mayita," Robye mentioned, while pressing a cloth against the wound, "but I wasn't sure."

"I remember thinking it."

"There, you're all done, Claudius," Robye said, helping him pull on his coat. "There's a much bigger hole in that sleeve than in your arm. You're a lucky guy."

"I know. Thanks."

"All right, Santa. I'm not going to make you suffer any longer," Robye laughed, raking away all the ice. "Let's see about that leg. How does it feel?"

"I'd say it feels pretty frozen," he muttered, sitting up.

"Okay, you old crank," Robye laughed, "let's see if you can walk." Looking toward Claudius, he said. "You get on one side and I'll do the other, just in case."

"In case, what?" Claudius asked, reaching toward Santa.

"In case it is a broken leg."

"You didn't say anything about a broken leg," Claudius said.

"You were out cold," Robye finished.

"Is anyone going to help me up?" Santa complained. "I'm about to grow to the floor."

As soon as he was standing upright, Santa aimed for the entrance.

"Well, it's obviously not broken," Robye sighed with relief. He grinned, watching Santa hobble across the room. "There is no need to be in such a hurry, Santa."

"Why not?" He asked, turning around. With an, "Ouch, that hurt," he grabbed at his leg. "I want to see what kind of damage that storm caused."

"We're iced in. We won't be leaving here for a while," Robye answered. "It's probably a good thing too, by the way you're walking."

"I'm walking just fine," he said, cautiously turning around.

"Oh, sure you are," Robye said, grinning. "Why don't you come join us then? Claudius and I have worked up quite an appetite from all the excitement."

"Uh! Oh! If you say so," Santa groaned, hobbling with great effort toward them.

"Do you need some help?" Claudius asked, looking up.

"Oh, I guess," Santa answered, dragging his leg.

"Do you want me to feed you, too?" Robye giggled.

"Hold it, Robye," Claudius said, rubbing his ears. "Listen!"

Looking from one to the other, they all became quiet. Santa put his hand up as a caution.

"I heard it again. It's more like a feeling."

"Maybe your ears were having a growth spurt," Robye suggested, testing the length of his own. "Mine are stunted, I think. I started getting a little growth and then that was it."

"Sh-h!" Santa warned. "I'm hearing something, too."

"I wasn't sure," Claudius said. "It was so faint, I nearly missed it."

"It's Dalt! He's outside."

"How can you tell, Santa?" Robye asked. "How would he know we were in here?"

Santa turned to him, then back.

"Of course he would know," Robye thought, shaking his head.

"Come on, you two. Hurry and help me up," Santa cried. "I need to get closer to the entrance.

They lifted Santa to his feet then quickly ran toward the door.

As soon as his foot touched the floor, Santa screamed out in pain. "I don't think I can do this. The whole side of my leg is yelling back at me, now."

Robye ran back to him, reaching for his arm. "You shouldn't be on that foot then. It's a bad bruise, Santa and you're trying to push it too hard. It needs iced, again."

"Get me to the door," Santa demanded. "We'll do the ice thing after I talk to Dalt."

"All right, Santa," Claudius said, going toward the other side. He glanced at Robye with a shrug. "Here, let me help you."

"Careful with that injured arm, Claudius," Robye cautioned, "it may not strong enough to hold his weight. Why don't you switch sides with me?"

"Good idea! Thanks for the reminder," he nodded, going to the other side of Santa.

"Quiet!" Santa growled, looking up with a frown. After shrugging off his helpers hands, he turned back to the barrier. "I can hardly hear what Ari's saying." He pushed his head against the ice and pressed his ear next to it. "Oh yes, much better now. Ari's voice is really faint but I can hear him now. He's trying to tell me something."

"What is he saying?" Robye asked, looking from Santa to Claudius, then back.

Santa repeated the message as he listened. "Danger, you're in danger! Go! Leave now." Quite shaken, Santa looked up. "I could hear him squawking and screaming but I couldn't understand what he was saying, at first. Finally I heard 'danger, danger'. He wouldn't say that if he didn't mean it." Pushing away from the barrier, he stared at the two for a second then said carefully, "he came to warn us; we must get out of here."

"That makes no sense," Claudius frowned. "I don't see any kind of danger that we're in."

After his eyes met theirs, Santa looked down, feeling a nudge against his feet. "There's water coming from somewhere, it's pooling around me---I'm standing in it."

"Oh, yes it does," Robye cried, getting quite agitated. "I'm beginning to hear a faint rumble; I don't know how to describe it but it seems to be coming closer. I can't imagine what would make a sound like that."

"I hear the ringing in my ears," Claudius answered, "of course, but it's there all the time."

"Not that, you duff," Robye yelled over the elevated noise level. "The water---the water Santa is standing in, didn't just appear, it came from somewhere."

"Get serious, you two," Santa cautioned. "We've got a problem here."

"I'm trying to---find---where the water is coming from?" His eyes followed a slight trickle to the center of the room and a slightly larger pool. "It's from here." He looked up, yelling. "Over here!"

"What?" Both Santa and Claudius cried, going toward him.

"Oh, I know what it is," Robye cried, over the deafening roar that was bouncing off each wall of the cavern, magnifying in volume as it rolled through the space. The water must have broken through the ice in the underground waterways. It's racking down through all the tunnels, pushing furiously toward us."

"The floor is shaking, too." Claudius's voice had reached a high pitched scream. "Everything is vibrating---making all those rocks fall loose. Do you see---they're dropping off the walls, everywhere---all around us. This place is going to collapse."

"Cut it," Santa hissed. "Don't you dare panic on me. We have a problem and I see no answer to it---yet." His eyes flicked to the entrance. "It's hard to know how much ice is blocking us in." Gently touching his leg, he yelped, "Ouch!" then looking down he added, "and I'm worthless at best."

Claudius sat flat on the floor, propping his forehead against his knees and took a few deep breaths. After a deep sigh, he opened his eyes.

"I know, I know! We're thinking," Robye quipped. Suddenly pointing toward the place they had been eating, he yelled. "Would you look at that? We have more trails of water coming in here."

When a small trickle began to pool in front of Claudius, he looked up. "It's a fast melt too, for some reason."

"It could be because it's warmer in the fall," Santa yelled over the noise. "Do you think it's seeping in from the opening?"

"Maybe a little," Claudius answered, studying the flow, "but the majority is coming from the back; not the front."

"You're probably right, Claudius," Santa agreed. "I saw a little seepage. That's all."

"So, it's coming from both directions," Robye said, "and the noise level means it's getting pretty close."

"I would say so," Santa said, limping back toward the others.

"There's one thing I'm thinking," Robye said, pacing around the small water pockets, "and I'm afraid we're about find out."

"What's that?" Claudius said.

"This cavern is a mouth to the underground river system. There may be more but I'm sure this is one of them. The small water pockets that have suddenly appeared all across this cavern floor and keep getting larger and larger, makes me think that the path must go right through here."

"So the melted ice has the river flowing again?" Santa interrupted.

"Yes, I'm sure of it---and it's a downhill slope," Robye added. "I don't know if there are hot springs feeding into these tunnels, adding to the massive amount of water coming down or if it's melted ice , or what caused it. I can tell you this, though, the way everything around us is vibrating and shaking means the water is picking up speed as it gets closer."

"---and the earsplitting roar is kind of like ice and snow rolling down the side of a mountain, only a lot louder." Claudius cried over the noise.

"Oh no," Robye cried out, frantically picking up rock after rock that had fallen to the floor. Choosing one that had a slight point on one end, he ran to the barricade and began pounding it against the ice. "I just thought of something else," he panted. "We're on a waterfall crest. We've got to make a hole and get out of here."

"I was wondering about that," Santa said, leaning his ear against the barrier then pounding on it sharply two or three times with a rock.

"What is all the commotion out here?" Mr. Twiddler said, poking his head out of Santa's pocket. "I was right in the most exciting part of my book when all your infernal noise interrupted me."

"Sorry, Mr. Twiddler," Santa panted, dropping the rock beside him, "but I'm listening for a hollow sound when I tap the ice. It might indicate a crack or some kind of weak place to break through."

"Oh, I see," said Mr. Twiddler, dropping back through the fur pocket cuff.

"Well, I don't get it," Claudius said, wiping the ice chips from under his knees. He began pounding at the wall again.

"Give me a second and I'll tell you," Robye answered. "Just think about it. All this ice that has us trapped inside here---," he spread his fingers in a sweeping motion.

"The ice blades that stacked up against the door; yes, yes I know. Go on."

"When all that ice breaks loose, and it will you know, the pressure of the rushing water charging through the underground tunnels will blast it away. What I'm expecting is when the force of the water reaches this cavern, it will immediately flood up and slam through that opening. It will explode water all the way down the mountain."

"Yes, we know all that," Claudius said. "We're going to get smashed up against the ceiling of this hole and be crushed to death. Why else would you think I'd be chipping at this ice, with little to no chance of getting through it in time?"

"If we find a weak spot and break through, there is still a possibility of us escaping before the water hits," Santa reminded them.

Robye glared at the others, shaking his head. "Do you know what will happen to us? We'll be tossed out that door and thrown down the mountain side."

"You mean the waterfall crest?" Santa said.

Mr. Twiddler popped his head out. While tying the purple string around his ears, he looked toward Robye and Claudius then at Santa.

"You'd better get back inside, Mr. Twiddler. It's not safe out here," Santa urged. "I need to fasten the pocket so you won't fall out."

Mr. Twiddler dropped back inside, saying nothing.

"Yes," Robye answered. "If we're still in here when the rushing water hits we will be forced through the opening and pushed down the mountainside with all the water, rocks and everything else as part of the waterfall."

"Oh no, here it comes. We can't beat the water now, even if we did have a way out." Claudius screamed. The water was gushing across the floor; it was already flooded and climbing up the walls."

"I have an idea. No time to explain. There is a way we can get out of here," Santa said, touching his left ear. "Stay calm and do exactly what I do. We've run out of options; this has to work."

"What's the plan?" They cried.

"To save our lives; that's all the plan I have, so just grab hold and hang on tight," Santa commanded. "Stick with me---don't let go."

"We're with you," Claudius cried out, hooking his arm under Santa's shoulder.

"Do as he said; hang on. Just do it!" Robye yelled, grabbing for Santa's other side.

For a few tenacious seconds Claudius floundered, clutching only air while trying to reach out for Robye. Once they touched, his arms swung out and locked in place. With only the thought of survival in mind, the three clung by sheer might to each other.

With the rage of a ferocious storm the waves raced in and slammed against the tunnel walls, pushing the flood of water across the floor. Minutes later the cavern's air-filled open space was engulfed by measured inches of water against the wall. The raging waves crashed with a vengeance into everything in its path. Knocked to their knees, the boys grappled for strength to hang on, as they tumbled uncontrollably through the water. Time stood still. They stopped spinning. Their senses had been magnified and the tremors from deep within the earth vibrated through their bodies. Suddenly they were immobile, pressed tight against the ceiling. The water was still. It pushed with a force that nearly stopped their breath.

With a sudden crunch and rumble, they felt a release of pressure. They dropped, following the water as it raced toward the barricade. It slammed through the ice and spewed out the opening.

"Eyes closed," Santa screamed. "Up, up!"

The entrance was clear. Without boundaries the thunderous water raced down the mountainside, toward the valley below.

Barely escaping the raging flood, a circle of warmth passed through Santa and his friends. Hand in hand they floated upward, through mellow waves of color.

Their eyes sprung open when a familiar voice said, "where are you going?"

"Ari," Santa cried out, looking around excitedly, "where are you?"

"Behind you, Santa," Ari said. "I heard your call for help. Where are you going?"

"We're to meet Dalt but I don't know where that would be," Santa answered. "We were stranded in the cavern when I heard him speak."

"I know," Ari replied. "I'll take you there."

Chapter Seventeen
Gates of Re

"DALT ISN'T HERE," CLAUDIUS SAID, sounding out his disappointed. "I don't see him." He rolled over on his side and searched around until Santa and Robye were in view. After checking his injury for damage, he slipped the sleeve back over his arm and gave it a pat. With wrinkle crossed his brow. tHe winced then looked up. "Where are we anyway?"

"I have no idea, Claudius," Robye answered. "From what Santa told us, Ari was taking us to meet him. I expected Dalt to be waiting on us, just as you were."

"That was my understanding, Robye," Santa said, peering between the bushes and small trees where they had landed. "He's not failed us yet."

Glancing over toward Claudius, Robye noticed the grimace on his friend's face and asked, "Is there something wrong with your arm? It's bothering you again, isn't it? Maybe I should examine it for you."

"I guess. I fell on it when we landed," he admitted, slipping the coat sleeve down from the wound. "It really doesn't hurt, though. It just feels scratchy when I move it."

Robye carefully removed the bandages and examined the cut. After gently pressing the skin next to it, he asked, "how does it feel now? It doesn't seem to have any swelling or fever. Actually it looks pretty well healed; you don't even have a scar."

"The itchy feel is gone, now," Claudius said, quite surprised. "What did you do?"

"I took off the nasty bandage was all," Robye laughed. "That's probably why you were having some discomfort."

"Do you think?" Claudius said, slipping his arm back into the sleeve. "It feels a lot better without the bandage, though."

With a sharp yelp, he shook his arm out of the sleeve again, glaring at Claudius. "Ouch! There's something that keeps sticking into me."

"I don't know what it could be, Claudius. Your wound is healed," Robye frowned with concern. "I'll look again, if you like."

The sleeve turned inside-out when Claudius slipped off the coat. With a snicker, he laughed, holding it up for Robye to see. "Oh, ho, I see what it is already. Would you look at all that dried blood; it's all over the lining. That icky stuff must be what has been sticking into me."

Robye let out a sigh of relief. "Well, who would have thought?"

"You were a bit busy, taking care of the two of us."

"Speaking of that," Robye said, somewhat concerned, "where did Santa go? I need to check his bruise. He was in a lot of pain before we left the cavern."

"He left a few minutes ago," Claudius answered, trimming the dried blood off his coat. "He said he was going to find a place to sit down."

"Did you see where he went? His leg must still be giving him trouble."

"Over by those trees, I think," Claudius nodded. "Mr. Twiddler was on his shoulder, as usual."

"Oh my gosh," Robye gasped, "Mr. Twiddler. He could have drowned in that deluge. I didn't even think about him."

"He's fine; he did just fine, I tell you. His house didn't even get wet in Santa's pocket." Claudius said. Then waving his hands about, he added. "He came through it better than the rest of us. I, for one, have bruises and scrapes all over me, I think."

"I'm kind of achy, too. We're lucky to get out of there alive."

"You are so right about that." Then looking toward Robye, he added, "Santa's still not walking very steady, you know."

"I had noticed that, too. Those ice blades hit him pretty hard." Robye stood, shielding his eyes with both hands, searching between the bushes and underbrush. "I don't see him anywhere. I can't imagine him going very far, though."

"Oh, I see him. He's over there," Claudius pointed, "behind that chunky old stump; looks like it's from that tree laying beside it Do you see him?"

"I think I see the stump," said Robye, still searching.

"Now, do you see those three huge tree trunks all grown together?"

"No! All I see is " He stumbled and looked down.

A massive gnarl of roots lay across the ground. Some segments had intertwined with other foliage, pushing its roots out of the soil. Grayed and split by the weather, the gnarls of wood lay in huge clumps, weaving in and out of the ground and stretching in all directions. Patches of snow still clung to the shade.

"Is he sitting on the ground, or what? I still don't see him," Robye said, stepping over a patch of crusty snow.

"Yeah, it looked like to me," Claudius said, examining the coat lining. He trimmed it a bit more then turned it to the right side. After slipping the coat back on, he wriggled his arm around inside the sleeve. "There, that's better---no scratching."

Hearing nothing Claudius had said, Robye turned to face him. "Are you coming?" He growled.

"All right, all right, I'm right behind you," Claudius snapped a little too sharply. Mellowing somewhat, he added. "I needed to finish trimming the blood out of my lining."

"Oh sorry, I knew that. I wasn't thinking," Robye apologized. "I'm worried about Santa. He's never acted like this, before."

"Let's go check on him," Claudius suggested. "We'll both keep an eye on him."

"Good idea," Robye said, heading toward the tree stump. "When you were talking about those three trees, I was looking for something much smaller. Those trees are so huge I mistook them for a boulder or wall, or something."

"Didn't you notice the bark on the trunk, and all those limbs; they've still got some leaves on them. Besides all that, I saw you trip over some of the roots that were sticking out of the ground."

"Hey, don't rack on me, Claudius," Robye growled. He stepped over another chunk of root then glanced up through the limbs of the tree. "I hadn't even seen a tree until after we left the old city---well," he hesitated, "in books but that doesn't count."

"Guess you're right," Claudius grinned. "I couldn't believe you'd miss something that big, though."

"The size of a wall," Robye quipped."

"Yeah, right!"

"Dalt hasn't shown up, yet?" Robye called out.

"Not yet," Santa answered.

"Where do you suppose he is, Santa?"

"I don't know," he said, speaking as if in a trance.

Robye immediately noticed the glazed, far-away look to Santa's eyes.

"What happened?" Claudius asked. "We've only been separated a few minutes.

A light snow was beginning to fall, clinging to the red curls around Santa's koyt. He reached up to his shoulder and held out his hand for Mr. Twiddler then slipped him in his pocket. "There seems to be a chill in the air." He sat, watching all the footprints they had made fill up with the sparkling white snow.

"So, have you heard from him?"

"No, not yet," he said. His gaze slipped through the branches, toward the open sky.

"You seem to be staring at something. What is it?" Claudius asked, sitting down beside him.

"Oh, I don't know; nothing I guess," Santa said. Still watching the snow-flakes swirl down, he added. "I was just wondering why we were sent here. I haven't seen Dalt, or heard from him either. It concerns me a bit. We've put our trust in him and Ari for a lot of miles."

"Do you know where we are?" Robye asked. He perched himself on the log beside the stump, leaned back and crossed his legs. "We're on the side of some mountain. I know because I looked over the edge and it's nearly straight down."

"What were you looking for?" Santa asked, gently massaging his leg.

"I was trying to see the waterfall we escaped from, but I couldn't find it," Robye said, observing the light touch Santa was using on his injury.

"Do you suppose it's on the other side of that mountain," he asked, pointing at the one across the valley.

"Probably not, Claudius," Robye said, turning toward him. "The shadow was in front of us, remember? The waterfall crest was only two days up from that little path we'd been following around the base."

"Yeah, I know. There wasn't much snow down there; not much up here either, for that matter." He walked over to a rocky ledge and looked down. "I can't believe the trees and bushes and stuff---and all the way up the mountain side; strange how green everything is, too."

"Don't forget," Robye reminded, "we've been traveling more south ever since Dalt told us about the shadows. That's probably why."

"I noticed that some of the bushes were still in bloom. That seemed strange to me."

"I saw that too, Claudius," Robye said. "I was disappointed about the waterfall, though, I was hoping to see it."

"I tried to find it; never did. I had to look for myself, I guess."

"Maybe it's not the right mountain."

"Maybe not! We have no idea how far Ari brought us," Claudius pointed out.

"Are you feeling any better, Santa," Robye asked, "you were looking a bit whipped a few minutes ago. How is your leg? Does it hurt much?"

"I think it's fine; just a little stiff," he answered. "I'm not sure how it will do on a long walk, though."

"Would you like for me to examine it?"

"After we find a campsite, maybe," Santa said, looking down. Noticing a movement by the stump, he reached toward it.

Just then Mr. Twiddler hooked both arms out the edge of the pocket. "Did I hear you say camp? It's about time."

"You agree with that?" Santa laughed, reaching out again. "Oh, look what I found---a blue fairy. It seems to have an injured wing."

"It sure is a tiny thing," Robye said, looking over Santa's shoulder, "much smaller than Mr. Twiddler."

Claudius slipped in closer to the stump and looked down. "Would you look at how tiny he is."

"I know," Santa said.

"Oh, poor thing," Claudius crooned, "something is wrong with his wing."

Robye placed a leaf for the fairy to get on. "Can you fix it---the wing, I mean?"

"I don't know yet," Santa said, reaching out. "Oh come on little one. I won't hurt you," he coaxed, curling his finger toward the small figure.

Sticking his head through the fur, Mr. Twiddler peeked out. "By all the noise, I had to see what all the excitement was about. Did you find something good?"

"I found this little fellow. He's got a broken wing," Santa said, glancing toward Mr. Twiddler. Looking back, he reached for the leaf and held his hand out to the fairy.

"Oh no, oh no-o-o, oh, Santa! No, no, no!" Mr. Twiddler screamed in terror. "Don't touch! He'll put a spell on you."

With ferocious black eyes, the blue fairy glared at Mr. Twiddler then gazed pitifully back at Santa.

"But he's hurt, Mr. Twiddler. We must help him," Santa said, gently caressing the small being.

"Oh, Santa," Mr. Twiddler wailed, "you should not have touched him." His face had paled and his body shook with fear. Without another word he dropped back into the pocket.

Once the blue fairy was back on the leaf, Santa placed it at his feet. With huge, sad eyes he turned his head toward Santa, moaning and groaning in pain. "I can't leave him like this," he thought.

With Robye and Claudius crowding in to watch, Santa mended the blue fairy's wing.

The moment they all touched the blue fairy squealed with wicked delight. "You are now in my power." In a frenzy of excitement, he flew out of Santa's hand, looping and twirling in the air. With a point of his finger a hidden door, at the base of the three trees, flew open. In an instant they were all tossed through it to the other side.

The blue fairy, now a midnight black, with menacing joy began taunting his prisoners. Darting and dashing, like a ferocious bee, he maliciously poked at their eyes and nose then zoomed in circles around their heads.

"Where are we?" Santa asked, pushing himself to a sitting position and swatting his hands in front of his face. "How did we get here?"

"Through the door in the three trees, of course," the fairy said, with an evil grin. He spun around each of them, nipping at their ears. "Follow me!" He commanded.

From his sprawled position on the ground, Robye rolled over to his knees and started to stand. Looking toward Santa, he asked, "where are we going?"

"You are not to speak, underling," the fairy jeered. "A servant, you are."

"They are not servants, they're friends," Santa said sharply. "Ouch!" He growled, pushing against his injured leg. A couple of attempts later, he managed to get to his feet.

"Well, who is to speak?" The blue fairy squawked.

"About what?" Santa asked, pushing the fairy from in front of his face.

"Only one is to speak to the queen."

"To what queen and for what reason?" Santa cried.

"So, you are to speak," the fairy laughed, gleefully streaking from side to side.

"What is it you want? We've done nothing to harm you. We were only waiting for a friend."

"A friend, you say," the fairy squealed. "Why do you think the queen has summoned you?"

"We have no idea," Claudius spoke up.

"Silence, you insolent!"

Looking toward Santa, his black eyes dancing with mischief, he said, "follow me. The queen awaits your arrival."

"What is this place?" Santa cried, staring at the stark remains of huge, ornate buildings that had fallen to shambles, as they passed. "The whole city is in ruin. What happened here?"

"The queen's palace is just ahead. Now come along; no lagging," he giggled. Buzzing and pecking at his prisoners, the fairy pressed them forward, up a steep flight of polished marble stairs. At the top were two tall, ornately carved doors with large, golden hinges. They were slowly swinging open.

Beyond the doors was a spacious entry hall, plain of trim but decorated with garlands of flowers and sheer silks. A decorative carpet led to the middle of the room where a lady of striking appearance was sitting in an ornate chair, a few steps above the entry level. Her slightly adorned, pale face was slim and attractive. With carefully styled white hair, she was regally crowned with a small, jeweled tiara that nearly hid her slim, pointed ears. She was dressed in a plain but quite beautiful gown of white. A purple velvet robe, trimmed with gold and silver embroidery, was draped across her shoulders and flowed to either side, as she sat waiting for them to approach.

As soon as they reached the steps, Santa's eyes were drawn beyond the queen's ladies in waiting and rested on the two guards who were standing in the shadows to her right. Each wore a uniform of blue tights and a fitted red jacket. The glitter from the jacket's silver trim caught his attention. Suddenly his eyes were drawn to the rather small boy, standing in shackles between them.

"Hermes?" He whispered. "That can't be." Visibly shaken, he looked again.

The boy moved slightly then lifted his eyes toward the guards.

"It is him." When the thought registered in his mind, Santa's eyes lit up and he cried out excitedly, "Her-m-e-s."

The boy turned at the sound of his name. He smiled in recognition, but said nothing.

"How did you--? Where---?" Santa cried. As he spoke, silver bracelets curled around his wrists and ankles. He looked down then toward the queen, saying nothing.

"The silver bonds you are wearing can only be removed by your Gift of Merit," she said, observing each of the prisoners. "It is a law beyond my powers. If you are believed, the ropes will fall."

Feeling quite ignored, the sparkle in the blue fairy's eyes turned fiery red. "After all," he thought, spitefully, "I did capture these vermin. It's my right to be allowed to speak." Ducking quickly, he flew in front of the queen, "not to mention the trouble I took to relocate her subjects. She should thank me."

"Queen Daira, of the Wickie Nation, your humble servant has come to request audience." The blue fairy said, buzzing around her face. His eyes began to sparkle a brilliant shade of blue, again. Darting forward, he bowed deep in a most graceful manner.

The queen's eyes followed the blue fairy, as if in a trance.

"The evacuation of your city; is it doing well?" He inquired, with a regal flair. From a hidden glance, his eyes burned through Santa, defiantly.

"Well known for being a safe haven," he continued, "the city of At il was notified of your need. Preparations have been made for the arrival of your subjects."

Quite shaken by the fairy's report, Queen Daira spoke. "By what orders were those actions taken?"

"By your need, of course," the blue fairy said. "The citizens of Wickie have no home. I took it upon myself to assist with the matter." Dancing in the air above her head, the chameleon fairy turned black. With menacing eyes, he glared again at Santa.

Spoken in Queen Daira's native Wickie language, Santa requested permission to speak. "Your highness," he said, accepting the floor with her permission, "what charges are held against us?"

"Your guilt is by association," she answered, motioning toward Hermes." The youth, held captive by my guards, was found to be sitting at the base of the magic well. Since then, my time has been entertained by numerous citizens who saw him climb through the Gates of Re, releasing the underground waters which flooded my city. Should you look through my window, you will see it still flows. By this act, many of our homes have been destroyed."

"With respect, may I interrupt?" Santa said.

"Speak," the queen said.

"The old city, At il, would not be friendly to your subjects."

"He speaks lies," the blue fairy raged."

"You speak as if you know," she said.

"I do not lie," Santa said, in the language of her youth. "Your way of determining truth from deceitfulness is honorable."

The shackles fell, releasing him from bondage.

"Your Gift of Merit has been accepted," the queen announced. "My language will not permit an untruth."

After observing the chains at his feet, Santa nodded slightly in reply.

"Continue," she said.

"I have no knowledge of the event causing your disaster, but the prisoner's version may be worth taking into account."

The queen listened.

When Santa had finished speaking, she turned to the guards. "Bring the prisoner forward."

They bowed to the queen then did as she requested. One guard stepped forward, holding a book of records.

"Your name must be recorded," he said.

"Hermes Potts."

"Your age must be recorded."

"Nine years old," he trembled.

"Where is your home?"

"I have none."

"The guard stood back, closing the book.

"Now, Hermes Potts, tell me who opened the Gates of Re?" The queen asked.

"He did," Hermes said, pointing above his head. "The blue fairy did. He's black now, though."

In fury, the fairy spun around Hermes head, pecking and nipping at his ears.

Without a sound, a net of silver spun through the air and landed on top of the fairy. He screamed in a fit of fury and rage.

When his eyes met with the queen's, he fell silent.

The queen's attention returned to the prisoner. "It seems your mother's brooch was lost while you were fishing."

"Yes'um," Hermes said, staring at his feet. "I didn't mean to lose it."

"I know Hermes. That's all right," she said, softly. "Were you in the water when you lost it?"

"Yes, one time when I went fishing. I went down there every day---it was the only thing I had of my mother's." He began to cry.

After a few moments, she asked. "The brooch was in the bottom of the pond? How did you ever find it?"

"I went in to get one of the poles from building the sleigh. There were three left in the water. I wanted to show Santa how we made them bend." Hermes shuffled from one foot to the other. "That was when I saw it." Looking into her eyes, tears fell down his cheeks. "It was all tied up in weeds. I had to dig it out."

She waited for him to continue.

"All of a sudden, water started coming into the pond, really fast. It was going round and round but I couldn't move my feet." He looked at her face then back down to his hands. A big hole was right under me. I fell into it. I screamed. I was so scared."

"What happened then?" She said, gently.

"That was when I met the blue fairy. He was right there. He was all beautiful, with sparkly blue eyes. He smiled at me and took my hand. He said he was sent to save me. He did too, I guess."

"What did you do after that?"

"He led me through a lot of tunnels and stuff. He knew just where to turn and everything. We walked for a long, long time." Hermes hesitated, looking toward his friends then back to the queen. "There was water in some of them. He called them underground waterways."

"Do you know where he came from?"

"The blue fairy? Oh no, he was just there. He never did tell me his name, either."

"Did you think that was unusual?" She asked, quietly.

"Not as unusual as the way he went on about the Gates of Re. From the time I met him, that was all he talked about. He said he knew we could get out because he had the key. He showed it to me, too. It was around his neck." Hermes laughed. "He doesn't know how to hide things, either."

"Your mother's brooch; do you have it?" The queen asked.

"Yes! It's in my pocket. Would you like to see?" Hermes said, proudly.

"I would. Yes," she said.

The restraints tightened when he moved his arm. "I'm sorry," he said, looking up. "I cannot reach it."

"Would you give it as a gift?" She asked.

For a moment Hermes studied Queen Daira's face then, bowing down with respect, he said quietly. "It would be an honor," he said quietly.

The silver ropes fell to the floor.

The blue fairy clawed at the silver net, screaming. "No, no, no, he is my subject. He must do as I say."

"Your Gift of Merit has been accepted," she said with a smile. "The key the blue fairy holds will no longer open the Gates of Re." She held the brooch toward Hermes. "This is now the key and you are to keep it, always."

"You knew where we were?" Santa asked.

"Yes, of course," the queen answered. "You were in the Valley of Deception. Beneath the Enchanted Pond is where the other, of the two Gates of Re, is located."

He nodded.

"Many years ago, our elders were forced to relocate the Wickie nation, in an effort to escape annihilation of our race." She noticed the net over the blue fairy had moved slightly and touched her hands together. It slipped back in place. "Between the gates, there is a network of underground tunnels. The only two ways to leave those tunnels are through the Gates of Re. The Enchanted Pond protects one gate and the other is here at the well. They both must be unlocked for either to open. Only incorrigible prisoners are incarcerated between those two gates. The blue fairy is one of those hopeless inmates."

"What caused the gates to open, if it is supposed to be so secure?" Robye asked.

"The Valley of Deception does not usually appear. When it does, it means a prisoner has discovered a method of escape. Heated water pressure, causing steam and the increased whirlpool motion, were indications that the key had been compromised."

"So, when Hermes was caught in the pond it kept the blue fairy from escaping," Robye deduced, moving slightly. He winced when the chains around his waist tightened.

"That seems to be true," Queen Daira said thoughtfully.

"So he was used as a key for escape?" Robye said, glaring at the silver cloth. "That little piece of worthless---!"

Robye's silver chains fell to the floor.

"Your Gift of Merit has been accepted," the queen smiled. "I believe you have discovered the flaw in the Gates of Re."

"I didn't mean to let the blue fairy loose---or, or get my friends in trouble." Tears filled Hermes eyes.

"I know," said the queen. "You had nothing to do with the disaster of our city. You were tricked into opening the gate."

"My apology," Santa said, respectfully.

"You may speak," the queen said.

"When we first arrived in your city, it seemed unusual that the streets were empty of residents."

"I'm sure you also noticed that many of the homes had been destroyed," Queen Dairia answered. "We were forced to evacuate the city. Without my knowledge, the blue fairy arranged for their transfer to At il. Although you warned me of the dangers, I cannot change the destination until after their arrival."

"That would be too late." Santa's face paled, in horror. "Magic does not work within At il's walls."

"We've got to do something," Robye cried. "If they go through the city entrance, they will be doomed. Their magic will disappear. They will be prisoners forever. We can't let that happen."

"Ha, ha, ha," the blue fairy giggled. "It serves them right."

"Maybe I can help," Claudius said, turning to the queen. "Where are they now? If I can get to them in time, the camp of my family would be a safe haven."

His shackles fell to the floor.

"Your Gift of Merit has been accepted," she smiled. "Thank you for offering to assist. What do you need to know?"

"How many residents did you have living here, and how much time do I have?"

"There are three groups of two hundred. The first has just arrived outside At il city gates and should be entering momentarily. The other two are not far behind."

"Maybe we should assist you, Claudius," Santa suggested.

"I have a plan," he answered. "It would be much faster if I went alone."

"If that is your choice," Santa said, "you must go."

With a bow of regard, Claudius cried, "At il! Up! Up!" and leaving everyone behind, he disappeared.

"The blue fairy must now be attended," Queen Daira said. Putting her hands together, the silver net floated toward her, with the prisoner intact.

Hermes looked up toward Santa's face. "Is the blue fairy a monster?" He asked.

"I would say he is," Santa answered.

"I was just wondering," Hermes said, watching the silver net settle in Queen Daira's hands.

"Mr. Twiddler tried to stop me," Santa began. "He warned me about touching him." With a gasp, he cried. "Oh, my goodness, he's still in my pocket!"

"It's about time you gave me a little credit," Mr. Twiddler squeaked, pushing his head through the furry opening. "If you had listened, but oh no-o-o, not you."

"Say," Santa laughed, "what about your house? You used to live on a lamp post."

"Life was more simple, back then," he muttered.

"Oh, okay! I could take you back," Santa offered, with a grin.

"I think I'll pass. It sounds too much like work," Mr. Twiddler snorted.

Queen Daira smiled at the two. "I'm sure you're aware of our small prisoner's fate." She said, holding the silver net toward Santa. "He must be returned to the Enchanted Pond and through the Gate of Re."

The blue fairy screamed, furiously shaking the net. "You must not listen to her. She lies---it is all lies! You are my subjects; you must not listen to her."

Placing her hands together, he became quiet. "All his needs are met within the net," she said. "He will try to persuade you otherwise. Do not let him trick you."

"I'm not going to any Enchanted Pond," Mr. Twiddler cried out, defiantly.

With a quick smile toward Santa, the queen said, "I agree with his concern. You may place your friend's house on the mantel by my chair. He will be safe until your return."

"If he would be no bother to you," Santa said, taking Mr. Twiddler and the house from his pocket, "the offer is accepted."

She nodded in confirmation. "When you get to the pond, wait until the whirlpool beats strongly against the side, clearing the bottom of any water." Should fear or anticipation of your surroundings slow you down, you could be drawn into the vortex with the prisoner. You will have only moments to close the gate. Hermes will be here to turn the key at the well."

"How will I know if the gate is locked?"

"Your escape will be jeopardized if you wait," she warned. "Get out of the Enchanted Pond before the water rises."

Turning to Robye, Santa said. "We should go. There is little time."

"The silver net must be returned as evidence of the prisoner's incarceration."

Turning to Robye, Santa said. "We have a lot to do." He placed a hand on Robye's shoulder and commanded. "To the Enchanted Pond, up, up!" Feeling nothing, he opened his eyes. They were still in the presence of the queen.

"I've never been very good at transporting. Robye, you give it a try."

Robye cried out the command. The result was the same.

"One more time; we'll do it together," Santa said, decidedly. "Maybe we should go to the steps."

They ran through the tall doors and beyond the palace landing. Wisps of snowflakes tumbled down their cheeks as they peered toward the haze-coated sky. "To the Enchanted Pond, up, up!" They cried in unison.

Shuffling down the palace steps, they looked at each other in desperation. "We're grounded," Robye said, gruffly. "Without magic we have no way to get there in time."

"You're not permitted to use transporting," the queen advised, stepping through the palace doors. "Your prisoner could use it to escape."

"Wait!" Santa cried. "Did you hear something?" A look of excitement spread over his face.

"I wish I had," Robye said, staring at Santa, quite discouraged.

"Come on!" Santa yelled, running down the rest of the steps, to the courtyard below. "I think it was Dalt. He was calling me. Maybe he knows of a way we can get there."

Robye ran down the steps and across the courtyard, just a few seconds behind Santa. When he reached the street, he came to an immediate halt. He stared in amazement at the sight in front of him.

Santa was standing beside the sleigh from the Garden of Deception. At the helm was Dalt, followed by three of his ladies. They were all draped in garlands of golden light. "I understand you are looking for a ride," said Dalt to Santa, with a nod of his antlers.

"Speed is of the essence. We must return to the Garden of Deception immediately and our use of magic is not an option." He heard Santa reply. "We may not use transporting as a means of travel, should our prisoner find a way to escape."

"Your prisoner cannot jeopardize my magic. The secure return of your prisoner through the Gate of Re in the pond will be done." Dalt assured Santa. "Queen Daira told me of your dilemma."

As soon as Robye and Santa had scrambled into the sleigh, Dalt and his girls began a slow circle around Queen Dairia's castle. Santa turned to Robye. "You must keep the knot secure," he explained, placing the silver net in Robye's hands. "The blue fairy keeps trying to slip out. He's managed to untie it twice, already."

"Ouch! He's got something inside that net and keeps jabbing at my fingers," Robye yelled.

"I know! He's mean. He doesn't give up, either." Santa said, picking up the reins of light. "Hold the knot really tight and put the bottom flat against your palm. He doesn't have as much room to move around that way."

"Thanks, I'll try anything, at this point," Robye said, squeezing the silver net close to his hand.

"All right, Dalt," Santa cried, holding up the reins, "let's see what you can do."

Dalt shook his antlers forward. An instant later, the sleigh had lifted straight above the castle and was speeding across the valley. Queen Dairia and the mountain with two shadows was now behind them.

A rush of wind blew through Robye's hair, tossing his ponytail from side to side. Tightening his grip on the silver net he looked up, crying out and instant later. "Oh my gosh, Santa, we're up in the air and flying like a bird." He looked over the edge, staring at the trees as they whizzed by, then quickly back inside. He pushed his head against the back of the seat, sitting very still.

"What's wrong, Robye," Santa asked, turning toward him.

"Air sick," Dalt advised.

"Oh," Santa said.

"I'm fine, now." Robye said. "The blue fairy stopped nicking me, for a minute anyway."

"Still there?"

"Oh yes, he's still in there. Giving him no room to move seems to be working."

"It's amazing how Dalt and his ladies pulled this sleigh up in the air."

"It sounds like you're feeling better."

"Yeah! Dalt did something. I don't know what he did---or how I know---,"

"That's the way he is," Santa said, watching the four reindeer effortlessly glide toward the range of mountains ahead.

Moments later, lost in the thrill of the ride, Robye's eyes glistened with excitement. "We are flying across the sky like a shooting star. Unbelievable!"

"Yes we are, Robye. Amazing, huh?" Santa laughed, lifting the reins. "I guess Dalt knows the way to the Valley of Deception."

"Of course!" Dalt answered with a tilt of his antlers.

Chapter Eighteen

Mist of Light

"I DIDN'T THINK THE BLUE fairy was ever going to let go of me," Santa said to Robye, as they waded toward the shore. "He kept snapping at my fingers, every time the water was swirling into me. I kept slipping in that slim on the bottom of the pond; nearly fell into that void two or three times, myself. When that hole got small enough I just held him inside until it closed." Once out of the water, he squeezed his hair and pushed it out of his eyes then jumped off the pond wall. After crossing the narrow beach, he ran through the field of dried weeds and brush, toward Dalt and the girls. "Come on, Robye," he cried, leaping into the seat of the sleigh.

"Yeah, I know," Robye said, piling in the seat beside him. "There was a barb on the end of that pick he'd been jabbing and poking me with; it got all twisted up in the net. I didn't think he'd ever let it loose. He sure put up a fight. Once he was below that gate, it's a good thing it closed like it did."

"I nearly didn't make it out of the water," Santa laughed, grabbing his coat and settling into the seat. The reins of light dropped to his hands. "Then when that water started spinning up the sides, I thought I was going to drown before I could get out of there. The waves kept knocking me down, I don't know how many times. Just about the time I'd get to the ledge and start to the climb out, I'd get hit again."

"I know. I kept trying to grab your hand, thought maybe that would help, but you'd get another attack from those waves and disappear from sight. I'd try again and the same thing would happen all over again," Robye laughed, grabbing hold of the sleigh. He slid into his seat, pulling his coat from beneath him. "It's cold out here when you're wet."

"Br-r-r, I know," Santa said, closing the front of his coat. "I'm sure glad that ordeal is over."

"Me too," Robye said. "I've got the silver net; the pick, too, by the way. That's the main thing. It's right here in my pocket."

"Now to get it to Queen Daira," Santa said, raising the reins.

"Claudius is in trouble, Santa," Dalt said with lowered antlers. "He was captured while trying to rescue the Wickie citizens."

"All of them?" Santa cried, pushing his fingers through the unruly locks of copper curls. He jammed the koyt on his head and pulled it down tight.

"I do not know."

Turning toward Robye, Santa relayed Dalts message. His voice was tight with fear as he spoke. "Dalt just told me that Claudius and the Wickies were inside the old city walls."

"Oh, no," Robye moaned, "what happened? Oh, never mind; it doesn't matter. Let's go."

"Any ideas?" Santa asked; his voice still tight.

With Santa's quick flick of the reins, Dalt and his ladies quickly began their ascent and headed toward the old city.

"We need some kind of rescue plan before we get there," Santa urged.

"I'm thinking, I'm thinking," Robye answered. After a few quiet moments, he said. "Hm-m! Actually, I do have an idea. It just might work, too."

"Dalt, we're going to At el," Santa cried out. "We're working on a plan; we'll know what to do when we get there."

"We are already on the way." His antlers perked up as the sleigh picked up speed. With a slight lurch, it tilted slightly back then aimed for the clouds.

"We have a powerful lot of magic attached to this sleigh," Robye said, thinking aloud; yours, mine and Dalt's."

"Don't forget to include my girls," Dalt nodded.

"Dalt reminded me," Santa laughed. "His girls have magic, as well."

"I didn't know about that," Robye said.

"We all have a lot of magic between us," Santa agreed. "Go on with your thought."

"What if we flew over the city and---."

"We cannot fly over the city. This sleigh would crash within seconds of crossing over the walls," Santa argued.

"Why do you think that?" Robye blurted out. Then realizing what Santa meant, he said, "Oh, I get what you mean; it would act like a magnet and destroy all of our magic."

"I'm sure of it," Santa said.

"Then, oh yes, this is a better idea yet," Robye said, excitedly, "what if we flew from the outer perimeter, making circles around the city---,"

"a-n-d draw them closer and closer together, going inward toward the center of the city?" Santa suggested.

"You know," Robye cried out excitedly, "I think it could work."

"It's worth a try, Robye," Santa exclaimed, "let's do it." Grabbing tighter to the reins, he called, "Dalt---."

"I heard," Dalt signaled. "I'm beginning the first lap around the city as you speak."

Then from far above, a familiar voice commanded. "Where are you going?"

Santa's head jerked suddenly toward the sound. "It's Ari," he cried, pulling off his koyt. "Where is he? I don't see him."

Turning in his seat and staring directly above, Robye pointed excitedly toward the eagle. "Santa, he's flying over your head."

"Where are you going?" The eagle asked again.

"To At il; to the old city," Santa called back. "Claudius needs our help; he's trying to stop the Wickie residents from entering the old city."

"Use your magic," Ari spoke again. He flew around the sleigh, tilted his wings and disappeared.

With a puzzled frown, Robye asked. "What do you suppose he meant by that?"

"By what I'm doing, I think." Santa said, pushing the koyt in his pocket. "Do you see what is happening below us?" Holding his hand over the side of the sleigh again, he watched sparkling dust flow through his fingers and downward, forming a mist of light over the city. "See if you can catch some of it, Robye. It's fun."

"It tickles my hands," Robye giggled. "What is it anyway?"

"As near as I can determine, it is the magic that was stolen from all of those who entered the old city and could not leave."

"Your ears are glowing, Santa. Did you know that?"

"Then I must have been right in my assumption. They began to feel warm when Dalt began circling the old city." He reached up, touching the slight point of one ear. "You have a bit of a glow yourself."

"Really? I hadn't noticed."

"My mother said you would have nice, strong ears. Remember? She would have been proud of those."

Touching his ears, Robye's face turned slightly pink. He then extended his arms out over the edge of the sleigh and watched the tiny dots of confetti-size lights drift through the air.

"Say, look! All those sparkles are covering the whole city. They are getting thicker and thicker, the more we sift the air," Santa laughed. "I'd say we're breaking up that energy cloud pretty good; it's activating the magic again."

"Can you imagine how many years it's been suspended up here?" Robye reflected.

"No idea," Santa answered, "forever, I guess. Everyone's magic has been stored up above the city, in this invisible cloud. Without remembering or knowing of it, the magic was never missed or searched for. Discovery was not even a concern."

"How did you know about the cloud?"

"With Ari's help, I just knew."

"All he said was 'use your magic', wasn't it?"

"The use of magic hadn't occurred to me. Depending on it as a solution for anything takes repetition I guess, before it becomes second-nature." Santa said with a grin. "When he reminded me, I seemed to know what to do."

"I know what you mean. I still need to think first before I use it," Robye admitted. "We've been stifled all our lives."

"Not any more, I hope." Glancing over Dalt's antlers, Santa guided the sleigh closer to the ground. "Oh, look at the city," he cried out happily. "Everything is beginning to glow since the energy cloud collapsed." After drawing the sleigh to a halt, he jumped to the ground.

"Oh, my gosh, Santa," Robye cried out, "look over there; around the city! There's no barricade; it's disappeared. There's no wall of ice around the city anymore; it's gone---disappeared. There's no guard shack, either. All the steps, everything---it's all gone."

"That's unreal. I had no idea we were barricaded in by fear." Santa exclaimed, staring in all directions. "What about the guards? Surely not them, too."

"I've not seen any guards since we landed," Robye called out, pacing back and forth across the imaginary barricade line. "Are you sure we're in the right town?"

"I'm wondering the same thing," he thought. Reaching down, he picked up a well-worn piece of wood and turned it over. On it was written in block letters, At il. Taken aback by the proof, he gasped. Holding the placard in front of him, he called to Robye. "Look what I found."

"Hello there Fox, we've been expecting you." A voice said behind him.

Santa whirled around. "Oh, my gosh Joshua, where did you come from? You are a sight to see." He exclaimed, reaching out to his friend. "How did you know---?"

"---that you'd be coming back? Why, your friend, Storg, er Claudius, of course," Joshua said. "We helped him rescue your Wickie friends. Some of them were on the steps, right outside the city. Tim and Matt and some of the guys kept the guards occupied while he got all them turned around and back off the steps. You should have seen it."

Catching Robye's eye, Santa motioned for him to join them. "You remember Wolf, don't you, Josh?"

"His true name is Robye, as mine is Santa."

"Claudius caught me up on that," Joshua said, turning to Robye.

"Say there, Josh, it's good to see you. We just got here," Robye said, pushing a hand forward in greeting. "Did you see us land? The sleigh---," he pointed, "---over there---we flew, that's how we got into the city."

"The reindeer, Dalt and his girls flew us in," Santa explained. "Before we could land, we had to circle the city and break up the cloud of magic above it. That's where it had been stored for all these years."

Dalt nodded his antlers toward Joshua then went back to nibbling at the moss and grasses, growing close by.

"Unbelievable," Joshua said, trying to take everything in.

"Dalt has been our friend and guide since we left At il."

"Amazing---and he flew you to the city---for real?"

"Yes," Santa smiled, "for real."

"What's that piece of board you holding, Santa?" Robye asked. "It seems pretty important, the way you're holding it."

"It's the placard with the city name on it," Santa said, slightly embarrassed. "I found it on the ground about the time Joshua arrived. It's changed so much around here, I wasn't sure we'd come to the right place."

"What does it say? I'd never seen it up close." Said Robye, leaning toward it.

Santa turned the board with the writing upward and placed it on the ground. They all gathered close to examine it. The first two letters, At, were clear enough to read as well as the il, but the letters between were all but faded away. "I can't seem to make any of the letters out---after the 'l' might possibly be an 'a' and an 'n', I don't know," Santa finally said.

"Maybe there is something in these documents that will help us out," Joshua said, digging through his coat for them. "I found some sealed packets in your father's desk drawer with your name on them." He retrieved the well-worn packages from an inside pocket and unfolded them. "I thought it best I keep them for you," he added, placing them in Santa's hand. "It's a good thing I did because your father's office was ransacked and demolished a couple of days later. I have no idea if anything is left; I never went back to see."

Santa took the rolled packages and carefully removed the cloth covering from the first one. While scanning down the page, his face began to pale. Finally tearing his eyes from the page, he murmured, just above a whisper. "The name of this city is Attiland. It's named after a place called Attilaree, where my father was in line to become king. From what I'm reading, he had a younger brother who was spurned by my mother when he made advances---my parents were married and I was almost three years old when all this happened."

"What was his brother's name?" Joshua asked, curiously.

"I don't know," Santa said, scanning down the page again. "Oh, here it is, Nicholas Eugene Claus, why?"

"I was just wondering. I've see a strangers come through here a few times. I thought maybe I might have seen him. Are there any pictures?"

"No pictures, just a lot of details I'll read over later."

"What else does it say?" Robye urged.

"Well, it seems his brother duped him into visiting At il, or rather Attiland, as we now know it. Once he was out of the way, my mother and I were no longer welcome, so we came here." Staring into nothingness, the document draped across his hand, Santa began remembering. "It finally fits together," he said. "Do you remember my telling you about my parents having to leave here on two different occasions?"

"You said you were so scared. Yeah, and there was something about being pinched and you couldn't stop crying. Sure, I remember you telling us about that, why?" Robye said.

"It says in here that a few years later my father was summoned by his brother, who was now king, to return to Attilaree---." Santa dropped to the ground, tears streaming down his face. "Oh no," he moaned. "That can't be true."

"What does it say?" Joshua asked, kneeling down beside him.

"My mother, she's an elf you know,"

"Yes," Robye said, rubbing his shoulders.

"My mother was banned from her family, she had to stay here---," he sobbed.

Not knowing what else to do, Robye sat down beside him.

"Adrian, the little cripple girl that Sara Sue was taking care of, is my sister."

"She's what?" Robye cried. "Is that all?"

"No," Santa groaned, "that's not all. Nicholas is the father. My father's brother forced himself on her then disposed of her---and the rest of us, here in the old city."

"I need to find my parents," Robye said, jumping to his feet.

"I know you do. Dalt said you'll find them at the university. We should leave before dusk. I'll meet you at the old hideaway."

"What about Hermes' mother?"

"Dalt just told me that she and Sara Sue are with Adrian at the Kroll camp. Since their magic is stronger and much more refined than what the elves here in Attiland know how to use," Santa answered, getting to his feet. "Maribel, you remember Claudius's aunt, she's trying to cure Adrian's cripple foot."

"You have another parchment to unroll," Robye reminded him. "Aren't you curious about it?"

"Yes, but I'd like to share it. When you return, I'll open it," Santa said, reaching to unhook Dalt and his girls from the sleigh. "Besides, I have a lot to digest from the first one."

With a nod Dalt and his girls continued to nudge, through the rocks and patches of snow, seeking out their favorite plants to nibble on.

Turning toward the university, Santa watched as Robye climbed the steps toward the door then motioned to Joshua. They walked past the field of small igloos; most had now been disposed of, Santa noticed. They continued on, putting the cross-street behind them. His eyes then searched the family back yard for his old swing. It was still hanging, rocking in the breeze. He paused, catching his breath. His throat ached with pain but he went on by. Before long he was standing under the lamp, at the bottom of the hill, looking up at the old hideaway. "It seemed like such a long walk when we were here before," he said.

"You were living in fear," Joshua reminded him.

"I was happy, though. I thought I was," he answered.

"You had good parents."

"The best," he agreed, looking about. "Where is everyone? The town looks empty."

"Most of the people are at the Kroll camp, or at the university, learning how to use their magic. Our friends are in the hideaway, though. They've planned a celebration and are waiting on our arrival. I'm surprised they're so quiet."

"You weren't supposed to tell him," a young boy yelled, running down the hill. "Hi, I'm Daniel. I'm the lookout. I was supposed to tell them when I saw you coming this way." He laughed. "I guess I messed that up." With a sudden gust of noise, he yelled, "Hello, everyone, Fox is back!"

"Josh told us you were coming," a girl cried out, bounding down the hill, with three others following close behind. "Hi, I'm Beth, she said, nearly running into him."

"I'm Amy and this is Cassie."

"My name is Gracie. We've been helping with the food collecting since you've been gone. It's good to meet you, finally."

"And you, too," Santa said, quite surprised at their bubbling disposition.

"Come on up," Cassie urged, excitedly. "We've all been waiting since your arrival."

"You saw me coming?"

"Well, not exactly," Mark said, stepping through the entrance to the hideaway, "we felt the difference in our spirit. Joshua said you gave us back our magic. When the barricade disappeared---,"

"---and the security shack, we knew it had to be true," Tim added, shaking his hand. "Most of us had no idea we were elves; that we had magic and all that stuff."

"I didn't know until I left the city," Santa admitted.

"I heard you changed your name," Tom said, crowding between the others. "Santa, am I right?"

"Yes, that's true. Just before my mother died, she told me my true name was Sandor, the same as my father. We changed it a little but everyone seems to like it."

"Are you going to stay?"

"I'm afraid not. We must leave before sunset."

"Is Josh going with you?"

"I'm not that easy to get rid of," Joshua laughed.

"Santa and I are traveling together," Robye said, joining the crowd.

"Speaking of that, we should be leaving," Santa announced.

"Not until we give you our surprise."

"I could never disappoint you," he said, watching a large bag being passed toward him.

Reaching inside, he pulled out the gift. "Oh my goodness, it's a new koyt," he exclaimed happily.

"All our names are on it," a voice called out.

"Try it on," another voice cried.

After looking it over, recognizing the names, Santa lifted it over his head and pulled it on. Confetti poured over his hair and down his face, under his collar and onto the ground around him.

Everyone laughed and cheered as he headed toward the hideaway door. At a glance, he saw Dalt and his girls waiting beneath the street lamp. "Come Robye, it's time to go," he said, waving back to everyone. They ran down the hill and jumped in the sleigh as it left the ground. "Come out and watch the sky," he cried, as they left the hideaway behind.

"You're a natural behind those reins." Robye said, admirably.

"I don't know how I know. It surprises me too." Santa said, flicking the reins. "Dalt, we must go back to the Valley of Deception!"

With a nod, Dalt turned and lifted the sleigh high into the sky.

Hearing a crunch, Santa reached in his pocket and pulled out the other roll of parchment. "I guess I should open this other package," he said unrolling it with care.

"I was wondering when your curiosity would get to you," Robye said, looking over his shoulder.

"Oh, look, Robye, it's birth records for both Adrian and myself," he said, "and what is this other document? I can't believe it---it's a map from where I was born. It's a map of Attilaree. It's a real place on a real map."

"Oh Santa, oh no, you forgot Claudius" Robye yelled out suddenly.

"Claudius is well ahead of us, Robye. He and the residents have already left the old city for the Wickie nation."

"You say?" Robye said, quite surprised.

"Hang on! The Valley of Deception is just below" Santa yelled.

"Alre-a-dy?" Robye cried out.

With an abrupt landing, the sleigh stopped. Robye and Santa were thrown out. They rescued themselves just in time to see Dalt and his ladies disappear. They watched the sleigh fling itself straight up and land inside the disappearing Valley of Deception.

Santa grinned, "I may have to work on my landings."

"It seems we're stranded," Robye said, dolefully taking note of their situation.

"Oh, I don't think so. Put your arm around my shoulder," Santa laughed. "We must return to the Wickie Nation."

"It didn't work the last time," Roby complained.

"Let's try anyway. Hang on," Santa said.

"Up, up," they both cried.

A cloud of floating color instantly flashed by and when they opened their eyes, Queen Dairia's palace had come in to view. As they landed, Hermes and Claudius were racing toward them.

"It's about time you got here," Claudius yelled. "We thought maybe you were lost."

"Or the Valley of Deception had eaten you up," Hermes giggled.

"Oh no. Oh no, no! I had to talk Robye out of walking back up the mountain," Santa laughed.

"Not true, not true," Robye argued playfully. "I was not too sure I wanted to ride with him after the last landing in the sleigh."

"Oh, come on you two and check out all the improvements we've done around here," Claudius invited. "All the Wickie residents have now returned to their homes. The city cleanup is nearly complete, as well."

"Yeah, and the key to the Gates of Re worked perfectly, too," Hermes said, proudly holding up his mother's brooch. "See the silver chain Queen Daira gave me. She said I should never lose it again."

"Where is the queen?" Santa asked curiously. "We should pay our respects."

"She said for me to apologize on her behalf," Claudius said, quite formally. "It seems she's been detained."

"Yeah, detained all right," Hermes chuckled. "She and Mr. Twiddler are in the palace kitchen. He's teaching her staff the fine art of gourmet cooking."

"I should have guessed." Santa laughed.

Chapter Nineteen

Free Fall

"WHEN ARE WE GOING TO find our new home?" Hermes asked, for the tenth time. Holding his hands out, the snowflakes slipped between his fingers as they melted. He looked up, waiting for Santa to answer.

"I don't know," he said, walking along beside him. "I wish I had an answer for you."

"Queen Daira invited us to stay at the Wickie Nation, you know." Glaring down at his feet, Hermes slid his boots through the new-fallen snow, making a path of fine, narrow ridges. "There wasn't even any snow in their city. It was warm, too."

"I know, Hermes," Santa said, patiently. "To stay was very tempting."

"Well!"

"Hermes," he began, again, "remember the pact we all agreed on?"

"I know, but the 'children of the night' are free, right?"

"That is true, Hermes. There are no longer any prisoners of the city but what about all the other children," Santa said gently, "those who don't have magic?"

"We don't know any of them," Hermes muttered.

"Yes we do. We know all of them."

"If you say so," Hermes answered. Squatting down, he pulled his hands through the snow and squeezed some of it into balls.

Santa slipped down beside him, adding a couple snowballs to the pile.

After tossing one into a tree, Hermes giggled, dusting the snow from his hair.

"Good toss," Santa chuckled, taking aim across the brook.

"It fell down on my head."

"They do that when you stand under them."

"H-m-m, I missed. You're much better at target shooting than I am, Hermes."

"I do it all the time. Lots of practice; that's what you said I should do."

"It's working, too," Santa said.

Looking up, Hermes said. "Do you miss being called Fox? I like Hermes a lot but I miss Hawk sometimes."

"Fox was a long time ago. Santa is a good name, I think."

"Hermes makes me real. I like that."

"I do, too," Santa answered. He pointed at a crevice in the wall of rock. "Do you think you can hit that shadow up there?"

"Probably. My aim has gotten pretty good," Hermes grinned. After making a few tosses, he turned toward Santa. "I hit all five of them. What do you think of that?"

"Excellent shots," Santa answered, patting him on the shoulder. "What about that little stump; do you think you can hit it?"

"I don't know. That's a long way from here." After loading his arms with the small snowballs, he said. "We're never going to find a home, are we?" A couple of the snowballs dropped to the ground. He didn't bother to pick them up.

From a distance Robye and Claudius watched Hermes walked away. "Santa and Hermes are really into a heavy conversation," Robye said, looking toward Claudius. "I wonder what Hermes is whining about, now?"

They watched Hermes throw the rest of the snowballs at a nearby bush then, with his head hung low, slide his boots slowly through the snow

"What's up with Hermes?" Robye asked, walking up beside Santa.

"He wanted to know about a new home. I didn't have an answer," Santa said.

"We've been curious about that, too," Claudius said. "Now that the guards are gone, we don't have them to worry about."

"I know," Santa answered. "They disappeared when the old city fell. I didn't know they were bound by the walls."

"What about going back?" Robye suggested.

"I'll admit, that thought has crossed my mind," Santa said, "but I believe there was purpose to our flight. While in the old city, we helped the children find courage; something to believe in." His eyes turned toward the two. "If we could give a child a bit of happiness, even for one day, don't you think it would be worth it?"

"I know we all took that vow," Robye agreed, "but do you really think it can be done?"

"I do," Santa answered, "but I just don't know where."

"Or how, would be something to consider, as well," Claudius said.

"I think the 'how' will come when the 'where' is found," Santa said, with a smile. "We are now capable of a lot of unexplored magic, you know."

"Speaking of magic, Claudius, I have a question that has been bothering me for a while," Robye said.

"What would that be?" He said. "I may have an answer."

"There were three times, that I can think of, when you came into the old city and your magic was not taken away from you."

"That is correct," Claudius answered with a grin. "I was wondering when that question would come up."

"You and your family were outside the old city when you first visited Hermes at his window."

"Yes, that's true. The second was when I met 'the children of the night', and the last, as you know, was during the Wickie rescue."

"Yes! How did you keep your magic?" Robye quizzed. "On anyone else, their magic would have disappeared. Is it because you are a Kroll?"

"Easy explanation," Claudius laughed, "but being a Kroll had nothing to do with it. You see, our clan has traveled so much, after our near annihilation, that we try never to take chances. We always sent a clone of ourselves into a questionable situation. My father and grandfather did the same when they visited the governor."

"Your family visited Santa's father? I didn't know that."

"He told me about it, Robye," Santa said. "I was surprised, too."

"While we're on that subject, I'd like to clear my conscience," Claudius said, hesitantly. "We did not visit At il by accident. There were so many rumors, about your old city being such a safe haven, it seemed too good to be true. We were sent by other nations to see if it was a ruse. Sorry to say the ruse was correct. It was awful that so many years had passed before the At il situation was discovered."

"No one even knew we existed?" Santa cried out in shock.

"Not really. It was kept pretty quiet," Claudius said. "My grandfather heard a rumor about your town a few months before our visit."

"Oh, really?"

"But it was quite by accident, Santa. He was negotiating a reindeer trade with a small group of nomads. They wanted one of our bucks for breeding and we were low on slaughter stock; I think that was it. Neither party could understand the other's language very well. He kept hearing the word elf in the background conversation. We had friends who were elves and were afraid they may have been attacked, like we were, so he asked. I guess they thought we wanted to go there. They made sure we knew At il was only open to the elf population. That's how we heard about it. Actually our interest was in locating our clan members."

"At il laws were our life; it was all we had ever known," Robye said quietly.

"My family granted me permission to visit Hermes at his window, as a matter of safety. I'm sorry I could not share any of this information before now. We do have powerful magic but we also have powerful enemies. The near loss of our clan is proof of that."

"I'm sure I would have done the same thing," Santa said.

"He's right! Don't worry about it," Robye grinned. "We couldn't have made this trip without you."

Claudius looked to the others with a smile. "Wow, I feel better! It's so good to get that bit of information off my chest."

"Why were you still looking?" Santa asked. "You knew you weren't planning to stay."

"After the search for our lost clan members, you're right," Claudius said. "The rumors were that At il was the ideal home for elves. Nothing fit. Elves are normally so meticulous and tidy. They would have never put up with the conditions of your city."

"Have you found any of them," Robye asked, "your clan members?"

"Some. It's been so long since our clan was disbanded, I'm not sure we'll find many more."

"I'm so sorry," Robye said.

"How is the pitching arm?" Claudius asked, as Hermes joined them.

"Not too bad. The snow is too dry; it doesn't stick together very well," Hermes answered. "I didn't know you were still looking for your family, Claudius."

"It's not my family, Hermes. You met all of them. Many members of the Kroll tribe are still missing, though."

"I'm sorry, Claudius," Hermes said, quietly. "I miss my mother, too. She's the only family I've ever had."

"Your mother was at the Kroll campsite, we told you about it, Hermes," Santa reminded him. "Robye didn't get to see his parents either, but it's good to know they are all doing well."

"I didn't get to see her, though. I miss her a lot."

Santa reached down, placing his arm across Hermes shoulders. "I know you do. She'd be so proud of you."

Hermes dropped his head slightly then added. "You know it didn't really make me mad when she stole my clothes. I knew she was trying to protect me. She thought I'd get in trouble if I hung around with you."

"Oh, we knew that, didn't we Santa?" Robye said.

"You didn't act like it. You were always teasing me."

"Well, you'll have to admit, some of the things you wore were quite unusual," Santa said, trying to hide his grin. "The time you wore gloves with lace trim all over them, for example."

"They were warm, so there!" Hermes glared.

Claudius smiled down at Hermes. "Your mother must be a very nice lady."

"She's the best. When I lost her brooch in the pond, it was almost like she was gone." He pressed the flower-shaped pin against his chest. "Most people in the old city didn't even have a family."

"That was something I thought unusual, too," Claudius cut in.

"What do you mean," asked Hermes, "unusual---how?"

"I've always wondered where all the children came from."

"Uh, I'd never thought of that, before."

"I know a little bit about that," Santa said.

A look of surprise covered Hermes face. "You do?"

"Yes, many times I'd hear my folks talk about the abandoned children found on the city steps. It happened quite often, you know."

"I cannot imagine anyone doing that," Claudius said, his face twisted with agitation. He became quiet trying to control the flood of anger that passed through him. Finally focusing on a distant rock formation, he said. "I think I'll take a walk. I need to clear my head."

Robye glanced at Santa then back to Claudius as he left them standing and raced across the clearing. "He got pretty upset about that, didn't he?"

"I know," Santa answered. "His family ties are much different than we're accustomed to."

Hermes scuffed along beside them, watching Claudius in the distance. A little later he slid between Robye and Santa, trying to match footsteps with them. Looking up, he said, "I can't wait to be as big as you."

"You nearly are, Hermes. You've grown a lot since we left the old city," Santa said.

"Guiding us through that tunnel in the wall was pretty grown up," Robye noted.

"I was scared, though."

"I'm not surprised. Stepping into the unknown is always fearful," Santa answered. "We all get scared sometimes."

"We're a family now," Robye said, hugging Hermes shoulders. "We take care of each other. We've been doing that for a while, now."

"Not when I'm hungry," Hermes giggled. "You're always saying 'not again,' or 'Break time; Hermes is hungry, we've got to stop,' don't you?"

"Yeah, I guess I do," Robye laughed. "It makes for a good excuse to stop, though."

"Hey, where did Claudius go?" Hermes asked, suddenly. "I saw him walking on that tall, rocky ridge a while ago. He's not there, anymore; he disappeared."

"He's out there somewhere, Hermes. I wouldn't worry, too much," Santa said, glancing between the bank of bushes and trees along the grass-coated base of the ledge. "You know how he enjoys exploring. I wouldn't be surprised if he wasn't looking for us a place to camp."

"They are easier to spot in the daylight," Robye added.

"Robye, did you know your ears were glowing?" Hermes said, staring in awe.

"They've been doing that every once in a while; since we flew over the old city." He reached up, touching the left ear with his fingers. "They get to feeling kind of warm."

"Why are they doing that?" Hermes touched one of his long slim ears. "Mine don't feel warm."

"I think they glow when we are capable of receiving new magic," Santa said, thoughtfully. "When our magic was stored above the city, it matured as we did. Now that it has been released, we are receiving it in small doses, giving us time to make discoveries, as well as learning to control the usage. We wouldn't be able to do that if all was given back at once. Nature is good about those things. At least that is my theory."

"So, when you transported over the old city, your ears---? That doesn't make sense," Hermes argued.

"We didn't transport, Hermes, we flew," Robye corrected him.

"No way---how? I don't see any wings on your back," Hermes giggled, peeking at Santa's face. "You are teasing, right?"

"It's true, Hermes. Robye's not making a funny," Santa said, quite seriously. He took another step then squeezed between two large rocks, heading further up the hill.

"Dalt came to our rescue. Santa and I rode in the old sleigh we built---," Robye began. He tried to follow Santa then changed his mind, going further around the rocks. Slipping on the gravel, he groaned, nearly losing his balance then caught hold of a small boulder before he fell.

Noticing a signal from Claudius, Santa waved in return. He left Hermes and Robye deep in conversation concerning the best way to navigate the rocky climb and headed in his direction.

"Did you find anything of interest?" He called, raking his hands across some bushes. Catching hold of the limbs, he pulled forward for leverage and aimed for the narrow plateau where Claudius was standing.

"There are some rock formations in the valley below me, but not much different than what you've seen. I like watching the mystery lights from up here though."

"They are truly beautiful from up here. The spectacular shapes and colors; I never get tired of the way they pulse across the open fields. We missed that in the old city."

"Look across the valley, though. See how they're draping right across the top; it's like a huge curtain floating in the wind," Claudius pointed out. "Sometimes they have a kind of tail that sweeps between the mountain ranges; not doing it today, though."

Santa laughed. "You have way too much energy sometimes, for the rest of us to keep up with, Claudius. It has been many days since we left The Wickie Nation and I think we are all getting a bit worn. What do you think about finding a place suitable for a long stop, maybe two or three days?"

"I've been feeling the wear, too," Claudius agreed. "The last couple of stops have been rather difficult, I must admit. These rocky ridges usually have some good caves. I'll keep an eye out."

Santa jumped off the ledge and started back down the hill, searching for Hermes and Robye as he descended

"Say, look at that," Claudius called out to him. "There's a big fog bank rolling in." After motioning toward it, he jumped off the ledge and followed Santa down the steep bank. "It wasn't there a few minutes ago; it's coming in fast."

Stopping at the bottom, Santa watched Claudius climb down the rocky hill. "I don't suppose you had a chance to find a campsite? With a fog like that, we should probably stop soon."

"I did see a place not far from here. It seemed rather interesting. Maybe I should check it out. Okay?"

"With all the fog, we'll have a hard time keeping track of each other if you leave us behind," Santa said, a little apprehensive. "Just keep that in mind."

"I know," Claudius said.

"Maybe we should stay close together," Santa suggested. "I'm sure we'll find a place to stop."

"That is probably a good idea. Where are Robye and Hermes?" He asked, quickly looking about. "Oh, there you are."

"You didn't see us coming," Robye laughed.

"I really didn't think you'd be too far away," Claudius stated.

"Not in this kind of weather," Robye pointed out. "It's not a good idea to mess around with heavy fog."

"Yeah, we wouldn't want to lose anyone," Hermes laughed, sliding between them.

"Say, how would you like to try a new way of transporting?" Claudius said, thoughtfully. "It seems like a good time to try it."

"What do we have to do?" Robye asked.

"I have to keep sight of my landing location so we'd better hurry before the fog gets too thick for me to see it."

"What?" Santa exclaimed, apprehensively. "We don't need to take chances on getting split up."

"No chances taken. Queen Daira showed me a few tricks of magic while we were visiting," Claudius said, quickly. "Hang on to each other and I'll show you. Is everyone ready?"

"I guess," Santa said, placing his hand on Hermes shoulder.

"Good!" Claudius yelled. He nodded his head forward. A few moments later, with no sensation of movement, they were standing between tall pillars of rock. A hidden crevice between the rocks was directly in front of them. "Say, that was great. It worked just like she said it would."

"How did you do that?" Santa cried out, touching his face to make sure he was all there. "That was remarkable."

"With a little practice, it's easy enough to do," Claudius said. "It's kind of like Hermes sliding from place to place."

"I've never gotten the hang of that, either," Robye scowled.

"You're trying too hard," Hermes piped up. "It's easy; I do it all the time."

"I know," Robye growled.

"I don't know how you find all these cozy places to camp," Santa said, "but you always come through."

"It's no secret. I like to study rock formations and the shadows around them. It takes a lot of the guesswork out of the hunt," Claudius laughed. "Come on! Let's see what you've found before Hermes starts yelling he's hungry."

Hermes glared at Robye. "I didn't say a word."

"I heard you think it," Robye laughed.

"Not this time," Hermes growled.

"Oops," Robye giggled. "It must have been me. I'm hungry enough to eat about anything."

"Me too," Santa smiled, taking Mr. Twiddler out of his pocket. "On my shoulder, okay?"

"You did interrupt my reading," Mr. Twiddler complained, "but my palate could be entertained by a bit of food."

Santa grinned as he repeated, "on my shoulder?"

"Oh, that would work quite nicely," Mr. Twiddler agreed, busily tying his ears with a purple string.

"Claudius? Where did you stash the supplies?" Robye yelled, rummaging through the stack of canvas bags. "I don't see them anywhere."

"Right there in my knapsack. Just dump it all out." Reaching over Robye's shoulder, Claudius sorted through the contents. "There you are," he said to himself, picking up a small thin square. "You were really trying hard to stay out of sight, weren't you?"

"And what is that?" Santa asked, watching him unfold it.

"It isn't much bigger than my book," Mr. Twiddler said, inspecting the square. "Something special, I guess?"

"Yes it is. It's our cooking stone," Claudius twittered.

"It's your cooking stone," Mr. Twiddler squawked, "oh, really?"

"Um hum," Claudius said, glancing toward Santa. "When you told us about At il magic being transferred into the cloud above the city, I got to playing around with the idea." He began opening the square and as he did the cooking stone shape began to restore. "I found a way to transfer all the weight out of our supplies. I've been trying to figure it out ever since we left the Wickie Nation. This was my first time being successful." Reaching around the stone, he placed it on the floor. Immediately, the fire began to flame up around the edges.

"So where is the weight?" Hermes asked. "How did you carry it?"

"I didn't. It was in a cloud above my head," Claudius smiled. "Amazing, huh?"

"Quite creative, I'd say," Santa grinned.

"I have some herbs you might like to try on that roast," Mr. Twiddler suggested, jumping to the small table in front of Claudius. "Queen Daira gave me a nice supply."

"You're the gourmet cook, Mr. Twiddler," Claudius said. "Just tell me what to do."

Hermes stood watching Claudius follow Mr. Twiddlers instructions. After a few minutes he took the stack of bowls and plates from one of the supply bags and began placing them on the small table.

"Now put a cover over the food and turn the heat down to a simmer," Mr. Twiddler said. "I'll tell you when to test it."

Finally turning to Santa, Hermes said. "Sorry, what I said about the children. I guess I never thought about any others, only those in the old city."

"I'm not sure I had either until we left. Our world was pretty small, back then." Looking sideways at Hermes, Santa asked. "What brought that up anyway?"

"I've been doing a lot of thinking," Hermes answered. "Are you really talking about all the children, everywhere?"

"It would be nice, don't you think?"

"Yeah, but---?"

Santa laughed when he noticed Hermes' expression. "Oh, no, not every day, I'm only speaking of one day each year. Wouldn't it be nice to put a smile on each child's face and make them feel special."

"My mother used to make me feel special."

"I'm sure she did," Robye said, coming up from behind. "We were very fortunate, Hermes."

"Do you think I'll ever see her again?" Hermes asked.

"I think it's possible, now that the city walls are down," Santa said, kindly. "We do know she's alive and well, so there's a good chance you'll get back together."

"What day should be the special one?" Hermes asked.

"Oh, that is the easy part," Santa smiled. "That would be Christmas of course. It already belongs to them."

Coming back from the cave entrance, Claudius said, excitedly. "The fog has lifted and the sun is shining, this morning. I thought this day might be lost to the weather. Unbelievable!"

"I vote we have a play day," Santa laughed. "We have a good camp for tonight---."

"---and a delicious meal behind us," Robye said, rubbing his stomach. "Maybe you can show me again, how to do that slide, Hermes. What do you think?"

"We can always try," Hermes snickered. "You need to limber up and not work so hard at it. Come on. I'll show you."

"I want to learn how to do those short jumps, Claudius," Santa said. "That was quite fascinating."

"I'm not going," Mr. Twiddler stated, quite stubbornly. "I'll just finish my book."

"We all stick together, Mr. Twiddler," Santa said, gently. "We haven't had a fun day in a long time. You wouldn't want to squelch that, now would you?"

After an appropriate hesitation, he whined. "Oh, just put my house back in your pocket. I'll read in there, I guess."

"Good! That's settled then." Santa reached for the house as Mr. Twiddler jumped inside. "Come on everyone, before Mr. Twiddler changes his mind."

"Just look at you, leave all the supplies behind," Mr. Twiddler growled. "I thought I taught you better."

"I did not," Claudius smirked. "They are all collected, right here with me. You just can't see them anymore."

"Oh!" Mr. Twiddler said, ducking back into the pocket.

"Where are Robye and Hermes, Claudius? Do you have any idea?" Santa asked.

"I think they've already left. Should be out there , somewhere."

Shading his eyes, Santa glanced out the door of the shelter. "It is a beautiful, bright sunny day." He declared. "I can't wait to get out there."

"Well come on, we'll find them," Claudius urged. "That sun sure did burn off that cloud of fog, pretty quick. I thought we were in for a big snow storm or something."

"Do you see them?"

"They just went over that small rise," Claudius pointed.

"They're all the way out there already, huh?" Santa said, looking across the field.

Glancing over at Santa, Claudius asked. "Do you still want me to show you the short leaps? They're really easy once you get the hang of it."

"Everything is easy," Santa muttered, "once you get the hang of it." Looking toward Claudius, he said, "I guess I'm ready to give it a try."

"Now, what you do is first find your target," Claudius said, speaking very slowly."

"I've got it, Claudius. I understand that part. It's the rest I don't get."

"Uh, okay," Claudius laughed. "I had to tease you a bit."

"You're full of it, you know."

"Yeah," he quipped.

"Okay," Santa laughed, "let's see if I can do this."

"Now, what you do first---."

Santa belted him with a huge snow ball.

They both laughed.

"Okay" Santa said, aiming his vision toward a small hill ahead of him. "I see a shadow just passed that rise over there. Is that good?"

"If it suits you, it will be good," Claudius said. "Now, stare at it. Don't lose sight of it for a second."

"Are you sure it will work?"

"You won't know until you try," Claudius laughed.

Santa disappeared.

Claudius was gone a few seconds later.

"Ouch! Oh, oh!" Santa cried out as he slipped into darkness. Down he plunged, through the open space, with no control as he fell. Seconds later, he forced his eyes open. Blurring shades of dark and gray were speeding by, "Not good," he thought, squeezing them closed again.

From somewhere below, he heard a scream. He forced his mind to listen. "I've heard that voice before," he thought. "I can't be dreaming, I can feel the air pushing into me." His eyes blinked open again. He could see nothing but blackness.

He heard the voice again. "Robye---it sounds like Robye. I must be dreaming."

"Look out! I'm down here. Don't ---No-o-o---."

After an eternity of tumbling and rolling, Santa's body stopped with a sudden thud. "Oh, my arm," he heard himself cry out. His eyes flew open. "Where am I? Who?"

"It's me, Santa. You fell on my leg," Robye howled. "You're crushing my leg."

"How did you get in here? Where are we?" Santa cried, trying to shift his weight.

"I don't know, Santa. I just got here, too. Oh, oh my leg," Robye moaned. "You've got to get off of it."

"I would if I could, give me a minute. It doesn't feel like there's much room to move," Santa grunted. Slipping carefully to one side, he managed to change positions.

"Oh, that's better," Robye said, rubbing his thigh. "It was in a pinch."

"Do you know where we are?" Santa questioned, sliding his hand around in front of him. It feels like we've landed on a ledge. We're down in some kind of hole."

"That's what I thought. Hermes was teaching me to do that magical skimming he does all the time and it got away from me."

"Claudius was helping me out; same thing," Santa growled. "I need to see what is below us. Have you looked over the edge?"

"No, not yet," Robye said, rubbing his leg.

After some careful maneuvering, Santa managed to look over the side of their perch. "You don't want to, either." Drawing in a breath that sounded like gravel in his ears, he managed to say," it's straight down for as far as I can see."

"You're in front of me; let me see," Said Robye, leaning over Santa's legs. He looked over the edge and gasped. "All I see is a lot of space with no bottom."

I don't know how we managed to land on this same little ledge and not fall all the way to the bottom."

"Just lucky, I guess," Robye said, cautiously leaning back. "I think we have a problem, here."

"We should be able to transport out, though."

"Probably not," Robye reminded him. "I remember you telling me about your escape off the old city wall."

"Oh, you're right. That was quite a challenge," Santa said, looking up toward the opening. "We do have a bit of a dilemma, don't we?"

"I'd say we do."

"Since Claudius taught me that new bit of magic, maybe it would work to get us out."

"To go down but not up, maybe. You must see the exact spot you want to land on." Robye winced, pushing himself away from the edge. "We could be in more of a squeeze than we are now. We have no idea what is down there."

"You're probably right," Santa said, trying to gather his wits. "There must be a way out of this mess." He peeked over the ledge, again. "There a canyon of ice down there. My eyes are finally adjusting to the dark; I'm beginning to get a visual. There's a huge split down there, with a wall of ice on each side. I can't see either end of it from here; I don't know how far the split goes."

"Where are we?" Mr. Twiddler asked, climbing out of Santa's pocket. "My, my, you do have us in a fix."

"I was trying out a new piece of magic and fell through a crevice in the ice," Santa told him. "We are now sitting precariously on a slab of rock somewhere beneath the surface of a long gorge."

"Like I said before, you do have us in a fix," Mr. Twiddler said, taking the purple string out of the fur-trimmed pocket. "What are you going to do now?" He reached up and tied it around his ears.

"Hel-l-o, down there," a voice cried out.

Mr. Twiddler jerked around. "What was that?"

"Is everyone okay?"

"I can see them, Claudius." Another voice yelled. "Do you see them,? They're right against that wall. See, right over there."

"Oh yeah, I do now."

"Who's up there?" Santa cried, straining to turn his head and look above him.

"It's us; Claudius and Hermes. Are you all right?"

"We're fine; no broken bones. We can't get out," Santa yelled back.

"Don't worry about that," Claudius called back. "We're coming down. I can see you. Turn your light so we can find our way down there."

"What do you mean?" Robye called back. "There's no light down here."

"Santa, it's your hand; I see it waving all around," he yelled back. "Point it this way so we can get to you."

Santa raised his hand above his head and looked up. Sure enough, there was a thin beam of light registered on the two faces staring into the passage. "I'll say," he gasped.

Moments later, Hermes and Claudius appeared on the ledge, below.

"How did you see us?" Santa asked.

"A light was glowing around the split in the ice you fell through," Claudius laughed.

"We weren't very far from it," Hermes giggled. "We nearly fell in the same place."

"Now we're all stuck in here," Robye growled, pressing up closer to the wall.

"Oh, I don't think so," Claudius chuckled. "I can show you how to get out. I only came down to rescue you."

"I was wondering if there was a way to get to the bottom of this gorge---without falling, that is?" Santa questioned. "Falling would not be my preference for landing. I'd really like to explore a bit of it."

"I'm sure we can," Claudius said. "Hold on and I'll take you."

"I'm not going down there. We're in enough trouble," Robye complained.

"We should all go together," Santa reminded him.

"Oh, yeah I guess," he answered, reaching for Hermes shoulder.

"We need a beam of light, Santa," Claudius said, holding to Robye's arm.

"You've got it," Santa said. He leaned over the ledge, pointing his hand toward the bottom.

"Wow," Hermes cried, as they landed. "What a place."

"I'll say," Claudius said, noting all the stalagmites and stalactites standing like posts along the chasm floor. "Who would have ever guessed the snow would be hiding such a place."

"Oh, my gosh! This is spectacular," Robye yelled, hearing the echo of his voice.

Santa pointed his hand, illuminating the wide, rugged valley lying between the mountainous walls of ice. As far as the light would reach, he saw no end to the massive gorge in either direction. He looked to the others then back at the majestic vision in front of him. Unbelievable as it seemed, they were standing far below the harsh, Arctic surface in a wonderland of ice. His face glowed with excitement. He turned to the others and said. "I think we've found our new home. Does everyone agree?"

"Do you really mean it, Santa," Hermes asked, his eyes sparkling, "we're going to live here?"

"You've got my vote," Robye laughed, swinging Hermes off the floor.

"Watch that stuff," Hermes snickered, "I'm all grown up---." He giggled, "well maybe tomorrow I will be."

Claudius stood, breathlessly staring. "I vote 'yes' of course."

Mr. Twiddler crawled out of Santa's pocket, tying the purple string around his ears and looked up. "What's all the commotion about?"

"It's about time you came out of hiding, Mr. Twiddler," Santa exclaimed, placing him on his shoulder. "What do you think of our new home? Did you ever see such a sight?"

"I believe you're living up to your name, Santa," Mr. Twiddler snickered, dropping to a sitting position. He crossed his legs and allowed his eyes to follow Santa's light beam, uncovering a spectacular play on ice along the monumental canyon walls. "First class is what I say. First class"

They all laughed.

---and so the legend begins.

Epilogue

Long ago, in a far-away land, a boy was testing fate
When he jumped into a toy-filled sleigh and rode swiftly on his way.
He reached out for the reins of light, to guide his reindeer band.
To his great surprise and with twinkling eyes, sweet magic warmed
his hands.
It flowed throughout his gentle soul and filled his heart with cheer.
He laughed aloud and said. "I'm proud, this is my premiere year.
So long I have been waiting, my ride to be unfurled,
So I could bring some Christmas joy to every boy and girl."

The sleigh was lifted up in flight
As he flew into the endless night;
He was surrounded by the Northern Lights.
The moon appeared so clear and bright,
Beneath the stars, that pointed right
For him to make his long, long flight.

The forest creatures all looked up; they paused from frisky play,
And the birds came out from winter nests to cheer him on his way.
He felt the forces from below and said. "It's right for me.
This is a dream I've had since birth; it is my destiny.
All children need one special day for happiness to show
And feel the magic in their hearts, with time to let it grow.
I know I'm only Santa Claus; I have no claim to fame
But the magic day of Christmas is for children, I proclaim."

CPSIA information can be obtained at www.ICGtesting.com
Printed in the USA
LVOW092059081211

258501LV00002B/2/P